June Tate was born in Southampton in the 1930s and spent the early years of her childhood in the Cotswolds before returning to Southampton after the Second World War was declared. After leaving school she became a hairdresser and spent several years working on cruise ships, first on the *Queen Mary* and then on the *Mauritania*, meeting many Hollywood film stars and VIPs on her travels. After her marriage to an airline pilot she lived in Sussex and Hampshire before moving to live in Portugal.

June and her husband Alan, who have two adult children, now live in Sussex.

Also by June Tate

Riches of the Heart

No One Promised Me Tomorrow

June Tate

HEADLINE

First published in 1999
by HEADLINE BOOK PUBLISHING

First published in paperback in 1999
by HEADLINE BOOK PUBLISHING

10 9 8 7 6 5

ISBN 0 7472 5910 0

Typeset by
Letterpart Limited, Reigate, Surrey

Printed and bound in Great Britain by
Mackays of Chatham plc, Chatham, Kent

HEADLINE BOOK PUBLISHING
A division of the Hodder Headline Group
338 Euston Road
London NW1 3BH

www.headline.co.uk
www.hodderheadline.com

To my dearest friend Patsie and her husband Robert. I love you both. And in memory of Mary, my mother.

With heartfelt thanks to: Marion Donaldson, my
brilliant editor and a lovely lady; Judith Murdoch, my
agent, who is always there for me; and my family,
Beverley, Maxine and Alan, for their constant love and
encouragement.

Prologue

She looked around in despair as she joined the line of new women prisoners as they left the building, dressed now in their shabby and worn prison garments. She drew her cape around her to shut out the cold December air.

They were led by a prison warder across the quadrangle. In the dim lights she could just make out the silhouette of the tall brick wall surrounding the area. The rolled barbed wire along the top of the wall looked sharp and menacing.

She waited, heart thumping, for yet another door to be unlocked. The key grated as it turned. Then the sudden flood of bright light blinded her for a moment as they were led into the main prison.

There were four tiers of landings, with cell doors lining the walls. Women warders walked around in their navy uniforms, keys jangling from their leather belts. It was an alien stark world and she was gripped by fear.

She followed the warder to the second tier, her ill-fitting shoes clattering on the iron staircase. They stopped outside a cell door and the officer unlocked it, shoving her roughly inside.

The smell of stale urine clogged her sinuses and she wanted to retch. She saw the cockroaches scuttling across the floor and was appalled. Then she looked up and saw the other two women staring at her.

Lily desperately wanted to turn and run, but the door behind her was firmly locked . . .

Chapter One

'Miss Pickford. Thank you for coming, please take a seat.'

Lily looked at the tight-drawn features of the manager of the National Provincial Bank and with concern asked, 'Are you all right? You don't look very well.'

Alan Bennet took a clean white handkerchief from his pocket, mopped his brow, sat down and cleared his throat. 'I don't quite know where to begin, Miss Pickford,' he said. 'But I have some very bad news, I'm afraid.'

Lily frowned. 'About what?'

'The company that you invested your money with has gone into liquidation.'

She looked at first puzzled, then horrified. 'You mean it's gone bust?'

He nodded. 'I'm afraid so.'

'And my investment?'

'Worthless.' Wringing his hands, Bennet said, 'I'm just as shattered as you are, Miss Pickford. When I recommended the company it looked solid. I put a lot of my own money in it, too. I'm liable to lose my house and maybe my job, as I recommended it to several of my clients. One or two are coming in this morning and I'm not looking forward to breaking the news to them, either.'

3

Lily sat motionless, stunned. She heard him speaking through a rushing noise in her ears and tried to get her mind around his words, but nothing made sense. 'You mean that every penny of my inheritance has gone?'

'You – we – may get a small percentage back on our investment once the receivers have been through the books, if there is anything to be salvaged, but it could take a very long time.'

'Oh my God!' Lily took a packet of cigarettes from her handbag. The manager walked around the desk and lit one for her. Her fingers were trembling as she held the cigarette. 'What happened?'

'The textile firm was doing well, making money. It had the potential to make huge profits with added investment paying for further expansion. The books were fine and the plans drawn up for its future were watertight. That's when the owner started to look for investors.' He paused to wipe the sweat from his brow. 'For a while things went well, as you know, with dividends being paid, but eventually the owner became greedy and instead of paying out the profits, he started to cook the books . . . and now he's run off with all the money. Disappeared! There are no funds to carry on and the receiver can't find a way to rescue the company – so they've put it into liquidation.' He returned to his seat. 'If you remember, I did advise you not to put all your money into one company,' he said tentatively.

'I do remember,' said Lily. 'I should have listened to you.'

'But you still have the Club Valletta,' he said, trying to encourage her.

Lily closed her eyes as if to keep out the world that suddenly had collapsed around her. This couldn't be true. This was a nightmare! She'd wake up in a minute and all would be well. She gripped the arms of the chair in desperation, opened her eyes and saw Alan Bennet looking at her apprehensively. Overwhelmed by a feeling of panic, she started to shake. She had to get out of the room; she needed to be alone. Getting quickly to her feet, she told him, 'I have to go away and think about this. I – I'll be in touch.' Then she turned abruptly and made for the door.

Once outside the bank, Lily clutched at the rail as her legs seemed unable to hold her. She suddenly felt hot and faint and gasped for air. All the money that Vittorio had left her in his will, her security, her future . . . *gone*. She sat down on the steps of the bank and put her hands to her head. What on earth was she to do? But her head was buzzing, her temples sweating. She fought the waves of nausea that threatened to overcome her.

How could life be so cruel? She'd pulled herself out of the gutter once before and certainly had no intention of returning to it! Lily remembered that night seven years ago now, when her violent father threw her out of the house on the eve of her sixteenth birthday, after she had found the courage to refuse his sexual abuse. How well she recalled her early struggle to survive on the dockland streets of Southampton until she was rescued by Rachel Cohen, a second-hand clothes dealer who had offered her a job and lodgings in her shop. Eventually she had fallen for the charms of Vittorio Teglia, one of the town's biggest villains. Known to all as 'The Maltese', Vittorio had given the young Lily a life of luxury, a child and his love. She still felt the pain of his untimely death, but he had left her and Victoria, their daughter, well provided for, knowing the hardships of being unmarried with a baby. The legacy had cushioned her against his loss. But now . . . now she was once again in dire trouble. How ever was she to survive *and* provide for her daughter?

As Lily sat on the steps, pulling the jacket of her smart

blue suit around herself for comfort, she was lost to the comings and goings of other people, oblivious to the strange looks sent in her direction by the bank's other clients making their way inside and out of the building. One or two of them frowned uneasily, having been summoned to meet the manager themselves, wondering if bad news awaited them too, for it was obvious to all who looked in her direction that this smartly dressed, attractive young woman was deeply distressed.

Eventually Lily rose to her feet and walked slowly down the steps of the bank, then made her way on trembling legs along Bernard Street and back to the Club Valletta. She moved in a haze, unaware of the sights and sounds around her – the flower-vendor, the rag and bone man, the cry of the seagulls, the call of the ships' funnels, the whistle of the goods train making its way into Southampton's dock gates . . . She heard none of these things.

She didn't remember walking home, but when she entered the Club Valletta, she stood in the elegant dining room and leaned on the bar, looking around at the room. This had been her pride and joy. The original Club Valletta had been run by Vittorio, but when it burned down, costing The Maltese his life, she and Rachel, using the insurance money from the old place, had opened this hotel, named after Vittorio's club in his memory. It was two buildings knocked into one, with fourteen letting rooms as well as Lily's rooms and next to her bedroom, Victoria's nursery.

For a moment she put the bitter news behind her, recalling the pleasure of furnishing the club tastefully and with flare. Rich velvet drapes hung at the windows, and the tables were covered in the finest damask cloths, with dainty flowers set at their centre. A soft green carpet matched the drapes and complemented the flower-bedecked small stage set up in one corner. Wall lights gave the room a cosy ambience. The new Club Valletta had attracted local businessmen, the Shipping Federation used it for private functions, and despite the fact that it was located in the heart of Southampton's docklands, the Club had thrived with a reputation for fine cuisine and a hostess who was both efficient and personable.

But despite all that, business was now dropping off, for everyone was feeling the pinch financially in this troubled year of 1926. Clients were cutting down on business lunches and firms were curbing their expenses. The General Strike had caused chaos in the country; now there was an international recession and business people were decidedly nervous about the future. This had only added to Lily's problems.

Now Lily made her way upstairs to her office and sat in her leather chair behind the desk. She removed her cloche hat and ran her fingers through her bobbed hair. How the hell was she going to manage now? Her head was spinning, searching for ideas, but her mind was muddled. It was at that moment that Rachel Cohen, her partner – a short plump, smartly dressed soul – came into the room and spoke to her.

'Lily! A ghost you look. What's the matter?'

Lily gazed across the desk at the elderly Jewish woman and said, 'I've lost all my money. The textile company I invested in has gone bust . . . I'm broke!'

'Oy vey! You mean you got nothing left?'

Lily shook her head. 'I have a bit put by in another bank account, but it's only enough to live on for two or three months. But really all I have is a club that's losing money, an overdraft at the bank and no way of paying it off unless business picks up.'

Rachel moved swiftly over to the sideboard, and pouring two brandies, handed one to Lily. 'Here, darling. Drink this. In shock you are. Me too!'

The two women sipped the fiery liquid, silent, both lost in their own thoughts. Rachel glanced across at the lovely young woman who looked so worried, her blue eyes clouded, her shoulders slumped. Lily was usually so full of ideas, so full of life – and the older woman's heart ached for her. She herself had invested a lot of money to stock the club bar and wine cellar when the Club first opened, and she too was having to watch every penny. Rachel had £100 in her account, but that was all – and that had been salted away for her retirement. She'd seriously considered selling her house and buying a smaller one, and now she would have to do so.

'You can have what money I've got if it will help,' she said.

'Certainly not!' said Lily immediately. 'You'll need that one day – maybe sooner than you think, the way things are going.' She frowned. 'I just need time to think. There *must* be a way round all of this.' Putting down her glass and picking up a sheet of paper she said, 'Anyway, life goes on. I need to talk to Chef about today's menus.' She kissed Rachel on the cheek. 'See you later.'

But first Lily made her way to the nursery on the top floor, where Victoria, her three-year-old daughter, was stumbling around in a discarded pair of her mother's shoes, a feather boa around her neck, an old hat on her head, singing, 'My Old Man Said Follow the Van'. She looked up as Lily entered the room and staggered over to her with a big smile on her face.

'Mama! I'm Marie Lloyd.'

Looking up at Nanny Gordon who was ironing in the background, Lily winked and said, 'When are you ever Victoria Teglia, I wonder?' She picked up her daughter and held her close, smoothing her jet-black hair, kissing the smooth olive skin, so like her father's.

8

Tears of frustration rose as she thought of her present position. She loved this child with every fibre of her being. She wanted to protect her for ever. Keep her in a glass case away from the trials and tribulations of the world. Vittorio, Victoria's father, had left a trust for his child to pay for her education, and at twenty-five, Victoria would have come into her own inheritance, but the stocks in which he'd so carefully invested to swell the fund had plummeted – and with it his daughter's future. At the time, Lily had felt sorry that Vittorio's carefully laid plans had misfired, but she hadn't been too concerned because her own financial investments had promised a secure future for them both, but now . . . now there was absolutely nothing.

Lily tweaked her daughter's nose and said, 'I've got to go and see the chef. Would you like to come with me?'

The child's face lit up with delight. Graham, the chef, was a particular favourite of hers. He always made such a fuss of her, feeding her delicacies whenever they met. 'Oh yes, please,' she said.

'Well, we'd better put your own shoes on or else you'll break your neck,' Lily joked as she bent down to remove the oversized ones. She tickled the soles of Victoria's feet as she did so, sending the child into hysterical laughter.

'No, Mama,' she begged through her laughter. 'Stop it, please.'

Lily pretended to nibble her toes through the cotton socks, ' "No, Mama, no",' she mimicked. ' "Leave my toes alone".'

With much giggling and many hugs and kisses, the pair eventually made their way downstairs.

Walking into the kitchen, Lily saw the chef doling out bowls of soup to two men standing just inside the back door. He handed them each a hunk of bread to go with it. Then, catching hold of Lily's arm, he led her to the other end of the room.

'Look, Miss Lily,' Graham hissed. 'It's all very well for you to tell these poor sods to come to the back door for something to eat, but you know we can't afford it as business stands.'

She looked over at the men eagerly devouring their food. She knew what it was like to be starving, not to have eaten for days.

'Surely you couldn't ask me to leave them on the streets without anything,' she said gently. 'Look at the medals on that bloke's chest. He's been through a war and what has he got? Bugger all for his trouble. "A land for heroes" they were promised, and where do they end up? Selling matches on street corners! They have no dignity, no pride. Surely a drop of soup and a piece of bread doesn't cost that much?'

Graham shook his head in resignation. 'You'll be wanting me to give them a three-course meal soon!'

Lily couldn't help but laugh at the indignation in his voice. 'Now you're being silly, I'm not *that* bad a businesswoman.'

The chef didn't appear totally convinced. Looking down at Victoria he said, 'Your mother will bankrupt us one day.' He ruffled the child's hair and picking up the end of the feather boa asked, 'What's all this, then?'

She smiled at him. 'I'm Marie Lloyd. This is the way I dress when I sing.'

'Oh, I see. Well, why don't you go through to the dining room and stand on the stage and practise, then when I've talked to your mother, I'll give you some ice cream. How about that?'

She beamed at him. 'Yes, please.'

'Away you go then.'

Graham shook his head and smiled as she ran off. 'What a

woman she'll be when she grows up!' Turning to Lily he asked, 'What about today's menu?'

'I see you've taken the salmon off and replaced it with trout,' she remarked.

'I'm trying to cut down the costs and the wastage, Miss Lily, but I'm still using the best steak for the Boeuf Bourguignon. And as always, the vegetables are fresh.'

She nodded her approval. 'I know things are difficult, but let's hope we have a few more clients. The Shipping Federation have cancelled their luncheon, by the way – they hope to have it at a later date, but that doesn't help us much, does it?'

'No, I'm afraid not.'

She handed him the menus. 'That's fine. I'd better go and find Victoria.'

'Don't forget to bring her back for her ice cream.'

With a smile she said, 'Do you honestly think she'll let me forget?'

While Victoria was in the kitchen eating, Lily sat at the bar in the dining room and looked around. What could she offer that would bring in more business? She wracked her brains. What would men be eager to spend their money on, apart from a good meal? She knew from her days with Vittorio that men would always find money for a woman. His brothel had been a success, but she was determined not to go down that road again. She'd left the world of prostitution way behind her and had spent too long building a respectable reputation: she wasn't going to throw that away for anything.

She strolled into the assembly room, next to the bar, kept for various meetings by private companies. It was a fair size, but these days it was empty more than it was full. It was wasted space – and wasted space cost money, which she couldn't afford. Lily strolled around looking at it, wondering how best to use it. Suddenly she could picture it all. Of course, why hadn't she thought of it before! The room was perfect. It was a brilliant idea! This would be a way to save all their futures. Then she frowned. It would be taking a considerable risk, but after all, life was a gamble. And as far as she was concerned, at the moment it was shit or bust!

Through the open door she saw Detective Inspector Chadwick enter the club with his sidekick Sergeant Green and went forward to meet them. The senior policeman was as usual wearing his raincoat and trilby hat, whilst the other was dressed in a suit that just about buttoned over his substantial paunch. She liked Chadwick and had got to know him over the last few years as he did his rounds. He smiled as she walked towards him.

'Hello, Lily. How are you?'

'Fine, thanks. To what do I owe the pleasure?' She nodded to Green.

'There's been a spate of burglaries in the area. Have you had any trouble?' he asked.

'Not so far,' said Lily. 'As you know, we are very careful with our security. The doors are thick and the windows locked, but of course I do have a night porter on duty, which would deter most burglars.'

He looked at her with interest. He knew this vibrant young woman very well and sensed that something was amiss. 'Is everything else all right? You look a bit pensive today.'

'Well,' she said slowly, running her hand through her hair, 'I was thinking about the business. You know that everyone is suffering at the moment and I was wondering if I could get a licence to open a gambling club in the assembly room.'

He didn't look at all happy about her suggestion. 'I can't see why that would be a problem – the Club has a good reputation. But what sort of gambling?'

'I thought I could set the room up with a few roulette tables.'

'Is it what you really want?'

'No, it isn't,' she said. 'But I've got to do something.'

'If you do this, Lily, you must realise that your type of clientele will change radically. The people who like to gamble are not the sort you're used to looking after. You may get a few of your usual business executives, but the men who gamble are a mixed bunch, especially the ones who get rich with shady money.'

She looked at him and with a shrug said, 'Look, I can't afford to be fussy. All I want to do is survive.'

He was not impressed. 'I wish you could think of an alternative, but if you can't, then I shall wish you luck – but for goodness' sake, be careful. You start going down this road and it will undoubtedly lead to trouble. I've seen it all before.' He pursed his lips. 'I would hate to be the one to have to close you down.'

'Oh for God's sake,' retorted Lily, irked by his negative approach, 'I'm only going to have gambling on the premises! It will be all legal and above board. I'm not holding a bloody orgy!'

'The day you do, you can invite me,' chipped in Sergeant Green, who was immediately quashed by the stern look from his superior.

'Just take care,' was Chadwick's parting shot as he left the Club.

Take care? sniffed Lily. Of course I'll bloody well take care! But at least it was a possible way out of her problems. First, however, she had to discuss it with Rachel. She collected Victoria from the kitchen, wiping the ring of ice cream from her mouth, and took her back to Nanny Gordon to be washed.

In the office, later that day, Rachel sat listening to Lily's idea, her face getting longer by the minute. 'A gambling club! My life, where do you get such ideas?'

'Look,' said Lily, her blue eyes bright, 'I know it's not what we wanted in the beginning, but times are desperate. We have to give it a try.' She sat back in her chair and said defiantly, 'If we don't do something, the business will go under. We have no choice. There's enough room to put three roulette tables in the assembly room, which should bring in the punters. They'll get hungry, the dining room will be busy and the bar should make a small fortune.'

'You haven't thought this through, Lily. OK you open, but where are you going to get the money to cover the winners' bets? You've got to have a substantial float to start with.'

Twiddling a strand of her dark hair, Lily decided, 'I'll sell my jewellery. That ought to bring in enough to stake us for a month, maybe two. If it doesn't pay by then, we'll have to close anyway.'

Rachel looked across at her. 'You'd be willing to sell the things that Vittorio gave you?' she asked quietly. 'What about your diamond and emerald ring, the one that was his mother's?'

Lily stared back at her. 'What good are diamonds and emeralds if we have no food, no roof over our heads – tell me that!'

'What about the cost of the tables?'

Lily's mouth tightened into a determined line. 'I'll find the money somehow.' She tried hard to make her old friend understand. 'Look, if we don't do something quickly, we'll have to sell up. There will be sod all left after we pay off the overdraft. How will I be able to afford to feed and clothe Victoria? What will I do? Where will we live – in some seedy room somewhere? I'd have to find work to pay the rent and buy food. Things are desperate – it's the only chance we have!'

The elderly Jewess looked at Lily who was suddenly so fired with enthusiasm. She loved this young girl whom she'd first met when Lily was sixteen. She'd seen her struggle to make a better life for herself. How far she'd come from those dark days – and look at her now. Beautiful, once again fighting to survive. She still felt guilty that it was her son Manny who had destroyed Vittorio's living by setting fire to his Club; the fact that Vittorio had died in the fire, trying to rescue her waster of a son, was a heavy burden for her to carry. Who was she to stand in Lily's way?

'That's what you think. All right – we give it a try.'

Lily was surprised at such a quick capitulation. 'You're sure?'

'Sure? No, I ain't sure, but as you said, do we have a choice? No, we don't have a choice.'

At that moment a waiter appeared at the door of the office. 'Excuse me, Miss Pickford, but Sergeant Green is downstairs asking for you.'

Frowning Lily said, 'Sergeant Green? What the hell does he want now?'

The waiter shrugged. 'Don't know, miss. He never said.'

Getting to her feet, Lily went down the stairs to the bar.

Archie Green was a big bluff man, his face puffed and red from drinking too much beer. He'd been in the Force for years and he knew he'd never rise any higher than his present position, but he wasn't too worried. He had a few irons in the fire and now he'd got an idea to put to Lily that should earn him a few quid.

'I'm off duty,' he said immediately when Lily appeared beside him, 'and I have a business proposition you might be interested in.'

'If you're off duty then I can offer you a pint,' she said pleasantly, and asked the barman to pour him one. She was puzzled: what did the man want? They sat down at one of the tables.

'I was interested to hear about your new idea, when we spoke earlier this morning,' Sergeant Green began.

'Your boss didn't seem to like it,' said Lily shortly.

'Yes, well, you know old Chadwick. His brain is beginning to go with his hair. I was just thinking, if business is bad, the cost of the tables is going to be a great consideration. It just so happens that I know a couple of blokes who make and service these tables for various clubs and casinos. They'd be willing to hire you three.'

Lily looked sceptical. 'And what's in it for them?'

Green laughed. 'Ever the businesswoman! They would want a small percentage of the take. They could also find the croupiers for you. Everything would be taken care of.'

'Yes, I bet it would,' said Lily scathingly. 'Do you take me for a fool? Their tables, their croupiers. They could be fiddling and I wouldn't even know.'

'No, it's not like that at all. You can hire your own staff, as soon as you get it up and running, but this would save time until you get sorted. It's up to you,' he said with a casual shrug and sipped at his pint. 'I could bring Percy Gates round to see you and you could have a chinwag. You're under no obligation.'

It made sense, Lily thought to herself. To buy the tables she'd have no other recourse but to go to the bank for finance, and she wasn't at all sure she'd get their backing, although she hadn't voiced these concerns to Rachel. It wouldn't do any harm to see this bloke. 'All right then. When?'

'Tomorrow morning be convenient?'

'Yes,' said Lily. 'About ten o'clock.'

Looking well pleased with himself, Green said, 'Fine. I'll arrange it.' He emptied the contents of his glass. 'Thanks. See you tomorrow.'

Lily watched him leave the club. Whereas she liked and respected DI Chadwick, she'd never particularly warmed to Green. He was a chancer, she thought, but as the situation stood, she'd no other choice. If she thought the deal was dodgy, she could turn it down.

Alone in bed that night, Lily tossed and turned. Sleep eluded her, with so many thoughts churning in her mind. She went over her hopes, her dreams of owning a small chain of exclusive hotels around the country. And now she was in danger of losing the one that she owned! Life was cruel, taking her out of the gutter, showing her a better life and now . . . It didn't bear thinking about. If her new plan failed, what would happen then? The Club would have to be sold, she'd have to find a job, somewhere to live. Who would look after Victoria? She'd have to get rid of Nanny Gordon . . . This was too much. Agitated, Lily got out of bed, slipped into a dressing gown, walked to the nursery and quietly opened the door.

She crept over to the bed and knelt down beside it, gazing upon the sleeping features of her child and smiled as she saw Victoria's thumb stuck comfortingly in her mouth. Oh, if only life was that simple. She stretched out and gently touched the small hand, looking at the delicate fingers, the clean pink fingernails. Her child was such a perfect creature, so like Vittorio. Oh, if only he were here now. He would sort out her troubles. She needed his strength, longed to hear his deep mellifluous voice, to be held in his strong arms. To be comforted, to be loved.

She'd tried hard to make up to Victoria for the fact that she hadn't a father, but fortunately the child was surrounded by love – not only from her, but Rachel adored her and so did Nanny Gordon. She had a sunny temperament and brought great joy into all their lives. Lily *had* to succeed, for her daughter's sake. After all, hadn't she learned over the years that nothing was easy? You had to fight to survive in this world – especially in this area of Southampton. But her back was against the wall and she knew she'd have to take a chance if she was to pull through.

As promised, the next morning Sergeant Green arrived at the Club with Percy Gates. Lily was filled with a sense of unease when she was introduced to the man. She didn't like his smile – which wasn't genuine. It didn't reach his eyes which were fixed on Lily, carefully calculating her character, her strength, her weakness. He was far too smooth. She'd met many gamblers in the past and had learned never to trust them.

Percy Gates was a persuasive man. He began by telling her how, despite the bad times, there were always men who could find the cash for women and gambling.

'As you know, Miss Pickford,' he said, 'the poor will always be poor and the rich, rich, and in between are the men who make money in various ways and are prepared to spend it on their own enjoyment. They come from all walks of life – I'm telling you the truth for your own sake. But . . . they spend!'

'What do you mean exactly, from all walks of life?'

Gates looked Lily squarely in the eye. 'I'm saying they may not be the cream of society. Most of them are self-made men, that's all.'

Yes, I bet they are, thought Lily. Dodgy dealers, most of them no doubt – a few criminals too. She'd had enough dealings with the likes of them when she was the mistress of

18

Vittorio, and ever since had steered well clear of them as she built her own reputation. A respectable one. But she told herself, hers would be a respectable club; whatever her customers wanted, they would have to do it by the rules.

'Why don't you have two roulette tables and another for Black Jack?' Gates suggested. 'That way you'll give your punters a choice as to how they lose their money.'

Lily thought this was a good idea. 'Yes, perhaps you're right. But tell me, what do you get out of it all, Mr Gates? What's your cut?'

He gave a sly smile. 'You get the tables and the servicing of them when required. I will supply the croupiers, but you can replace them with your own whenever you like. For this I expect thirty-five per cent of the take.'

'Thirty!' said Lily immediately. 'And not a penny more. I'm supplying the venue and it's a classy one. There's a cabaret every Saturday, the food is excellent and the service first-class. Thirty per cent is all I'm prepared to pay.'

There was an expression of admiration on the face of Percy Gates. 'I heard you were a smart businesswoman,' he told her. 'All right – thirty it is.'

'One other thing,' said Lily, pointing a finger at him. 'These tables had better be kosher. If I find they're anything else, I'll call in the Fraud Squad, understand?'

'Perfectly. When do you want the tables installed?'

'Well, first I have to apply for a licence. I was told there shouldn't be a problem. I also need to turn the storage space in the assembly room into an office to use for the cash transactions, and I will have to install a secure safe. I'll use my own cashier,' she added quickly. 'I'll get back to you when I know.'

'Fine,' he said, holding out his hand. 'When you give me the nod, me and my partner will install the tables. I'll supply all the gambling chips so you've no need to buy them, either. They're part of the deal.'

Lily shook his sweaty hand and wished she didn't have to do business with such a man.

It was three weeks before Lily's application for a licence was granted, and business hadn't improved. She'd taken all her jewellery to be sold, telling herself she didn't need any of it to remind her of the man she'd loved. This helped to pay for a local builder, who quickly and cheaply transformed the stockroom. He changed the door, replacing it with a counter with a strong grill on the top as security. When this was nearly finished, Lily rang Gates telling him to bring the tables two days hence. During that time, the assembly room was cleared of furniture and thoroughly cleaned, ready for the tables to be set up. Percy and Bert his partner came personally to see them installed.

Despite her misgivings, Lily looked at the finished room with pleasure. It was attractive and just the right size for such a venture. There was enough room around the tables for the punters to gamble in comfort, and by the walls a few tables and chairs were set up, for any who wished to sit. She bit on her bottom lip. This was her last chance. If they didn't make it in a month, six weeks at the most, she would be penniless.

Finally, Lily hired a retired accountant to work at the cash desk, impressing on him the importance of keeping the books up to date. 'I want to know at the end of every night how much we've won ... or lost, to the last farthing. Understand?'

'Yes, Miss Pickford. You have nothing to worry about on that score, I can assure you.'

She instructed two waiters assigned to the room, 'As soon

as anyone has an empty glass, I want you beside them taking
an order for another drink. The same applies to the tables.
I've not put too many in because I want people to use the bar
and dining room.'

'Yes, miss. We understand.'

'I hope you do. The more drinks you sell, the more tips
you make.'

They both grinned at her, knowing she was speaking the
truth. There wouldn't be many empty glasses if they had their
way.

Sandy, Lily's longtime friend and Club pianist, walked in
and stood beside her. 'You've set this up well. It looks very
smart,' he complimented her gently.

She tucked an arm through his. 'God, I hope so. We need
to make money – and quickly.'

Sandy knew that things were bad. He used to play the
piano at lunchtimes only, as during the evenings there used to
be Harry, with his five-piece band. Regretfully the band had
been dismissed as trade dropped off. Now Lily sang to
Sandy's accompaniment, on Saturday nights.

He patted her arm. 'Well, girl, you can but try.' Seeing her
worried frown, he teased, 'Listen to me. Remember the old
days when you didn't have a farthing to your name and we
went round the pubs, you singing, me playing?'

She gave a soft chuckle. 'You old tart, how could I forget.
God, Sandy! Those were good days. The two of us only had a
few pennies to rub together, but we survived, didn't we?'

He grinned broadly. 'You in my frocks. I was so jealous
that you were able to wear them in public but I could only put
them on in the house behind closed doors.'

'Well, dearie,' said Lily, 'if you'd worn them outside,
you'd have been arrested for it, double quick. Imagine me
swanning down the nick to bail out "Mr Sandy Gilbert, the

cute redhead in the green frock". A right fool I'd have looked!'

'You cheeky monkey, Lily Pickford!'

They both laughed at the happy memories. 'You'll get by, darling,' said her friend. 'You're a survivor – haven't I always said so?'

She hugged him and kissed his cheek. 'Yes, you have, Sandy. You always have.'

Lily had advertised the opening of the gambling club in the *Southern Daily Echo*, on wall posters in the streets of Southampton, on a large hoarding in the High Street, and inside the Docks Railway Station. She'd had leaflets delivered to large offices, to the Cunard Building, and had paid newsagents to put leaflets inside their papers. There had been a few reservations from her regular clients, but one or two had thought it a good idea and said they might come along and try their luck. As one of them commented: 'At least here we know the game isn't crooked as it is in so many other places.'

She hastened to assure him that the Club Valletta was a respectable place still, and that wouldn't change. And she explained that the gambling room would remain separate and wouldn't encroach on those who just wished to dine.

As opening night arrived, Lily was decidedly nervous. She chose her gown with care, not sure what image to create. Victoria sat on her mother's bed in her nightclothes watching Lily change from one gown to another.

As Lily put on a wine-coloured dress with a square neck and dropped waistline embroidered with bugle beads, Victoria clapped her hands in delight. 'You look pretty in that, Mama,' she said.

Lily turned first one way then the other. 'Will it do? Shall I wear this one?'

'Yes, yes,' said Victoria.

'Right, but before I finish getting ready, I'll take you off to bed. Come along.' She picked the child up and took her next door to her room where Nanny was waiting. Tucking Victoria into her bed, Lily kissed her. 'Sleep tight. See you in the morning.'

Eventually Lily was ready. Full of nerves, she walked downstairs to the new gaming room and looked around, pleased with the transition. She greeted the three croupiers, all young men in their twenties, who were smartly dressed in black trousers, white shirts and bow ties.

Bill, the oldest of the three, looked at her, introduced himself and said, 'Don't worry, Miss Pickford. It may take a while to get going, but a lovely place like this will soon be packed out. You see, a lot of gambling clubs are seedy, but this place has class.' He winked. 'Gamblers like a bit of class, even if they don't have any themselves.'

She liked the look of him. He had a pleasant face, his fair hair was sleeked back and there was an air of competence about him that was reassuring.

She smiled warmly at him. 'Listen, Bill, I expect to make a small fortune *tonight*, never mind waiting for it to get going!'

'Are you going to sing this evening, Miss Pickford? I've heard you've got a lovely voice.'

She gave him a cheeky look. 'I see you're well versed in the art of flattery, young man. You'll go far.'

His cheeks flushed slightly at her words. 'I hope we both go far, miss.'

'And I hope you're right,' she said. And walked back to the bar to await her first punters.

As Bill turned away, his smile instantly faded. He frowned, rubbed his chin then shook his head and muttered beneath his breath, 'Bloody Percy Gates!'

Chapter Two

Business in the new gambling club picked up even quicker than Lily could have anticipated, mainly due to the plush surroundings. The clientele were impressed by the tasteful elegance. And DI Chadwick had been correct: the punters *were* from a different class than the high-toned businessmen who'd been her regulars. They were more boisterous, lacking in social graces and sometimes crude, but Lily was well able to deal with them. They admired her spirit and despite the fact that her clothes were both expensive and classy, they recognised in her the mark of their own. She was of the streets, as they were.

The only men who gave her any feeling of disquiet were three brothers, who arrived on opening night and had become regulars at the tables. They were the Giffords, who came from gypsy stock and had made their money from horse trading and fairgrounds. Dark and swarthy in appearance, the brothers, Jake, Bart and Quinn, didn't observe any particular dress code but their own.

They walked through the main entrance on the first evening, dressed in corduroy jackets, bright waistcoats and colourful neckerchiefs. Lily heard their noisy entrance and when she saw their mode of dress, walked quickly over to them. She said to the oldest of the three: 'Good evening, what can I do for you?'

Quinn Gifford, the brother to whom she spoke, grinned at her, his gaze observing every detail of her. He was very much taken by the young lady who stood before him. 'We, me brothers and me, have seen the adverts and we want a bit of a flutter.' He looked around. 'Nice place you've got. Is the food any good?'

'We have a fine chef and a reputation second to none for our dining room, but I'm very sorry, gentlemen,' she looked at the other two men, 'I can't allow you to use my hotel or the gaming room because you are unsuitably attired.'

Jake, the youngest of the Giffords, stepped forward. 'Unsuitably what?'

'I'm afraid, gentlemen, I must insist you wear ties if you wish to use my establishment.'

'Bugger that!' exclaimed Jake. 'My money's as good as anyone else's. In the other clubs they don't complain.'

His manner was belligerent but Lily didn't hesitate in her response. 'I'm not interested in other places, but in mine you have to wear a tie. We have some for sale, if you would like to purchase one each. If not, I'll have to ask you to leave.' She stood defiant and resolute.

Quinn looked at her with interest and admiration. It wasn't usual for anyone to stand up to the Giffords with their fearful reputation. He looked into the bright blue eyes of this sparky woman and was intrigued. But his two brothers were angry. Bart, the third man, glowered at Lily.

'Then as far as I'm concerned, you can stuff your club!'

He turned to walk away, but Quinn caught hold of his arm. 'Hang about. We're not going anywhere.' He gazed intently at Lily beneath hooded eyes. 'We'll take three of your ties, miss.' He undid his neckerchief and motioned to the others to do the same.

Lily, with a sense of relief, obliged.

The other two brothers grumbled loudly about this indignity but Quinn ignored them. 'We'll have a table for three,' he said.

Lily led them to an empty table and beckoned the waiter over to take their order.

The Giffords caused a few of their fellow diners to look at them askance as they devoured their food in an unseemly manner. Like pigs at a trough, thought Lily as she watched from a distance.

They were on their last course when Lily, with Sandy's accompaniment, took to the stage to sing. All the time she was aware of Quinn's eyes upon her, watching her every move.

As she sang 'I'm Always Chasing Rainbows', her clear voice filled the room causing a hush among the diners, and when she followed it with 'What Do You Want To Make Those Eyes At Me For?' flirting with her customers from the stage, she looked at Quinn who smiled back at her with delight. But when she sang the poignant 'It Had To Be You', she avoided looking in his direction, aware that he was taking far more interest in her than she liked or wanted.

Eventually the Giffords made their way into the gaming room. Later when Lily went in to check on the proceedings, she saw that Jake and Bart were losing heavily, but that Quinn was having a modicum of success. When he saw Lily he beckoned her over, calling to one of the young waiters to get her a drink. He ignored her refusal, gazing at her, a broad grin on his face. 'I'm real glad that me and me brothers decided to come here tonight.' He pulled at his tie, loosening it. 'Even if I do have to wear this damned thing. You'll be seeing a lot more of us, that I can promise.'

Lily sipped her drink out of politeness before she made her excuses and returned to the bar in the other room. There was something very menacing about Quinn Gifford, and she wasn't at all sure she wanted him or his brothers as regular customers.

Over the course of the next few weeks, the Giffords came in every Saturday night. They didn't always have a meal, but went mainly straight to the gaming room, yet Quinn always made a point of coming in and standing at the bar, watching Lily closely as she sang to the punters.

She was aware that this man had taken a shine to her and she found his constant gaze unnerving. She tried to keep him at a distance but when she visited the gaming room, he would appear at her side, or if he was playing the tables, he would call her over to stand beside him to bring him luck. He said little, but Lily with her long experience of men, recognised the predatory look in his eyes.

One Saturday night, the younger brothers both lost and won as they played the tables, but Quinn seemed to have a great deal of luck. He won at the roulette tables then at Black Jack, and Lily was counting the cost, praying that he would lose some of his substantial winnings before the night was out.

Jake and Bart took their money to the bar and started drinking heavily, but Quinn went over to the Black Jack table again and started to play. Beside him another punter who was losing steadily and was more than a little inebriated, started to complain about the other man's astonishing run of luck.

As the dealer pushed yet another pile of chips towards Quinn, the man muttered, 'This is getting ridiculous. You win much more and I'll begin to think the cards are marked.' He glared at Quinn. 'You running some kind of deal with him?' He nodded towards the dealer.

Quinn just stared at the man. 'When I was losing the other night and you was winning, you didn't think so,' he growled.

'That was the other night,' retorted the punter.

The dealer, quietly but firmly said, 'Perhaps you'd better stop for tonight, sir. The cards are running against you. It happens.'

The man was about to argue but he saw the baleful look on Quinn's face and decided to retire gracefully.

Lily, now standing at the bar, ever watchful, saw the man stagger out of the door and heard him berating the staff about a rigged game. She made her way to the gambling room and walked over to Bill who was working on the roulette table. 'Is there some sort of trouble?' she asked quietly.

He shook his head. 'No, Miss Pickford. Just a drunken punter who's on a losing streak.'

She stood and watched the game from a distance and was pleased to see Quinn lose some of the money he'd won earlier. While she watched she was able to study him, unobserved. He was of medium height but very stocky in build. A powerful man, it was obvious. His jet-black hair was curly and wild, growing long into his neck. In a coarse way he was quite handsome. She noticed the nails of his broad strong hands were caked with dirt, but on his right hand he wore a large signet ring with a single diamond in the centre. In one ear hung a gold earring.

She heaved a sigh of relief as he lost another hand of cards. She wasn't yet in a financial position to recover if someone had a run on the tables, and although there was a cash limit, the Giffords had made a hole in her takings tonight. What's more, Jake and Bart were now getting riotously drunk next door at the bar.

Lily left the room and approached them. 'Why don't you call it a night, boys?' she suggested. 'You'll have such a hangover tomorrow you won't be able to work.'

Jake, the younger of the two, put an arm around her

shoulders. She saw the barman stiffen, ready to intervene, but she shook her head. 'Let me call you a taxi, Mr Gifford.'

He looked at her through bleary eyes and gave her a stupid alcoholic grin. 'You can call me Jake. In fac', you can call me whatever you like, darlin'. Why don't you come home with me?' he leered.

At that moment Quinn appeared at his side and roughly pulled his brother away from Lily. 'Time to go,' he stated in a tone so menacing that there was no argument from the other two.

'I'll call a taxi,' said Lily quickly.

'No need,' said Quinn shortly. 'I've got the truck outside. I'd better get these two away afore they throw up over the carpet.' And then with an arm around each of his brothers, he half carried them towards the door.

'Whew! Thank goodness for that,' said Lily, as they left the premises.

Sandy had been watching the little drama. 'You'd better keep an eye on those three,' he warned her. 'They have a really bad reputation, especially Quinn. He's been inside, you know, for beating up some man who upset him.'

Lily felt a shiver run down her spine. She was able to cope with most situations, but Quinn made her decidedly nervous. She sensed that he had a volatile nature and hoped that it wouldn't ever erupt inside her club. She needed to keep out of trouble with the local police if she was to survive.

The club was slowly making money even with Percy Gates's cut, and Lily could at last see a light at the end of her tunnel – except for one thing. Two strangers had started using the club. They came in about twice a week. She didn't know them and not one of her staff had seen them before, but the thing that began to worry Lily was the fact that they seldom lost at the tables.

30

Using her usual hostessing skills, she chatted to them but found they were both very close-mouthed. Many of her punters didn't like to talk about themselves, but these two were almost defensive if they were questioned, which made her suspicious. She took to watching the tables, the croupiers and the dealer of the Black Jack table, but saw nothing untoward. Yet she had a gut feeling that things were not right. Some of the regulars were also beginning to complain and suggest that this long winning streak was not kosher, then the punters would lose a hand and the mutterings would stop, but Lily was still uneasy and her takings were dropping.

The Giffords had not been in the club for a couple of weeks but when they arrived the following Saturday, they told Lily they'd been away at horse fairs around the country and were ready for a good night out. Once again, Lily was aware of the constant gaze from Quinn's dark eyes.

This particular night the club was full. There was a party of men out celebrating the impending marriage of one of their midst. They gambled for a while but just before the cabaret they all sat in the dining room, drinking champagne and eating, with much laughter and ribaldry about the coming event.

Lily was surprised to see all the Giffords standing at the bar, drinking, observing the riotous behaviour. She stood in the middle of the stage, her black sequinned dress twinkling in the lights, nodded to Sandy sitting at the piano and began to sing 'The Bells Are Ringing For Me And My Gal', which brought forth even more comments from the stag party. Lily could see the thunderous expression on Quinn's face and her stomach tightened. God, don't let him be a problem, she prayed. She was easily able to cope with the revellers; they were not belligerent, only full of high spirits and she'd dealt

31

with this sort of audience over the years without any trouble.

She started to sing 'He'll Come Along One Day, The Man I Love', when to her surprise one of the men began to climb unsteadily up onto the stage, yelling, 'Here I am. I'm the man you love, darling.'

Within seconds, before Lily could handle the situation in her own way and with humour, Quinn had crossed the room, leapt on the man's back and dragged him off the stage. All hell broke loose as his companions jumped to their feet to defend their friend, who by now was being punched in the face by Quinn. The other two brothers sprang to Quinn's defence and there was mayhem. Tables were overturned, chairs thrown, glasses broken. The barman had no choice but to call the police.

As the drunken revellers and the Giffords were driven away in the police van, Lily looked around the room in horror, seeing the broken furniture, the mess of squashed food on the carpet, the splintered glass. It would cost a great deal to put it right.

At that moment DI Chadwick entered the Club. He looked around at the chaos then at Lily. 'Don't say I didn't warn you,' he said.

She turned on him, fury blazing in her eyes. 'All right! Yes, you warned me.'

'It was inevitable, Lily, I'm afraid. Especially with the Giffords around.'

'Quinn was only trying to protect me,' she argued. 'Some drunk climbed up onto the stage. Quinn thought I was in trouble.'

Chadwick raised an eyebrow and looked sceptical. 'He must fancy you, my dear Lily, because normally to see a woman in trouble wouldn't make him turn a hair . . . But to other things. If this happens again, you know your licence will be in jeopardy, don't you?'

She sighed wearily. 'Yes, I thought as much. But it won't happen again.'

'You can't guarantee that!' he said sharply. 'You'd better get a couple of men to keep things under control. But be careful, I don't want to have to deal with complaints from clients of yours with broken arms.'

'Thanks for the vote of confidence,' she snapped.

He gave a wry smile, rubbed the top of his balding head and said, 'Look, Lily. I don't want to see you in trouble, I know you're having a tough time. Just watch your step, that's all.' He made his way to the exit without another word.

Lily closed the Club for the rest of the night and the staff started the thankless task of clearing the debris.

Rachel arrived at the Club Valletta the next morning unaware of the fracas as she'd gone home early the previous night. She looked with horror over her spectacles at the sight of carpenters mending broken chairs, the staff still finding broken glass in a carpet that was being washed by many willing hands.

'What the bloody hell happened here?' she exclaimed.

Lily wearily ran a hand through her hair. 'You may well ask. There was a fight. Quinn Gifford started on one of the stag party that was booked in, and who was climbing onto the stage. He didn't give me a chance to sort it myself, he just went wild and beat him up. It turned into a free for all, I'm afraid.'

Shaking her head Rachel remarked, 'How much will it cost to put it right?'

'Too bloody much!' said Lily furiously. 'It'll take all our profits, and these past weeks will have been for nothing. We're hanging on by the skin of our teeth as it is. This is the sort of thing that could close us down – I could kill that hot-tempered bastard.'

'I've heard about the Giffords,' said her friend as she looked at the mess. 'Trouble with a capital T. You'll bar them, of course.'

Lily looked at her with surprise. 'Bar them? No, of course not, they spend too much money. But the next time they come in, I'll give them a good talking to. Tell them if this happens again, *then* they'll be out on their ears.'

Victoria came running down the stairs at that moment, calling for her mother. Lily scooped her up in her arms, afraid she'd get broken glass in her feet. 'You must go to the nursery and play, darling,' she urged.

'You promised to take me to see the trains, Mama,' pleaded the child.

'I'll be up in half an hour,' Lily promised.

When later she took Victoria to the docks station, she was pleased for the distraction. Seeing the delight on her daughter's face as the trains arrived, her pleasure as she watched them belch steam as they left the platform, Lily was able to put her own problems to one side.

They walked along the Esplanade and picked up small shells from the shore, then threw bread to the noisy and hungry gulls before returning to the Club, Lily skipping alongside her child, singing songs. These moments were very precious to both of them. Victoria ran eagerly up the stairs when they arrived home, to show off her spoils to Nanny Gordon.

The next evening the Club reopened with the dining room once again in a pristine condition, albeit with a few less tables and chairs, but with two burly men watching for any trouble. Ready to defuse any situation.

Lily was talking to the head waiter when she saw Quinn Gifford come into the club. He was alone. Her eyes blazing, Lily marched over to him. 'Come to apologise, have you?'

He just looked steadily at her. 'The magistrates fined me this morning for causing a disturbance.' Then he put his hand into the back pocket of his trousers and pulled out a bundle of white five-pound notes. He handed it to her and in his rough voice said, 'This should cover the damage.'

Looking at the money, Lily realised it was a generous amount. She asked, 'Why did you have to come storming in like an avenging angel? I could have handled it. The men were only tipsy, they weren't looking for trouble, just a bit of fun. You could have cost me my licence!'

There was anger in his dark eyes as he snapped, 'They had no right to behave like that. Not to you. That drunk could have hurt you.'

Lily was disconcerted. She knew that Quinn thought he was protecting her, but she didn't want him guarding her like this. There was an unhealthy feeling of possession in his actions, and that was the last thing she wanted.

She held up the money. 'I'll take this, thanks – the damage last night will cost a pretty penny. But any more trouble, and you and your two brothers will be barred from my premises.'

The corners of Quinn's mouth turned up as he tried to hide a smile, but there was menace in his voice as he said, 'My brothers and I go where we like and when we like.' He caught hold of her wrist in a grip of iron. 'You need someone to watch over you, Lily, my girl. A woman on her own in this part of the world isn't safe. You saw that last night.'

Snatching her hand away she flew at him. 'Now you listen to me, Quinn Gifford. I've been looking out for myself for years. I don't need some wild gypsy telling me how to run my life. You go back to your horses where you belong, but if you come in here again, you behave like a human being.'

He slowly studied her face. 'Oh, I'm human all right, Lily.' He lowered his gaze and looked at her shapely body, her full breasts and slim legs.

Lily felt as if he'd stripped her naked. This made her even more angry. 'Don't get any crazy ideas, Quinn, because you haven't a chance in hell.'

He raised an eyebrow and quietly said, 'Don't be too sure.' Then he walked towards the door, paused and told her, 'I'll be back.'

Outside the Club, Quinn walked down the road towards his old truck and climbed into the driving seat. He took a cheroot from his shirt pocket, struck a match against the leg of his trousers and lit the small cigar. He leaned back and slowly blew out the smoke, smiling to himself as he did so. Fiery little madam, that Lily Pickford. My, how her blue eyes flashed when she was angry. Her nostrils flared too. There was a woman with passion in her soul – passion he'd like to unleash. He would very much like to see her without all her finery, her posh frocks. His eyes narrowed as he visualised her soft body, her full breasts, her long legs and the hidden private places that he would like to explore. He felt himself harden at his lecherous thoughts. One day he'd find out for himself. He had to have her, some way. And one day he would.

Lily had too much on her plate to worry about Quinn Gifford. By now she was convinced that there was something going on with the dealer of the Black Jack table, for the two strangers were in again and winning. She went to a drawer behind the bar and produced a brand new pack of cards and took them into the gaming room. She handed them to the dealer. 'Use these from now on,' she said.

He made no comment, and didn't seem a bit fussed as he took off the wrapping. The game continued, but the men soon moved to one of the roulette tables and were again successful.

She watched several games and sensed the restlessness of the other punters. It seemed that only the ones who placed their bets on the same numbers as the strangers, won. But for all that, Lily couldn't find fault in the way the game was being handled. She wandered back to the bar in the dining room to think.

Standing at the bar she looked around the room and saw a small group of gentlemen enter the Club; she studied them with interest. They were well dressed in tailored lounge suits, and of a better class than those who nowadays frequented the Club Valletta. The tallest of them had an air about him, a look of intelligence, an elegance. He gazed around the dining room with interest as the head waiter showed them to a table. After they'd placed their order, they continued to look around and appeared to be discussing the décor, the one man pointing out one or two special touches – the drapes at the window, the cutlery and table settings. Lily was intrigued.

Towards the end of the meal, her curiosity getting the better of her, Lily sauntered over to their table and introduced herself. 'I'm Lily Pickford, the owner of the Club Valletta. I don't think we've had the pleasure of your company before, gentlemen.'

The four men rose from their seats. The man who had impressed her introduced himself. 'Good evening, Miss Pickford. I'm Luke Longford and these are some of my colleagues. Won't you join us for coffee?'

Lily accepted the invitation and sat down.

Luke smiled at her. 'We've been admiring the décor. This really is an excellent place. Very tasteful, very classy.' He hesitated for a moment, then went on: 'Forgive me for saying so, but your clientele seems out of place in such opulent surroundings.'

With a wry smile Lily said, 'I totally agree with you.'

Luke was surprised.

'But you see, gentlemen, business has been difficult for everyone and I had to make adjustments.'

'Like what, exactly?' asked one in a soft Scottish burr.

'I had to put in a gambling club.'

Luke smiled sympathetically. 'We all have to survive, of course, but . . . it does seem a pity.'

'Where are you gentlemen from?' asked Lily.

'We work for the Cunard Company on the *Mauritania*,' he explained. 'I'm a Chief Steward, Ian is the Second Engineer, and the others are pursers.'

'What an interesting life you must lead,' said Lily.

Luke shrugged. 'Every job has its problems, Miss Pickford.'

'Call me Lily. Yes, nothing is easy, is it?'

During the next half-hour, Lily had an interesting conversation with the men, finding in Luke especially a like mind. They exchanged business ideas, talked about the difficulties of finding good staff and working within a budget. He had a strong personality, a great sense of humour, and he made her laugh. She looked at his green eyes twinkling as he told of his travels, his business problems, and she was intrigued by the man. She hadn't enjoyed herself so much for a long time.

Reluctantly, Lily finally got up from the table. 'I must go and look at the gaming room,' she told them all. 'Do any of you gamble?'

They all shook their heads. 'Not me,' grinned Ian. 'I'm a canny Scot.'

Luke rose from his seat. 'I don't gamble – it's a fool's game – but I'd like to take a look around, if I may?'

'Of course.' Lily led him to the other room and left him to wander. She saw him watching the Black Jack table where one of the strangers was still winning, then he went across to one of the roulette tables and observed for a while. Eventually he stood by the second table where the other stranger was playing . . . and wining fairly steadily. Lily saw him frown. He walked over to her, took her arm and led her out of the room.

'Lily,' he said quietly and earnestly, 'I have worked on ships all my life so I've had quite a bit to do with casinos, and I'm telling you the game is not running right. I'm sure it's crooked.' He saw the look of horror on her face. 'I'm not saying for a moment that you knew about this but tell me, where did you get the tables and the staff?'

She found a quiet corner and told him about Percy Gates.

'Are these the staff he supplied?'

Lily nodded. 'I didn't think it was necessary to employ others, as things were going well. But I have to confess, these past two weeks I've had my suspicions, but I can't prove anything.'

Luke took a pen and card from his pocket. 'I'll give you the number of a friend of mine who's retired. Get him in to check the tables over. He's a genius. If there's anything amiss, he'll find it.'

She thanked him. 'I'll get in touch with him tomorrow.'

Luke smiled at her. 'I wish I could stay longer, I've enjoyed meeting you so much, but I must return to the ship. We're off on a short cruise but when I get back, I'll come and see you, if I may?'

'I'd like that very much,' said Lily. 'And thanks.'

'Be careful,' he said. 'I wouldn't like to see you in any kind of trouble.' He lifted her hand to his lips and kissed it softly. Then he left the club with his friends.

★ ★ ★

The following day, Lily rang the number that Luke had given her, only to be told that Mr Granger would be away for two days. She left a message for him to call her on his return, saying that the matter was urgent. Then she placed an advert in the local paper for croupiers and thought that at least she'd started the ball rolling in the right direction.

But for Lily, it was too late. The following evening, the Club Valletta was raided.

Chapter Three

Lily was startled as a dozen policemen rushed through the door of the Club Valletta, led by DI Chadwick.

'What the hell's going on?' she demanded.

Chadwick held a document in his hand. 'This is a search warrant. We've had complaints from some of your punters,' he told her. 'They say you're running a crooked game here. We have to take the tables away for inspection, and all the cards used in the Black Jack game.'

As she looked at the policeman, Lily felt the blood drain from her face, knowing that her worst fears were soon to be realised.

The police made their way to the gaming room, with Lily following in their wake. They asked the punters to pick up their chips and cash them in. The cards were removed from Bill the croupier at the Black Jack table, to his consternation. The clients began voicing their anger, milling around Lily, pushing and shoving, demanding an explanation. An argument erupted between two punters: one accused the other of stealing his chips. Blows were exchanged. It was chaos! The tables were removed, a chair was knocked over, a glass broken. Lily tried to calm everyone, but there was nothing she could do to stem their ire.

Chadwick caught hold of her by the arm and led her safely

out of the gaming room. 'I'm afraid we'll have to close the Club,' he said. 'You can't reopen until after our enquiries have been completed.' He hesitated. 'If, of course, we do find anything untoward, then I'm afraid you'll lose your licence altogether.'

'Can't I even open the dining room?' she asked, stunned.

'No, I'm afraid not.'

'But what about these people who are still eating?' She looked around the restaurant at the diners who were watching the scene with curiosity and dismay.

'They can finish their meal, but the bar will have to be closed as your licence has been suspended, pending our enquiries.'

'I do hope you're not expecting *me* to vacate the premises?' she snapped. 'After all, this is my home. Victoria is asleep on the top floor and I'm not going to disturb her for anyone!'

There was sympathy in Chadwick's expression. He placed a hand on her arm and said softly, 'No, of course not. You can remain in residence, but you can't open for business. I'm sorry, Lily, but when someone comes to the station and makes a complaint, we have to look into it . . . and there has been more than one, I have to tell you.'

As he was talking to her, the punters from the now-defunct gaming room pushed past, complaining bitterly. The tables were even now being taken out of the club. Lily's lips were pursed as she said, 'All right. You have a job to do, I suppose. Well, all I can say is get on with it and get it over with.'

She walked away, looking for Bill the senior croupier. She saw him skulking in a corner and pointed a finger at him. 'You!' she said coldly. 'In my office – now.'

Bill followed her up the stairs to the first floor and stood in the office, looking very perturbed.

'Right!' said Lily. 'What's going on?'

'I don't know what you mean, Miss Pickford.'

'Don't give me that crap,' she scoffed. 'For two weeks now I've had my suspicions about the game being rigged. I'm not a fool. Who were those two blokes that kept winning?'

He looked down at the floor.

'Were they friends of Percy Gates?'

He looked at her in surprise. 'How did you know that?'

'I didn't, but there had to be some tie-up with him.' She was furious. 'That rotten sneaky bastard! I never liked him from the first. So . . . what are the police going to find? You might as well tell me. I'm going to lose my licence, I have a right to know.'

'The cards of the Black Jack table were marked,' he said quietly.

'And the roulette tables?'

'Only one of them was doctored,' he admitted. 'The other was straight.'

'Is that supposed to make me feel better?' Lily retorted.

He looked away. 'No, miss.'

'You realise of course that you'll probably be taken to court over this?'

'Yes, I know,' he said with a note of resignation.

'You don't seem very bothered about it,' said Lily, somewhat surprised and a little suspicious.

'No, miss.' He looked up at her, his eyes full of guilt. 'I'm really sorry about this, Miss Pickford.'

'A lot of bloody good that'll do. But tell me, why don't you seem bothered about going to court?'

'It's all part of the deal with Gates.'

'Deal! What deal?' Lily's voice was filled with anger.

'Well, miss, if I was to get caught, Gates looks after me financially.'

'In other words, you take the rap for him. Is that it?'

He nodded.

'Not this time,' snapped Lily. 'Not when I tell the police about this conversation.'

'Then I'll deny it ever took place.'

'You what?' She couldn't believe what he was saying.

His face was pale and drawn. 'Look, Miss Pickford, I've got a family – a wife and two kids. If I spill the beans on Gates, he'll do them harm – he's told me as much. I can't let that happen.'

Lily ran a hand through her hair. 'The wicked bastard. But the police are bound to go to his place when I tell them where I got the tables.'

'That won't bother him none, miss. All the stuff there will be kosher and he'll deny all knowledge of it, by putting all the blame on me. Oh, he's a crafty bugger all right. All you have to do is to deny any knowledge of the offence.'

'But I'll lose my licence anyway. And I *didn't* know anything about it.'

'No, of course you didn't. The police will realise that. Perhaps they'll let you open again, without the gaming room.'

Lily closed her eyes; she had a raging headache. 'Get out of here. I've got to see the rest of the staff.'

He quickly scuttled away.

She walked down the stairs to see the staff gathered together in the kitchen doorway, talking. They stopped as soon as they saw her. Moving towards them she said, 'Please, let's go into the kitchen away from the few punters we still have. Look, I'm sorry but it seems that at the moment, I'm out of business and you're out of a job. I don't know what's going to happen in the future, but I suggest that when those who are still eating have finished, you clear away then go home. The bar has been closed so no more alcohol can be served. Come back in the morning and I'll make up your wages.'

There were mutterings among the staff and one of them asked, 'What's going on? We have a right to know if it means losing our jobs!'

Lily stared at the woman. 'The gambling tables have been removed for inspection. The police think there's something wrong with them.'

The same person asked, 'And is there?'

Lily was annoyed by the note of accusation in the voice. 'Not as far as I was aware. I run an honest game here.' But she knew from the discontented murmurings that there were a few members of her staff who doubted it. 'I think that you should all look for new jobs,' she continued. 'If I'm allowed to open again, I'll advertise. And of course any of you who want to come back will be given preference.' She gave a brave smile. 'And thank you all for your loyalty through what have been difficult times. Now, if you would go about your work until those in the dining room have finished their meal, you can then go home.'

At that, Lily left them to it and walked over to the bar where she collapsed on one of the high stools. Sandy came and sat beside her.

'First thing tomorrow morning,' he said, 'call your solicitor.'

'Yes, I will. What do you think will happen?' she asked her old friend.

'Well, first of all, *was* the game crooked?' asked Sandy.

She nodded. 'It seems it was. I had my suspicions but I couldn't see how.'

'Then, my love, you are what is known as "in the shit".'

'How am I going to make a living?' she asked. 'I've got

Victoria to consider and Rachel. Oh my God! Rachel! She doesn't know.'

'For goodness' sake don't ring her tonight,' Sandy entreated. 'There's no point in spoiling her night's sleep as well. Call her first thing in the morning.'

Alone in her room that night, Lily lay on top of her bed, fully clothed, trying to sort out the future. I suppose they'll fine me, she thought. With any luck she could cover it, but after that, what should she do? She would definitely lose her licence, then she'd be forced to sell the property, the proceeds of which would only be enough to pay off the overdraft at the bank. She'd be left penniless! What the hell could she do then to make a living? She had no idea. And what about Rachel? Poor Rachel had her money tied up in the Valletta, too. She stood to lose her investment as well. God! What a nightmare.

Eventually Lily undressed, climbed into bed and tried to sleep – but to no avail. When, through complete exhaustion, she did drop off, it was to be beset by nightmares of the Club, the police, and Quinn Gifford. She jerked awake, her body wet with perspiration, overcome by a feeling of impending doom. A feeling so strong that no matter what she did, she couldn't shake it off.

Picking up the telephone early the following morning, Lily rang Rachel's number and told her the bad news.

The Jewess didn't fuss. 'Right,' she said. 'I'll be there in an hour.'

The Club seemed empty and desolate when Rachel opened the door and let herself in. The staff had left everything tidy, but they'd taken off the tablecloths and napkins and the tables looked bare and clinical. She made her way upstairs to the office, where Lily was sitting at the desk making up the wages. Seeing Lily putting money into brown envelopes brought home the seriousness of the situation to Rachel.

'So . . . out of business, are we?'

Looking up, Lily said angrily, 'That bloody Gates has fitted us up good and proper.'

'Bloody *shyster*!' snapped Rachel.

Lily explained what Bill had told her the night before. How Gates had carefully covered his own tracks.

'But surely we can at least inform the police?' argued Rachel.

'First of all I need to consult my solicitor when he comes,' said Lily. 'Then we must do whatever he advises.'

Drawing up a chair, Rachel said, 'OK, I'll give you a hand with the wages, then we'll see what your Mr Williams has to say. Getting too worried, it don't help, not at this moment.'

Richard Williams, the solicitor, was more than concerned when he heard the news. Sitting in the office later that morning talking to the two women about their problems, he explained, 'You may get away with a fine, Miss Pickford, but I think you should know that running a crooked game is tantamount to fraud, which is a custodial charge. You could go to prison.'

'But I didn't know!' Lily was aghast. 'I explained to you how I was duped by that bastard Gates.'

'I know, my dear, but we can't prove anything if what the croupier says is true. No doubt the police will be vigilant in their search, but when it comes down to the bottom line, it's your name over the door. You are responsible for what happens on these premises.'

Lily's face was ashen as she said, 'I can't go to jail – I've got a young daughter to look after.'

Mr Williams looked grave. 'You must be prepared for such

an event. Have you anyone who could care for her if the worst was to happen?'

Lily looked at him with horror; she couldn't believe what she was being told. She tried to clear her mind, to face up to all eventualities. She must make plans, just in case. 'Rachel?' She turned to her friend, her eyes pleading for help.

Rachel looked at her with a worried expression. 'Now listen, darling, don't you get into a state about this. Victoria is safe. The worst comes to the worst, with me she'll live. Now don't you fret.'

Richard Williams turned towards the Jewess. 'And you, Mrs Cohen, being Miss Pickford's business partner, you too will most probably be held liable.'

'Oy vey!' Rachel held her hands to her face in horror. 'Me, go to prison?'

'In your case there is little likelihood of that. You used to leave quite early and didn't have anything to do with the gambling side. But a fine is more than likely.'

'My life!' said Rachel in despair. 'What will the Rabbi say?'

'When do you think we'll hear from the police, Mr Williams?' asked Lily in a choked voice.

'Within the week, I would think. Now I want both of you to come to my office this afternoon and make a statement. We must get the facts right and then I can prepare my case for the court.' He rose from his seat. 'I'm very sorry for your trouble. Can you come about three o'clock?'

'What else have we to do?' sighed Lily. She got up from her seat and saw the man off the premises. Returning to the office she said to Rachel, 'How the devil am I going to pay his fees? I'll need a barrister and I don't have the money.'

Rachel walked over to her, and putting a comforting arm around her shoulders she said, 'Now listen, darling. Worst situations we've been in together. Don't worry. You can use my retirement money.'

Lily was horrified. 'But you'll need that!'

Rachel shrugged. 'I've already put my house on the market – with business as it was I couldn't afford it. If it sells I'll find a smaller place.'

Putting her arms around her friend, Lily said, 'Oh Rachel, I'm so sorry. We had such plans, you and me. Remember – a string of hotels?'

Rachel was philosophical about it. 'Maybe I'm too old for all that anyway.'

'Rubbish!' exclaimed Lily. 'You'll never be too old for anything.'

The front doorbell interrupted their conversation. 'I hope that's not a punter,' said Lily. 'It would break my heart to have to turn him away.'

But when she made her way downstairs and opened the door, she was surprised to find DI Chadwick standing there. 'Come to arrest me, have you?' she snapped.

'I'm here unofficially, Lily. Can I have a quick word?'

'Why not? I'm a lady of leisure now.'

They sat at one of the tables in the empty dining room. 'I just want you to know that our experts have found that one of the roulette tables is weighted and that the Black Jack cards are marked.'

'But that had nothing to do with me!' exclaimed Lily. 'It was that bastard Gates.'

'I know,' he said. 'We've been suspicious of him for a while now, but we can't pin anything on him. We have to have proof.'

'What about Bill, the croupier?' she asked. Then told him of her conversation with the young man.

'We've already interviewed him. He won't say a word

against Gates – he's too scared,' explained Chadwick. 'Without his testimony we have nothing.'

Lily's shoulders slumped. 'So I'm up the bloody creek.'

'I'm afraid it looks that way. I'm really sorry, but my hands are tied. But I want you to know, Lily, that I'm after Gates. I'll keep after him and one day he'll make a mistake. Then I'll have him.'

She looked at him, grateful for his sympathy. 'But in the meantime, I'm out of business. It doesn't seem fair.'

He stood up. 'That's life, Lily, and you of all people must know that.'

She let him out of the door and went to report her conversation to Rachel.

'Try not to worry, darling,' said her friend. 'A day at a time we'll take it. What else can we do?'

'Come on,' said Lily. 'Let's go and spend some time with Victoria. I'll have to have a word with Nanny Gordon – I can't possibly afford to keep her on now. I need to explain the situation to her.'

Victoria was having her breakfast and insisted that the two sat and had a cup of tea with her. She produced her child's teapot and cups and very carefully poured out the lukewarm tea Nanny Gordon had put into the pot.

Looking at Rachel she asked, 'Do you take sugar?'

Trying to keep a straight face Rachel replied, 'In a cup that small, just a half a teaspoon, please.'

The child carefully complied with the request, then smiling at her mother she said, 'Mama doesn't need any sugar, do you?'

'No,' smiled Lily and gave her stock reply: 'Because I'm sweet enough.'

Leaving Rachel to play with Victoria, Lily took the nanny aside and explained the situation. Poor Nanny Gordon was shocked but she stood tall and dignified and said, 'I quite understand, Miss Lily. I can find another situation, but I would like to stay with you all until after you go to court. Unpaid, of course.'

Lily hugged her. 'Thank you, Nanny.'

Eventually, Lily and Rachel were taken to the magistrates' court and charged. They both pleaded not guilty, and were released on police bail, to appear at the next quarter sessions. As the day drew nearer, they both became increasingly nervous.

Rachel Cohen's case was heard first. The judge, after hearing the facts, fined her eighty pounds, saying he felt she held no responsibility for the gambling but as a partner in the business, she should have been aware of everything that happened on the premises. Then Lily's case was called.

She sat in the dock, pale and anxious, dressed soberly in a grey two-piece, an overcoat and a small black felt hat. She tried to stop her legs trembling as she waited for the first witness to be called.

Percy Gates was brought in and swore his innocence. The two croupiers took the oath and denied all knowledge of the dirty dealings. Finally, Bill stood pale and taut in the witness box and pleaded guilty to running a crooked game. But Lily could scarcely believe her ears when he was asked by the police prosecutor, 'Did Lily Pickford have any knowledge of these crooked dealings?' and he answered: 'Yes, she knew.'

She turned to her barrister and breathed, 'That bastard's lying. I knew nothing!'

'I know,' he said.

When it was Lily's turn, she took the oath and stood in the

witness box gripping the edge tightly until her knuckles were white.

Her barrister put the case that she was innocent. That she was a dupe, who had unknowingly been used. That the croupier was not telling the truth. But the judge wasn't impressed, despite Lily's determined effort to be convincing when she was cross-questioned.

'Do you mean to tell me, Miss Pickford,' the prosecutor asked, 'that when these men continued to win, night after night, enough for some of your clients to question the validity of the game, that you had no suspicions?'

She looked at him. 'Yes sir, I did have my suspicions, but no matter how closely I watched, I couldn't see how it could be done. I couldn't accuse anyone without any proof.'

He frowned. 'How long did this feeling of suspicion continue before the police closed your premises?'

'About two weeks, sir.' She saw Richard Williams shake his head.

'Yet you allowed the gambling club to remain open?'

'Yes, sir. You see, as I said, I had no proof.'

'You thought it more beneficial to remain open.'

Lily looked puzzled. 'I don't know what you mean, sir.'

He looked at her with some disdain. 'It seems to me, Miss Pickford, if you were innocent as you claim, you would have closed the gaming room as soon as you thought something was wrong, whether you had proof or not! But of course, if you were to benefit from the proceedings yourself, then it would have been in your own interest to remain open.'

'That's not true! How could I benefit? They were taking my profits!'

'Not if you had some arrangement.'

Lily was furious. 'I had no such arrangement. I run an honest place.'

'But surely,' he argued, 'if you were entirely innocent, you would have considered your clients, not wanting them to be cheated. Wouldn't it have been the actions of an innocent party to close the gambling club until you had a chance to prove your suspicions?'

'I did call someone to check the tables, but he was away. The police raided my establishment before I could do anything.'

In a voice heavy with sarcasm he said, 'How very convenient. No further questions.'

When Lily eventually stepped down from the witness box and returned to the dock, she watched the judge refer to his notes. She didn't like the harsh expression on his face. He's going to give me a hefty fine, she thought. God! How on earth will I pay it?

The judge finally spoke to her. 'I have decided after listening to the evidence that you are guilty of duping the public of their money. It is not, after all, your first experience in this field. Your previous association with the father of your child, a known gambler, would have given you an insight into this world, which makes your plea of innocence doubtful. This is a most serious offence and one this court will not tolerate. I am here to protect the public and I fully intend to do so. Therefore you are sentenced to serve six months in prison.'

Chapter Four

The judge's verdict shocked Lily. They were going to shut her away! What about Victoria? What would happen to her? Rachel had said she would look after her if the worst came to the worst, but what would happen if Victoria wanted her and she wasn't there? How would her old friend be able to explain, so that the child wouldn't be frightened? She put her hands to her face in despair. She'd been expecting a similar fine to Rachel's, albeit a heavier one. Although her solicitor had warned her of the possibility of imprisonment, she'd not seriously contemplated such a thing. She looked across the courtroom towards Rachel, a look of disbelief and horror mirrored in her eyes.

The Jewish woman's face was white. She tried to smile at Lily but her bottom lip trembled.

One of the two policewomen standing behind her, touched Lily's arm. 'This way,' she said coldly.

Lily blindly followed her down the steps into a small room with a wooden table and two chairs. 'Your solicitor will want a word with you,' she was told.

'Can I see my friend, Mrs Cohen?'

'Speak to your solicitor. We'll be here for the rest of the day, before we go to Brookmans.'

'Brookmans?' queried Lily

'The women's prison just outside of Winchester,' was the short reply. The officer left the room and Lily heard the key turn in the lock.

With trembling fingers she opened her handbag and took out a packet of cigarettes, then lit one with her gold lighter. As she placed it on the table she saw the initials carved there by previous prisoners. She ran a finger over them, wondering what was the story behind them. Were the people who carved them as frightened as she felt at this moment? She looked around the stark room with its whitewashed walls and stone floor. There was only one window but it was heavily barred. Even on a warm day this room would have a chill about it, and today it was cold. Lily shivered and pulled her warm woollen coat around her.

The door was unlocked and Richard Williams hurried in and took a seat opposite her. 'I'm so sorry, my dear. We were unfortunate in our judge this morning. He abominates gambling in any form.'

Lily exploded, her fear turning to anger. 'Are you trying to tell me that but for some sanctimonious old fool, I might still be free?'

He shrugged. 'There's no guarantee of course, ever.'

'That swine Percy Gates! If I live to be a hundred I'll get him for this.'

Mr Williams looked worried. 'Hush, Lily. You let the warders hear you make those kind of threats once you're inside, you'll make it worse for yourself.'

'Worse! How can anything be worse than losing my freedom for something I didn't do?' she cried. 'And there's Victoria! Rachel said she'd care for her. I need to talk to her.' Her head was buzzing and she was finding it hard to concentrate.

'And the club?' asked Williams.

'It'll have to be sold. I must see Rachel.'

The solicitor said, 'She's outside . . . with Victoria.'

Lily's eyes widened. 'Victoria's here?'

He looked somewhat abashed. 'Well, I wasn't at all sure how it would go today, so I took the liberty of having the child wait with her nanny, just in case things went the wrong way. I thought you'd like to see her before . . .'

'Before they shut me away? You might have made it clearer that this could happen.'

'I did warn you, Miss Pickford.'

There was a lump in her throat as she asked, 'Can I see her now?'

'Yes. Mrs Cohen will bring her in.' He looked at his client with concern. 'These next few months are going to be very hard for you, but try to keep your spirits up . . . and try to keep out of trouble. Then you'll probably get some time off for good behaviour.'

'Whatever do you mean?' she asked.

He let out a deep sigh. 'You're high-spirited and won't take kindly to authority, especially after being your own boss for so long. Just learn to be patient. Keep your head down and a still tongue is my advice to you.'

She leaned towards him. 'And my advice to you, Mr Williams,' she retorted, 'is to keep after Detective Inspector Chadwick. He knows that Gates is crooked, but he doesn't have the proof. You make certain he keeps looking so you can get me off this stretch!'

He rose from his chair. 'I certainly will, you can be sure of it.' He paused. 'I'm sorry it turned out this way. I'll keep in touch.' He patted her shoulder. 'Good luck, Lily.'

As the door was locked behind him, Lily was feeling distraught. Why did she have to appear before this particular judge? Why couldn't he have been taken ill this morning?

Then she could be with Victoria. Tears welled in her eyes as she realised she wouldn't see her beloved daughter for months. The child was bound to fret. Nothing seemed real in this nightmare world. It was as if she was watching a picture unfold before her, as if all this was happening to someone else and she was just an onlooker. She bravely brushed away the tears as she heard the door being unlocked. As she turned, she saw Rachel walk into the room, holding Victoria by the hand. The child ran forward.

'Mama, why are you in here?'

Lily gathered her daughter to her and held her close, breathing in the scent of her. Taking a deep breath to steady her voice, she sat the child on her knee and said softly, 'Look, darling. I have to go away on business for a little while. You can go and stay with Rachel. It'll be like a holiday.'

'And Nanny Gordon too?'

Lily slowly shook her head. 'No, darling. Nanny has to go home.'

The child's bottom lip trembled, which almost broke Lily's heart.

'Have I been a naughty girl?'

She hugged her. 'No, of course not! Nanny has to go and see her own Mama and I'll soon be back.'

Victoria looked up at her with eyes that were anxious. 'You'll come home soon, won't you?'

Lily cupped the dear face in her hands and kissed her. 'Of course I will and then we'll have a great time.' She looked pleadingly at Rachel.

'Come, darling,' Rachel said. 'I'll take you outside to Nanny. Mama and I need to talk.'

Victoria threw her arms around her mother and gave her a smacking kiss. 'Goodbye, Mama, I love you lots,' she said.

Lily's voice caught in her throat. 'I love you too, darling. Be a good girl.'

Rachel took the child from the room then returned a few moments later. The elderly Jewess looked shattered and suddenly much older.

Lily got up and opened her arms.

The other woman walked quickly towards her and held her tightly. 'Oh Lily, my darling. Such a terrible thing. Ay yi! What is to happen to you now?'

Although she was desperately needing to be comforted by her dear friend, it was quickly apparent to Lily that she was the one who had to be strong for both of them.

Leading Rachel towards a chair she said, 'Now don't you worry. Six months isn't a lifetime and according to Mr Williams, I won't even serve that long.'

Rachel mopped her tears with a lace-edged handkerchief. 'What do we do with the club? We have bills to pay and no money. Well, not much. We have to pay the butcher and the veg man out of that. There's not nearly enough to cover the overdraft and the bank will surely call that in.'

Putting a comforting hand over Rachel's, Lily said, 'You'll have to sell everything. The furniture, fittings. The building if necessary.'

'My life! Such a waste,' said the older woman sadly. 'Nanny will help me to pack your personal things and Victoria's, but of course then she'll have to look for another position.' This was not the time, thought Rachel, to tell Lily that she had a buyer for her own house and was looking for something smaller. If she had to live in a box, Victoria would be loved and cared for.

'At least I know you've got a home and enough money for your old age,' said Lily now, as if on cue. 'Thank God for that! We will just have to fight to live another day.'

Her savings had been used to pay her fine, but that was another thing the Jewess kept from her friend. Didn't she have enough to worry about? Instead she said, 'I'll come and see you in prison when I'm allowed.'

At that moment the policewoman intervened. 'Time to go,' she told Rachel.

The two women clung together for a moment, then Lily was once more alone.

Suddenly the whole implication of the judge's verdict sank in. She was to be shut away. Her freedom, which she prized so highly, would be taken from her. How could this happen when she was innocent? How could they take the word of Percy Gates and his croupier against hers? But of course, the judge had been fairly scathing about her chequered past. After all, she had been the mistress of the biggest villain in the docklands . . . and she was an unmarried mother. Such a stigma would certainly have coloured his view. But shut away, for months! How was she going to cope?

Several hours passed before Lily was at last taken to the police van with four other women. She'd been given sandwiches and a cup of weak tea whilst she waited but now, in a daze, she was on her way.

Inside the van, the other occupants looked grimly at one another, but no one spoke. One was obviously a prostitute and kept fluffing up her hair and powdering her nose, and Lily suspected this was not the first time she'd made such a journey. The other three women seemed ordinary enough, varying in age and from their shabby clothes, from the lower classes of humanity. Two of them appeared nervous – one in particular was constantly wringing her hands – and Lily wondered just what their individual crimes were. They mainly just stared into space, each lost in their own thoughts.

The two policewomen sitting in their navy uniforms didn't utter a word either. They seemed bored by the whole procedure, yet they remained watchful of their charges.

The atmosphere was claustrophobic and tense. Through the high windows of the van, Lily tried to catch a glimpse of the outside world in the impending dusk, knowing it would be some time before she saw it again. She saw the roofs of the buildings of Southampton gradually disappear as they journeyed into the countryside and she tried to picture everything she saw. It was like trying to fill her mind with the nicer things of life to remember during her incarceration. But all she could see were the bare limbs and branches of the trees, devoid of leaves, moving in the cold December air. Stripped of their identity, as she soon would be.

Eventually the Black Maria swung right into the entrance to the prison and stopped, waiting for the huge gates to open. As the vehicle moved into the courtyard, Lily heard the gates clang behind her. It had an ominous resonance, like the sound of doom. The gates of hell. And she was on the inside. The first few hours of her arrival at Brookmans Prison would live with her for ever. Carved in her soul.

She and the other prisoners were hustled into a room that had the word *Reception* on the door. Once inside the room, the policewomen who had accompanied them on the journey, handed them over to the prison warders, exchanging gossip and pleasantries with their colleagues, strangely animated now they were among their own kind. Eventually, laughing and joking, they signed some legal-looking documents and left.

The room was sizeable, with wooden cubicles down one side, each containing a wooden bench against the wall. Lily and her companions were shown into a separate cubicle, and the door was closed behind them.

Lily sat on the hard bench, her shoulders hunched, her feelings numb. She shifted to try and get comfortable, but the bench was unyielding. In the dim light of the bare light-bulb, she peered at the writings on the wall: *I love Jack. Fuck the judge. I'm innocent* and *God get me out of this hell-hole.* The same sentiments that echoed in her own mind. It was bitterly cold, and when the door opened and a tin mug of weak tea was handed to her with two pieces of dry bread, she was grateful, hoping the tea would warm her, but it tasted foul and the bread stuck in her throat.

Eventually a hardfaced prison warder opened the door and thrust a white hospital-like garment at her. Lily was to take off all her own things, fold them neatly and put the white thing on. With a cruel grin the woman looked at her fine clothes and sneered, 'The style might not be quite up to your standards, *my lady*, but you're a criminal like all the rest and you'll be dressed like all the others! We don't put up with any airs and graces here.'

Lily removed her wrapover coat and two-piece suit, her silk underwear and stockings, then put on the gown, which resembled a shroud. Made of washed-out, torn cotton, it had short sleeves but hung down well below her calves and was done up with ties down the back. Lily felt the cold from the bricks of the wall seep through the flimsy material as she leaned against it. She shivered, both with the cold and with nerves, but compressed her lips together in a determined line. She would get through this. Live one day at a time. After all, no one had ever promised her a tomorrow. All she wanted was to serve her sentence, get out of this dreadful place and be with Victoria. That was her main aim and to do so, she'd tolerate whatever was before her. But at least she had the knowledge that Rachel would love and care for her child. Thank God for that. It would bring her at least a crumb of comfort during the months that stretched before her.

'Outside,' snapped the warder, taking her clothes from her as she opened the door of the cubicle. She held her prisoner's arm in a vice-like grip. Lily tried to shake it off.

'I can manage to walk by myself,' she protested, but the woman ignored her and took her along the passage with the others all dressed in the same white gowns. They were led to a small room where a female officer sat behind the desk. She asked Lily the date of her birth, her occupation and her next of kin.

'Miss Victoria Teglia.' She gave them Rachel's address, then watched as the contents of her handbag were emptied on the desk and carefully listed before her. She was handed her powder compact and her lipstick.

'Thank you,' she said quietly.

Then she was weighed and searched, before being superficially examined by a woman doctor. Her head was examined roughly for lice, and her body for VD. The humiliation was almost more than she could bear. Eventually she was led away to have a bath.

The bath-house had several baths within wooden partitions, but there were no doors so the wardens could see everybody. She was handed a piece of green soap, a towel, toothbrush, comb and a clean handkerchief.

Lily smothered herself with soap trying to wash away the degradation she was feeling as her prison clothes were placed by the doorway.

The warder who had taken her own clothes from her glared at her and with a snide smile said, 'You call me Miss Cole and you obey the rules if you want to stay out of trouble. I don't like trouble, best remember that!'

Lily looked at the garments with despair. Once she put those on, she thought, she'd lose her own identity. Lily

Pickford would be no more. Now she would be just a number. She washed her hair in the soap as instructed and thought, No one can do that to me. I'll never be just a number. Never!

She dried herself as best she could with the thin towel and picked up the woollen vest and knickers, unlike the silk she was used to next to her skin. Over this she put the grey cotton and wool mix dress, at least two sizes too big. Then a grey cardigan. She picked up a pair of thick lisle stockings that were clean but well worn, and the garters that came with them. She turned up her nose at them. There was a dark grey woollen cloak that offered some comfort against the cold.

From here she was taken to a place with shelves of worn shoes and told to choose a pair. The shoes were mainly black but a few were brown, the shape of different feet imprinted still upon them.

'Hurry up!' snapped the warder. 'We haven't got all day.'

Lily managed to find a pair that didn't fit too badly, then waited as she and the other prisoners were handed their bedding. A clean sheet, one pillowcase and two blankets. Plus a long cotton nightdress which looked too big and had a tear in it that had been badly mended.

'Follow me,' said Miss Cole, and marched towards a door which was unlocked and which clanged shut behind them. They stepped outside into a courtyard enclosed by high walls, into the dark of the night, and made for a tall building, where once again the door was unlocked for them. Now they were inside the main prison.

Lily looked around with trepidation, blinded by the light for a moment. There were four tiers of landings, with cell doors lining the walls. Women warders walked around in their navy prison uniforms, bunches of keys jingling against their leather belts. It was an alien stark world and Lily was filled with a sense of foreboding.

What am I doing here? She asked herself. I don't belong here, I'm innocent! She wanted to scream out loud and tell everyone there had been a mistake. Make them believe her. Make them take her away from this awful place.

She followed the warder up to the second tier, her ill-fitting shoes clattering against the iron staircase and stone floors. They stopped outside a cell and the warder unlocked it.

'Make up your bunk,' Cole ordered, and gave Lily a shove.

Clutching her bedding, Lily stumbled into the cell. The smell of stale urine made her want to retch. She looked around. The room had a single bed on one side and on the other, two beds, one on top of the other, bunk-style. The lower one was bare with just a mattress, but the top one was occupied. Lily saw for the first time her fellow cellmates.

Stretched out on the bunk was a young woman who looked at her with interest. On the single bed sat a woman of about thirty-five, a dumpy-looking soul whose hair was drawn back tightly on her head. She smiled shyly, and Lily immediately noticed the vague expression on her face and behind her eyes. But the young woman on the top bunk sat up with a smile of welcome. She was young, plump and pretty, with bright blue-grey eyes and brown hair. Climbing down she said, 'Thank Gawd! Somebody young. We was dreading getting some old biddy.' She held out her hand. 'I'm Madge – Madge Brooks. You'll be sleeping under me.' She indicated the dumpy woman. 'This here is Hetty ... What's your name, love?'

'Lily Pickford.' She put her bedding down on the lumpy mattress beside the tin plate, tin mug and spoon, and looked around the cell. In the corner stood a bucket half filled with water and two others with lids on, yet the stench was unbelievable. Under the bed, she could see cockroaches scuttling over the stone floor and around the chamber pots. Above a table was a high window with iron bars.

Her face was white with anger. She was filled with rage. How dare they put her in this place! 'This is disgusting!' she declared. 'Surely they don't expect people to live among this?' She indicated the buckets.

'You'll soon get used to it,' said Madge.

'I'll never get used to it!' retorted Lily. 'It's filthy. And it's unhealthy.'

'What did you expect – the fucking Ritz? How long have you got here?'

'Six months,' said Lily.

'Is that all?' said Madge disparagingly. 'Six months is nothing in this place. Now you listen to me, girl. Some of us have got a lot longer to put up with these conditions, and we don't want you whining on about it, reminding us how bad it is. So just keep your mouth shut and do your time. Understand?'

Lily could see the logic of the other woman's argument, but the shock of the surroundings was hard to take, and the cold acceptance from Madge was unbelievable. How could you put up with this? No human being should be expected to do so. But at the same time she realised there was nothing she could do about it. It wasn't the first time she'd been faced with degradation and had had to survive. And she didn't want to upset these women with whom she would have to live. Life was going to be tough enough without that. 'Yes, you're right. It's just a bit of a shock to the system, that's all.'

Madge asked, 'Your first time, is it?'

'First *and* last time!'

Her cellmate laughed. 'We all say that, Lily love. Look,

66

better get your bunk made up or the screws will start giving you aggro. Especially Miss bloody Cole. A right bitch she can be. It's best to keep out of their bad books. They can make life in here even more hellish than it already is. Hurry up, they'll be bringing the cocoa round soon. Then it's lights out.'

'What time is it?' asked Lily.

'Buggered if I know,' said Madge. 'But lights out is at eight o'clock.' At the look of surprise on Lily's face she said, 'Yeah, I know. But they gets us up in the morning at six.'

'What happens then?'

'You get washed and dressed.'

Lily looked around. 'Where do you get washed?'

Madge pointed to a bowl and jug under the table. 'We take turns using this. The bucket with the water is for washing so don't throw anything in it. Then after, we slop out.'

'Slop out?' Lily asked with a puzzled look.

Madge indicated the lidded buckets. 'Those are emptied twice a day. In the morning and in the afternoon.'

Lily could feel the stench filling her nostrils and lungs, and fought to keep down the bile. She had to be strong if she was to keep her sanity in this place.

Hetty had been sitting on her bed listening to the conversation. She looked at Lily and said, 'You're a pretty lady.'

The childlike voice touched a part of Lily deeply, because it reminded her of Victoria.

'Thank you, Hetty. That's a pretty name, too.'

Hetty beamed with happiness.

As she started to make her bed, Madge leaned closer. 'Hetty's all right. Just a little backward, bit short of a full shilling if you know what I mean, but she ain't no trouble . . . if you don't upset her.'

Lily resisted the impulse to ask what happened then.

'I'll show you the ropes, until you find your own way,' said Madge. 'I can remember my first time.'

Lily looked at her with surprise. Madge could only be about twenty. 'How many times have you been inside?' she asked.

Completely unfazed, the other girl replied, 'This is my third. Me dad's in Pentonville.'

'Whatever for?'

'Thieving, same as me. He's always in and out of some prison or other. And I suppose I'll be doing the same.'

Lily looked at the girl and thought what a shame that she seemed so resigned to such a fate. 'Don't you want to go straight? Do you like prison so much?'

'It's not a case of liking – it's a case of survival. Thieving's the only way I know to earn any money to keep the bread on the table at home.'

'But when you're in here, you're not doing that, are you?' reasoned Lily.

Madge grinned at her. 'I know. It's a bugger, ain't it? What did you get sent down for, love?'

'Someone fixed the roulette tables in the club I run. I didn't know, but still they gave me six months.'

Madge threw her a crafty look. 'And you didn't know a thing about it . . . in your own club?'

Lily glared at her. 'That's right. You can believe it or not – I don't give a damn.'

At that moment there was a sound of activity outside in the corridor. 'Cocoa!' was the cry.

Hetty stood up, waiting, with her mug in her hand. Madge picked up Lily's and handed it to her. 'It's bloody awful but at least it's warm.'

The cell door was unlocked and a warder stood with a pail

and ladled the cocoa into each cup, then locked the door behind her.

'I don't think I'll ever be able to live in a house again with locked doors,' Lily protested.

'You'd better,' said Madge dryly, 'else you'll have the likes of my dad calling on you!'

The cocoa was watery and tasted strange. Lily took a sip, then emptied it into one of the buckets. 'Ugh,' she grimaced.

With a sly smile, Madge promised, 'In a month's time, you'll drink it without batting an eyelid.'

Lily looked at the others, dressed in the same drab prison garb as herself. Their individual personalities had been taken away. It was a painful reminder of her lost freedom.

She undressed and crawled beneath the sheet, pulling the blankets up to her chin. She'd put the grey cloak over her as well, to keep out the chill. God, she'd freeze to death before the night was out. A shaft of moonlight seemed to illuminate the cell, emphasizing the cold stark walls. Dear God, she thought, how am I going to live here in the confines of this dreadful place? Six months might not seem a long time to the likes of Madge, but to her it was a lifetime. She turned on her side and saw Hetty, on the bottom bed opposite hers, staring at her. She turned over to get away from those eyes, her own filling with tears of despair.

And then the screaming began.

As cries of wretchedness rent the air, Lily cringed in her bed. God! Was this some kind of madhouse she'd been sent to? She covered her ears, to no avail. Angry voices echoed down the corridors, abusive language was hurled from one cell to another. Demoniacal laughter reverberated, moans and wailing continued relentlessly. The rattle of keys clinked as cell doors were opened, followed by cries of pain . . . the warders' angry orders could clearly be heard.

'Shut your face or you'll be sorry!'

It was mayhem and madness.

Lily covered her head with her pillow, but somehow she couldn't shut out the ugly sounds. Eventually she fell asleep through sheer exhaustion.

Chapter Five

Bart Gifford lumbered into the untidy kitchen-cum-living room at the Giffords' farm; he was in his stockinged feet, having removed his boots at the back door. His mother was stirring a huge pot of stew over the open fire in the grate. Quinn was sitting at the long, roughly hewn kitchen table, loudly slurping his mug of tea.

Bart took the local paper from beneath his arm and threw it on the table. 'Your girlfriend's been sent down for six months,' he proclaimed.

Quinn frowned. 'What the 'ell you talking about?'

'That Lily Pickford. Been sent to Brookmans.'

Grabbing the paper, Quinn saw the headlines: *Hotel Owner Sent To Prison*. Beneath it was a picture of Lily, smiling.

Bart looked over his brother's shoulder. 'Bet she ain't smiling now,' he sniggered.

Leaping to his feet, Quinn grabbed him by his shirt and punched him on the jaw, sending him flying across the room. Rosie Gifford looked up from her stewpot with a startled expression, but when she saw that Bart was sitting up rubbing his chin, she turned away.

'What the bloody 'ell did you do that for?' he asked.

Quinn just growled angrily at him and continued to read slowly, laboriously pointing out every word to himself. 'It says here the gambling table was fixed and the cards marked. So that's why the Club has closed. I went down there several times, but nobody I spoke to knew exactly what had happened.' His mouth tightened and his brow furrowed. 'My Lily wouldn't run a crooked game! There must be some mistake.'

'*Your* Lily!' Bart looked at him with amazement. 'Your Lily my arse! She wouldn't touch you with a bleedin' barge-pole.'

His dark eyes shining with anger, Quinn said, 'I've got plans for her and me. I'll just have to wait a bit longer, that's all.'

Bart snorted. 'You lost your marbles, or what? Remember what the club looked like?' He gazed around at the untidy room. 'You think she'd live here after the Club? She's used to luxury, a bit of class. She's had money.'

'Well, she ain't got the Club now. At least, it's been closed. She's got nothing, no livelihood, a prison record as well . . . and anyway, I've got plenty of money. I can provide for her. You'd like some help in the house, wouldn't you, Ma?'

Rosie Gifford pushed away the grey straggling hair from her forehead and gave a toothless grin. 'You thinking of taking a wench then, son?'

Quinn rubbed the rough growth on his chin. 'Yeah. Take a look at her picture. What do you think?'

The old crone looked hard at the paper and slowly, as she studied it, her smile of amusement faded. She covered the picture with her hand and closed her eyes for a moment. When she opened them, she looked at Quinn. 'You keep away from her, son. Keep well away.'

His eyes narrowed, knowing the power of the gift she'd been born with. 'Why? Why do you say that?'

She gripped his shoulder. 'You lust after her, it'll be your undoing. You want a woman, choose a village girl or pay for a whore, but leave her be or you'll regret it.' She returned to her cooking.

Quinn lit a cheroot and continued to study Lily's picture. He knew he should heed his mother's warning but he looked into the smiling eyes of Lily Pickford and knew he couldn't.

Rachel Cohen was surrounded by packing cases, trying to keep Victoria from undoing the things that she'd just wrapped in newspaper.

'No, Victoria! Put that back, please. You're making things harder for me. I'm having to do everything twice!' She wearily wiped her brow, realising that looking after a three-year-old was tiring and she was getting old.

She gave the child some wax crayons and a sheet of writing paper. 'Here – draw a nice picture for your Mama. Draw the new house we're moving to.'

Victoria looked up. 'When is Mama coming home?'

The plaintive note in the child's voice pulled at Rachel's heartstrings. 'Not yet, darling. But soon.'

With tears brimming in her eyes, the little girl asked, 'Doesn't she love me any more?'

The Jewess gathered her to her ample bosom. 'Of course she does, and she's longing to see you.'

Thus mollified, Victoria allowed her tears to be dried and she sat at the table where she studiously began to draw.

Rachel continued to pack her precious china. Tomorrow a man was coming to buy some of her furniture. The new house was much smaller than this large Edwardian home that had been hers for so long; she was loath to leave it, but since the closure of the Club Valletta, she was fighting to survive. The money for the furniture would pay off the wine merchant and the brewery, which had been her responsibility. Unless she paid her debts, the companies had threatened to make her bankrupt. But they had agreed to wait another month.

She let out a deep sigh. Now that Nanny Gordon had left she was finding it very tiring looking after an energetic child. But she wouldn't have it any other way. Lily was like a daughter to her and she'd do everything in her power to help.

A loud knocking on the front door interrupted her work. 'All right already,' she called as she walked towards it.

Outside stood a man and a woman holding a sheaf of papers. The gentleman was dressed in a grey suit and wearing a trilby hat, which he removed.

'The doorbell isn't good enough for you?' demanded Rachel.

The man spoke first. 'Mrs Rachel Cohen?'

'Who's asking?'

'I'm from The Protection of Children Society,' he said. 'You have in your household Victoria Teglia, the daughter of Miss Lily Pickford?'

Rachel looked at him and then at the imperious features on the face of the tall skinny woman standing beside him, and felt suddenly apprehensive.

'That's right.'

'May we come in, please?'

She looked past him and saw a parked car at the gate and a policeman standing by the bonnet.

'Yes,' she said, and stepped aside. 'In here.' She led them to a well-furnished front parlour, moving an empty packing case out of the way. 'You'd better sit down and tell me what this is all about.'

The woman sat on the edge of the seat, unbuttoned her long black coat, her back straight, her mouth in a tight line. 'You were the partner of Miss Pickford at the Club Valletta?'

'Yes that's right, it's not a secret,' said Rachel. 'But what has it to do with you?'

'You were fined for running an illegal game?'

Rachel's stomach tightened. 'It was a set-up. We didn't know,' she protested.

'That was not the opinion of the court,' snapped the woman.

Rachel had a sudden desire to slap her hard to remove the sanctimonious expression from her face.

The man intervened at this point. 'In short, Mrs Cohen, Victoria's mother is in prison and it has been decided that you are not a suitable person to oversee the child's welfare.'

'I'm not suitable?' Rachel's face flushed with anger. 'How dare you speak to me like that! I love Victoria. She has a nice home. She's well fed and cared for. There's something wrong with that?'

The woman looked at the packing case. 'Are you moving?'

'Yes,' replied Rachel reluctantly.

'And why is that?'

The Jewess bristled. How dare this sourpuss question her? In any case she wasn't going to reveal her dire financial state to a stranger. 'This house is too big for me,' she replied.

'And the one you're moving to . . . how many bedrooms does it have?'

'Two. One for me and one for Victoria!'

The woman sniffed loudly and took the papers from her associate's hand and waved them in front of Rachel. 'Here we have a court order to take away the child and put her with foster parents.'

Rachel felt the blood drain from her face. She took the papers and read them. She looked at her visitors over the top of her spectacles. 'You want to take her away?' she asked, in all but a whisper.

'Yes,' said the woman, her voice cold and hard. 'Pack her things and we'll take her now.'

'You can't do that! I promised Lily I'd take care of her.'

'You have no choice in the matter,' the woman said sharply.

Rachel appealed to the man sitting beside the hard-faced woman.

'Victoria is already missing her mother. At least she knows me. Since the day she was born I've loved her – distraught she'll be. A baby yet she is . . . Please don't do this!'

There was an expression of sympathy in his eyes, but his voice was firm as he said, 'I'm sorry, Mrs Cohen. It would be better if you did this calmly. Try and explain to the child. If she sees you're upset it will only make it worse.'

'Upset!' Rachel's face was flushed with anger. 'You say you are from a society to protect children, yet you take her to strangers!'

'Mrs Cohen!' exclaimed the woman impatiently. 'Either *you* do it or *I* will.'

Rachel leapt to her feet so suddenly the woman sat back in the chair with a look of alarm. 'You don't touch her!' She walked towards the door. 'You wait here. This will take time, but I'm telling you, I'll contest this decision.'

She walked unsteadily to the room where Victoria was intent on her drawings. She knelt beside her. 'I've got a nice surprise for you, darling,' she said. 'You're going away for a lovely holiday to stay with some kind people while I move house.'

The child's eyes widened with surprise. 'A holiday?'

'Yes,' said Rachel. She took her to the bathroom where she washed her hands and face and told her to be a good girl whilst she was away and that when she, Rachel, was ready she'd come for her and take her to the new house. 'Such a surprise you'll have!'

The child was excited for a time, helping her choose her

clothes to be packed in a small case, but when she went downstairs and saw the two strangers waiting for her she started to cry.

'Rachel!' she cried as she clung to her. 'I don't want to go. I want to stay here with you.'

The woman went to get hold of her but Rachel stepped forward. 'Don't touch her!' she spat and picked Victoria up. Walking slowly towards the door she opened it. 'Look, darling, a nice policeman has come to give you a ride in his car. You have a lovely time and I'll see you as soon as I can.' She held the child close to her and with a choked voice she said, 'I love you and I'll come for you very soon. I promise.' She handed Victoria into the waiting arms of the man.

Victoria's cries nearly destroyed her. She clasped her hands tightly together to stop herself from trying to snatch back the child, knowing it would be pointless. She closed her eyes as the car drove away, and tears were streaming down her cheeks.

Once the car was out of sight, Rachel telephoned Richard Williams, Lily's solicitor, but the news wasn't good. When she read him the official letter left with her, he said there was nothing he could do. She sat on the settee wondering how on earth she was going to break the news to Lily. Her brain was numb. She kept asking what she could have done to stop Victoria from being taken away, and although she knew she had had no choice, she was filled with guilt that such a terrible thing could have happened.

She picked up the telephone directory and found the number of Brookmans Prison. The least she could do was try to get an extra visit to tell Lily about this terrible business.

Lily's first few days spent in the prison had been a revelation. The first morning she woke, she was about to put on her

77

shoes when Hetty stopped her and tipped them upside down. Lily grimaced as a couple of cockroaches fell out, only to be trodden on as they scuttled away. The crunch of them beneath Hetty's feet had turned her stomach. As did the half-cold lumpy porridge served for breakfast.

The three cellmates had washed and dressed then walked down the two flights of iron stairs to a hall lined with long tables and benches. The porridge was brought round in pails and scooped out with a ladle before being slammed on each plate. Lily looked at hers and felt the bile rise to her throat at the sight. She pushed her plate away and started to eat the two slices of bread, scraped with rancid margarine.

Hetty, who was sitting opposite Lily, looked at the discarded plate and asked with a simple smile, 'Can I have it?'

She nodded and pushed the plate towards her.

The woman sitting next to Lily said, 'You'd better get used to it, girl. You don't eat you'll get sick.'

'I'll be sick if I do,' retorted Lily.

Leaning towards her the prisoner said, 'You want to get out of here in one piece, don't you?'

'Of course.'

'Then you have to try and keep well. Even if it chokes you, you must have a little of everything. You have to keep going, keep strong; it's the only way. Believe me, I know.'

'How long have you been inside?' asked Lily.

'Ten years,' she said in a flat voice.

'Christ!' exclaimed Lily. 'I'd never be able to stand being shut away for that long. I'd top myself.'

The woman looked at her coldly. 'You think I haven't tried?' She held out her hands, palm upwards, and showed the deep scars across her wrists. 'But I decided in the end that this life is better than none at all.'

'How much longer do you have?' asked Lily.

'Another five,' she said and turned away.

Hetty had cleaned every scrap of porridge from Lily's plate and pushed it back towards her. 'Thanks ever so,' she said. 'It was lovely.'

She smiled at Hetty. 'I'll make a deal with you,' she said. 'Whatever I don't want, you can have. OK?'

The beam of happiness on Hetty's face touched her. Although a grown woman, there was such an air of innocence and childishness about her that Lily felt drawn to her.

At that moment a big, broad, short-haired prisoner, with more the look of a man than a woman with her coarse features, walked past the table and shoved Hetty in the back. 'Been stuffing your face again have you, you fat pig!'

Lily saw the happiness fade from Hetty's face, to be replaced by a look of fear. She was furious. She looked at the woman and snapped, 'Leave her alone! She wasn't troubling you.'

A hush descended over the hall.

Belle Chisholm looked at her with amusement. 'You're new here, ain't you?'

'What's it to you?' asked Lily defiantly.

'I'll let your stupidity pass this time. Give the others a chance to put you in the picture. But you cross me a second time and you'll be sorry.' She walked away with two other prisoners following in her wake.

'Who the bloody hell does she think she is?' asked Lily angrily.

'That's Belle Chisholm,' said Madge in hushed tones. 'She runs the place.'

Lily looked at her in surprise. 'Runs the place? What a load of crap. The screws run the place.'

'Oh my God,' said Madge, 'what a lot you have to learn, Lily Pickford. Belle is top dog here. She's got that Cole woman for a lover as well, and what Belle says goes among the inmates. She's a lifer with nothing to lose. A few have tried to cross her, but they've always come off worse. Keep out of her way.'

Lily's fighting spirit rose. 'Look, Madge, believe it or not but I'm here through no fault of my own. I am innocent of the charges brought against me. That's bad enough, nevertheless if I was guilty, a triple murderer or even a minor pickpocket, no one tells me what to do. The warders, all right, but another prisoner? Not on your life! I've had to struggle too many years to survive, and no one, but *no one* runs my life!'

Madge and Hetty looked at one another. 'Oh my Gawd,' said Madge. 'I can see trouble ahead.'

Miss Cole walked over to the table and glared at Lily. 'Already making trouble are you, Pickford?'

Lily returned her gaze without flinching. 'I'm not making trouble. I just don't like bullies . . . in or out of uniform!'

Cole leaned over the table. 'Watch your mouth, girl. The only winners in here are the screws. Remember that!' She walked away.

The others had watched the confrontation with bated breath, but when Cole had gone, there were a few cruel remarks thrown in Lily's direction.

'Think you're bloody Lady Muck, do you? Well, in here we don't put up with no airs and graces.'

'Think you're better than us, dearie? Is that it?' called another. 'You're just a fucking con like us all.'

Lily was shaken by the sudden hostility around her. She glared at her tormentors. 'No, I don't think I'm better than anyone, but I *am* a human being – something you all seem to have forgotten!' She stood up and left the table as the bell rang. Hetty for her part, followed Lily back to the cells like a puppy at its master's heels.

When they returned to the cell, Madge and Hetty showed her where they had to empty the slops. They walked to the end of the corridor where there were three toilets. There they emptied the stinking contents of the buckets, swilled them out and refilled the one used for washing with clean water.

'What a bloody awful way to live,' muttered Lily beneath her breath.

She'd had to suffer in her life, she thought. Even having to resort to prostitution to save herself from starvation, but she couldn't help but think that even those days were more dignified than this existence.

Later she was taken to a room with the others and given a needle and cotton, some rough material, and shown how to make mail bags.

'And don't lose the needle,' snapped the warder. 'They're all counted at the end of the shift.'

Lily stuck out her tongue at the receding figure of the woman, much to Madge and Hetty's amusement.

'Quiet there!' ordered the woman.

Later, as they filed into the dining room, Lily was sucking her finger which was raw from trying to push the sewing needle through the thick material. 'Why don't they supply us with a thimble?' she grumbled.

'Try and get hold of a cotton reel and use the edge of that to push the needle through,' advised Madge. 'Anyway, at least you get paid a few bob at the end of the week, so you can buy a packet of fags. And in any case, it's better than working in the laundry which is hot and sticky.'

Lily had been dying for a cigarette ever since she'd arrived, and the contents of her bag had been emptied, her cigarettes with them. 'Where do you get the fags?' she asked.

'They open a shop once a week,' said Hetty. 'I always buys chocolate 'cos I don't smoke.'

After lunch they went outside to exercise. It was cold in the yard as they all trooped around in twos. A few of the cons sat around talking, but most kept on the move. Lily looked up at the cold grey sky. It looked as forbidding as the walls which enclosed the prison. Would they look any better on a bright day, she wondered, but doubted it very much. Nothing could bring cheer to this hell-hole. She felt even more depressed when she realised that in a few weeks' time it would be Christmas – a time for families. This year Victoria would be old enough to understand more and Lily had been planning so many things they could do together. Visit the shops, see Father Christmas. Her heart was heavy as she continued to walk. There would be little Christmas spirit here, that was for sure. But at least Victoria would be with Rachel. That at least was some consolation.

That night she slept fitfully with the thoughts of being inside on Christmas Day, when she had longed to see Victoria's face as she opened her presents.

The following day passed as the one before, except that in the morning Lily and Madge were sent to scrub down one of the stone passages. Madge at one end, Lily at the other. On her hands and knees she scrubbed away, lost in her own thoughts when she heard footsteps approaching. Miss Cole stopped in front of her.

With a sneer she said, 'This is a come-down for you, isn't it, my lady? A pretty girl like you should be doing less menial work.'

Lily looked at her distrustfully. She'd been around the streets too long not to recognise the inference. 'I'm fine,' she said. 'Just fine.'

Cole smiled slowly and putting out her hand, she went to smooth Lily's hair. 'I could make life in here very easy for you, darling. You'd just have to be nice to me.' She cupped Lily's face in her hands and whispered, 'I'd be nice to you. I know how to make a woman very happy.'

Lily grabbed the warder's wrist and glaring at her said, 'You lay a finger on me, you twisted bitch, it'll be the last time you touch anyone!'

The woman snatched her hand away and beneath slitted eyes said, 'Have it your own way.' She peered into the bucket. 'Change that water – it's filthy.' She kicked the bucket and sent it flying, the water spilling over the floor. 'And make sure you mop all that up first,' she commanded. Then walked away laughing loudly.

Lily fought to keep her anger under control, remembering Richard Williams's words of warning. That bitch Cole would love to see her retaliate – well, she wouldn't give her the satisfaction.

Madge, who had been watching the scene, got to her feet and came rushing down the corridor. 'You all right, girl?'

Shaken as well as furious, Lily nodded. 'By Christ, I'd really have to be desperate to fancy her.'

'Just as well,' said her friend. 'Belle Chisholm is a very jealous woman. She wouldn't like anyone else taking up Old Mother Cole's affection. She'd bloody kill them.'

'I've had to do a lot of things in my time to survive, but never that.'

'We all have our limitations, eh?' said Madge. 'But in here, desperation makes you go a little bit crazy sometimes.'

'I can't afford that luxury,' said Lily with a wry smile. 'I have a child waiting for me.' But her smile faded when she thought of the warder. She wouldn't take the rejection kindly. That was another enemy she'd made.

On the second floor, Belle Chisholm had looked down and observed the exchange between Lily and Cole; she was seething with rage. Her lips curled in a cruel smile. This new upstart needed teaching a lesson. She'd heard on the prison grapevine all about Lily Pickford. Here for a short time, worried about her child. Well, she could make things very difficult for her. If she chose, she could cause Pickford to lose her time off for good behaviour. She liked the idea of that. It would give her great satisfaction. With another glance at Lily busily scrubbing the floor, Belle ambled away.

When they'd finished, Lily and Madge were sent back to the sewing room with the others. As she sat at her table and picked up yet another mail bag, Lily wondered just how prisoners serving a long term, like the woman who'd spoken to her in the dining room, could keep their sanity, doing the same thing day in day out. She thanked God she was only here for a short time, and vowed to keep telling herself this to get her through the daily grind.

An hour later, another warder came into the room and after a whispered conversation with the officer on duty, Lily's name was called.

Everyone looked up in surprise.

'Come here, Pickford.'

Lily rose from the chair, looked at her friends with a worried frown and followed the woman down the corridor. Was this anything to do with Miss Cole, she wondered. She was taken to a room and waited before a door whilst the screw unlocked it.

'Inside,' she was told. 'You've got a visitor.'

Before she could say anything, she was pushed into the room and the officer stepped inside the room and locked the door behind her.

'What's going on?' she asked.

'Sit down,' she was told.

Lily did so, wondering who was coming to see her and why. At that moment the door on the other side of the room opened and Rachel entered.

Lily looked at her with surprise, then apprehension when she saw the expression on her friend's face. 'Rachel! What on earth are you doing here?'

Wringing her hands, Rachel hurried over to the chair opposite to her and sat down. She caught hold of Lily's hands in a steel-like grip. 'It's Victoria. They've taken her away!'

Chapter Six

Lily stared at Rachel, her face devoid of colour. 'What do you mean, they've taken her away? Who's taken her away?'

Rachel told her the whole sorry story, her eyes brimming with tears. 'I couldn't stop them, darling. I tried. Honest to God, I tried.'

Despite her own anguish, Lily attempted to comfort her friend. 'I'm sure you did.' But her voice broke as she asked, 'Where are they taking my baby?'

'To foster parents. I ain't good enough to take care of her, they said.' She wiped her nose. 'I rang Richard Williams, but there was nothing he could do.'

Lily put her elbows on the table, cradled her head in her hands and closed her eyes. Was this nightmare never to end? She could visualise the face of her beloved child. Would she be frightened? Would the strangers who had her now, comfort her? What would happen if Victoria was unwell and cried for her mother, as children do? At least with Rachel, Victoria would have felt secure. But now . . .

Rummaging around in her bag, Rachel produced a slip of paper and handed it to Lily. 'Here is the address of the foster parents. I rang The Protection of Children's office and they gave it to me. They said for you to write to Victoria and then it could be read to her. I left some envelopes and stamps at the office for you. They said they'd give you prison paper to write on.'

Lily took the note and read the address. 'Paynes Road in Shirley. Well, at least it's a decent area. You'll be able to visit her, see that she's all right?'

Rachel was crestfallen. 'I'm afraid not, darling. When I suggested it, they said it would be too upsetting for Victoria and as it's for a short time they think it best to leave her be.' Seeing the expression of dismay on Lily's face, she added: 'I took a tram to Shirley though and walked past the house. It looked clean and cared for.' She caught hold of Lily's hand. 'Try not to worry.'

'My poor baby. I'll write to her tonight. Thanks for coming, Rachel.'

The warder stepped forward. 'Time's up, ladies.'

The two women rose from their seats and hugged one another. 'I'm so sorry about Victoria,' said Rachel.

Poor Lily was so overcome, she was unable to speak. She held the older woman close to her, feeling a moment's comfort before she released her hold, turned quickly away and hurried out of the room, tears of anguish pouring down her cheeks.

She was led back to the others and to the mail bags, the unsympathetic warder telling her sharply to, 'Pull yourself together.'

She didn't look at anyone as she entered the room, but sat down, brushed the tears away and picked up the material. But try as she might, she couldn't concentrate and kept making mistakes. Her emotions were in turmoil. First she was filled with desolation and despair, then fury that this could have happened. She couldn't understand the reasoning behind it. Rachel not good enough? What rubbish! The officer in charge started berating her for not getting on with her work.

Madge immediately came to her cellmate's defence. 'For Christ's sake, get off her back. Can't you see she's had some bad news? You fucking screws, you're all the same. Power bloody crazy. Leave her be, do you hear?' She got up from her seat and went over to Lily. 'You all right, love?'

Lily just shook her head.

Madge patted her on the shoulder, and returned to her seat with a baleful glare at the warder, who walked away.

There was total silence in the sewing room. It was as though the deep misery that Lily was feeling spread through the place like Scotch mist. Everyone was relieved when the bell went for lunch.

The women filed silently into the dining room and sat down. The meat stew was ladled out in the same fashion as the porridge in the mornings. The gravy was watery. Fine shreds of cabbage, an occasional slice of carrot floated in it with the odd piece of meat. Another large pan held potatoes.

Madge sat beside Lily and cajoled her into eating a little. Hetty watched from across the table with anxious eyes keeping the others from bothering her. In their own way they protected her.

It wasn't until they all went outside into the exercise yard that anyone spoke. Madge tucked her arm through Lily's as they walked side by side and led her away to a corner, Hetty following close behind them.

'Come on, darlin', what's happened? You need to tell someone or you'll flip your lid – and in here, that wouldn't be wise.'

Looking straight ahead of her, Lily said, 'My daughter's been put with foster parents. She's only three years old. And there's nothing that can be done about it.'

Madge pursed her lips. 'Then you'll just have to wait until you gets out. I'm sorry if that sounds harsh, but that's how it is when you're a con.' Her voice softened as she tried to comfort Lily. 'Besides, the people fostering her will have been chosen especially for the job. They'll know how to care for her properly. You just tell yourself you're in here for a short time only, then you'll be together again.'

Hetty stood beside them, in silent contemplation.

'Thanks,' she said. 'That's sound advice.'

With a wry smile, Madge said, 'Oh, I've got a lot of that. Pity I didn't listen to myself years ago, eh?'

As they continued their daily exercise, Lily concentrated on the future. She'd have to find work and that was a worry. If people knew she'd been inside, they wouldn't employ her. So . . . she wouldn't tell anyone! But she'd need to find something that would pay well enough to care for Victoria too. Wages were low and she'd have to fight to survive one way or another.

When they returned to their cell, Hetty sidled up to Lily who was sitting disconsolately on her bed and sat beside her. Shyly she said, 'I'm sorry you're unhappy.'

Lily looked into her soulful eyes and caught hold of Hetty's hand. 'Thanks.'

Hetty's face broke into a wide smile, then she said, 'I was unhappy once. But I'm all right now.'

'When was that?' asked Lily.

The smile faded. 'When I was at home with me mum.' She shook her head dolefully. 'Me mum hated me, you see. She said I wasn't right in the head, not like me brother. She loved him all right . . . but not me. Yes,' she said in a matter-of-fact manner, 'she bought him lots of toys, clothes and things but she never bought me anything. Only a pet rabbit once, that's all.'

Lily looked across the cell at Madge who raised her eyebrows but said nothing. 'I'm really sorry,' she said.

Despite her own unhappiness she could feel compassion and pity for the other woman.

Hetty looked suddenly petulant. 'That Belle Chisholm don't like me either, but that don't matter, 'cos I hates her!'

Putting an arm around Hetty's shoulders Lily said, 'I shouldn't think Belle Chisholm likes anyone but herself!'

Hetty gave a childlike chortle. 'That's funny. Fancy liking yourself!' She looked at Lily with adoring eyes and said, 'I wish I was pretty like you.'

Looking at the dumpy figure beside her, her heart went out to her. She gently touched the dark-blonde hair drawn so tightly back from Hetty's face it was like a band round her head. 'You have pretty hair.'

Her cellmate looked amazed. 'Me? My hair?'

'Yes,' said Lily. 'If you washed it and it was cut in a nice shape and worn loose, it would look lovely.' She looked up at the top bunk opposite and asked Madge, 'What are the chances of getting a pair of scissors?' When she'd been on the streets, she'd cut her own hair often enough and had become quite skilful.

'I could nick a pair after they count them when we've finished the mail bags tomorrow,' said her friend, 'if you keep the warder talking – but we'd have to put them back as we filed in the next morning, first thing.'

Lily smiled at Hetty. 'How about I cut it for you tomorrow night? You're down on the rota to have a bath. Wash your hair at the same time and we'll see what we can do. What do you say?'

Hetty jumped up from the bed and clapped her hands with childish delight. 'Oh Lily, would you really?' She clasped her hands together. 'I can hardly wait for tomorrow.'

Seeing the sheer joy on Hetty's face helped to lift Lily's deep feeling of gloom. 'You can use a bit of my lipstick too.'

'Oh my goodness,' said Madge. 'We won't know you.'

Putting her hand over her mouth, Hetty's eyes widened. 'Me wear lipstick? Could I really?'

'You certainly can,' said Lily.

'Yeah,' said Madge, now carried away with the idea. 'We'll turn you into a regular *femme fatale*.'

'What's that when it's out?' asked Hetty with an anxious look.

'It means a woman with a special attraction. A vamp.'

There was a mischievous look on Hetty's plump face. 'Go on,' she said.

'You wait and see,' said Lily. Suddenly weary from the trauma of the day, she undressed and climbed into bed. She looked around at the soulless room that was to be her home for the next few months and shut her eyes, at the same time wondering what sort of a place Victoria was in. She hoped that Madge was right and that the foster parents understood the needs and fears of a small child. She closed her eyes and made an earnest prayer for the happiness and safety of her daughter.

Little Victoria Teglia sat on the wet sheet on her narrow bed and cried. The door was thrown open and Gladys Parker stormed in. She was tall and angular with a narrow mean mouth, her mid-brown hair coiled tightly into a bun in the nape of her neck. 'Stop making that row,' she said. Then she saw the sheet. 'You dirty girl!'

Victoria cowered away from her as Gladys grabbed her by the arm and hauled her off the bed.

'Well, that's the last sheet you have. I'm not going to keep washing them. They don't pay me enough money for that. Sometimes I don't think it's worth all the trouble!' But Gladys knew that without the allowance from the Society, she'd have to forego the little extras she now enjoyed.

The child whimpered, 'I want my Mama.'

'Your mama's locked away in prison and you won't be seeing her for a long time,' she sneered. She stripped the sheet off the bed and with an angry look at the child said, 'And don't forget what I said about when that woman calls tomorrow!' She went out of the room, slamming the door behind her.

Victoria put her thumb in her mouth and sat on the floor in the corner, quietly sobbing.

The next day, Gladys Parker opened the door to the woman from The Children's Society with a warm smile. 'Please come in. We've been expecting you.'

Ethel Giles entered the house, her back stiff as a ramrod; she was wearing the same sour expression, the same black coat. She'd been sent by her boss to check that young Victoria Teglia was being well cared for.

Victoria was seated on a stool, waiting, her little face puckered with the effort to hold back her tears. She'd been threatened with punishment if she misbehaved and had been told exactly what to say.

Miss Giles sat on a nearby chair and looked at the child. Sulky little thing, she thought. But she was well dressed in a warm frock and a woollen cardigan and looked as if she'd been well taken care of.

'Are you happy here, Victoria?' she asked.

'Of course you are, aren't you?' chipped in Gladys Parker quickly.

'Let the child answer for herself,' instructed the visitor. 'Are you happy here?' she repeated.

The child nodded.

'Speak up,' she was ordered.

'Yes, thank you,' whispered Victoria.

Miss Giles looked around the room. It was clean. Although not nearly as opulent as that Jewish woman's home, it was comfortable. The brass candlesticks were shining in the reflection of the fire burning in the range and the antimacassars were spotless, hanging over the backs of the easy chairs. China ornaments decorated the mantelpiece. Everything was carefully in place and precise. As was the woman of the house. It was obvious that all was well.

'Right then. I'll get back to my office and make my report.' She picked up her handbag and looked at Victoria. 'You make sure you behave yourself,' she said. 'It was very good of Mrs Parker to look after you. You just remember that!' She walked towards the door without a backward glance and therefore didn't see the tears brimming in Victoria's soulful eyes.

Gladys Parker breathed a sigh of relief as she closed the front door. She walked back into the living room where Victoria sat still hardly daring to move, the tears falling silently down her cheeks.

'Now don't start,' barked the woman. Walking over to the biscuit barrel, she took out one and gave it to Victoria. 'Here,' she said. 'Now don't you move until I get back. I've got to go down to the shop.'

Victoria didn't stir, but sat holding the biscuit in her hand, her little mind confused. Why didn't her Mama come and take her away? Where was Rachel? She said she'd come soon. Was it because she was naughty and wet her bed? She didn't like it here and the nasty lady frightened her. The tears continued to fall.

Madge successfully removed a pair of scissors from the sewing room the following day and put them in her pocket, winking at Lily who was busy chatting to the officer on duty.

Later that evening, Hetty prepared to have her bath; she was filled with excitement.

'Now remember,' warned Madge as she was leaving the cell, 'you don't utter a word about this to anyone, or we'll all be for the high jump.'

There was a look of cunning in Hetty's eyes. She shook her head and with a solemn expression put her fingers to her lips. 'Shh,' she whispered and left.

'Do you think she'll remember?' asked Lily anxiously.

'Oh yes,' said Madge with conviction. 'Hetty may be a bit backward but she's bright enough in other ways. When she wants to, she can be quite crafty.'

When Hetty returned, Madge kept watch for the screws whilst Lily sat Hetty down at the table and began to cut her hair much shorter. To her surprise, once she'd put a bit of shape into it, removing the weight from the long straggly tresses, it became apparent that Hetty had a natural curl. Lily primped the damp hair with her comb and fingers after towel-drying it, brushed and pampered it until it was finished. Then, taking her lipstick from her bag, she carefully followed the shape of Hetty's lips. The transformation was quite startling.

Although Hetty was a dumpy creature, she had a face that was childlike and innocent. Without the severity of her previous hairstyle, she looked much younger and more attractive.

Lily stepped back and admired her work.

Hetty stood before them, nervous and anxious.

'You look a smasher, girl,' said Madge.

With a bewildered look, Hetty said, 'I do?'

Madge squeezed her arm. 'You look really lovely.'

Lily took her compact from her belongings and handed it to Hetty. 'See for yourself.'

The woman hesitated, then with a shy smile she looked at her reflection. Her expression of joyful surprise was almost comical and the others burst into laughter.

'Is that really me?' asked Hetty. Breathless with excitement.

'That's really you,' said Lily. 'I told you you had pretty hair.'

Hetty grabbed her in a clumsy bearlike hug. 'Oh thank you. Thank you.'

Lily felt the tears prick her eyes. 'You're welcome.'

'What are we going to say in the morning when the screws notice?' asked Madge. 'They'll know it's been cut.'

'Mm,' said Lily. 'Hetty, you'll have to cover your head with a scarf. Tell them you're cold. Then when we've put the scissors back, you can uncover it.'

'But how will we explain it?' pressed Madge.

With a toss of her hair, Lily laughed and said, 'We'll tell them it's a bleedin' miracle. How can they argue if we don't have the scissors on us?' She paused. 'What about the hair I cut off?' she asked. 'I'd forgotten about that.'

'We'll get rid of it when we empty the slops in the morning.'

It all worked according to plan. Madge slipped the scissors back into the box unobserved, as she gathered her mail-bag material. At lunchtime as they trooped into the dining room, there were a few murmurs as Hetty pranced behind Lily, hand on hip, smiling at everyone.

'Bloody hell,' said one of the inmates. 'Is that you, Hetty Richards? What's happened to your hair?'

'It's a miracle,' said Hetty artfully. 'I woke up this morning and that is what had happened.'

Her cellmates smothered their laughter.

But Belle Chisholm wasn't amused. 'You mind you don't

wake up one morning to find it's your throat that's been cut – not your hair!'

Hetty's expression of joy faded.

To see the simple gentle creature bullied this way incensed Lily. She turned on Belle, letting go of all the frustration that was festering inside her. 'That's all you're good for, isn't it?' she raved. 'You swan around this place, followed by these stupid creatures who haven't got a brain between them, and you have to pick on someone who isn't capable of standing up for herself . . . Well, try me instead!' She pushed Belle in the chest, sending her staggering backwards.

For a moment the big ugly woman was taken aback but when she saw all the others waiting for her reaction she glared at Lily. 'I've told you before, but it seems you haven't learned a thing. I'm top dog here.'

Lily's eyes blazed. 'Top dog, my arse! All you are is a bloody bully. Well, you don't frighten *me*. And you'd better know now – *no one* tells me what to do, certainly not the likes of you. I've *stepped* in better things than you!'

Belle moved towards Lily in a menacing fashion, her fists raised to strike her, but at the same time, Madge stepped forward and stood between them. 'You take her on, you'll have to deal with me too.'

At that moment Miss Cole came over. 'Break it up, you lot. What's going on?'

Belle looked at her, then glared at Lily. 'Miss bloody Pickford here keeps forgetting her place. She's getting very lippy.'

The warder looked at Lily. 'Is that right?'

'If you like,' said Lily. 'I just don't take kindly to bullies, that's all.'

'Is that right, Miss Hoity Toity.' Cole grabbed the front of Lily's dress and drew her close, her eyes blazing with anger and hatred. 'Now you listen to me, you little bitch. I won't have any trouble on my shift. This is my last warning, Pickford. Any more from you and I'll put you on report. Now get back to your cell.'

Madge clutched Lily's arm as she stepped towards the woman. 'Come on,' she urged, and led her away.

Belle reluctantly lumbered off in the direction of her cell, cursing to herself.

Hetty clung to Lily. 'You shouldn't have done that,' she said. 'Belle is big trouble. I was all right, honest.'

Lily put an arm around her. 'It's all right, love. She doesn't scare me.'

Madge looked at her. 'You'd better watch your back in future, girl.'

'I will,' said Lily. 'Thanks for standing up for me like that.'

Madge shrugged. 'I hate the bitch. She doesn't scare me either, I've been around prisons too often, but I know enough to be careful because she can be dangerous. She's a lifer with nothing to lose. And watch out for Cole. She's not to be trusted either. Just keep your eyes peeled, that's all.'

Lily knew she'd made a dangerous enemy in Belle Chisholm, but she was determined to stand up for herself. It was bad enough to be incarcerated in this dreadful place through no fault of her own, but if she was forced to be here, no one was going to destroy her spirit. It was the only thing she had left.

Two days later all the inmates of Brookmans were excused work detail as it was Christmas Day. The atmosphere in the prison was heavy and depressing, with everyone visualising how their families would be together. Some no doubt, without the traditional fayre because of lack of money, but at least free to celebrate in their own way.

The Governor of Brookmans had scheduled an extra half an hour for the exercise period, thinking to keep the inmates on the march instead of brooding in their cells.

It was bitterly cold, but most of the cons elected to be outside, all wrapped up in their cloaks, hoods up, walking around like a secret order of monks to keep warm, puffing on their weekly supply of cigarettes. But there was a feeling of unrest in the air that Lily didn't like. She could understand it, if everyone was feeling like her. Her thoughts were full of Victoria, wondering if the people caring for her had a nice Christmas tree and were there presents there?

She'd written to Victoria, telling her how much she loved and missed her. She'd also written to Rachel and asked her to send some of Victoria's toys to the house, but her heart was heavy.

When the inmates filed into the dining room at lunchtime, there was a feeling of doom about the place. Instead of the usual loud chatter, backbiting and noise, it was strangely silent. There was a Christmas dinner of sorts – a thin slice of turkey on each plate, one roast potato as hard as a rock, some overcooked sprouts and carrots and a small piece of suet pudding with a scattering of sultanas.

Lily couldn't stand the atmosphere any longer. 'Do you know any carols?' she asked Madge.

With a look of puzzlement she said, 'Yes, I suppose I can remember a few. Why?'

'Because we're going to sing some,' she said and began with 'Once In Royal David's City'. Everyone around her looked startled, but when they heard the pure tones of Lily's fine singing voice, one by one they began to join in, with the exception of Belle Chisholm and her cronies, who remained silent.

The atmosphere lightened at last and everyone began to

relax and enjoy themselves. For the wardens who were on duty it was a great relief. Christmas Day was usually fraught with trouble. After a few carols Lily began to sing 'When Irish Eyes Are Smiling' and 'You Made Me Love You', finishing with a rousing, 'When You Wore A Tulip'. The air was filled with the sound of voices, if not in tune, at least in unison.

When the bell rang for the end of the meal, which had been extended as things were going so well, everyone filed out in a happier frame of mind. But Belle Chisholm was seething with jealousy. She edged her way forward and jabbed Lily sharply in the back with her finger.

'Who do you think you are – fucking Vesta Tilley?'

'No! But I know who you are, dearie. You're one of the ruins that Cromwell knocked about a bit,' she retorted, quoting one of Vesta's songs.

Belle's face was puce with anger, but before she could retaliate, the senior warden on duty who'd seen the exchange, and who was not going to have her watch spoilt by any confrontation on the part of Belle Chisholm, came quickly over.

'Move along, Chisholm. Get back to your cell . . . and you, Pickford. Now! On your way.'

Madge tucked her arm through Lily's as they were escorted back to their cells. 'I really enjoyed meself,' she said. 'I didn't know you could sing.'

'I used to earn my living doing it,' confided Lily.

'Well, I'd pay to hear you, love,' said Madge.

If I can't get a job, thought Lily, I may be forced to try again. But she knew she wouldn't earn enough to keep her and Victoria. My baby. What sort of a Christmas did you have? She wondered.

Victoria's Christmas was miserable. There was no Christmas tree. There were no presents. She sat at the table with Gladys Parker and her husband, eating her meagre portion of roast chicken with a few vegetables. Her mother's letters were read by Gladys and immediately torn up and stuffed in the dustbin. The toys Rachel had sent were pushed into the cupboard under the stairs, to sell on. After lunch the child was given a peeled orange and bundled off to her room where she sat in the corner eating the fruit slowly, not even knowing it was Christmas Day, wondering where her mother was.

Chapter Seven

Luke Longford walked down the gangway on his ship, whistling to himself as he made for the taxi rank. 'Club Valletta in Oxford Street, please.'

The driver turned and looked at him. 'Blimey, mate! Where have you been?'

'What do you mean?'

'The Club's been closed down these past few weeks.'

'Closed?'

'Yes,' said the driver. 'Lily Pickford was done for running a crooked game. She's in prison, doing a six-month stretch.'

Luke was shattered.

The driver was all ready for a good gossip. 'Her partner, Rachel Cohen, was fined – but poor Lily was sent down.'

'This Rachel Cohen . . . do you know where she lives?'

'Yes, I often used to run her home.'

'Take me there,' said Luke.

Rachel was very surprised to see a well-dressed stranger on her doorstep.

'Mrs Cohen?' asked Luke.

'Yes, that's me.'

'My name is Luke Longford. I'm the Chief Steward from

the *Mauritania*. I wonder if I could have a few words with you about Miss Pickford?'

Looking the man up and down, Rachel liked what she saw and was intrigued by the request. 'You'd better come in,' she said, and led him into her living room, which now contained only two armchairs and an occasional table. 'Sit down,' she said. 'You'll have to excuse the bareness of the room, but I'm about to move to a smaller house and I've sold off a lot of my stuff.'

'That's all right, Mrs Cohen.' He took a cigarette case from his pocket. 'May I?' he asked.

'Of course.'

He began to explain. 'Before I sailed on my cruise, I went to the Club and spoke with Lily. I warned her that I thought the tables in the gambling room were fixed and I gave her the address of a friend and advised her to have them checked. Today I heard the terrible news that she's in prison.'

Rachel nodded. 'It's true. But as far as I know, the tables weren't seen to.' She told him the whole story.

Luke shook his head. 'Perhaps she didn't have time to contact him.' He sat back in the chair, a frown creasing his brow. 'What a terrible thing to happen. And this Percy Gates has got away with it all?'

'Yes. The rotten *shyster*! The police know he's behind it, but they haven't any proof. I had to sell everything in the Club and I think I may have a buyer for the premises. Some man wants to turn it into a Merchant Navy Club – a posh seamen's mission. Poor Lily has nothing left when she comes out. We'll have to pay off the bank loan, you see. Then there's little Victoria.'

'Victoria?'

'Her daughter.' Rachel then told him what had happened regarding Victoria.

'Oh my God!' said Luke. 'I didn't know she had a child. What a terrible time it must have been.'

'Lily is devastated.'

'What about Lily's husband?' Luke asked.

'Victoria's father died when she was but a few months old,' ventured Rachel without giving too much away.

'Is there any chance that I can see Miss Pickford?' he asked.

'I've booked a visit with her in a couple of days' time. I've got a pass for two. Our friend Sandy was coming with me, but his sister's been taken ill.'

Luke leaned forward. 'Would you mind very much if I came with you? I'm on leave for two weeks and I'd like to see her.'

'Why, Mr Longford? Why do you want to see Lily?'

'I know she didn't have anything to do with this scam. When I told her I suspected the game was fixed, she was horrified. If she could give me all the details, then perhaps I could help in some way.' He raised his eyebrows. 'I do have some very useful contacts – and who knows? It's worth a try, don't you think?'

Rachel looked uncertain. 'I'm not at all sure it's a good idea.' At his look of surprise, she added, 'Prison is an appalling place to be, even when you're an innocent. It can remove all vestige of pride. It's bad enough for prisoners to see those close to them, but a stranger . . . even worse. Unless there's a very good reason to be there.'

'There's no guarantee that I can help, of course, but it infuriates me to see someone like Lily who is innocent, incarcerated.'

'Well, all right. I'd never forgive myself if I turned down your offer and denied Lily a chance.' Rachel sat back in her chair and changed the subject. 'So how are you spending your leave?'

He smiled and told her of his plans. 'I'm looking for a suitable property myself. I intend to open a very special hotel in Southampton which will be expensive, and exclusive. As you know, Mrs Cohen, there are always people who can afford the best, whatever the financial climate of the country, and I'm going to give it to them. I've worked all my life with such a plan in mind, and now I have the money to do it.'

'Why don't you buy the Club?' asked Rachel.

'It's not big enough.' He hesitated. 'Please don't be offended, but I need a smarter, more classy location.'

'What's to be offended about! You know what you want. Now about Lily . . . we go on Wednesday. The prison is near Winchester and we need to get a train, so you can pick me up at twelve-thirty.'

He shook her hand warmly. 'You won't regret this, I can assure you.'

'I'd better not!' she warned.

Visiting day always filled Brookmans Prison with tension. Those who knew they were to see their family or friends were excited. Those who were uncertain about receiving visitors at all were taut with anxiety, and others who knew they would be sitting alone in their cells were filled with anger at their rejection. The prison warders were on alert to quash any riotous behaviour.

Madge was smartening herself up to see her mother, and Lily was ready, waiting anxiously for any news that Rachel might have for her.

Hetty sat on her bed, happily watching all the activity around her. But she remained behind as the others were led away. She waved at Lily, who glanced back at her.

To Madge, Lily whispered: 'Doesn't anyone come to see Hetty, ever?'

Her cellmate just shook her head.

The two of them sat side by side at the long table and waited anxiously for the visitors to be let in. They looked up at the large timepiece on the wall as every second ticked away until the hands reached two o'clock, when the doors were opened under the watchful eyes of the prison officers. The outsiders swarmed in, gazing around, searching for their particular inmate, hurrying over to them so as not to waste a precious moment of their time.

It was with some surprise that Lily realised Rachel had a companion with her, and she was filled with horror when she recognised Luke Longford. The blood drained from her face with embarrassment and shame. She wanted to get out of her chair and flee, but so anxious was she for news that she sat still, her hands gripped tightly together in her lap.

Rachel and Luke sat opposite her. He was the first to speak.

'Forgive me for this dreadful intrusion, Lily. I'm sure I'm the last person you'd want to see, but I do have something important to ask you. However, I'll let you speak to Rachel first.'

He moved his chair back a little so as to appear, in such a crowded place, to give the two women a modicum of privacy.

'Any news of Victoria?' asked Lily immediately.

'The authorities tell me that she's settled well and is happy,' said her friend. 'But they still won't let me visit.'

Lily shook her head. 'Victoria will feel abandoned.'

Rachel tried to cheer her. 'Children are really resilient, darling. Just think – it's not for ever. Only a few months.'

'But what if she forgets about me?' asked Lily, her voice breaking. 'What will I do then?'

'She'll never forget her Mama, darling. Please try not to worry. You'll only make yourself ill.'

As the two women talked over their problems, Luke sat back and watched. Even in her drab prison garb, Lily managed to look stunning, despite the paleness of her skin, the circles beneath her eyes. Yet he sensed a new vulnerability about her. He wanted to take her into his arms and hold her. Comfort her. Tell her that everything would be all right . . . eventually. He was filled with outrage at the injustice that had put this innocent woman in here. God alone knew just what life was like behind these bars.

He looked around at the other inmates, at their visitors. There was a rich tapestry of life in this room at the moment and he was curious enough to wonder what was the story behind each and every one of them.

Lily's voice broke through his thoughts. 'What did you want to say to me badly enough to bring you to this godforsaken place, Luke?'

He moved his chair closer. 'I was shocked to hear about you, Lily. Didn't you get in touch with my friend to check the tables?'

'He was away. I left a message but that night I was raided.' She smiled wryly. 'Just imagine, if you'd come into the club a couple of days earlier, none of this would have happened.'

Luke shook his head. 'Life is full of ifs. Quickly, tell me again about the arrangement with this Gates.'

Lily repeated the tale. 'It was Sergeant Green who put me on to him.'

'Who's Green?' asked Luke.

'He's with the local police force.'

Luke raised his eyebrows in surprise. 'A crooked copper, eh? Do the police force know?'

She shrugged. 'I think I mentioned it to DI Chadwick, I can't be sure.'

'I'll ask about, see if I can help in any way.'

Puzzled, Lily asked, 'Why? Why would you want to?'

'I have no time for criminals! And it makes me angry to see you here when you are innocent.'

'Thanks, Luke, but really I think you're wasting your time. Chadwick knows about Gates. He's watching him, but I've heard nothing. I'll be out soon anyway,' she said somewhat dismissively.

Luke felt disappointed. He rose from his chair. 'I'll leave you two alone.' Then he added, 'I'll give Rachel a number where you can contact me. Good luck, Lily.'

She just glanced at him. 'Goodbye, Luke.'

As he walked away, Rachel snapped, 'Was that really necessary? He's only trying to help.'

'It's a waste of time, Rachel. All I want right now is to get out of here and have my baby returned to me. I can't think of anything else!'

Patting her hand, her old friend said, 'No, of course. I'm sorry, I didn't think. Stupid I was to bring him.'

With a half-smile Lily said, 'No. It's all right. You thought you were doing the right thing.'

Rachel told Lily about the prospective buyer for the Club. 'Keep your fingers crossed, darling,' said the Jewess. 'The creditors are getting edgy, and the bank have called in the overdraft, but are waiting for the sale.'

'I'm sorry to have put all this on to you.'

'My life! What's the matter? You know of any Jew who can't sort out finance?'

The bell for the end of visiting time rang out, but today, for Lily, it was a welcome relief. She'd felt exposed, seeing Luke. Stripped of her dignity, filled with shame. Right now she just wanted to retreat to her cell and nurse her shattered pride.

Just as she was about to leave, a row broke out between

another prisoner and her male visitor. The woman hit the man in the face. He bellowed with rage and took hold of her by her hair, yelling abuse. The warders rushed in and separated them.

Rachel was horrified by the scene and clasped her hands to her chest, her anxiety turning her face pale. 'My God, Lily. What sort of people are in here?'

'Most of them are very ordinary,' she tried to explain. 'But emotions are very fragile and just beneath the surface. That's why this sort of thing happens.' They watched as the warders tried to drag the prisoner away, kicking and screaming. The officers soon had control and the room was cleared of visitors.

Lily thanked God that Luke was not here to witness such a scene. She would have died. It was bad enough that Rachel had done so.

The inmates filed back to the cells, their minds full of what had transpired during visiting time. On many occasions what had been awaited with so much eagerness, ended with bitter recriminations, family issues and disappointment. Such was the case it seemed in the cell on the second tier of the prison.

Lily flung herself onto her bed, filled with despair at the thought of Victoria being kept away from those she loved. The Club was being sold, which was the end to all her dreams, and she was angry at having what little dignity she retained, taken from her by Luke's visit.

Madge was disgruntled after being told off by her mother for being in prison and not out thieving, putting food on the table. 'That's bloody great, that is,' she said angrily. 'It was because I was trying to look after me mum I ended up inside again. A lot of thanks I get.' She lit a cigarette and puffed on it.

'What's wrong with your mother – is she ill?' asked Lily.

'No, she's as fit as a fiddle. Why?'

'Then tell her to get a bloody job!'

'That would be a first,' Madge declared.

'Then why go thieving?' said Lily sharply. 'You're going round in circles. Send your mother out to work and you go and get an honest job.'

Madge looked at her with surprise. 'An honest job?'

'Have you ever tried?' asked Lily.

She shook her head. 'No. Thieving's all I know.'

'How do you know what you are capable of, if you haven't tried something else? Look, Madge, your mother's lazy. You're a nice-looking girl, bright. For Christ's sake, do you want to end up inside for the rest of your life?'

'No, of course not!'

'Then do something about it, before it's too late.' Lily was furious with Madge for throwing away her freedom needlessly, especially as she herself was here, an innocent victim.

Madge sat down on the chair in front of the table and pondered on this. Maybe Lily was right. She didn't want to end up like her father . . . an old lag. And she was pissed off by the constant carping of her mother. Her cellmate's statement about her mother was correct, she was a lazy cow and spent more money in the pub than she did on food. If Lily Pickford told her she was bright and could do it, well maybe, just maybe, she could.

Hetty asked shyly, 'Did you have a nice visit, Lily?'

Madge said, 'Bloody hell, you should have seen the man that came to see her. What a beautiful geezer! I wouldn't kick him out of my bed, I can tell you.'

'Is he your boyfriend?' asked Hetty.

'No. I've only met him once and he had no bloody right coming here today!' She was still seething at the indignity of it all.

Madge looked at the angry expression on her face. 'He must have had a good reason. No one comes to a prison to while away an hour.'

'He wants to try and help me.'

'You lucky thing.'

'Yes, maybe. But I've got other things on my mind. Victoria has to stay with her foster parents and that's all I can think about at this moment.' She turned to her friend and with a rueful smile said, 'I'm sorry I flew off the handle.'

'That's all right, love,' said Madge. 'In any case, you spoke the truth. It's time I did something with my life.'

Luke and Rachel were sitting on the train heading for Southampton.

'I should perhaps have written to Lily instead of going to see her. That was a mistake,' said Luke.

'Yes, I think perhaps you're right,' agreed Rachel.

His eyes clouded. 'It makes me furious to think she's there because of this man Gates.'

'Well, I blame Sergeant Green myself,' said Rachel. 'It was all his bloody idea.'

Luke felt compelled to try to help Lily. 'Would you think it an imposition if I went along to see this Chadwick and find out what's going on?' asked Luke. 'And perhaps mention this Green. It might be important.'

'You do whatever you like, young man. I'm as anxious to see Lily out of that hole as much as anyone.'

The following day, Luke was ushered into an interview room to await DI Chadwick, who joined him a few minutes later. The two men shook hands.

'Sorry about this place, but everywhere else is busy right now and you made a point of saying you wanted to see me in private.'

'That's right,' said Luke, and introduced himself. 'I've been to see Miss Lily Pickford at Brookmans.'

Chadwick became very interested. 'How is she?'

'I'm sure you don't need to ask me that. How would you feel in her position? The woman is innocent of the charges brought before the court and shouldn't be in that dreadful dump.'

'I'm sure you're right, but I didn't have the proof to put Gates away, and the croupier took the rap for him, implicating Lily in his testimony. There was no proof of Lily's innocence. But believe me, we're watching Gates like a hawk.'

Leaning forward Luke said, 'Are you aware that your Sergeant Green had a finger in this particular pie?'

Chadwick frowned. 'What are you saying?'

Luke explained what he'd learned yesterday from Lily.

'This has never come up before,' the officer said with a scowl of anger. If there was one thing that Chadwick could not tolerate, it was a bent copper. 'If this is true, then I'll have to look into it very carefully.' He paused. 'Gates is such a smart bastard, but if Green is mixed up in this, he could be the weak link. I'll have to tread very carefully so as not to spook him.' He rose from his seat and proffered his hand. 'Thanks for coming in, Mr Longford.'

'Not at all,' said Luke. 'I just want to see justice done.'

With a grim expression Chadwick said, 'We all want that, believe me.'

Chapter Eight

Quinn Gifford was sitting at the kitchen table, laboriously writing a letter.

Dear Lily, When you come out of prison you can come and live with me at my farm. Don't you worry about nothing. From now on I'm going to take care of you. You let me know the date you get out and I will come and meet you and bring you home. Quinn Gifford.

Then he put a kiss beside his signature and sat back with a satisfied smile. There! That ought to please her. She wouldn't have any worries now. He scrabbled around until he found an old and creased envelope and smoothed it to the best of his ability and addressed it. He'd put that into the mail tomorrow, first thing.

When she received the letter, Lily sat on her bed and opened it. The contents first filled her with horror and then anger. Who did this man think he was? Whatever gave him the impression she'd be in the least bit interested in sharing his life? She remembered the last time she'd seen him in the Club, when he gave her the money to pay for the damages he'd caused. She remembered too the hungry look in his eye. Well, at least whilst she was in here, he couldn't get to her, and once she was out . . . she'd keep well out of his way.

★ ★ ★

Three months had passed since Lily had been sent to prison. With the help of her cellmates, she'd settled to the routine and as Madge had prophesied, she even drank the nightly cocoa without complaint.

Miss Cole picked on her whenever she could, giving her every menial task that was available, and Belle Chisholm was still a thorn in her side, making snide remarks which Lily treated with the contempt they deserved, but she made sure she was never alone when Belle was around, thus preserving her own safety. Belle had striven time and time again to bait Lily, to trick her into a fight so that she lost her time off for good behaviour, but somehow she had been thwarted at every turn, mainly due to the vigilance of the senior warder, who was aware of her efforts and had no time for Belle Chisholm. One day, however, the inevitable happened.

During the exercise period, Belle and her mates dogged Lily's steps all around the parade ground, sniping at her, needling her, all of which she ignored until Belle started on about her daughter.

'Suppose you think you'll be able to have her back once you get out of here,' sneered Belle. 'Well, the authorities aren't fools. They'll know you're not a fit mother. They'll probably send your little darling to some institution or other.'

Lily could stand no more. She hurled herself at the big ugly woman, taking Belle completely by surprise. Lily hammered into her, punching her, pulling her hair, screaming at her in her fury.

The duty warders pulled them apart and they were sent separately before the Governor, who looked at Lily in disgust.

'I expected more from you, Pickford. I won't have this disgraceful sort of thing in my prison. You'll lose your time off for good behaviour. You'll serve your full six months.'

Lily was devastated.

Madge and Hetty tried to comfort her when she returned to her cell, but she cursed herself for her foolishness and she cursed Belle Chisholm, who had also lost her privileges, through the débâcle.

Lily was unaware of the frustration and anger of the lifer, who was still seething about this upstart, Lily Pickford, who had dared to cross her. Belle watched her, constantly waiting for an opportunity to pay her back in some way. Fired by Lily's stand, one or two other inmates who still had a bit of courage had also crossed Belle, but in a minor way that was easily dealt with by the big woman and her minions, but nevertheless, Belle felt her tight grip of fear slipping. And she didn't like it.

In particular it infuriated her to see the kindness Lily showed to Hetty Richards who, until Lily arrived, had been Belle's favourite whipping boy. But since the scene between herself and the newcomer, after Hetty showed off her new hairdo, Belle had left her alone. But as she watched the friendship grow between the two, she knew she could get back at Lily through Hetty. And she waited for the opportunity.

The following day at lunchtime, she saw Hetty tucking in enthusiastically to her meal and looking across from her own table, she called, 'You enjoying that, Hetty?'

Hetty in her innocence looked back at Belle and smiled. 'Yes, thanks. It's lovely.'

Madge and Lily were watchful, wondering what the lifer was up to.

'Yeah. Very tasty,' said Belle loudly. 'I knew you'd like it – it's better than the rabbit stew your mother used to make.'

The sudden scream of rage from Hetty took everyone by

surprise. The usually gentle creature went berserk. She swiped her plate off the table, then did the same with everyone else's. It was chaos. Lily, Madge and all those sitting beside them, were covered in their food, their uniforms dripping in gravy and potatoes.

Across the room, Belle Chisholm's laughter echoed raucously. With a cry of rage, Hetty leapt over the bench, and ran to the table where Belle was sitting. She hurled herself at the big woman, her hands round her throat.

'You wicked bugger,' Hetty screamed. 'I'll kill you for this!'

Madge and Lily rushed over, trying to pull Hetty away, but in her rage she was as strong as any man and held on to her victim. Belle was puce in the face, gasping for breath. Prison warders soon descended on them, dragging Hetty away as she screamed abuse at her tormentor.

Lily watched, stunned by the change in the gentle soul she knew. She glared at the lifer, knowing that there was more going on here than she understood, and wondered what it was. Everybody was sent back to their cells. Those who'd been splattered with food were told to change; they would be given clean clothes.

Sitting on her bed wrapped in her prison cloak waiting for a clean dress, Lily looked at Madge and asked, 'What the devil was all that about? Hetty went crazy. I couldn't believe it. She was like a maniac.'

'That bloody Belle!' snapped Madge. 'That wicked bitch knew exactly what she was doing.'

'Well, for God's sake will you tell me why, because I don't understand any of it,' asked Lily.

With a deep sigh her friend began to explain. 'As you know from Hetty herself, her mother didn't love her. She spoilt the son something rotten, but she did buy Hetty a pet rabbit one day. Perhaps she had a moment of guilt. Anyway, Hetty adored this animal. It was the only thing she loved and which loved her in return.' At the look of surprise on Lily's face she said, 'Rabbits are affectionate creatures.'

'But what's the connection?' asked Lily with a puzzled frown.

'One day after an argument, Hetty's mother killed the rabbit and cooked it!'

'Oh no,' breathed Lily. 'Poor Hetty.'

'Poor mother! Hetty took a kitchen knife to her and stabbed her to death.'

Lily's eyes opened wide. 'Our Hetty?'

With a sardonic grin, Madge said, 'Yes. That quiet soul who you would think wouldn't hurt a fly. Well, normally she wouldn't as long as nothing is done to anything she loves.'

'But what'll happen to her now?'

'They'll give her a sedative, put her in solitary confinement for a couple of days and then bring her back here.'

'Has something like this happened before then?' asked Lily.

'Once or twice,' said Madge nonchalantly. 'But there's nothing to worry about. She's not really dangerous in the normal way; in fact, she's harmless usually – you've seen that for yourself. She only gets riled if anyone baits her like that bitch did today. She'd never harm either of us. She loves us, especially you.'

Lily lay back on her bed and thought how awful life was for some people. Her own problems paled into insignificance in comparison. Poor dear Hetty. Even though she'd seen her today, wreaking havoc, Lily could only feel deep pity for her and anger bordering on hatred for Belle Chisholm for the deliberate way she'd led her into the trap. How vicious. How cruel. She felt somewhat mollified when the next morning she heard the Prison Governor had put Belle into solitary too.

When Hetty returned to her cell and her friends a week later, she walked in with a big smile as if nothing untoward had happened. Indeed, she seemed to have forgotten all about it and neither of them mentioned the incident.

But Belle Chisholm, still in her solitary state, seethed with rage. All this was Lily Pickford's fault. When she got out of here and back onto the tier, she'd do for the little slag once and for all.

She heard the key turn in the lock of her cell door. The door opened and the warder called, 'Come on out, Chisholm. Go back to your own cell, get your things and go and have a bath. You stink of sweat.'

'What time is it?' Belle asked.

'Ten o'clock. When you've had your bath, wait in your cell. Then when the bell goes you can join the others for lunch. After, you can exercise as usual. But you keep your nose clean, Chisholm. The Governor isn't best pleased with you.'

'Now ain't that a shame?' she answered scornfully.

She made her way down the corridor and waited for the officer to unlock the doors along the way, until she was back in the central part of the prison. There were one or two inmates slopping out, others scrubbing the corridor floors, but the main body of prisoners were off working in the laundry and the sewing room, making mail bags.

Belle sat on her bunk and took from beneath her pillow her cigarettes and lit one. She breathed in the nicotine like a drug. In solitary you weren't allowed such luxuries. She hated being shut away. She needed to be free, to walk among her peers, to make her mark. She enjoyed the position she'd made for herself and no one was going to change that. She smirked. Who did that Lily Pickford think she was? She was here on a minor misdemeanour, not a serious crime like Belle. Well, she had a position to uphold and it was about time that jumped-up madam learned who was boss.

When she'd finished her cigarette, Belle walked down to the bath-house. She glanced at the list on the noticeboard with interest. Lily Pickford's name was down for a bath tomorrow afternoon. A cruel smile spread across the big woman's countenance. How very convenient, she gloated.

As the bell for lunch sounded, the inmates filed into the dining room. Madge nudged Lily. 'Your friend Belle is out,' she murmured.

Lily didn't look around, but glanced anxiously at Hetty. Fortunately, the young woman seemed unaware of the presence of her old enemy. When eventually she did see her, she looked very warily at Belle, who ignored them all.

'She's being very quiet,' said Lily, with some relief.

'Mm,' said Madge. 'That's when she's at her most dangerous. She's usually planning something. You just watch your back, girl.'

In the exercise yard, Belle was as usual surrounded by her fans. She was smiling at them, holding court. She looked across at Lily and stared hard at her.

Lily felt a shiver run down her back. The cold expression in the other's eyes chilled her to the bone.

The following day was Sunday and the workshops were closed. Madge was reading and Hetty was brushing her hair. Lily collected her towel, soap and flannel and said, 'Right, I'm off to have a bath. See you both later.'

She walked down the two flights of stairs escorted by a warder, who handed her over to Miss Cole who was on duty in the bath-house. The other two baths were occupied and

Lily made her way to the third cubicle and started to run the water. She'd got used to bathing in a cubicle without a door, but she always sat with her back to the taps so she could see anyone passing.

Miss Cole poked her head round the partition. 'All right, Pickford. I'll just tick your name off my list – and don't take too long,' she snapped. 'I've got to go to the office. By the time I come back, I expect you to be finished. And don't forget to clean the bath after you!'

Lily ignored the woman. She was only allowed one bath a week and she wasn't going to be rushed. She ran the bathwater, slipped out of her uniform and folded it neatly, putting it on the floor, then stepped into the warm water and relaxed. She covered her body with soap and rinsed the suds away. She vaguely heard the others being hurried along by Cole, made to empty their bathwater, as she lay immersed up to her neck, lost in her own little world. It was suddenly very quiet, so different from the general hubbub of the main prison. It was absolute bliss. She closed her eyes.

When she heard the door of the bath-house open, she assumed it was the next person on the list, but a sudden sixth sense made her open her eyes, just in time to see Belle Chisholm and her two mates rush into the cubicle. She didn't have time to scream as they pushed her under the water and held her there.

Lily struggled for all she was worth. In her terror and panic, she grabbed at the hands that held her throat, her shoulders, trying to loosen their hold, but to no avail. My God, I'm going to die, she thought. Just as she felt that her lungs were going to burst and that she would surely drown, the hands that gripped her released their hold. She came to the surface coughing and spluttering, fighting to breathe, gasping for breath. As she held onto the side of the bath trying to fill her lungs with air, she was aware of Hetty, standing resolute, her face flushed with rage, swinging a galvanised pail at the heads of her attackers, who were screaming with fear.

Two of them went down under the rain of blows, bleeding from the head. Belle Chisholm was holding up her arms to protect herself, but Hetty's anger gave her the strength of ten and Belle fell to the floor, bleeding profusely.

Lily scrambled from the bath in time to stop Hetty bringing the pail down on Belle's upturned face. 'No, Hetty! That's enough. You'll kill her!'

The woman stopped at the sound of her friend's voice.

At that moment two prison officers rushed in, alerted by the noise, followed by Cole, who looked with surprise at the scene before her. They grabbed hold of Hetty and dragged her away, kicking and yelling. Lily ran after them, leaving puddles of water in her wake. 'Don't you hurt her,' she cried. 'She's just saved my life!'

Other warders appeared. 'What's going on?' the senior one asked.

Pointing to Belle and her two mates, the naked Lily panted, 'These buggers tried to drown me and Hetty saved me. But for her, I'd be dead now.' She looked across at Miss Cole. 'You left me alone. You wicked bitch! You knew what was going to happen, didn't you? Belle Chisholm put you up to this!'

Cole looked at her grimly. 'Don't be so bloody stupid. Of course I didn't.'

Nothing could silence Lily. 'All because I wouldn't play your dirty little games. You couldn't wait to pay me off!'

The senior officer said, 'Get dressed, Pickford. Then wait outside the Governor's office. I'll have to report this. And you, Cole. Come with me.'

Belle sat dazed on the floor, blood pouring from a wound on her head. She was hauled to her feet, as were her accomplices, and led away.

Lily dressed herself and made her way to the office of the Governor, and sat on a chair outside. She was shaking. She put her hands between her knees in an effort to control her limbs, but couldn't stop trembling.

Inside the office was the sound of raised voices and as the door opened, the senior officer came storming out and Lily was ushered in.

'Sit down, Pickford,' said the Governor. 'Now what the devil's going on?'

Lily filled her in with the details of the attack. 'Please, Ma'am, don't punish Hetty Richards. She saved my life.'

'Don't worry about Richards, she won't be punished. But tell me, why has Belle Chisholm got it in for you in particular?'

'Because I stood up to her. She was baiting Hetty and I wouldn't stand for it. The woman's a bully, picking on the weak. It didn't seem right.'

The middle-aged woman behind the desk looked coldly at Lily. 'What do you expect? This isn't some cosy girls' school, this is a women's prison, full of criminals – like you!'

Lily returned the cold gaze with her own and said quietly, 'I am not a criminal, Ma'am. I'm innocent of the charges brought against me.'

'If I believed everyone in here, Pickford, we haven't a guilty person behind these walls!'

'What about Belle?' asked Lily.

'She is to be transferred to another gaol. She's having her head stitched at the moment, then she'll leave. I'm doing this for the peaceful running of Brookmans. I won't put up with this behaviour.'

'And Miss Cole?' persisted Lily.

'What about Miss Cole?'

'I reckon she knew what was going to happen. She left me alone deliberately.'

'Why would she do such a thing?'

'Because I wouldn't touch her with a barge-pole. She's a bloody dyke!'

'Have you any proof of this?'

Lily shook her head. 'But I know.'

'That's not good enough,' said the Governor. 'You can't make such a serious allegation without proof. That's slander. You don't want to be involved in any more trouble, do you?'

Lily looked straight at the Governor. 'I can't believe you're the only one who doesn't know about Cole and Chisholm. You're too intelligent for that.'

The Governor ignored her remarks and called in the officer waiting outside. 'Take Pickford to the doctor and get her checked over, then escort her back to her cell.' She glared at Lily. 'I don't want to see you in here again. Now off you go!'

The doctor was satisfied that Lily was fine, apart from the shock she'd suffered, and advised her to rest. 'There's not much wrong with you, young woman,' he said. 'You've the constitution of an ox.'

Whilst Lily was being examined, the Governor called Miss Cole before her. The warder stood in front of her superior with a worried expression.

'Chisholm is being transferred,' she was told. 'I don't want to hear of any tearful goodbyes between you!'

Cole looked startled. 'I don't know what you mean, Ma'am.'

'Don't take me for a fool. I've given you far too much leeway in the past. Keep your mind on the job, is my advice

125

to you. One more whisper about you and you'll be on suspension. Do I make myself clear?'

'Yes, Ma'am.'

'Then get back on duty.' The Governor watched Cole leave the office, knowing she should have sorted the woman out long before this. The anger of her senior officer had forced her into action. Now perhaps the prison would run more smoothly, with Chisholm being transferred.

When Lily returned to her cell, Madge rushed over to her. 'What on earth happened?' she asked. 'We heard rumours but they were very garbled.'

Lily filled her in with the details.

'That wicked bitch!' raged Madge. 'I told you she was scheming, didn't I? Thank God for Hetty. What's going to happen to her?'

At that moment, their missing friend was escorted back to the cell. She walked in, a smile on her face.

'Hetty!' said Lily and threw her arms around her. 'How can I ever thank you?'

Her saviour grinned broadly. 'I knew she was up to something. I heard one of her mates talking. When I realised you were going to be alone, I guessed.' She gave them a haughty look. 'I'm not daft, you know!'

They both burst out laughing.

'No, indeed you're not. In fact, you're a crafty little bugger,' said Madge.

This pleased Hetty. 'Yeah. I'm a crafty little bugger, that's what I am!'

Lily produced a packet of biscuits she'd bought with her money earned from sewing mail bags. 'Let's celebrate,' she said. 'We'll have a picnic . . . Oh, I forgot the best bit of news!'

They looked at her expectantly.

'Belle Chisholm is being transferred – as of today!'

The others cheered loudly, bringing the warder on duty over to see what was going on. 'Nothing,' they all said in unison. 'Nothing at all.'

The warder shook her head and walked away.

The three of them were in a party mood. Lily was so grateful to be alive and filled with relief that Hetty would no longer be tormented by the lifer.

They started to talk about the time when they got out of prison.

'I'm definitely going to try and go straight,' declared Madge. 'I don't want to be like me old man.'

'That's great,' said Lily. 'I hope you make it.'

'I'm going to have a bloody good try. I think I'll move to another town where I'm not known. Away from me mum and her grasping ways.'

'What about a job as a barmaid, or something like that . . . A waitress maybe,' suggested Lily.

'I don't know how to wait on tables.'

'I'll teach you,' said Lily. 'There's nothing to it.'

'Right. You're on.'

'Tomorrow in the dining room,' said Lily, 'I'll borrow a tray and show you.'

Hetty, of course, didn't join in the conversation. She didn't know if she'd ever be released, and the others were aware that if she was, she would probably end up in some institution or other. But at least she was safe now from the evil attentions of Belle.

As Lily lay in bed that night she thought how strange it was. Desperate as she was to get out of this place, when she did, she would miss the camaraderie that had grown between them all . . . and the affection.

The following lunchtime Lily, true to her word, gave Madge a lesson on how to wait the tables. The warders went along with the plan, passing ribald remarks about her becoming an honest citizen. Miss Cole stood silently watching, but she didn't join in. After the reprimand from the Governor for neglecting her duty, and an unspoken threat about her sexual deviations, she knew she'd better watch her step – for a while anyway.

With a tray borrowed from the kitchen, Madge carried plates. Moved food from one plate to another, with a fork and a spoon held in one hand. She wasn't very successful at first, dropping Hetty's potatoes in her lap, much to the amusement of the screws. But gradually she got the hang of it and as the days passed, she became very adept.

Lily's final weeks slowly went by, and came the day of her release. She'd been told that morning, after breakfast, that she'd to report with an officer to the reception room. There she would be given her clothes and belongings and released.

There was a sombre mood in the cell early that morning as the women washed and dressed. Lily was feeling very emotional, knowing that she could so easily have been incarcerated with women who would not have been so friendly.

'I'll write to you,' she said to Madge.

'I'd like that,' she said.

'Look – when you get out, why don't you get in touch with me, come to Southampton. Make a new start.'

Madge's eyes lit up with happiness. 'Could I really?'

'Why not?' said Lily. With a broad grin she added, 'After all, there are plenty of places in need of a good waitress.'

Madge hugged her with glee. 'I'm going to miss you.'

Lily looked at Hetty who was watching her with a slightly perplexed expression. Lily took from her pocket her lipstick, and powder compact and gave them to her. 'Now you make sure you brush your hair and put on your lipstick every morning after you wash, OK?'

Hetty grasped them to her as if they were the crown jewels. 'Thanks, Lily. I'll miss you too.'

Putting her arms around Hetty, Lily said, 'I know. I'll send you a postcard.' They walked together down to the dining room without speaking.

Lily looked at her plate of lumpy porridge and pushed it across to Hetty. She sipped the weak tea and thought of the proper cup she would have at Rachel's. God, it had better taste nicer than this, she thought. The meal passed in complete silence. No one could bring themselves to make conversation.

As she was about to leave the dining room, Lily turned around and with an impish grin burst into song. 'Goodbyee, don't cryee, wipe a tear, baby dear, from your eyee!' She picked up the hem of her shabby prison uniform and pranced around as she sang. There was good-humoured uproar from the other prisoners. Cries of, 'Get out of here! We'll keep your bed warm and . . . find us a few randy men and send them back.'

In the reception room, an officer stood with Lily's clothes in a pile. Her handbag and contents, once again checked. Then she was put in a room to get changed. The softness of her underwear felt strange against her skin. Her fine stockings after the thick lisle ones were like gossamer. She quickly slipped back into her two-piece suit, put on her overcoat and combed her hair until she was led away to the main entrance, where a small door was open in the huge gate and she stepped outside Brookmans and to freedom.

It was a fine June morning and she felt slightly ridiculous dressed in winter clothes. She slipped the blue woollen coat off and looked up at the few clouds in the sky. She held wide her arms and twisted round. 'I'm free as a bird,' she cried, then looked about for Rachel.

Her old friend was standing by a taxi, across from the prison. Lily rushed to her and clung to her dear friend, tears streaming down her cheeks.

Rachel was crying also. She held Lily's face between her hands and kissed her. 'My darling. How good it is to see you.'

But Lily was too full for words.

'Come, let's get into the taxi and go to the station,' said Rachel.

'No,' said Lily. 'Let's go to the nearest hotel where I can have a decent breakfast – and a strong cup of tea. I saved some of the money I earned sewing mail bags, so it's my treat . . . and then we can make plans.'

And that's what they did.

Seated in the dining room of the hotel, Lily lovingly smoothed the white tablecloth, poured the tea from its elegant pot. Spread the butter and marmalade thickly onto her toast and tucked into her eggs and bacon. She looked at Rachel and said gleefully, 'You have no idea just how good this is.'

'I'm sure I haven't. How are you, Lily? Really?'

With a broad grin, Lily assured her friend, 'I'm fine, honestly. Now I'm out it doesn't seem that long, but inside every day seemed to stretch for ever.' She squeezed Rachel's hand. 'Oh, it is good to see you! I know you came to Brookmans regularly, but it wasn't the same, being watched all the time by po-faced warders. When we've finished here, we'll get the train and go and see about getting Victoria home. Have you the address of this Children's Society?'

'Yes, I have.'

'Right,' said Lily with determination. 'That's what we'll do.'

Chapter Nine

Lily pushed open the office door of The Protection of Children Society and said to the secretary, 'My name is Lily Pickford and I want to see Ethel Giles.'

'Do you have an appointment?' asked the girl airily.

'No, I don't.'

'Then I'm afraid you'll have to make one.'

With a determined look Lily said, 'No, I'm afraid that won't do at all. I need to see Miss Giles today.' She saw a couple of chairs against the wall and sat in one. 'I'll wait,' she said.

The secretary saw the set of Lily's jaw and decided it wouldn't be worth trying to argue. She rose from her chair, knocked on Miss Giles's door and entered, closing it behind her.

Lily waited, smoothing the pleats in her skirt in an effort to allay her impatience.

After a few minutes, the young girl came out. 'You may go in,' she said.

'How very kind of you,' said Lily, but there was a note of mockery in her voice that was not lost on the young woman, who returned to her desk and sat down.

Ethel Giles looked up from her papers as Lily entered the office and walked towards her. 'Miss Pickford, what can I do for you?'

Observing the narrow mouth of the imperious-looking woman, Lily felt she'd have to step carefully. She sat in the chair opposite. 'I've come out of Brookmans today and naturally I'm anxious to see my daughter and take her home.'

'I'm afraid that's not possible.'

'What do you mean, it's not possible? I don't understand. A child should be with its mother and as of this morning, I'm free.'

'And where will you be living?'

'I'll be staying with Rachel Cohen, until further notice.'

'Do you have a job . . . any means of supporting your child, or yourself?'

Lily's heart sank. It was obvious from the woman's attitude that she was going to be difficult. 'Not at the moment, no, but I can get a job easily enough!'

Miss Giles raised her eyebrows. 'Really? You think it will be that simple, do you? You seem to forget that now you have a prison record.'

Lily's mouth tightened, but she remained calm. 'Are you telling me that until I'm working and earning a wage, you won't let me have my daughter?'

Ethel Giles, who enjoyed the feeling of power her position gave her, smiled in triumph. 'That's right.'

'But at least let me see her,' pleaded Lily.

'I really don't think that would be very wise, do you? After all, she hasn't seen you for several months, then if you turn up for a visit and leave again, it will only be upsetting for the child. No, I don't think we can allow that.'

Lily was furious but she controlled her temper. This was not the person to upset. After all, she was holding all the cards . . . at the moment.

'Very well,' she said with as much dignity as she could muster. 'I'll be seeing you very soon, when I have found a job, then I hope there will be no reason for you to keep us apart.'

'If you are gainfully employed, Miss Pickford, then it will be different.'

'Is she all right?' Lily asked anxiously.

'Your daughter is being looked after very well, as are all the children in our care.'

Lily rose from her chair. 'Thank you,' she said and left the room.

Rachel, who had been waiting outside, saw the look of thunder on Lily's face and knew that things had not gone well in the meeting.

'She won't let me have Victoria until I'm employed and earning, and what's more, she won't let me visit with her either! She says it will upset Victoria too much.'

'Well, I suppose she's right in a way,' reasoned Rachel.

Lily shot her an angry look.

'Think about it, darling. If you go to see her, she'll expect you to take her home with you. If you can't . . .'

With a deep sigh, Lily conceded. 'I shall take the first job that I can find. I want my baby back.'

'Of course you do, it's only natural. What do you want to do now?'

'Now we go and see Detective Inspector Chadwick!'

'Right,' said Rachel. 'Come on.'

They made their way to the police station and asked to see the detective.

He ushered them into his office. 'It's good to see you, Lily,' he said with a welcoming smile. 'Sit down, and you, Mrs Cohen.'

'So what's happening about that bastard Gates?' she demanded.

Chadwick sat back in his seat. 'I'm happy to tell you, Lily, that things are beginning to move in the right direction.'

'What do you mean?'

'Well, when Luke Longford came to see me . . .'

'Just a minute,' Lily interrupted. 'What do you mean about him seeing you?'

'He came in here after he'd visited you in Brookmans. He told me that Sergeant Green had been the one to put the idea of renting the tables from Gates to you.'

'Yes, that's right,' said Lily.

'But you never told me that,' said the policeman.

She frowned. 'Didn't I? But he only introduced us. I thought it was pure coincidence that he knew of the bloke. I really didn't think it was important.'

He shook his head. 'I can't believe you were that naive, Lily. He's up to his neck in the scam. Anyway, we've been keeping a watch on Gates and Green.' He looked suddenly angry. 'To think one of the Force had something to do with this. It makes my blood boil!'

'I never liked him anyway,' said Lily. 'I always thought he was a bit fly.'

'Then why did you have anything to do with him?'

She shrugged. 'I was in a desperate situation. The Club would have had to have closed if I couldn't come up with some idea or other. Anyway . . . what's going on?'

'We're gathering information and proof. Gates is a clever bugger, but Green is the weak link. When I've got enough evidence against him, then I can call him in and face him with it. Green will sing like a canary. Then I'll have them both, and what's more important, I can clear your good name.'

'That would be great. It would mean that Victoria could grow up without the stigma of a mother with a prison record, and it would make things a lot easier for me to find a decent job.'

He looked at her with sympathy. 'I fully understand your problem, my dear. You have my word I'll get this sorted as soon as possible.'

Getting up from her chair, Lily shook the hand of the detective, then turning to her friend said, 'Come on, Rachel, let's go home.'

As they walked towards the tram stop Lily asked, 'What the devil made Luke Longford go to the police? I hardly know the man.'

Rachel gave a slow smile. 'It seems to me, darling, he wants to know you better. He was angry that you were innocent but still sent to prison.'

'Well, that makes two of us!' retorted Lily.

'Every time he docks, he gives me a call,' Rachel told her. 'He's looking for large premises to open as a posh hotel. I offered him the Club, but . . .' She shrugged. 'The area wasn't good enough. That man has big ideas. But let's talk about you. What sort of job will you look for, Lily dear?'

'The only thing I know – run a hotel, a boarding house, scrub floors, anything that'll bring in a wage. I want my daughter back!'

At that moment, Lily realised that they were standing at the wrong stop, but when she pointed this out to Rachel her friend said, 'No, this is fine. I've moved house.'

'You have?' said Lily with surprise. 'When?'

'A couple of months ago. I didn't tell you, you had too much else on your mind.'

The tram arrived and it was obvious that Rachel didn't want to be drawn further on the subject in public, so Lily remained silent, curiously watching the route the tram took, drinking in every detail of the streets of Southampton, as if she was seeing them for the first time. She looked in the shop windows at their display, watched a man grinding knives, sitting on his bicycle-like machine, with the back wheel raised, pedalling furiously to turn the grinding stone. Listened to the cries of the street vendors, selling from their barrows, calling their wares: 'Fresh fruit and veg. Cheapest prices anywhere!' And she thought this would be what she'd have to do in the future, hunt out the cheapest prices of everything if she and Victoria were to survive.

Rachel stood up and said, 'Here we are.'

They were in St Mary Street, the lower end of the town, in the poorer part. Lily frowned. This was a far cry from the more classy Polygon area where Rachel had lived previously. But she made no comment and followed her friend.

Rachel led her past the Kingsland Tavern and the Southampton Holiness Mission and turned into Bevois Street. At the third small house along, she stopped and put her key into the door.

Lily stepped into the living room. The house had two rooms up and two down. To her it was like walking back into her past. It was in such a house she had once lived with Fred, a pickpocket, who'd found her on the streets and taken her to live with him. At that time in her life it had been a godsend, but for her friend to leave her beautiful home for this . . . She shut the door behind her.

The fine furniture looked strangely out of place. The wallpaper was peeling, the paint cracked and flaking. The range however, was clean and shining, the furniture polished. The velvet drapes, far too long, were turned under at the bottom. Lily was horrified.

'I think we'd better sit down,' said Lily, 'and you can tell me exactly what's been going on.'

There was a set expression on the face of her friend, who took off her coat and hung it behind the door. She placed her handbag on the table and put the kettle on the hob of the blackleaded range, with its low fire.

The two women sat either side of the table. Lily looked around the room. There was Rachel's sideboard, settee and two armchairs, which crowded the small room, but Lily was aware that there were several beautiful pieces of furniture missing.

'I had to sell the house to pay the debts,' Rachel said without any preamble.

'What debts?' asked Lily. Completely shattered by events.

'I owed the wine merchant and the brewers. Bankruptcy, they threatened me with!'

'Couldn't you have paid them off when you sold the Club Valletta?'

'They wouldn't wait. So what choice did I have? I had no choice. Then I had my own personal accounts. As soon as people knew we were in trouble, they all screamed for money!'

Lily hardly dare ask. 'What about the proceeds of the Club?'

'Gone to pay off the overdraft and the other bills, the butcher, baker. The electric light.'

'What about the money you had saved for your retirement?'

'Most of it paid the court fine.'

Lily grasped her friend's hands. 'Oh Rachel, I'm so sorry.'

'What's to be sorry about, darling? It ain't your fault. I had enough to buy this fleapit, have it fumigated before I moved in. New wallpaper, I couldn't afford.'

'But how are we going to survive?'

'We got enough money to last us three weeks, if we go careful.' She hesitated. 'I was thinking of taking a lodger, but you and Victoria need a home.'

Lily was overcome. She too was in dire financial straits but at least she was young. Poor Rachel was in her early sixties, too old to find work.

'Well,' she said, her voice determined, 'as soon as I get a job, I'll find somewhere for Victoria and me to live and then you can get a lodger. I'll pay for our keep when I start work, of course, until we move out.' Her demeanour brightened. 'What's happened to my clothes?'

'Upstairs, packed in boxes.'

'Right!' Lily said. 'I'll have a sort through and sell some! That ought to raise a few bob.'

Rachel suddenly burst out laughing. 'Oy vey! How ridiculous is this? We started out together selling second-hand clothes to other people, and now you end up having to sell your own.'

Lily also saw the ludicrousness of the situation, and she too started to laugh. 'Oh Rachel, don't ever lose your sense of humour or we might as well die!'

'Then we could sell our bodies to the hospital!' The Jewess doubled up with laughter, rocking in her chair, holding her aching stomach. The two of them sat, mopping up their tears.

'Oh my life, I never thought I'd laugh again,' said Rachel, now recovered. 'A cup of tea is what we need.'

As her friend picked up the kettle, Lily thought, what I really need is a job! Rachel went into the scullery and returned with a huge bouquet of flowers. 'By the way, these arrived first thing this morning.' She handed them to Lily.

'They're beautiful, but who sent them?'

'You think I'm some kind of prophet?' retorted Rachel. 'How the hell should I know? Open the envelope attached to them.'

Lily read the card that was enclosed. *Welcome home. Best wishes, Luke Longford.* She looked up at Rachel. 'How did he know?' she asked.

'I told him when last we talked, just before I moved. I gave him this address.'

Raising her eyebrows, Lily said dryly, 'What's going on between you two?'

'Ha! Was it me that got the flowers? He's concerned about you and also he feels guilty about visiting you in prison. He feels it was the wrong thing to have done. The wrong time. He thinks he upset you . . . a gent the man is.'

Looking at the flowers Lily said, 'Well, he's very kind. I'll put them in water. Bloody hell! There's so many this place will look like a funeral parlour!' Fortunately Rachel had kept some of her large flower vases, and Lily arranged the beautiful summer blooms.

Afterwards, she searched around for the local paper from the previous night and turned to the Situations Vacant. Then settled down to study the column. She looked up with an anxious expression. 'There's nothing here that's suitable.'

'Friday's the best night,' said Rachel. 'The paper is full of jobs then.'

'What will I do if I can't find any work? I'll never see Victoria,' said Lily, filled with impatience and frustration.

'You'll find something, of course you will,' said Rachel, as she poured the tea.

The following morning, Lily sorted through her clothes and took a large bundle, including her fur coat, to a second-hand clothing shop. Here she haggled fiercely with the man behind the counter when he offered her a very low price.

'Now don't come it,' she said. 'You know as well as I do you'll make a mint on these. They're of the finest quality. I used to be in this business so I know just how much you can make. The fur coat alone's worth a packet! Now don't muck about. Give me a fair price or I'll take them somewhere else.'

Eventually she left the shabby shop, clutching eighteen

shillings and sixpence. Well, that would swell their meagre coffers until she found a job.

Lily wasn't the only one who was frustrated. Quinn Gifford cursed as he replaced the telephone receiver.

'What is it, son?' asked his mother Rosie, who sat by the fire, puffing on her clay pipe.

'Lily Pickford came out of Brookmans this morning,' he grumbled. 'I just rang the prison to find out the date of her release, 'cos I knew it was about now. She didn't damn well let me know! I told her I'd meet her and bring her home. I wrote and told her I'd take care of her.'

'She don't want you, Quinn.' She glared across the room at her eldest son. 'Why won't you listen to me? You and she weren't meant for each other. Leave her be and get on with yer life. I warned you of the consequences.' She puffed on her pipe, knowing her words were falling on deaf ears. 'She'll be the cause of your undoing if you don't listen. I won't tell you again.'

Looking into the burning embers of the fire, Rosie Gifford was filled with dread, knowing what was before them. Knowing that Quinn would go his own way and destroy them all by his stubbornness. She spat into the fire with anger and despair.

But Quinn was seething with rage. Who did she think she was, this Lily Pickford? He wanted her for himself. Had always done so, from the moment he'd first entered the Club Valletta and seen her standing by the bar, greeting her clients. He'd watched her perform on the stage and desired her so much, the pain of his longing had been almost more than he could bear. And by God he'd have her.

He lit up one of his cheroots and twisting his gold earring, started to scheme. Now where would she go? Who did she know? There was that little fat Jewish woman who was her partner. That would be a good place to start. He'd drive into the docklands and ask around, find out where she lived. He rose abruptly from his chair and walked out of the door without a word.

His mother didn't question him. She knew where he was going. He was taking the first steps down his own path of destruction. She wandered out across the untidy yard to the meadow, the grass long and overgrown, in need of attention. She sat beneath the chestnut tree and puffed on her clay pipe. To some this place might be a hovel, but to her it was her own piece of paradise and soon enough she knew she'd be denied the sight of it.

Luke Longford wandered around the first-class dining room of the *Mauritania*, checking that the passengers were happy and satisfied, the waiters were doing a good job and there were no problems with the food coming from the galley, but his mind wasn't on his work. Today was the day, according to Rachel Cohen, that Lily was to be released from prison.

Etched in his memory was the scene inside the gaol. He frowned at the thought of Lily having to mix with such people. How would it affect her, he wondered. She'd not been imprisoned for long, thank God, but having to live every day inside those walls with the other prisoners must leave a mark. He realised that of course, he knew absolutely nothing about her. He now knew she had a daughter, and he found himself wondering about the child's father. What was he like? The woman was a complete enigma, but totally fascinating ... How would she be feeling today, the day she'd been set free, back among her own kind? But who *were* her kind of people? The Club décor had been very sophisticated and tasteful, but why on earth had she opened it in the seedy docklands? Was there some kind of mystery about her?

The demands of the passengers took Luke's mind off Lily for the rest of the evening, and it wasn't until he retired to his cabin later that night that he again thought of her. He'd cabled some flowers to her, and hoped they would please. Perhaps when he docked in Southampton, she would come out to dinner with him. Give him a chance to apologise, further their association. Find out a little more about her. Answer a few questions that were puzzling him.

In Friday's edition of the *Southern Daily Echo*, Lily espied an advertisement that at last lifted her spirits. *Wanted: Waitress, Tivoli Restaurant. Above Bar.* She'd been there a few times in the past with Vittorio, but no one would probably remember. But in any case, she'd have to try.

The following morning, she picked out a navy-blue dress, with a white collar and pleated skirt. She polished her matching shoes and slipped them on, buttoning the bar over her instep. She pulled on a pair of white gloves, then made her way to the Tivoli. It was a nice morning and she decided to walk. She cut through Kingsland Market and threaded her way through the stalls set up side-by-side, smiling at the sharp banter exchanged between the stall-holders.

When she arrived at the entrance of the Tivoli restaurant, she took a deep breath and rang the bell. It was answered by a young woman.

'Yes?' she said.

'I would like to see the manager,' Lily said, with a smile.

'Can you tell me what it's about?'

'The advertisement for a waitress,' she replied.

The woman stepped back. 'You'd better come inside.'

Lily walked into the familiar surroundings, and thought wryly of her changed circumstances as she was led towards an office. Once she had been a client, fussed and waited on, now all she wanted was a job. She waited to be summoned.

The door opened and a smartly dressed man wearing a dark-grey lounge suit appeared and beckoned her inside. She recognised him as the restaurant manager. He indicated a chair, and she sat down, feeling more than a little nervous. It was a long time since she'd worked for anyone.

'What experience have you had?' he said, getting sharply down to business.

'I've worked in this line of business for several years.'

'You have references, of course?'

Lily was floored. Why hadn't she thought of that? How could she have been so stupid? But she was not to be caught out.

'I do, but I've not brought them with me. I can, of course, produce them whenever you like – later today, if you wish.'

The manager was rubbing his chin thoughtfully. 'Your face looks familiar. Have we ever met?'

She shook her head and said, 'No.' This wasn't exactly a lie. He'd waited on her and Vittorio from time to time, but they'd never had a conversation. However the man had a good memory. 'Aren't you Lily Pickford from the Club Valletta?' he said suddenly.

She felt her cheeks flush. 'Yes, that's right.'

He sat bolt upright in his chair. 'I'm sorry, Miss Pickford, but I couldn't possibly give you a position here.'

'Why not?' she asked. 'I've got the experience.'

'You also have a prison record!'

She wasn't going to lose her dignity by arguing her case. She got slowly to her feet. 'Thank you for seeing me,' she said politely, and walked out of the room. Once outside, she leaned against the wall as her legs were trembling.

She'd have to set her sights lower. Look for a place that

perhaps would be unaware of her existence. She walked slowly back to Rachel's house, realising that her troubles were far from over.

She spent the rest of the morning with Rachel, writing out false references, searching the paper again. She went after three other jobs over the next few days, without success. One was already suited and another asked if she had a criminal record. There was little point in lying. If they were that thorough they might check. She was getting desperate and money was short. She had thought of trying to sing around the pubs as she had in the old days, but Sandy, her pianist, was still staying with his sister in Bournemouth and without him, she doubted that the pub landlords would let her perform.

The final interview was going well she thought, until the manager asked where was her last place of employment and when . . . and why did she leave? She made up some sort of story, but let slip that she hadn't worked for the last six months. And the game was up. She made her excuses and left without admitting to her prison sentence.

Another week passed and Lily was really concerned now about her future survival. She went to yet another interview. This time she lied throughout. Gave the false references, made up a story about her previous job, saying the business had closed, and thought she'd done well, only to be told that there were several applicants and they'd let her know. She watched the postal delivery for the next three days but there was no letter for her.

Finally on the following Friday she saw another advert in the local paper: *Waitress wanted for small private hotel. Experience required. Mariner's Hotel, Chapel Road.* Lily was fraught with anxiety. How were she and Rachel going to survive if she didn't find work within the next seven days?

They were living as frugally as possible, making stew with cheap vegetables that were damaged and a piece of scrag end of lamb from the butcher, and making do with stale bread from the bakery, soaked in a little milk.

The address of this vacancy was in the docklands, a poor area. The clientele wouldn't be particular if they chose to stay here, so perhaps the management wouldn't be so fussy. She'd go first thing tomorrow.

Even the bright June sun couldn't disguise the scruffy façade of the Mariner's Hotel. The paint was peeling, the windows wanted cleaning and the road outside was covered in litter. A huge gasometer loomed behind the building, standing out against the skyline. Broken beer bottles lay in the gutter – the result of some drunken fight, no doubt, thought Lily, as she opened the door of the hotel.

Eddie Chapman looked up from behind the desk and saw an attractive young woman walk towards him, neatly dressed.

'Good morning,' he said. 'Can I help you?'

'I've come about the position of waitress.'

He was surprised. She was a touch better than his usual staff. Cleaner too. He wondered why she wasn't working at a better establishment than his.

Lily saw the expression on the face of the middle-aged man and hid a smile. Even in this dire situation she could see the funny side of things. This place couldn't be more different from the Club Valletta. She'd throw out the worn carpet that covered the floor for a start!

He ran a finger around the soiled collar of his shirt and said, 'Oh yes. Well, I'm Eddie Chapman, the owner. Please come through to the office.' He lifted the flap of the counter and led her through to an equally shabby room at the back.

The desk was a clutter of papers and bills. The chairs were

piled high with odd bits of clothing, and on the floor lay a tray containing dirty plates, congealed with food that must have been at least twenty-four hours old.

Lily picked up a jacket and shabby jumper off a chair, threw it disdainfully onto another and sat down. She looked at Eddie expectantly. 'Perhaps you could tell me about the post.'

He cleared his throat. For some reason he felt he was the one being interviewed. 'This hotel may not be one of the best,' he said defensively, 'but we are always pretty busy, being at the lower end of the market. Most of our guests are seamen and travellers. There are ten rooms and a dining room, plus a small bar. We serve breakfast and dinner – but we don't do teas.'

Lily thought that quite ridiculous. Only the smart hotels served teas, and by no stretch of the imagination was this place smart.

'What experience have you had?' he asked.

'I've spent several years in this business,' she answered. 'I can do silver service.' She could see that impressed him and realised that here, they probably didn't require such standards.

'I'll show you the dining room,' he said and led her towards a door.

Inside was a dining room of sorts, with some residents still eating their breakfast. Lily was appalled at the stained table linen and the appearance of the middle-aged waitress who was serving. Her black dress was creased and her small white apron, marked. Her hair was long, straggly and unwashed. Lily took a deep breath of disgust, but remained silent.

He then took her through to the kitchen, which was relatively clean, but dirty dishes were piled high. It was evident from the stale food on the plates that they had been left overnight. The owner said, 'The man who washes the dishes hasn't turned in again.'

Lily turned to him. 'Again?'

Eddie Chapman nodded. 'Yes, I know. I'm going to get a new man.' He walked her back to the reception area and saw her gazing around. 'Yes, the place could look better,' he conceded, 'but somehow, it's slowly gone downhill.'

Lily smiled at him. 'What a shame. It could be quite nice.'

'You're right, Miss Pickford, but you see, it's like this. This place was left to me by my father and I'm not getting any younger.' He paused. 'To be absolutely honest, I've got a dicky heart and the doctor says that I've got to ease up.'

'I'm sorry to hear that,' said Lily.

He studied her for a moment, then asked, 'Are you interested?'

She looked him squarely in the eye. 'I would very much like the job, Mr Chapman, but first you'd better know I've just come out of prison!'

Eddie Chapman couldn't have been more surprised. 'Well!' he said. 'You'd better come back to the office.' Once there he asked, 'How long were you inside?'

'Six months.'

'Then it can't have been for anything dreadful.'

'To be honest, someone fitted me up, but Detective Inspector Chadwick is hoping to be able to clear my name. If you want a reference, speak to him.'

'Are you serious, miss?'

'Oh yes,' said Lily. 'I'll wait while you do it, if you like.'

Eddie sat in his chair and shook his head. 'I like your style, girl,' he said, and smiled. 'Can you start on Monday morning?'

She was delighted. This place was the end, but at last she would be earning and then she could apply to have Victoria back.

'What are the hours and how much are you paying?' she asked.

'You work from seven-thirty until ten-thirty in the morning, and come back for six o'clock until ten. Twelve and six a week. You keep your own tips – I find that's better. There's no cheating then.'

'Thank you,' she said. 'That'll be fine. I'll see you on Monday morning.' At the door she hesitated and asked, 'Why did you give me the job?'

'Because you're honest.'

'But you haven't checked with DI Chadwick!'

He grinned at her. 'Oh, I probably will, but seeing as you was prepared to wait while I did so, you're either a first-class poker player, or honest. I think it's the latter.'

She gave him a cheeky grin and left with a feeling of relief mingled with expectation. She could see the potential of the Mariner's Hotel and there was nothing she loved more than a challenge. She dismissed from her mind the grotty surroundings. Business was business and given the chance, she could certainly improve Eddie Chapman's.

He was a nice man, she mused as she made her way to the tram stop. He had kind grey eyes but there was a pallor about his skin which showed his health was not as it should be.

She had a sudden longing to see Rachel's old house and caught a tram to take her there. As it made its way through The Bargate, she looked around at the shops, the buildings, the sky, her fellow passengers. She was free! Free to get on with her life. Now she had a job and could start the legal proceedings to win back the custody of her child.

For a moment she thought of her old cellmates and wondered how they were faring. Madge would soon be out, but poor Hetty would probably never have that privilege. She'd write to Madge tonight and send her address, and she must buy a picture postcard to send to Hetty, as she'd promised.

Getting off the tram, she walked along Bedford Place towards Wilton Avenue, looking in the windows of the shops. She admired the shoes in French's window, but it was the shop selling children's clothing that made her stop. Victoria must have grown a lot in the six months since she'd seen her. Lily felt a lump in her throat as her emotions welled up inside her. How she longed to see her baby. To hold her, bath her, see her in bed asleep, her thumb in her mouth. Tears filled her eyes and she quickly wiped them away with the back of her hand.

She stood across the road from Rachel's old house, observed the different net curtains at the window and was saddened to think of her old friend brought so low by circumstances. She was also beginning to consider the problem of just how she'd manage when she was working, if they moved out of Rachel's home. Who could she get to look after Victoria? There must be a reliable woman somewhere who for a small sum would take care of her daughter. She'd have to ask around, in readiness. But she put these worries behind her for the moment. This was not the time to fret about things, she told herself. She'd got a job and soon she would have her child back safe and sound. This was a day to celebrate!

Chapter Ten

Lily arrived at the Mariner's Hotel at seven-thirty the following Monday morning, dressed neatly in a black dress and a white apron hastily made out of a fancy tray-cloth.

Eddie Chapman greeted her with a smile. 'I'm pleased to see you're a good timekeeper. Come into the kitchen and I'll introduce you to the chef, who you'll report to in the future, and Dolly the other waitress.'

Lenny the chef, a man of rotund proportions in his forties, gave her a quick grin, but Dolly, still wearing her crumpled dress and dirty apron, just glared at her.

Eddie showed her where everything was and added, 'If you want to know anything else, just ask Dolly.'

Lily, with her astute knowledge of human nature knew there would be little help from the other woman, only resentment, but she was determined to do her best.

'Make up the tables ready for the evening meal before you knock off,' said Eddie. 'The chef will give you any other instructions. All right, Lily?'

She nodded. 'Yes thanks, I'll be fine.'

It was a busy morning. As she hurried back and forth to the kitchen, she thought what a great pity it was that the place didn't look better. If it did, it would probably bring in a better class of client. There was a strange mixture. Several seamen,

153

who appeared wearing their Navy sweaters, a few commercial travellers with worn and shabby suits. A couple of foreign seamen, and an engineer who had travelled down from Scotland and was waiting for his ship to dock that day.

Nevertheless, Lily smiled at them all and gave a cheerful word to everyone as she worked, serving them proficiently and quickly. None of them were used to eating in a high-class establishment comparable to the Club Valletta, so they had no complaints about the service, and were delighted to be looked after by such a charming, clean and pretty woman . . . especially after the doleful Dolly.

At the end of the session, Lily cleared her tables of dishes and dirty cutlery, then she took off the stained tablecloths and folded them up.

'What *do* you think you're doing?' asked Dolly.

'These are dirty,' said Lily. 'I'm sure there must be some clean ones somewhere. Where will I find them?'

'Who the bloody hell do you think you are?' Dolly glared at her. 'You've been in the place five minutes and already you're taking over!' She walked away to the kitchen in a huff.

Lily gathered up the soiled linen and followed her. 'You've got it all wrong,' she said, 'but I don't want to serve my customers on filthy table linen.'

Lenny looked up. 'What's the matter?'

Before Dolly could speak, Lily said, 'I just wanted to change the cloths on my tables, that's all. These are disgusting.'

He nodded. 'I quite agree. I asked Dolly to change them days ago. Go and ask Eddie for the keys to the linen cupboard. You'll find it on the first floor. First door on your right.'

'And these?' asked Lily, holding out the soiled ones.

'There's a basket just inside the door. The housekeeper

will see to them when she comes in at eight. You might as well change yours at the same time, Dolly,' he added.

'Get stuffed!' she said and walked out.

Lily pulled a face at the chef. 'Oh dear, I seem to have upset her.'

He shook his head. 'Don't you fret over her, girl. She's a miserable bitch, and a slut. If only Eddie would pull his bloody finger out, she'd have to change her ways.'

Eddie was only too delighted to give her the key for the clean linen. He looked a bit sheepish as he handed it over. 'This is another thing I've let slip,' he said.

'Don't you worry,' she said. 'You must look after your health.'

Having exchanged the linen, Lily set up her tables. Of Dolly there was no sign, but Lily didn't care. Hers looked fresh and inviting. The marked contrast would no doubt be noted by Dolly and her clients, and one way or another, she knew that soon the linen on the others would be changed.

At lunchtime, she walked towards the park on her way home. It was a lovely sunny day and the flowerbeds were ablaze with colour. As usual there was a lot of traffic in and out of the docks. Stewards off one of the liners, distinctive in their white jackets, were leaving the pubs, hurriedly making their way back to the ship that was preparing for yet another voyage across the Atlantic or another ocean, to foreign ports.

Although at times she'd longed to get away from the filth and the squalor of the area, it had a buzz about it. An excitement – an atmosphere all of its own, and Lily knew that wherever she went, this would always be home. She listened to the throaty roar of an ocean liner's funnels, as it heralded its departure, the shunting of the goods train, its high-pitched whistle of warning as it entered the dock gates, the cry of the paper boy, the tinny tune of the organ grinder. This was the music of the docklands – and she loved it.

When she arrived home, Rachel plied her with questions about her morning. She told her of her confrontation with Dolly.

'Ay yi!' exclaimed Rachel. 'Don't upset her too much. You need to stay in work until Victoria's home.'

Lily laughed at the consternation on the face of her friend. 'Don't worry. The chef's on my side and the owner too, I do believe.'

That evening, some of the residents being looked after by Dolly noticed the difference between Lily's clean tables and their own, and commented, bringing a flush of annoyance to the face of the older woman. She was furious. But the complaints were echoed by the others and soon Eddie received requests for clean linen.

Towards the end of the evening shift he sent for his waitress and demanded she change the tablecloths first thing in the morning.

She stormed into the now empty dining room and faced Lily. 'You interfering bitch!' she spat. 'Coming in here with your grand ideas. This isn't the bloody Savoy Hotel, you know. You can't make a silk purse out of a sow's ear.'

'No,' said Lily with a slow smile, 'but you can clean up the sty a little!'

On her way out of the hotel at the end of her shift, Lily said to Eddie, 'Goodnight. I'm sorry if I caused any trouble.'

'No, love. Don't you worry. My residents like you, you're like a breath of fresh air. See you tomorrow.'

Well, it was a beginning, thought Lily as she waited for the tram. If only Eddie would have the reception area painted and a new carpet laid, that would make a deal of difference. Mind you, she didn't know what the bedrooms were like.

She smiled to herself about the indignant Dolly. If she was running the place, that one would definitely be out on her ear!

Lily's legs ached and she was desperate to get home and soak in a hot bath. But now of course it would have to be the tin bath in front of the fire. Rachel's new abode didn't have a bathroom or any other amenities; the lavatory was outside in a shed. But never mind. It wasn't the first time she'd lived with these inconveniences. One day, she swore, somehow she'd fight her way back to a better life – the one she'd been used to these past years.

She was really tired and was grateful when at last she saw there was a tram coming. Her feet were killing her now and she didn't think she could have stood waiting for much longer. Had she not been so tired, she might have recognised the truck that was parked down the road a little way.

Quinn Gifford sat in the driving seat of his vehicle with a satisfied smile and watched Lily step onto the tram. It hadn't taken him long to discover Rachel Cohen's original address. When the new owner told him she'd moved, he'd hung about for the postal delivery and asked the postman for her new one, saying he owed her money and wanted to send it on. He was pleased when he realised that Lily was now living in a poorer area. It didn't make the contrast between her accommodation and his own farm that different, and he was filled with confidence.

He'd then parked several yards away from the house for days and watched for Lily. It was pure chance that he'd fallen asleep and stayed overnight, then seen her leave early this morning. It was so early that she had to be off to some job or other. The thing that had surprised him as he followed her tram journey, was the shabby destination ... the Mariner's Hotel! It was way below her expectations, he was sure. But with a prison record, she wouldn't have much choice, of course.

He put the truck into gear and headed for the farm. He now knew where he could find her and the hours she worked, having hung around all day. He was stiff from sitting so long and after an uncomfortable night, he needed a good sleep. Then he would plan his tactics. It was no good going after her like a bull at a gate. He would have to step carefully, mindful of his mother telling him that evidently Lily didn't want anything to do with him. Well, he'd charm her into wanting him. After all, he never usually had trouble getting a woman. All right, they weren't up to her standards, but before, he hadn't been that fussy – only wanting a woman to feed his sexual appetite. Not that he didn't want sex with her, but he wished her to be his woman and live with him. That was quite different.

Lily now had to give serious thought to Victoria's welfare when at last she was home living with her. The problem of finding work had pushed this concern to the back of her mind, but now she had to face up to it. She would of course pay Rachel rental and money towards her keep, but she knew that her friend could probably earn more with a lodger. It would be unfair to expect her to care for Victoria indefinitely; at her age it was too much to ask. She would make enquiries, see if there was someone around who she could afford. But twelve shillings and sixpence a week wouldn't stretch far, after paying rent, and buying food and clothes for her child who had probably grown out of the ones she had. She'd just have to pray that the tips from her customers would cover the shortfall.

As Lily sat at the table that night and ate her supper, she said to Rachel, 'At the beginning of next week I'll go back to see that old bitch Giles. I don't think she'll be impressed if I go before. I must have at least one week at the job under my belt. Then I just hope she'll let me have Victoria back.'

Rachel's eyes lit up with happiness and she looked across the table. 'We won't know ourselves when she comes home, will we?' But she warned, 'The child will probably take some time to settle.'

'What do you mean?' asked Lily.

'Think about it, my dear. She was taken away suddenly, to strangers. Then again she's moved. Only three years old she is, after all. A traumatic thing it was to have happened to her. She's bound to be unsettled, anxious. We'll have to tread carefully for a while.' There was a note of sadness and regret in her voice as she said, 'I blame myself. I should never have let her go.'

'Don't be silly,' said Lily, patting her shoulder. 'What choice did you have?'

Tears welled in the Jewess's eyes. 'I had no choice, but that don't make it right.'

'We must put all this behind us for Victoria's sake,' said Lily. 'I'm going to try and find someone to take care of her while I'm working.'

Rachel looked horrified. 'You can't do that, put her with another stranger! She'll be frightened to death.'

Lily's brow furrowed. 'I can't expect you to look after her. Besides, I'm going to look for a place to live, to give you your room back for a lodger.'

Poor Rachel looked very distressed. 'But my family you are . . . you and Victoria.'

'Look, love,' said Lily. 'We have to survive. You can't do

that on what I can afford to pay you.' She saw the unhappiness reflected in the face of her friend. 'We'll stay for a few weeks, until Victoria is settled, but then we really have to be sensible,' she said firmly. But deep down she had her own reservations as to how she herself would be able to cope.

On Friday evening, she rushed home clutching her pay packet and counted out her money with a sigh of relief. For the past week, Rachel and she had scraped an existence, living off soup made from cheap vegetables and the bones of a scrawny chicken which had fed them for days. She'd taken home stale bread rolls from the hotel from time to time and they'd wet them, warmed them on top of the range and scraped them with some of their precious margarine. Now at last they could buy something more substantial.

She handed over eleven shillings to her friend, leaving herself one shilling and sixpence. That ought to be enough to cover her tram fares and a packet of Woodbine cigarettes. She could have walked home to save the fare, but by the end of the day her feet ached so much, she couldn't face it.

'You've left yourself hardly anything,' Rachel protested.

Lily dug into her handbag and taking out her purse, tipped the contents onto the table. She counted up the pennies, a couple of threepenny pieces and the odd sixpence. 'I've got three and six here,' she said gleefully. 'My tips! I'm saving up to buy some clothes for Victoria.'

Rachel looked at the pitiful pile of coins. 'You won't get much for that!'

'I'll just have to see how much Victoria has grown, then I'll take her old stuff to the second-hand shop and swop them for something bigger.'

Her friend gazed fondly at her. This wonderful girl who'd been through so much was still a fighter. Somehow she would manage, but it would need a miracle to solve all their problems. If Lily did move away, she'd find life very difficult having to work and take care of a child. But at the moment they could keep their heads above water . . . just.

As she was leaving the Mariner's Hotel on the following Saturday night, a fight broke out between two sailors. It spilled out of the bar onto the pavement and Lily was caught in the middle of the mêlée as the companions of the two combatants piled in to add to the fisticuffs being exchanged. She was flung against the brick wall of the hotel, grazing her cheek in the process. She bunched her hand into a fist ready to defend herself, when one of the seamen pulled a knife. She froze. But before he could use this on his opponent, a large figure of a man pushed his way forward and picking up the man holding the knife by the scruff of his uniform, he lifted him off his feet and tossed him effortlessly into the road. Kicking the knife away.

'Now bugger off the lot of you!' he ordered.

The size and menace of the stranger defied argument and the band of men quickly dispersed. He came over to Lily. 'Are you all right, miss?'

Lily looked up at him, a smile of relief on her face. 'Yes, thank you, George. I'm fine.'

He looked at her with surprise. 'My God – it's Miss Lily. I didn't know it was you. I saw you get knocked down as you come out of the door.' For such a powerful man, his touch as he held her chin was surprisingly gentle as he studied her grazed cheek. 'You'd better bathe that when you gets home,' he advised. 'I read the paper and saw you was sent down. I was real sorry,' he said.

'Yes, well, we were fitted up by that Percy Gates,' she said bitterly. 'But the police are on to him so it's only a matter of time.'

161

There was a flash of anger in his eyes as he listened. 'Anything I can do?' he asked.

Lily knew exactly what he meant. George Coleman used to work for Vittorio as his fixer and had a fearsome reputation. No one dare owe Vittorio money for long: they were too scared of this man.

'No,' she replied hurriedly. More trouble was the last thing she needed, especially not at this moment in her life. 'Everything's in hand.'

'How's the baby?' he asked.

Lily explained the situation. 'I'm hoping to get her back very soon,' she said. 'The authorities put her with foster parents while I was inside.'

'I'd very much like to see her,' said George. 'She must have been only a few months old the last time I saw her.' His voice was filled with sadness. 'It was just after Mr Vittorio's funeral. I miss him, you know. I'd have died for that man.'

She touched his arm sympathetically. 'I know, George.' She paused. 'When Victoria's home and settled down, I'll get word to you.'

'What are you doing round here anyway?' he asked curiously.

'I've got a job as a waitress here.'

He looked appalled. 'But I don't understand.'

Lily explained about the loss of her inheritance and the Club losing money. And how she fell foul of Percy Gates.

George Coleman shook his head. 'What a bloody awful world, eh? You need any money, Miss Lily? I'll loan you some till you get back on your feet.'

She declined gracefully. She had no wish to be involved in the seedy world of George Coleman. She'd put all that behind her the day Vittorio died.

'I'd best be off,' she said.

'You want me to walk you home?' he asked.

'No, I'll be fine. You take care. It's nice seeing you.' She deliberately avoided telling him where she lived. She didn't want him to know everything about her decline.

As she walked away she saw two of the local prostitutes enter the Mariner's Hotel with their punters. Lily was horrified. If Eddie was letting the place be used as a knocking shop, he could lose his licence and she, with a prison sentence, could be in serious trouble if the place was ever raided. She vowed to have a word with her boss in the morning.

She tackled him as soon as she entered the hotel the following day. Knocking on his office door, she entered.

'Yes, Lily. What can I do for you?'

She came straight to the point. 'I'm worried about you losing your licence,' she said.

His eyes widened with surprise. 'You what?'

'Last night I was caught up in a fight outside.' She turned her face and pointed to her hurt cheek.

'My God! Are you all right?'

'Yes, that's not the point. As I was walking away, I saw a couple of toms walk in here with two of your guests.'

He looked abashed. 'I'm always meaning to put a stop to it, but . . .'

Lily liked Eddie Chapman. With a bit of help from her, he could do so much better.

'You get caught and that's curtains for you, you must know that?'

'Of course I do, but somehow I've lost heart in the place.' He looked at her with a quizzical expression. 'Why are you doing this, Lily? Why should you care if I lose my licence?'

She smiled slowly and looked around the reception area. 'I

hate to see a good business go to waste. You could do so much here, and it wouldn't cost a fortune to improve it.'

There was a sudden spark of interest in the man. 'Like what?'

Lily warmed to her subject. 'A coat of paint in the reception area would do wonders. And a new carpet.' She hesitated. 'Of course, I don't know what the bedrooms are like.'

He looked at the keyboard and took one down. 'Come with me. I'll show you.'

This place needs a bloody good clean, thought Lily as they entered the first room. She ran her finger along the mantel-piece. It was black with dust. She held it out for him to see. She shared her ideas with him. 'If the rooms were thoroughly cleaned and the beds had new covers, and the reception area freshened up, it would make a great difference. Residents don't care about a shabby stair-carpet if the rest is OK.'

'How do you know so much?' he asked.

'I told you,' said Lily. 'I've had a lot of experience in this business.'

As they walked back downstairs, Eddie said, 'I'll think about your ideas.'

'And what about the toms?'

'What do you suggest?'

'Have you a list of hotel rules in the rooms?' she asked.

'No.'

'Right,' she said. 'If you let me use the typewriter in your office, I'll type some out for you. Then we can pin them behind every door, have a set on the desk here, and then you're covered. You know . . . , *No loud music. No women in the room unless they're booked in and paid for.* All you have to do if someone comes in with a prostitute is show them the rules. If they want her, then let them pay for a separate room in her name. Make it legitimate.'

He looked at her with admiration. 'You're quite a girl, you know that?'

'Not at all. I can see things more clearly than you, that's all. I just have a few ideas that will work. And they will, I promise.' She left her boss alone to mull over her suggestions and went to the kitchen to report her arrival to the chef, thinking that if she could get Eddie Chapman to smarten the place up and by doing so, his trade improved, maybe, just maybe, she could persuade him to let her run the place. He wasn't well and if she could prove her capabilities to him, she'd be earning more money and could secure a wage that would keep her and Victoria, with enough left over to pay someone to look after her daughter whilst she worked.

Chapter Eleven

It was another ten days before Lily's wish was granted and she made her way to the court to apply to have her child restored to her. She entered the courthouse with great trepidation. Surely the magistrate wouldn't deny her the right to her child . . . would he? Rachel had wanted to accompany her but she had declined, saying she'd be better on her own. She was very surprised to see DI Chadwick sitting waiting and wondered why he was there. He gave her a friendly nod.

Lily was unable to afford a solicitor and spoke up on her own behalf, pleading her case. 'I'm now gainfully employed, sir,' she said. 'And I'm very anxious to have my child back with me. I've not been allowed to see her and I'm concerned that a longer period of time away from me, her mother, will have a bad effect on her. She'll think I don't love her any more.'

The magistrate with a stern expression said, 'You should have thought of that before you committed your crime.'

Lily swallowed on the words she wanted to say, protesting her innocence. This was not the time or place. 'Yes sir,' she said demurely. 'I will never be put in that position again. *Ever!* I love my child and want to provide her with a secure and happy home-life.'

To her great surprise, Detective Inspector Chadwick also

had a word on her behalf, saying that although she'd served time in prison, it had been her only misdemeanour. He didn't think she was a bad character and he had every confidence that she wouldn't offend again.

Tears filled Lily's eyes as she listened to him, and when at last the magistrate gave his permission for her to take possession of Victoria, she burst out crying with relief.

Chadwick came over to her and shook her hand.

'How can I ever thank you?' she asked.

'I owe you one, Lily. And I'm hoping before too long to right a wrong. The case is closing on Percy Gates. Then I shall set about restoring your good name.'

Despite her emotional turmoil, Lily had to smile. 'That's rich. I've been notorious for so long I don't think I'll ever have a good name.'

'One day you will . . . I give you my word.'

Lily was given the address of the foster parents, but it was explained to her that certain formalities had to be followed. She was told it would be a further two days before she could collect Victoria.

Her face fell. 'I thought I could collect her today,' she said to the policeman.

'Be realistic, love. Things have to be sorted out legally.' Seeing the disappointment on her face, Chadwick said, 'Look, I'll come with you in case of any difficulties, if you like. I'll pick you up in a police car on Tuesday morning.'

'That's very kind of you,' she beamed. 'It'll have to be after ten-thirty. That's when I finish my morning shift.'

'I'll pick you up there – it'll save time. The Mariner's Hotel, isn't it?'

She nodded, grateful for the support of her old friend.

The following two days were pure hell for Lily. She was so

restless, watching the clock, counting the minutes, the seconds. She cleaned her bedroom thoroughly. The single bed would be a bit crowded but there was no room for a larger one. At work she snapped at Dolly, who was being difficult as usual; she tried to lose herself in her work, but found it difficult to concentrate.

'What's the matter with you, mate?' demanded Lenny when she got two orders muddled.

She apologised. 'Sorry, chef. I've got a lot on my mind.'

'Then I suggest you keep it on your work instead!' he grumbled.

Eventually the day she longed for, arrived. She quickly tidied the dining room and prepared her tables for the evening meal, having arranged with Eddie to change her half day. She'd explained that there was a family crisis. He had agreed to her request but Dolly had given Lily a hard time for messing up her routine.

'You're a bloody pain,' she complained to Lily in the kitchen when she'd been told to change her day. 'Ever since you came here you've interfered with the running of things. We was all fine until you bloody arrived!'

Lily glared at her. She was tense and fraught as it was, and Dolly was just too much. 'For Christ sake, give your mouth a rest, will you! I've never in my life met a woman who whinged so much.' She swept out of the room, grabbing her jacket.

'Well!' declared the older woman in high dudgeon. 'Did you hear that, Chef?'

'Yes and she's right. Now get on with your work, will you!'

Outside, standing beside his car, was DI Chadwick. He greeted Lily with a broad smile and opened the car door for her. 'Get in, my dear.'

He could see she was frazzled and too choked for words and remained silent. Lily was grateful for his understanding. She sat in the vehicle with fingers all a-tremble, lit a cigarette to try to calm herself. She tried to take her mind off the drama of seeing Victoria again, by looking out at the passing scene.

Roger Chadwick drove them past the South Western Hotel, along the Western Esplanade, past the Royal Pier, the Old Walls and finally the West Station, before turning into Shirley Road. When shortly they turned right into Paynes Road, Lily's stomach tightened. I mustn't cry, she told herself. If I do, Victoria will be upset. Will she be pleased to see me, she wondered. Will she remember me . . .? So many tortuous thoughts ran through her mind during the journey which seemed absolutely endless.

At last the car drew up in front of a neat-looking house. The garden was tidy, Lily noticed, and the net curtains at the windows were clean. She breathed a sigh of relief. At least the people here were houseproud, so they must be decent folk.

She walked with the officer towards the front door, where he knocked on the shiny brass knocker.

The coldness in the eyes of the woman who opened it struck Lily as soon as she looked at her. And the bitter line of her mouth. She felt as if someone was gripping her heart in a glove of steel. 'I'm Lily Pickford,' she said. 'I've come to collect my daughter.'

Stepping back from the door, Gladys Parker said, 'You'd better come in. Victoria is all ready.'

With her stomach churning inside her, Lily followed the woman into the front parlour. There, sitting on a chair, her hands clasped tightly together, was Victoria. Lily stood in the doorway looking at her. My, how she'd grown, and her dark hair was longer, but whatever was wrong with her? Where was the happy bouncing child she knew? Victoria sat bolt upright, looking at Lily with an anxious expression on her pale and pinched face.

Lily looked immediately at Gladys Parker who was closely watching Victoria.

Walking slowly over to her child, Lily knelt down beside her and said softly, 'Hello, darling. Mama's come to take you home.'

Victoria looked at her with soulful eyes. For a moment there was a look of relief in them, then glancing at Gladys Parker, whose steely gaze was upon her, one of fear.

Lily caught hold of Victoria's little hands. 'You're coming home with me and you're never coming back here ever again. Do you understand, darling? You are never coming back to this house . . . *ever*.'

The tears brimmed in the child's eyes. 'Mama,' she whispered. 'Can I really come home with you, now?'

Gathering her daughter in her arms, Lily gently lifted her and held her close. 'Rachel is waiting for us.' She walked to the door, with Gladys Parker following in her wake.

As she stepped outside, Lily turned and looked at the woman. Softly, but with absolute conviction in her voice she said, 'If I find that you have been unkind to Victoria in any way, you have my word you'll pay dearly!' She turned away before the woman could reply.

Inside the car, Lily held Victoria close, stroking her dark hair. She said nothing, but could feel the tension in her baby and wondered just exactly what had happened inside that house for the past seven months. She vowed that however long it took, she'd find out.

When at last they arrived at the house in Bevois Street, Lily whispered to the detective, 'Tell Rachel to be gentle. Don't let her overwhelm Victoria, because something's not quite right here and I mean to get to the bottom of it.'

He nodded his understanding and getting out of the car, hurried to the front door which was already open. She saw him have a few hurried words with the anxious woman who had also waited for this day with so many happy expectations.

Lily carried Victoria who clung tightly to her, towards Rachel who stepped aside. DI Chadwick followed Lily.

Trying to sound normal and cheerful, Lily walked into the kitchen and sat down. 'Well, here we are, home at last,' she said, placing Victoria on her knee. 'Look, Rachel has made your favourite cucumber sandwiches and jam tarts.'

Victoria sat on her mother's knee and looked around at the small cramped room. She looked from Lily to Rachel, then at the jam tarts and her own toy tea-set, neatly laid out, and burst into tears. 'This isn't Rachel's house,' she said between sobs.

Lily rocked her gently and explained. 'Rachel sold her other house because it was too big, darling. Now she has this one.' She tried soothing her with soft words but her heart was heavy. Slowly, deep within her a fire of anger began to glow. She'd kill that woman who'd knocked every vestige of spirit out of Victoria. She would never forgive her.

Roger Chadwick quietly excused himself. 'I'll leave you to it,' he said. 'But I'll call in at the hotel tomorrow to see how the child is.' He looked at Victoria with some concern but made no comment. When at last Victoria's sobbing had stopped, Lily wiped her wet face with a flannel and asked Rachel to make them a cup of tea and a milky one for her daughter. She took off the child's coat and helped her to a drink. Then slowly encouraged her to eat something.

Rachel and Lily sat making quiet conversation, but both watching anxiously. Rachel looked at her young friend and raised her eyebrows in question but Lily just shook her head. She took Victoria to the toilet and then they settled back in comfortable chairs. Lily cradled her in her arms. The child fell into a deep sleep.

'Whatever is wrong?' asked Rachel at last.

'She's been ill treated,' stated Lily in an angry tone. 'And when I undress her I'm going to see if she's got any bruises. Of course, you don't need to beat a child to be cruel. But in time, with gentle probing, we'll discover what's behind all this. That woman was so cold, she could have sunk the bloody *Titanic* all by herself! I expected her to be subdued but not . . .' She couldn't continue.

'What was the woman like who took care of her?' asked Rachel.

'She looked thoroughly bad-tempered,' snapped Lily. 'But if she has been cruel, I'll make sure she never looks after another child, that's for certain! She certainly doesn't do it for the love of children, I'm sure. It's probably just for the money.'

Victoria slept for three hours and when she awoke, she looked around fearfully until she saw the familiar faces of those she loved. She let Rachel take her for a while to give her mother's arm a rest. Rachel got out one of her favourite books and read to her whilst Lily watched. They gave a sigh of relief when Victoria, thumb in her mouth, smiled at them. She only wanted some rusks and milk to eat later, but Lily was relieved to see her eat anything at all.

It was early evening when Lily in a matter-of-fact voice said, 'Well, young lady, best give you a nice wash before bedtime.'

Victoria nodded slowly.

'I've bought you some new pretty pyjamas. Look, they're airing on the fireguard. I'll show them to you when you're nice and clean. All right, darling?'

Again the child nodded.

Rachel watched as Lily took the kettle from the hob and went into the scullery, then started to undress her daughter, chatting away in an animated fashion, as she carefully scrutinised the small form for any signs of bruising. She gave a sigh of relief when there was not a mark to be seen, but Victoria remained silent. She carried her into the scullery wrapped in a towel.

Rachel sat and listened, but all she could hear was Lily's voice as she washed her. She shook her head sadly as she recalled the cheerful chatter from the little one in times past, and her heart was heavy.

Lily eventually returned to the living room. Picking up the pyjamas she showed them to Victoria. 'Look, darling. They've got little teddy bears on them.' She saw a spark of interest in Victoria's eyes and showed her how the bears were playing.

Her heart nearly burst with joy as Victoria smiled and said, 'Look, Mama! This one is eating a banana.'

Lily looked quickly at Rachel, who smiled back at her.

They both tucked Victoria into bed. Rachel kissed the little girl goodnight and said, 'I'll leave your Mama to put out the light.'

'No! No! Leave the light on. I don't want the light off!'

The panic in the child's voice shook both of them.

'All right, sweetie,' soothed Lily. 'I'll tell you what. We'll turn out the big light and put this bedside table-lamp on. It has a pretty pink shade and it makes a nice cosy glow. How about that?'

'Yes,' murmured Victoria.

'Mama will stay with you and read you a story. We'll leave the door open and then you can see the light in the hall.' She sat on the side of the bed and opened the book. 'Why don't you like the dark, Victoria?' she asked casually as she turned the pages.

'The cupboard was dark,' she replied softly. 'I didn't like it in there. I was frightened.'

The blood in Lily's veins turned to ice and she stiffened. But still turning the pages of the storybook she quietly asked, 'Why did she put you there?'

'She said I was a naughty girl.'

Lily could barely contain the rage that filled her being. She couldn't look at Rachel. 'Well, you know that won't happen here. That lady was the one who was naughty, not you. Now let's begin, shall we? Once upon a time . . .'

How she managed to read to Victoria, Lily didn't know, but she had to keep a totally calm exterior for the sake of her child. When eventually Victoria fell asleep, she walked down the stairs, filled with hatred for the woman who had treated her beloved daughter this way.

Rachel, who had left the room after the revelation, looked up as Lily entered the living room. 'That woman needs horsewhipping, and I'd love to be the one to give it to her!'

'You'd have to stand in line after me,' said Lily.

Rachel looked at Lily with horror. 'So cruel! How can anyone be so cruel?'

'At least there were no bruises on Victoria,' said Lily bitterly. 'Oh no. She wasn't physical in her abuse, but nevertheless she has done untold damage to that child. It will take months for her to recover from her ordeal . . . and even then she may well still suffer. Well, I intend to put a stop to this.'

'How?' asked Rachel.

'When Inspector Chadwick comes to the hotel tomorrow, I'll tell him – see if there is anything he can do. How many other children have suffered? It doesn't bear thinking about. That woman can't continue to get away with this.'

Victoria woke twice that night. Each time she'd wet the bed. Lily changed the linen and after, comforted her. 'It doesn't matter, darling. You couldn't help it.'

'You won't shut me away, will you?' the child begged.

'Never!' said Lily, as she held her close. 'You will never be shut away again, I promise.' At last the child slept.

'Poor baby,' said Rachel, who'd woken and heard Victoria. 'She wet the bed because she was frightened, then being shut away only made it worse. That woman has much to answer for.'

'And answer for it she will,' retorted Lily.

The following morning, Lily was loath to leave the sleeping child and go to work, but Rachel persuaded her. 'Look, darling. A living you have to make. I'll give Victoria her breakfast then later we'll come to the hotel and meet you. You can show her where you work, explain things to her. The outing will perhaps cheer her up.'

'Yes,' agreed Lily. 'That's a good idea. As long as she knows where I go, she'll be content.' Her eyes reflected her anxiety. 'I just hate to leave her like this.'

'Go!' demanded Rachel. 'With me she's fine. With me she's safe.' She cupped Lily's face in her hands and peered at her. 'Don't worry!'

When Roger Chadwick called at the Mariner's Hotel to enquire about young Victoria, Lily told him what had transpired. He was horrified.

'But the Society has a good reputation,' he said.

Lily's eyes flashed angrily. 'That's supposed to make me feel better?'

He shook his head. 'No, of course not, I didn't mean it that way. I'm just surprised, that's all.' A frown creased his forehead. 'This can't be allowed to continue,' he said. 'I'll start an investigation into this business at once.'

'How will you do that?' asked Lily.

'I'll put a man on it to trace any other children in the Society's care at present and in the past. Especially those in the care of that woman Parker. I need proof, Lily. When I get it then I can take it to the head of the Society.' He hesitated. 'Someone will have to question young Victoria at a later date.'

She nodded her approval. 'Let her settle down first,' she pleaded. 'Too many questions at the moment will only distress her more.'

He patted her arm. 'Don't you worry. I quite understand.'

Lily hoped that for once Dolly would steer clear of her, but the waitress was still smouldering with indignation, and apart from angry glares in Lily's direction she remained silent. However, when at last Rachel arrived with a subdued child to see Lily, Dolly's ears pricked up when she heard the child call Lily 'Mama'.

Lily introduced Victoria to Eddie and was pleased when her daughter softly said, 'Hello' even though she clung to her mother all the time. He didn't question Lily in any way, but gave the child a piece of chocolate from a bar on his desk, which endeared him to Lily.

When she made her way home, Lily walked happily beside Victoria, thrilled to feel at last the warmth of her child's hand in hers. Victoria clutched her hand in a tight grip, but as they neared their home, she noticed the grip didn't have the same intensity. When, later in the day, Lily explained that she had to return to the hotel to do some more work, but that Rachel would put her to bed and read her a story, there was not the same look of anxiety in the eyes of her daughter, just a trace of apprehension which Lily dispelled by taking her in her arms in a warm embrace.

'Mama will never leave you ever again,' she whispered, and was rewarded by a tight hug.

Lily stepped off the tram in a happier frame of mind and walked towards the hotel, but to her dismay, there, leaning nonchalantly against the wall, a cheroot in his mouth, Quinn Gifford waited.

Chapter Twelve

Quinn Gifford, dressed in his usual corduroy trousers, collarless shirt and bright neckerchief, gazed at Lily with a slow smile. His sultry good looks had appealed to many a wench, but there was a certain cruelty in his face that didn't escape Lily's notice.

'What are you doing here, Quinn?' she demanded, filled with unease.

He removed the cheroot from his mouth, slowly blowing out the smoke. The sun caught his gold earring, causing it to glint. 'I came to see how you're getting on,' he said softly. He gestured at the shabby frontage of the hotel. 'Come down a bit in the world ain't you, girl?'

'That's none of your business!'

He stood away from the wall and caught hold of her arm gently but firmly. 'You don't need to be here at all, you know that.'

She shook off his hold. 'Bugger off, Quinn. I don't want to see you hanging around again.'

There was an edge to his voice as he said, 'Don't be like that. I wrote and told you I'd take care of you. You can come and live with me at the farm. I've got plenty of money – enough for you and your babby. It's just the place to bring up a child. Good country air . . . I'll teach her to ride. Nice little thing, ain't she?'

Lily's blood ran cold. 'You've never seen her, so how do you know?'

There was a light of triumph in his eyes as he said, 'I saw her this morning, when she came here to see you. She needs a father, a man in her life – and so do you, Lily.'

Like a lioness with her cub, Lily sprang to defend herself and her child. 'We don't need anyone. I can take care of her and myself. My baby is my concern not anyone else's. Least of all yours!'

His wicked laugh echoed and his penetrating gaze was unnerving. 'I found you here easily enough. You can't hide from me, Lily Pickford, and like it or not, you *will* come and live with me, one day . . . both of you!'

He walked towards his truck which was parked a few feet away and with a backward glance said, 'I'll be seeing you.' She could still hear him laughing as he drove away.

She felt her heart thumping as she entered the hotel. Quinn's words sounded so threatening and she knew that he would do everything he could to possess her.

But the actions of the wild gypsy had not gone unobserved. George Coleman had just left the pub opposite where he'd had business with the landlord, and he'd seen the angry exchange between the two. It looked as if Lily was in trouble again. He knew of the Giffords – who didn't? – especially Quinn. George decided to keep a watchful eye on Lily for a while, in case she needed his help.

As Lily checked her dining tables before the next session, Dolly looked across the room and said, 'You've got a bloody cheek and no mistake.'

The sudden remark made Lily look up from her work. 'What?'

Dolly strolled over, a satisfied smirk on her face. 'You

swan in here with all your high-falutin' ideas, your Lady Muck airs, and all the time you've got a bastard child. You're no better than a whore!'

Ever since she became the mistress of Vittorio Teglia and eventually the unmarried mother of his child, Lily had met with many insults and she wasn't going to be upset by yet another from the likes of this pathetic woman. With hands on hips, Lily gave a broad grin. 'The trouble with you, Dolly, is that you're such a miserable bitch, I doubt if any man has ever asked you to open *your* legs!' She burst out laughing at the flush that coloured Dolly's cheeks and left the room chuckling gleefully.

When she arrived home later that night, she asked anxiously about Victoria. Rachel assured her that she was fine. 'A little quiet, of course. I stayed with her until she fell asleep.'

Lily crept up the stairs and peered in at the child. Victoria was sound asleep, her thumb in her mouth, her breathing even. Lily crossed over to the bed and kissed her forehead. She thought of Quinn's threats. She would never let him anywhere near Victoria. Ever.

When she went downstairs, Rachel said, 'I forgot. This letter and postcard came for you this morning.'

The postcard had a picture of Bournemouth on the front and she knew at once it came from Sandy. On the back he'd written:

I miss you, you old tart. This place is very dull. Thank goodness for the chorus boys appearing at the local variety theatre. I thought I would have to join a monastery. I'd heard about their habits! Love, Sandy.

Lily grinned broadly. He hadn't changed, but she missed him too. At least with his sister, he wouldn't have to worry about a job because she remembered Sandy saying she was worth a few bob. She put the card down and with a puzzled look at the envelope, opened it and with a cry of joy began to read,

Dear Lily, I'm getting out of Brookmans on Thursday of next week. Thank you for your letter. Hetty liked the postcard and sends her love. I've got your address and will come and see you. Do you know of anyone who needs a good waitress? I've been practising. Love, Madge.

With a broad smile Lily said, 'It's from Madge, my cellmate. She's coming here next week, and I might just know of a job for her . . .' .

Luke Longford sat in a taxi with one of the local estate agents.

'I think at last we've got just the kind of property you've been looking for,' he told Luke.

Luke was not particularly thrilled. How many times had he listened to exactly the same promise from others! But as the taxi drew to a halt outside a shabby, but large and impressive building, he became more than a little interested. A huge sign declared *The Regent Hotel*.

Paying off the taxi, the man led him to the main entrance and putting the key in the large padlock, unlocked it and then the door. 'Come in, sir,' he said.

Luke walked around the large foyer, then into the other rooms, looking at everything as he did so. He felt the excitement mounting as he inspected the kitchens and finally the bedrooms on the two floors. It was just what he wanted.

Turning to the agent he said, 'Would you mind waiting downstairs? I'd like to look around on my own.'

'Certainly, sir.'

At last he was alone. He re-inspected every room thoroughly. The structure looked sound enough. It would all have to be redecorated, of course, but in any case he would have his own ideas about the décor. Or Lily's ideas, for he fully intended to get her involved. As he walked around the ground floor he could picture it in his mind. This was exactly what he'd been looking for all this time! He'd have to get a surveyor in first, just to make sure the building was sound. If it was, then he'd go ahead and purchase it. Then . . . he could go to Lily with an offer.

The hotel was in an excellent position, overlooking Watts Park – a five-minute walk from the local shops and a ten-minute taxi ride to the docks and the large ocean-going liners. Perfect for sea-going passengers! Perfect for business people. Enough room to accommodate residents, a large dining room and a ballroom. An assembly room, just right for business conferences and private functions. It was ideal.

'Why wasn't I shown this property before?' demanded Luke when he rejoined the agent.

'Well, you see, sir, I was under the impression that someone had bought it.'

'I'll get a surveyor in, and subject to his report, we may have a deal – if we can come to an agreement about the price,' Luke told the agent.

'Right, sir. I can recommend a good surveyor if you need one.'

'No, thank you,' said Luke. 'I have my own. Right.' He held out his hand. 'I'll be in touch.'

He walked through the park, whistling with happiness. The floral displays with their vibrant colours seemed to match his mood. And poignantly, at the War Memorial was a single small posy. Luke's step was buoyant and he decided that this evening he'd call on Rachel and tell her his news and ask after Lily. He needed to know how she was. He desperately wanted to see her. If Rachel thought it prudent, he would ask Lily to dine with him.

But he was shocked when he arrived at the address Rachel had given him and saw the poor area. He'd visited her in the Polygon and knew it to be a decent part of the town, but this was decidedly seedy. Apprehensively, he knocked on the door.

Rachel was very pleased to see him, however, and ushered him into the kitchen-cum-living room. Looking around, Luke was aware that the furniture that crowded the room was of the highest quality, and he realised suddenly just how devastating it had been for the women after the demise of the Club Valletta. On the settee sat a little girl who looked at him with big brown eyes as she drank from a cup of milk and ate a biscuit.

'Victoria,' said Rachel, 'this gentleman is Luke Longford, a friend of your Mama's.'

Luke smiled at her and said, 'Hello.'

'Hello,' she said quietly and moved closer to Rachel who sat beside her.

'Lily's at work,' explained the Jewess. 'She's on until ten o'clock. She's working as a waitress at the Mariner's Hotel in Chapel Road.'

Luke frowned. 'That's near the dock gates,' he said.

'Yes, that's right.' Rachel lowered her voice. 'Difficult it was for her to find a job after being in . . . you know. But she had to take anything she could to get Victoria back to live with her.' She got up and made him a cup of tea.

'I hope that in the near future I will be in a position to offer her something much better,' Luke said. 'Something more in her line.' He smiled at Victoria. 'Your mother is a clever lady – did you know that?'

She nodded slowly.

'Today I was shown a property in Cumberland Place, which is just what I'm looking for. Now I need a surveyor to check it over. I'd like to talk to Lily about it. Perhaps I'll go to the Mariner's for a meal this evening,' he decided. 'It would give me a chance to see her and have a chat.'

'Why don't you?' encouraged Rachel. They sat and talked for a while until it was Victoria's bedtime. He ruffled the child's hair as he prepared to leave. 'Goodnight, young lady,' he said.

'Goodnight,' she answered with a shy smile.

It was with great surprise that Lily saw Luke enter the dining room of the Mariner's Hotel, an hour later. She was thankful that Eddie had done the reception area up earlier that week, because the place now didn't look so down-at-heel. But at the same time, she wished he wasn't here. Just like his visit to Brookmans Prison, she felt disadvantaged. He certainly stood out against the motley crew of residents in his fine lounge suit and she saw Dolly's ears prick up when Luke walked over to her and said, 'Hello, Lily. Do you have a table free for one?'

'How on earth did you know I was here?' She knew this was more than coincidence; this was not the sort of place the likes of Luke Longford frequented.

'I call in to see Rachel and she told me.'

'I see.' She led him to a quiet table away from the others and handed him the menu.

He couldn't help but compare the bill of fare to the comprehensive one he'd seen at the Club Valletta, but those days were over. 'What do you suggest?' he asked.

'The roast chicken is nice,' she said. 'The vegetables are fresh, served with roast potatoes. Would you like some soup to start with?'

He shook his head. 'No, just the chicken will be fine. Could I see the wine list?'

She handed him one with a modest selection and he chose half a bottle of Chardonnay.

Whilst Lily went to the kitchen he looked around, aware of curious stares from the other diners and the baleful look of the older, unkempt waitress. He wondered just how Lily would fit into such humble surroundings. Indelible in his mind was the image of an elegant woman, dressed expensively, surrounded by understated opulence.

She brought him his meal, opened the wine with panache and went to serve someone else. The new customer was coarse and loud. He eyed Lily up and down quite blatantly and muttered something to her which brought a flush to her cheeks, but Luke couldn't hear what the man said.

He finished his meal, which was surprisingly good, and ordered some apple crumble and coffee. As he drank his coffee, he saw Lily carry a pot over to the customer he'd watched earlier. He was appalled as the man put out his hand and rubbed it up Lily's leg. He was about to get up and remonstrate with him, but Lily just tipped the hot liquid in the pot over the man's hand. At the loud yell of pain, she leaned forward and spoke a few short words in his ear and walked away. With everyone in the dining room looking at him, the customer seemed to shrink in his chair in a very subdued manner. And when Lily returned with his bill, he paid it at once, then with a look of fury, left the room.

Luke was highly amused. It was apparent that Lily Pickford could take care of herself and strangely, she seemed to fit in comfortably with her surroundings, although there was still that certain something about her that made her different. It was as if she was a chameleon, able to blend in, wherever. But was it all a façade? Who was the *real* Lily Pickford? The elegant woman he'd first met or this perky waitress? Where did she come from? He was intrigued.

As he paid the bill he said, 'Can I meet you when you finish? Only I have something important to tell you that might well affect your future, if you are interested.'

She looked up at the handsome chief steward. There was something solid and dependable about him, yet she couldn't deny his physical attraction either. Especially the way the corners of his eyes crinkled as he smiled. He was very different from Quinn Gifford, for instance. Where the wild gypsy was attractive in his own way and wily, he was also uncouth; Luke was smooth and sophisticated and had class. She knew what Quinn wanted from her, but she was curious to know what exactly this man had in mind.

'I don't finish until ten o'clock,' she said.

'That's all right. I'll go along to the South Western Hotel, have a drink there and come back. I'll walk you home.'

Luke was waiting for her at the reception desk when Lily finished. Just as they turned to leave, Eddie handed a large brown teddy bear to her. 'This was left by a man who said he was a friend of yours,' he said.

She took it and read the label. *To Victoria. Love from Quinn*, it read. She felt the blood drain from her face. She handed it back to Eddie. 'Put it behind the counter,' she said quietly, and turned away. 'Ready?' she asked Luke and walked towards the exit.

As they strolled along Chapel Road to St Mary Street, Luke unfolded his future plans to her. His dreams. 'All my life I've worked to one end,' he explained. 'A smart, large, elegant and expensive hotel. Exclusive. Exquisite furnishings, excellent service, fine cuisine cooked by a chef who is innovative and clever. You see, Lily, as you know well, there are always the rich who can afford such luxuries. Those are the people who will be my clients.'

Lily hid a wry smile. Too right. There she was struggling

like thousands of others on a pittance, but there would always be the divide through class and money. She had been both wealthy and poor and she knew which she preferred!

'That sounds wonderful, Luke, and I'm very happy for you, but what exactly does this have to do with me?'

He stopped walking and catching hold of her arm said, 'When I buy the place, I want you to help me with the décor and choice of furnishings.'

She was completely taken aback. 'But you're well able to do that yourself, with your vast experience.'

'Yes, maybe, but I saw the Club. You have a natural flair for this. I need you, Lily.'

She was puzzled. 'Are you offering me a job?'

He burst out laughing. 'Of course! I'm sorry, didn't I make that clear? After the hotel is ready, then I'd like you as my manageress. I must have someone I can trust and who is up to the task. I'll pay you well.'

'I can't possibly work for you!'

His face fell. 'Why ever not?'

'For God's sake, Luke, I've got a prison record! If your wealthy clients get a whiff of that . . .'

'But you were innocent! And DI Chadwick hopes to clear your name.'

'But what if he doesn't?'

'It won't matter. *I* know you had nothing to do with the crooked tables and that's what counts. Those days are behind you anyway. The past is the past, we must look to the future.' He paused and gazed around at the shabby buildings, the rubbish-strewn street. 'Besides, it will take you away from all this. You don't belong here, Lily.'

He was so wrong, she thought. This was exactly the area in which she was born. It was on such streets she had been forced to sell her body. She lived with Fred, a pickpocket, who'd been her saviour, in a house like these, until she became the mistress of a wealthy villain. Just what sort of a picture did this attractive man have of her in his mind? Whatever it was, it was far from reality. And how would he feel if he discovered the real Lily Pickford? Would he still want her around? She thought not.

'Why should you be so interested in me?' she asked. 'You know nothing about me. This is our third meeting and one of those was in prison, yet you offer me a job with a great deal of responsibility.' She stared into his eyes. 'It doesn't make sense.'

The intensity of his gaze caused her heart to race. 'I agree. But deep inside me, I know it's the right decision. I want to get to know you better, Lily. Will you give me the chance?' He gently brushed her cheek.

Her skin tingled beneath his fingers. It was a long time since she'd been interested in a man, felt his touch. But there was something about *this* man. She could easily be drawn to him.

'I don't have a lot of free time,' she said. 'And there's Victoria.'

He smiled at her. 'Yes, I met her this evening.'

'Was she all right?'

'Yes, she was just off to bed. Look, why don't I take you both out to lunch tomorrow? We could drive to Hamble, sit by the river, have a picnic. Children like picnics. I'll get one of the chefs on board to make up a lunchbox for us. What do you say?'

He seemed so enthusiastic that she agreed. It would do Victoria the world of good and give Rachel a bit of peace and quiet.

'All right,' she decided. 'Pick us up at twelve o'clock.'

He caught hold of her shoulders, pulled her to him and

softly kissed her cheek. 'Thank you,' he said. 'Until tomorrow.'

As Lily settled down that night, with her arm over the sleeping form of her daughter, she wondered about Luke Longford. What did he see in her? He could have any woman. And it was all very well for him to include her in his plans, but so far they were pie in the sky. Nothing was settled; it could all fall through. No, she would just carry on, trying to keep her head above water. There was no use planning for a future. One day at a time was the best way, then there were no disappointments.

Snuggling down beneath the bedclothes, she smiled happily at the thought of her old friend Madge, soon to arrive. If she could get work, then perhaps they could find a place to live together, sharing the rent, leaving Rachel free to take in a lodger. The money that she was earning now was not enough to keep the three of them, and they were having to scrape for food. Victoria needed new shoes and there was no money for them. Still, if she lived with Madge, there would then be the problem of finding someone to look after Victoria when she was working. She'd asked around, but so far without success. She'd try again tomorrow.

Chapter Thirteen

The following day was bright and sunny with a gentle breeze, and Lily as she worked her morning shift was looking forward to the picnic. Victoria had been really excited when she'd been told about it that morning, and for the first time since she'd come home, had shown a bit of her old spirit.

Luke, dressed in casual beige trousers, shirt and blazer, collected Lily from the Mariner's after her morning stint, then drove her home in his new Morris Cowley. As she sat back in comfort, she breathed in the smell of the new leather upholstery. 'This is nice,' she said.

'I'm glad you like it – I picked it up last trip. I need a set of wheels. It makes for an easier life.'

Luke waited inside the house whilst Lily changed, chatting to Rachel and telling Victoria where they were going. He could see the excitement in the child's eyes. 'We'll search the seashore and see if we can find any shells, if you like.'

'Oh yes please,' she said.

Lily ran down the stairs and joined them. Her light patterned voile dress of pale lemon was slightly flared over a matching slip; her white stockings covered slender legs. She was a vision of the old Lily. One that Luke recognised.

'You look lovely,' he said, and she blushed at the compliment, thankful that she'd saved one or two dresses of quality.

Luke settled Lily and Victoria in the car then drove to Northam Bridge where he paid the toll for them to cross and drove on towards Hamble.

It was a beautiful July day. The sun glistened on the Hamble River. Yachts drifted by, their sails and spinnakers filled and billowing as they tacked first one way and then the other, making for Southampton Water and the Isle of Wight. Large gulls glided by, screeching loudly before diving to snatch bits of food. Seaweed clogged the edge of the water, flotsam floated by.

As Luke parked the car, Lily and Victoria alighted. The child ran to the edge of the shore, pointing excitedly towards a small yacht. 'Look, Mama!'

Lily watched the animation on Victoria's face with delight and relief. At last she was emerging from the dark. She walked over to her and they inspected the shore whilst Luke unpacked the rug and picnic basket, then he joined them. They began to collect seashells. He explained to the child how little creatures lived inside them, then he picked up some seaweed and let her smell it.

She turned up her tiny nose. 'Pooh! It's not very nice,' she giggled.

'It smells of the sea,' he explained.

In the far distance they saw an ocean liner making her way down towards Spithead, heading for the Atlantic Ocean and then on to America. Lily watched its elegant passage and looked at Luke. 'That to me seems such an exciting life. Why on earth would you want to leave it?'

They wandered back and settled on the rug as he tried to explain.

'It *is* a wonderful life. The sea is very much like a wilful woman that you love. One day full of passion and anger that is awesome, yet calm and serene another. It creeps into your veins, becomes part of your life. It has a fatal fascination of its own.' He took her hand in his. 'A life at sea is wonderful, interesting, exciting, different. It's like living in a private world where only those of you on board, belong. To walk around the deck of an ocean liner at night, at sea, with a full moon shining above you, is magical. To look out over the horizon, see the moon glimmering on the water, the wake of the ship leaving its trail behind, is one of the most romantic settings I know.' He grinned wickedly. 'They say that on water, people lose their inhibitions.'

She was curious. 'Do they?'

He laughed. 'Yes, I'm afraid they often do.'

She raised her eyebrows and with a quizzical expression asked, 'Did you?'

His eyes twinkled mischievously. 'Once or twice,' he admitted.

'Did it ever lead to marriage?'

He gently stroked her hand. 'No, Lily. I never had the time or the inclination. All that was important to me was to achieve my dream.' He let go of her and began to unpack the basket of food. 'But life at sea is unreal,' he continued.

'In what way?'

'As I explained, you're in a private world . . . it isn't normal. It only lasts one voyage, then it starts again on the next. Between trips you return to the real world. The danger is when you can't distinguish between the two.'

'And soon you'll be returning to the real world for good, if your plans come to fruition,' said Lily. 'I hope you won't be too disappointed.'

He looked intently at her. 'I think the future holds great promise.'

She sighed. 'We could all do with a bit of magic in our lives. At least you've had yours.'

He stopped his unpacking. 'And what about you, Lily? Has there never been a moment of magic in yours?'

She tried to think. She remembered the first time she sang in a pub for money, the applause at the end of her number – that had been magical. Her life with Vittorio had had its moments, but the first time she held Victoria in her arms . . . that was pure magic. She looked at him and with a broad smile said, 'Yes. I've had one or two.'

He chuckled softly. 'It seemed to me you were surprised by that.'

'As a matter of fact I was.' She looked at her daughter sitting playing with her shells. She would always be the best moment.

Luke laid out a splendid array. There was cold chicken, large slices of ham, smoked salmon that Rachel would die for, potato salad, lettuce, tomatoes. Spring onions cut in a special way so that the shortened green bits curled. Radishes cut into roses. Sticks of celery. Fresh rolls, curls of butter packed in a container. A lemon cut in slices. A selection of fruit, large luscious strawberries and a pot of cream, two bottles of wine and a bottle of fruit juice for Victoria. Knives and forks were wrapped in linen napkins and the plain white dishes were fine bone china. There was an ice box to keep the wine cooled. It reminded Lily of better days and how hungry she was and just how long it had been since she sat down to a proper meal!

Victoria was in her element. She sat as good as gold, almost swamped by the napkin tied around her neck to protect her best blue dress. She munched on the crisp celery, nibbled the chicken, cut into small pieces on her plate. Turned her nose up at the offer of smoked salmon. Enjoyed a banana, and drank the fresh orange juice.

When at last their appetites were satisfied, Luke poured

another glass of wine for both of them and said, 'Tell me about yourself, Lily.'

She hesitated. She didn't want to dispel his illusion, not at this moment. 'What's to tell? Once I was well off, now I'm not. But life's like that. Just when things are sailing along nicely,' she pointed to a passing yacht, 'like that, then life takes a swipe and your legs are knocked from under you.'

Victoria clambered to her feet and walked to the water's edge.

'Be careful,' Lily called. 'Don't move away from there.'

Looking at the child, Luke said, 'Tell me about her father.'

'Vittorio was Maltese. He came to this country as a boy. He was dynamic, well read, although mostly self-taught, and a fine businessman who appreciated the nice things in life. He had excellent taste.' She stared at Luke and said, 'He was good to me and I loved him, but he died when Victoria was three months old.'

'That's a very sad story,' he said.

She sipped her wine. 'Yes.'

As Lily sat watching her daughter, lost in her own thoughts, Luke pondered on this unusual woman. Such a young life but so full of tragedy and drama. Yet there burned within her a light that was so bright, he wondered just what force would ever be able to distinguish it. She was a survivor. And even now, working in that awful hotel, she shone. He'd seen that for himself the other evening. He wanted to take her in his arms, promise her a better future. A life such as she was accustomed to, but he held back. These were early days. She wasn't ready for that yet, he was sure. The woman had only just come out of prison, had had to cope with losing her child to strangers. Under that confident façade, he sensed there was a vulnerability. For some reason he doubted if there had been another man in her life since Vittorio. And he realised he wanted to know her better.

'Come on,' he said, covering the food with napkins and the rug to keep the flies off. 'Let's go and play with Victoria.'

They had a great time. Luke took off his shoes and socks, rolled up his trousers, and with Victoria, minus her socks and shoes, paddled in the water. Lily did likewise and joined them.

The pebbles were sharp and uncomfortable, but they ignored the discomfort. They returned to their place, hands full of seaweed to hang up outside the scullery door so they could tell what the weather was going to do – and more shells.

Eventually it was time to go home. And Lily found herself wondering just what Luke was going to do with the food that was left. It would feed the three of them for days. If he took it back to the ship it would be dumped and she couldn't bear to think of such a waste when she and Rachel were scraping two pennies together to produce some sort of meal . . . but how could she bring herself to ask for it? Luke had this certain picture of her in his mind. He knew she was having a hard time, but she was certain he couldn't possibly imagine the extent of her deprivation.

Her problem was solved for her. When they returned to Rachel's house, he took the picnic basket from the car. 'Take this with you, Lily. I have some business calls and I don't want this food hanging around the boot of the car. It'll go off and the car will smell.'

'Oh, right. Don't you worry about it – I'll see to it for you,' she said, trying to sound casual, yet filled with delight at such bounty. 'Will you come in for a cup of tea?'

There was a note of regret in his voice. 'Sadly, I don't have the time and we sail tomorrow, but I will come and see you next trip, if I may?'

'I'd like that. Thank you for a lovely afternoon. Thank Luke, Victoria.'

Clutching on to her seaweed, the little girl smiled at him, her eyes bright. 'Thank you, Luke. I've had a lovely time.'

He picked her up and kissed her. 'So did I.' He put her down and turned to Lily. He caught hold of her shoulders and gently pulled her to him. 'I've been wanting to do this all afternoon,' he said as he kissed her too.

As his lips closed over hers, Lily felt herself responding to his soft mouth. Her knees weakened as his lips moved over hers. The kiss was so much more than that of a friend, yet it wasn't one of a lover. But – it was filled with promise.

When at last he released her, his gaze held hers as he looked into her eyes. 'I can't wait until I can do that again.' As he got into the car, he smiled at her, started the engine and drove away.

Lily put her key into the lock and stepped into the living room, in a daze. Luke had taken her completely by surprise. She'd been so thrilled with the basket of food she was holding that the thought that he might kiss her had never entered her head.

'So, by the look of you both, you had a good time,' said Rachel from the depths of her chair. 'Me . . . I fell asleep.'

Lily was overcome with guilt. She knew that looking after a three-year-old was tiring, and was aware that, although Rachel loved her small charge, she was finding it all a bit too much.

'Perhaps this will make you feel better,' said Lily gleefully as she fetched a plate, unpacked the basket and put some chicken, smoked salmon and a tomato on it. 'Do you want some lettuce and potato salad?'

Rachel's eyes grew wide at the spoils. 'My life! Such a

feast,' she breathed as she squeezed a slice of lemon over the salmon.

'We have celery, radishes, spring onions too and some strawberries and cream, bananas, oranges,' said Lily, popping a large strawberry into her mouth, her eyes dancing with delight. 'Enough to feed us for days! Help yourself.'

'Mazeltov!' The Jewess cried as she put her fork into the salmon. 'This is manna from heaven.'

'Not quite, compliments of the Cunard Company more like!' quipped Lily.

Victoria waved her long piece of seaweed at Rachel. 'Look! We must hang it outside the door, Luke said. If it's dry the weather will be nice, if it's damp it's going to rain.'

'Such a miracle!' said Rachel. 'I'll know when to hang out the washing.' She looked knowingly at Lily. 'How is the handsome Mr Longford?'

Before Lily could answer, Victoria piped up, 'He kissed Mama!'

'Did he?' said the Jewess, then with a knowing look she asked the child, 'Did Mama kiss him back?'

'Oh yes.'

Lily felt her cheeks redden. She didn't look at her friend and Rachel said no more on the matter. But the corners of her mouth lifted in a slow smile of satisfaction.

To cover her confusion, Lily busied herself putting the rest of the picnic into the cool larder. She felt her mouth with the back of her hand. The pressure of Luke's kiss was still in her mind. Was the offer of a job a ploy, she wondered. Then chided herself for her cynicism. Over the years she'd learned a great deal about the male sex. Much of which she strove to forget, it was too sordid, but it had made her very wary. She brushed her doubts of Luke aside. She thought he was genuine, but she was concerned that when she told him the whole truth about herself, which if they were to work together, she felt it only fair to do, how would he react? She sensed that he had certain moral codes, and as she knew to her cost, a male ego could destroy relationships. She'd proved that years ago with a wild Irishman who'd loved her.

Whilst Lily had been enjoying herself on the shores of the Hamble River, the Gifford brothers had been together in The Grapes, a pub in Oxford Street, in Southampton's docklands, getting steadily drunk. Quinn was telling them of his future plans.

'Tomorrow I want you two to help me decorate the inside of the farm. The living room, my bedroom.'

Bart burst out laughing. 'What bloody living room? We ain't got one – unless you means the kitchen.'

Quinn glowered at him. 'Well, we live in it, don't we?'

'Yes . . . and so do half the bloody farmyard. If only Ma would keep the bleedin' hens out, it wouldn't get so dirty. They crap all over the place.'

'From tomorrow they don't. From tomorrow they stays in the yard.'

'Rosie won't like that,' he said, referring to their mother.

'If she don't like it she can go out in the yard with them,' retorted Quinn.

The two younger brothers looked at each other. What was going on here? 'What do we have to smarten the place up for anyway?' grumbled Bart.

Quinn gave an alcoholic grin. 'Because I'm thinking of getting wed!'

His brothers looked at him in astonishment. 'You? You once told me as long as Rosie was alive to cook for us and you had enough women to please you, you'd never get married,' protested Jake.

'Well, now I've changed me mind. I've found a wench and I wants her.'

'Do we know her?' asked Bart.

Quinn grinned with delight. 'Her name is Lily Pickford.'

There were roars of laughter from the other two. 'You don't stand a bloody chance,' jeered Bart. 'She's used to the good life. Remember the Club? The woman's got class.'

'She'd spit you out soon as look at you,' said Jake.

'She's fell on hard times,' Quinn informed them. 'Now she ain't got nothing. I can give her and her brat a home. And I've got the money to take care of her.'

'She's got a child?' asked Jake.

'Yeah.'

'But you hates kids!'

With a sly look, Quinn said, 'Yeah, but she don't know that.'

'There ain't no way she'd agree to marry you,' insisted Bart. 'You're wasting your time.'

Quinn winked at him knowingly. 'Don't you fret none. I've got it all worked out. There is a way, I've got it all planned. She'll beg to come to me. She won't have any other choice. Now drink up. It's time we went home.'

The two younger brothers looked at each other with concern. They knew Quinn so well. If he'd set his mind to a thing, he'd go to any lengths to achieve his ends. Many times it got them into trouble too.

As the three of them staggered out of the bar, George Coleman who'd been sitting nearby, frowned. He didn't like what he'd just heard. That Quinn Gifford had something up his sleeve and although he was ignorant, he had an astute mind . . . It was time he had a chat with Lily.

The following morning, George called at the hotel, enquiring for Lily at the reception desk. Eddie eyed the big man with some suspicion, but George told him he was a friend of hers.

'She'll be off duty in ten minutes,' he explained. 'I'll tell her you're here. What name shall I give?'

'George Coleman.'

Eddie Chapman was startled. There wasn't a person who lived in this area who didn't know who this man was. Although he'd never actually seen him before, he could now understand his reputation was well earned. Although George was wearing a hand-tailored suit, there was an air of menace about him and Eddie thought he'd hate to get on the wrong side of him. 'I'll go and tell her now,' he said, and hurried away.

Ten minutes later, Lily arrived. 'Hello, George. You wanted to see me?'

'Yes,' he said and led her outside. 'You been having trouble from Quinn Gifford?' he asked.

Lily was shaken.

'I saw him hanging around a while ago, waiting for you. I noticed the two of you talking. I was just coming out of the pub across the way.'

She explained what had transpired during their discussion. 'He was a punter at the Club Valletta,' she said. 'Now he's got it into his head he wants to look after me . . . and Victoria.'

George Coleman's eyes narrowed. 'Is that right? What did you tell him?'

'I told him to bugger off!'

He had to smile. Lily never did mince her words. 'It seems he has a mind to wed you, girl.'

Her face went white. '*What?*'

He nodded sagely. 'I overheard a conversation he had with his brothers, telling them.'

Lily was completely floored. Quinn Gifford frightened her, but she would never marry him. He could drag her to the altar in chains, but she would never utter a word when she got there! 'What am I going to do?' she asked.

'You? Nothing! My boys will sort him out.'

Lily grabbed his arm. 'No, George. No!' She had visions of Quinn Gifford's body being washed up on some shore when the tide went out. 'I don't want you to touch him. I'll think of something.'

'Now listen to me, Miss Lily. You can't handle a man like Gifford, he's a wicked bugger.'

'He can't force me to do something I don't want to, can he?'

'I wouldn't be too sure, girl. He's a crafty sod.'

'Was he drunk when he was talking about this?' asked Lily.

George nodded.

'Well then, that's all it was – drunken dreams. When he wakes up he'll have forgotten all about it.'

He could see she was adamant. It was useless to argue. 'Very well, if that's the way you want it.'

'I do. I don't want you or your boys to touch him. Thanks for being worried for me, but honestly, I can take care of myself. I've got to be off now. By the way, do you know of anyone reliable who could look after Victoria for a few hours while I'm at work and who doesn't charge much?'

'I'll ask around for you. If I hear of anyone I'll let you know.'

They parted company. As Lily made her way home she wondered why she hadn't thought to ask George Coleman before. Nothing happened on his patch, or anybody else's for that matter, that he didn't get to hear about. Secretly, she was filled with alarm at his news about Quinn. Marriage! Was the man crazy? The frightening thing was that she was convinced there was a hint of madness about him. And she was scared.

Chapter Fourteen

On the following Thursday afternoon, Lily was sitting reading to Victoria when there was a knock at the door. When she opened it, to her delight she saw Madge standing there, clutching a small suitcase.

'Madge!' She hugged her old friend and ushered her inside. 'How are you? When did you get out?'

'This morning. I can't tell you how wonderful it was to walk away from that bloody place!' She grinned. 'But of course, you know all about that.' She looked at Victoria who was studying the stranger with interest. 'And this young lady no doubt is your daughter.'

Lily's eyes shone with pride. 'Yes, this is Victoria.'

'Hello,' said the little one.

'Hello. My, but you're a pretty girl.' Madge looked across at Lily. 'I'll be frank with you, love. I need a job and a place to stay.'

Putting the kettle back on the hob, Lily said, 'Well, with a bit of luck, I might be able to do both for you. Tonight you can bunk on the settee, and if I get you a job, I had thought that you and me together – with Victoria, of course – might share a place, then we could halve the rent. What do you think?'

'It sounds like an answer to a prayer.'

Lily made a pot of tea and sat opposite Madge at the table. 'Does your mother know where you are?' she asked.

'No bloody fear! I scarpered as soon as they let me out. Look, Lily, I've only got the dress I'm standing up in. It's hardly suitable for a job interview.'

'You can borrow one of mine. I've got to go back on duty at six o'clock – you can come with me and see my boss.' She looked at Madge and in a firm voice said, 'But first you've got to give me your word you're going straight.'

'I promise, Lily. Honest to God! In Brookmans you gave me hope, and I don't want to go back inside again.' She gave a smile of satisfaction. 'The screws let me keep practising waiting at table after you left. I'm really good at it now.'

'How's Hetty?'

Madge's expression changed to one of concern. 'I hated to leave her, but the senior warder promised to look out for her.'

'Yes, she's not a bad soul,' said Lily, remembering how she'd tried to protect her against Belle Chisholm.

'What happens to Victoria when you go to work?'

'I share this place with my friend Rachel, who's out at the bakers at the moment. She's been looking after her. But times are hard with just me earning, trying to feed all three of us. We just about survive. If you and me get a place then Rachel can take in a lodger.'

'But what about your daughter?'

'A friend of mine is trying to find a woman who's reliable to look after her.'

The two of them spent the next hour chatting about their time together in Brookmans and Madge kept Lily up-to-date with all the latest happenings.

'I forgot to tell you,' she said suddenly. 'Old Cole was sacked!'

'No! What happened?'

'Well . . . she was up to her old tricks again with a young pretty girl, when the older sister of the girl came in to do a stretch. When she discovered what was going on, she filled our Miss Cole in. Blimey! You should have seen her. She had a real go at her, gave her a couple of real shiners! She lost a few teeth, too. There was a hell of a rumpus. Anyway, the Governor sacked her. We all cheered like mad!'

Lily started to laugh. 'I wish I'd been there. I'd have paid a week's wages to see her sorted out.'

In the midst of this hilarity, Rachel arrived and Lily introduced her to Madge. 'You don't mind if she camps out on the settee for a few days, do you?' asked Lily.

'No, of course not. I'll just go and put the bread away.' But as Rachel did so, it was with a heavy heart, knowing that now, Lily and Victoria would soon be leaving.

Lily arrived at the Mariner's Hotel later that evening with Madge in tow; Madge was wearing Lily's navy dress, which Eddie Chapman recognised as he greeted them. But before they could say a word, Dolly came bursting out of the dining room waving a cutting from a newspaper in her hand. 'I know all about you, Lily Pickford! Apart from having a bastard child, you're nothing but a bleedin' gaolbird. My sister gave me this article. You've been inside!' She turned to her boss. 'I bet you didn't know that!'

'You're wrong. Lily told me,' said Eddie calmly.

Dolly looked horrified. 'Yet you still took her on?'

'Yes, and she does a good job. I've been perfectly satisfied.'

Puffed up with righteous indignation, Dolly tore her apron off and plonked it on the desk. 'Well, I'm not bloody well going to work with criminals. I'm a lawful-abiding citizen, me, and I think it's disgusting!' She turned on her heel, made for the kitchen, grabbed her coat and left the building.

'Oh dear, Eddie,' said Lily, her eyes twinkling with amusement. 'It looks as if you need a new waitress. Can I introduce you to my friend Madge?'

The atmosphere in the dining room of the Mariner's lightened considerably over the next few days, with the two girls chatting happily with the customers. Dolly wasn't missed at all, and Eddie was delighted.

At the same time, George Coleman had called in and left the address of a woman he recommended who lived in French Street. Lily went to visit her and found a plump homely type, who said she would be only too pleased to look after little Victoria.

Lily explained her working hours, but it didn't seem to concern Betty Logan. 'Me husband does shiftwork, miss. I know it can be difficult.'

'But I don't finish until ten o'clock at night on the evening shift.'

'Don't worry, love. I'll bed the little one down on the settee and she can go to sleep until you come. But if she's sleepy when you collect her, you'll probably have to carry her.'

'I can get a tram most of the way,' explained Lily. A frown furrowed her brow. 'We'll give it a try and see how it goes. Of course, I'd have to bring Victoria to see you first.'

'Of course you would. I've got a four-year-old of me own so she'd have someone to play with.'

The next afternoon, Lily took Victoria along to the house. They knocked on the front door to be greeted by Betty, her hands covered in flour, a smudge of white on her nose, a small child at her knee.

'Come in,' she said. 'I'm just making a couple of steak and kidney pies for the workman's café along the road. I bake a couple of cakes a week for them too.' She chuckled and her ample proportions bounced as she did so. 'As you can see, love, I like me food and I love cooking, so I earn a few bob that way.' Looking at Victoria she asked, 'Want to help me, girlie? You and my Daisy can be my assistants.'

Victoria had a clean tea-cloth wrapped around her and very soon, she and the other child were helping roll out the scraps of pastry, cutting them into shapes, oblivious to everything else. Afterwards, the two children sat at the table with wax crayons, drawing pictures and chatting happily together whilst the two women shared a pot of tea.

Betty said, 'I don't think she'll mind coming here.'

Lily sat beside Victoria and said, 'When Mama goes to work, would you like to come here and play?'

'Oh yes,' she said quickly, then with an anxious look added, 'you will come and get me though, won't you?'

'I'll bring you in the morning, take you home at lunchtime and the same at night. While I work, you can play. But we go home to our own bed to sleep.'

Victoria gave the matter a great deal of thought, looked at Betty who smiled at her, then at Daisy, still busy with her crayons. 'Yes, all right.'

'If you don't like it, you can tell me and then you won't come any more.'

Looking at Betty, Victoria asked, 'Can we do some more cooking?'

'Why, bless me, child, of course. I cook every day. When you come again, we'll make some biscuits and you can take some home to your mum.'

Lily took the woman aside. 'How much will you charge me for looking after her?'

'Two bob a week, that all right?'

Lily was relieved; she was expecting it to be more. She didn't know of course that George Coleman had set the price and would be paying Betty a little extra on the understanding she kept their deal to herself.

There was now no reason why Lily and Madge shouldn't look for somewhere to share. The hardest part was telling Rachel. As she ate her poached egg on toast that night, Lily broke the news to her.

Rachel's face fell. 'Oh, Lily. I'll miss you both, so.'

'I know, darling, but you'll have more money coming in. There will only be the two of you to feed so you'll be better off. My money will stretch a bit further, which means I can buy the things that Victoria needs – well, after I've saved up for them. We'll visit each other, often.'

'Perhaps Victoria can come and sleep over once in a while?'

Her dearest friend sounded so desolate that Lily put her arms around her and gave her a hug. 'Of course – she'd love that. And I love you, you old trout. You're an important part of our lives – and that will never change. Now put an advert in the corner shop, today. I won't leave, of course, until you find someone to take the room.' Lily hoped it wouldn't take long. Rachel's little house was uncomfortably crowded with Madge there as well.

It was only a few days before a gentleman called to see Rachel. He was a stevedore in the docks, earning good money, unmarried and looking for a home. He arranged to move in the following week.

Lily and Madge went searching for accommodation and found a two-up, two-down near the Mariner's. After bartering with the landlord over the price of the rent, they settled on six shillings a week, starting from the following Monday.

When he asked for a deposit, Lily laughed at him. 'Don't be bloody silly – this is the docklands! Nobody gives a deposit. You'll get your money good and regular – not like some.' And with that he had to be satisfied.

During their mid-morning break the following Monday, Madge and Lily, hindered by Victoria, scrubbed and cleaned their new abode. The furniture was shabby, but everything else shone. The range gleamed as Lily finished the blackleading with a hard brush. Rag rugs were beaten, all the curtains were washed and the beds made up with linen Lily had saved from the Valletta. She and Victoria were to share the double bed and Madge was to sleep in the smaller room.

'Blimey, Lily – a room of me own. The only time I've ever had a bed to meself was when I was doing time.'

'Now,' said Lily. 'Let's work it out. The rent will be three shillings each, which leaves nine and six out of our wages and whatever tips we make. We buy our own food and share the other bills.'

'Suits me,' said Madge. And so it was.

It was still a struggle. Children grow so quickly, but Lily exchanged their things at the second-hand clothing shop, taking Madge along with her as she needed another dress for work. Victoria settled with Betty and came home with things she'd made – a few biscuits and the odd slice or two of cake, compliments of Betty Logan. These luxuries were much appreciated, as the tight budget didn't allow for them. Now Lily was living much nearer, so the journey home at night carrying the sleeping child was much easier.

Rachel's lodger was soon at home and was happy to pay a little extra to have his washing done. As Rachel put his clothes through the mangle outside in the yard, she would gaze at the seaweed, hanging, and was surprised at how efficient it was at predicting the weather.

Whilst Lily was rearranging her life, Luke Longford was planning a few changes himself. He walked around the building in Cumberland Place to take a final look before making his decision. The surveyor's report had been satisfactory and there were no major constructional changes to be made. Even as he walked from room to room, he knew he'd buy it. He visualised every area, furbished with elegant furniture, deep drapes at the windows, fine tableware, uniformed staff. Excellent food cooked by chefs with the best references, the finest skills. Here he would entertain the top people – folk with money. Whatever the economic climate of the country, there would always be those with full coffers only too ready to spend if the surroundings were right. And his would be.

Having completed his final tour, he turned to the estate agent and said, 'Right. Let's go back to your office. Then we can talk money.'

Early the next evening, Luke called on Rachel expecting to find Lily at home and was surprised to hear about the move. Rachel explained the reason behind the arrangement and gave him Lily's new address, saying she thought it was her night off.

As he made his way to College Street, Luke was depressed at the sight of the drab houses that were so alike. The only thing that differed was the state of the curtains at the windows. Barefoot children played, bowling wooden hoops, oblivious to anything but their own childish delight. For all the people with money who he planned to entertain in his hotel, there were still so many living in abject poverty, and he wondered why Stanley Baldwin and his government didn't do something for them.

How dreadful for such a woman as Lily to live like this, he thought, and he thanked God that at a later date he would be able to take her out of such surroundings by offering her a decent wage and a job in the better part of town. It couldn't be good for Victoria to start the formative years of her life here. And it must certainly break Lily's heart not to be able to offer her something better.

He glanced at the address on the slip of paper that Rachel had given him. Just a few houses further. As he looked along the road, a door of a house opened and out stepped a large figure of a man and behind him, Lily.

He could hear their conversation. 'Thanks for coming, George. I'm so grateful to you.'

'Not at all, girl. You know you only have to ask, any time. It was great to see how the baby I knew has grown. Her father would be so proud of her.'

Luke arrived at the house as the caller walked away.

'Luke!' said Lily with surprise. 'When did you dock?'

'Yesterday,' he said, watching the retreating figure. 'Is everything all right?'

Lily followed the direction of his gaze. 'Yes. Why?'

With a frown Luke said, 'He looks a real rough diamond.'

There was a sudden coolness in her attitude as Lily told him: 'He's an old and valued friend who used to work for Vittorio. You'd better come in.'

He quickly noted the tone of her voice and wisely said no more. As he was invited to take a seat, he glanced around the room. If anything, this place was worse than Rachel's. It was very clean, but that didn't alter the fact that the furniture, unlike Rachel's, was cheap and shabby.

Victoria could be heard upstairs chattering to someone, for

he could hear an answering voice. 'The little one sounds fine,' he said. 'Is she well?'

'Much better. Almost back to normal,' Lily answered with a smile.

At that moment the child herself wandered down the stairs, followed by a young woman who grinned broadly at him and said, 'Hello. Fancy seeing you again.'

There was indeed something familiar about her, but he couldn't place who she was. 'Have we met?'

'Yes,' said Madge, sitting at the table. 'When you visited Lily in Brookmans.'

'Oh, then.' At the back of his mind was a vague recollection of seeing her there. 'Were you visiting too?'

Madge laughed heartily. 'Lord bless you, no. I was an inmate! I shared a cell with Lily.'

Lily saw the look of consternation on the face of her visitor.

Madge got to her feet and said, 'I've got to pop to the local shop. I'll take Victoria with me, if you like.'

Lily agreed. When they'd gone, she turned to Luke and asked, 'What's wrong?'

'Is that young lady the person Rachel said you were sharing with?'

'Yes, what about it?'

'Do you think that's wise, to consort with a criminal? I'd have thought you wouldn't have wanted anything to remind you of that awful time.'

Lily's eyes blazed with anger. 'You have no idea, Luke Longford, what life in prison is like. Yes, it *was* a bloody awful time. You wouldn't believe what it was like. The cruelty and hardship that goes on. The perverted practices. I had a run-in with one of the screws who was a dyke. She hated my guts because I turned her down. She made my life hell and her girlfriend was so jealous she tried to kill me!'

He was shocked. 'Oh my God!'

'Let me tell you, if it wasn't for Madge and Hetty, who saved my life, I wouldn't be here now. They were my only friends.'

He tried to placate her. 'I'm sorry, Lily. I didn't mean to upset you. I'm sure you have every reason to be grateful to her. What was her crime, if I may ask?'

'Madge was a petty thief. Anyway, she's going straight now. I've got her a job at the Mariner's Hotel.'

'I admire your loyalty,' he said quietly, 'but I've been around, and I know that sometimes, people can let you down. I wouldn't like to see you get hurt.'

His genuine concern stemmed her anger. 'It's kind of you to worry about me, but sometimes in life, you have to have trust in someone. I think Madge has earned mine. Anyway – how was your trip?'

'Busy, but I really came to tell you that the surveyor's report on that property in Cumberland Place was satisfactory, so I've decided to buy it!' He couldn't hide the pride mirrored in his eyes, and Lily was really happy for him.

'That's wonderful – congratulations! Was it the place that used to be the Regent Hotel?'

'Yes, it is. It's quite big. I have great plans for it, Lily, but there's a lot to do. It needs redecorating from top to toe. The wiring has to be thoroughly checked and there are a few minor constructional changes that I want to make. But I really do need your help.'

She leaned back in her seat. 'You do? In what way?'

'I saw the Club Valletta, remember? You have a flair for décor and an eye for colour; I was really impressed. I want you to look around my place and give suggestions. I have several ideas of my own but I need you to help me with it.

What do you say? First of all I want your thoughts on the colour scheme. Then we have to see the place repainted and papered. Eventually we shall need new carpets, curtains, all new linen, cutlery, china, et cetera.' He laughed. 'What am I saying? We require everything! Furniture, beds – the lot! I need you desperately, Lily.'

With a note of anxiety in her voice she said, 'But Luke, you know I can't. What if your residents found out I have a prison record? It wouldn't be very good for your reputation – the reputation of the hotel.'

She noted the firmness in his jaw as he said, 'Let me worry about that.'

She shook her head slowly and touching his face gently she said, 'I know what it's like to have a dream, Luke. To see it come to fruition, only to have it destroyed before your eyes. It's devastating. I couldn't be responsible for that happening to you. I couldn't!'

He caught hold of her wrist and softly kissed the palm of her hand. 'Let me tell you about my dream, Lily.' She saw the brightness of his green eyes as he began. 'When I was sixteen, I joined the Cunard Company as a bellboy.'

Seeing the tall elegant figure reclining before her, Lily couldn't help but smile. 'You mean you wore one of those tight buttoned suits with a pillbox hat?'

He grinned at her. 'Indeed I did, and jolly smart I looked too. From that first day I had a vision of this big hotel – *my* hotel. A place of style, for people with taste and money to spend on the finest food, the best wines, superb service. I rose up through the catering division until I was a first-class waiter, wine waiter, Second Steward and up to my current lofty position as Chief Steward.' There was a twinkle in his eyes now. 'I saved every penny. One of my passengers was from the Vanderbilt family, the American millionaires. He wanted me to go to America and work as his majordomo, but I said no. When he knew what my plan was, he advised me about making money on the American stock market.'

'Blimey!' Lily's eyes opened wide. 'But that can be very risky.'

'True, but I was well advised and I made a lot of money. I'm now thirty-four. I know what I want, I can afford what I want, and I intend to have it. Nothing can stop me. My hotel will be the best, will have the best of everything . . . *you* are the best, Lily. And you are vital to my success. You can't turn me down.'

As Lily gazed at Luke, he reminded her in many ways of Vittorio. He had stature, presence, determination. But here, Luke was different. His travels had given him polish. Class. He spoke beautifully, in a firm determined voice, with just a trace of a Liverpudlian accent. He was a man who would command respect – demand it, even. And if he was as wealthy as he said – and he must be to have bought this property – he would have the financial strength to withstand anything. Even her prison record. The idea was exciting. Challenging. Then she remembered Eddie Chapman.

'But you know I have a job at the moment.'

'Is that a problem?'

She pursed her lips. 'To me it is. This man gave me a start, knowing I'd recently come out of prison. I'm not going to dump him, just like that.'

Luke considered this dilemma for a while then said, 'Look, at first I just need you to help me choose the colour schemes. There will be masses to do before I really need you all the time. Stay with your boss, but warn him about the future move. What do you say? It'll give him time to get organised.'

She paused. 'I do have Victoria's future to think of. And

this would be such a wonderful challenge. Something I'd really like to do.'

Luke didn't try to push her but waited patiently.

'All right,' she said suddenly. 'I'll do it. When do you sail again?'

'I left the Cunard Company as soon as the surveyor passed the place. I have just finished my last trip. I swallowed the anchor, as we seafarers say! Now I can dedicate all my time to getting things under way.'

Lily thought about it with a feeling of excitement in the pit of her stomach. She longed to do it, to get back into the environment where she felt most comfortable. She was used to dealing with all classes. Some of her old clients had been toffs. That didn't faze her, she could mix with them all, and it would take her away from the docklands, into the posh area of the town. No more seedy rooms and seedy clients. A new start for her, but most importantly for Victoria. And she wanted to see more of this charismatic man. For the first time since Vittorio's death, here was someone who interested her, and she knew she wasn't immune to his charm.

She smiled at him. 'I'll have a word with Eddie tomorrow morning,' she promised.

Luke held her hands between his and looked into her eyes. The intensity of his gaze was disconcerting, but he didn't comment about the sudden flush to her cheeks. 'Thank you, Lily. You won't regret it, I promise you. You and I are going to do great things together. We'll make a formidable team, you just see.' He took her into his arms. 'I've thought about you a lot whilst I've been away. The voyage seemed endless. I couldn't wait to get home. To see you.'

He pulled her towards him and kissed her gently. 'I hope you thought of me once in a while.'

'Of course I did,' she murmured as his lips again covered hers.

'Come out with me,' he said eagerly. 'I've packed all my stuff and moved into the Dolphin Hotel until my place is ready. Come and have dinner with me. Let's celebrate, talk, then perhaps we can get to know each other even better.'

'I can't, Luke. There's Victoria.'

'Of course, how foolish of me to forget,' he apologised. 'Can I pick you up after work tomorrow morning instead . . . and Victoria too, naturally. Then we could take a look at the hotel and discuss the colour schemes and the wallpaper.' He held her hands in his. 'I really do value your opinion, Lily.'

Despite his suave exterior and air of confidence, she sensed in him a frisson of uncertainty and could appreciate his feelings. When she was doing up the Club Valletta she would have liked a second opinion to assure her her choices were right. She smiled at him. 'Just after ten o'clock will be fine.'

At that moment Madge and Victoria returned.

Luke took from his pocket a box of American candies and gave them to the child and another small packet, wrapped in exquisite paper, for Lily. 'I hope you like it,' he said, and opened the door. 'Until tomorrow then.'

As Lily closed the door behind him, Madge rushed forward. 'Open it! I'm dying to see what he's brought you.'

Inside the wrapping was a bottle of Chanel No. 5. Lily started to chuckle.

'What's so funny?' asked Madge.

'Here we are, living in squalor and I'm going to be wearing Chanel!'

'Listen, love,' said Madge. 'You play your cards right and you'll be moving back up in the world.'

Lily helped Victoria unwrap her sweets and wondered if

perhaps Madge was right. It would be nice.

'He fancies you something rotten, you know,' said Madge with a cheeky grin. 'I saw the way he looked at you.'

'For goodness' sake behave!' Lily chided as she began to prepare a meal. But she hoped that her friend was right in her assumption.

Luke was a little disappointed as he walked away. He'd so been looking forward to sharing a celebration with Lily, but of course he realised, with a small child, a social life would be difficult. He frowned as he thought about the man leaving Lily's as he arrived and wondered just what such a person did in the employ of Victoria's father. What sort of business was he involved with? If ever a man looked as if he were a villain, that one did.

But then Luke gave a slow smile of contentment. When Lily worked for him he'd see more of her – much more. He was still intrigued by this woman. And still as mystified. He had this mental picture of her – of an elegant woman in beautiful clothes, set against sophisticated surroundings – which was how she had looked when first he'd met her. He found it hard to relate to the same woman living in such a drab household in this godforsaken area. As soon as he took her away from here, then once again she would be the woman he had in his fantasy. His Lily.

Chapter Fifteen

Lily was very impressed as she was shown around the old Regent Hotel by Luke the next morning. He showed her all the bedrooms on the two floors upstairs before they inspected the public rooms downstairs.

'I want to make an opening here, knock the two rooms into one,' he said, 'and turn this into a reading-cum-smoking room. I want a real masculine feel to it.'

'Then I suggest you have big leather chairs,' said Lily immediately. 'Heavy flocked wallpaper, wall lights and a nice log fire in the winter, with brass fire dogs and a fender. Low tables and table-lamps, but bright enough to read by. A deep rich maroon-coloured carpet, pictures on the wall . . . hunting scenes would be nice.'

He looked at her in astonishment. 'How can you do that?'

'What?'

'See everything so clearly?'

'I don't honestly know,' she admitted.

They studied the colour charts from the paint companies and pored over books of wallpaper patterns. She was impressed by his choice. Luke wasn't going to stint on anything.

Victoria sat on the floor looking at the pretty paper, telling them which ones she liked, which amused them considerably.

They discussed the type of furnishings for each of the rooms and Luke told her he knew of an antiques warehouse in London which sold furniture from stately homes and old Cunard stock as well. 'I'll go there and see what they have whilst all the preparation goes on.'

Lily walked into the foyer and gazed out of the window across the park. She was excited at the prospect of the job ahead. It was one she would relish ... but her joy was cut short as in the distance she saw the parked truck belonging to Quinn Gifford. Her heart seemed to miss a beat and she turned away quickly.

'What is it, Lily?' Luke asked, seeing the sudden change in her expression. He too looked out of the window, but to him everything seemed normal.

'Nothing,' she said. 'Someone just walked over my grave, that's all.'

But as they left the hotel, she glanced over her shoulder to see the truck pull away and the grinning figure of the gypsy, sitting at the steering wheel. Waving to her as he passed by.

George Coleman had had enough. He knew that Quinn had been stalking Lily and despite her protestations, he felt it was time this fellow was taught a lesson. And the sooner the better.

Frank and Charlie, two of George Coleman's men, were waiting for their boss in the bar of the Glasgow Hotel in the Southampton docklands. Charlie looked across the room at a couple of the local prostitutes. One of them met his gaze and with an inviting smile, got up from her seat and walked towards him.

'She's got you picked out as her next punter,' warned Frank.

Charlie leered at his mate. 'I wouldn't mind giving her a

good screwing, if I had the time.'

Frank looked at her with disdain. 'She'd look a damn sight better if she had a good wash and combed her hair,' he retorted.

'Hello, darlin',' said the young girl, sidling up to Charlie. She eyed him up and down then squeezed his biceps. 'My, but you're a big fellow. Nice muscles.' She rubbed herself up against him and slipped her hand down to his crotch. 'Or are you all mouth and trousers?'

He put his hand on her plump bottom. 'I've got more than enough to satisfy you, girl,' he boasted.

At that moment George Coleman walked into the bar. Everyone stepped aside to allow him to pass. It was like the opening of the Red Sea – such was the man's reputation. 'On your way,' he said to the girl. 'We men need to talk.'

Miffed at being done out of a likely punter, the girl glared at him. 'And what if I don't want to go?'

'Piss off before you get into trouble,' he threatened.

Her friend rushed over and grabbing her by the arm, dragged her away. 'Don't be a bloody fool. That's George Coleman!'

'Oh shit!' exclaimed the girl and sat down, her complexion turning pale.

George ordered a pint of beer and then said, 'We have a job to do. Someone is giving a friend of mine a lot of aggro and has to be stopped.'

'Stopped permanently?' asked Charlie.

'No, just given a warning.'

'Anyone we know?' Frank asked.

'Yes, you know him,' said George, taking a drink of his beer. 'Quinn Gifford. The gypsy.'

'Bloody hell,' said Charlie. 'He's a mad bugger when he's riled. How are we going about this, guv?'

'Well, it has to be today. There's an important horse-sale on in Ringwood this afternoon and I know for a fact he'll be there because I rang the farm earlier today saying I wanted to buy a horse. I've arranged to meet him.' He smiled to himself. 'Under a false name, of course.'

Frank grinned. 'Of course . . . So what's the plan?'

'We'll just have to pick our moment. I want to get him away on his own, without the brothers seeing. I've no quarrel with them. Then we'll take Quinn back to my warehouse in the docks and deal with him. Make him see sense.'

'How much sense?' asked Charlie.

'Oh, he'll see reason by the time we're done with him. But don't get too carried away. We don't want to snuff him.' He finished his beer. 'Come on then, we'd best be on our way.' He looked across at the young prostitute and then at Charlie. 'Christ! Can't you do better than that?' He strode out of the bar.

There was a huge crowd at the horse-sale. Horse-boxes filled the car park. Gentlemen farmers, horse-trainers, breeders and ordinary family members wandered around the ground. Gypsies with their colourful caravans were there too, and notices were placed outside one announcing that Madame Lillian would read the crystal ball for one shilling and sixpence. Or Gypsy Lee would foretell the future, at another. Home-made pegs were being sold as well as lucky heather. Hurdy-gurdy men were winding their music machines, churning out tinny tunes, others were selling balloons to the children. An Italian ice-cream man called his wares from a cart. The place had a festive air about it.

Inside one large building was a selling ring, and when George and his men arrived, they could hear the auctioneer already into the bidding. They wandered around until they saw the Gifford brothers watching.

Quinn bid for a fine white stallion and stayed with the sale until his was the highest offer. George saw the look of satisfaction on his swarthy face as he went to pay for the horse.

George gave the nod to his men and they followed Quinn out of the building. They watched as he went to collect the handsome beast. Saw him pat the horse, talk to it, feed it a carrot until he took hold of the halter and led it away.

They followed behind at a distance.

Bart and Jake were just unloading two ponies as Quinn waited. They admired their new acquisition.

'You did well there, brother,' said Jake.

Quinn just muttered, 'You take these two to the ring, while I load this beauty. I'll come back in and see what price we get on the ponies.'

George sent one of his men over to Quinn.

'Lovely animal you've got there,' said Frank. 'Can I have a look at him?'

Thinking he might be able to make a quick profit, Quinn allowed him into the horse-box.

Frank stroked the horse's flanks, felt his back legs then his front. 'Seems sound enough,' he said. 'Is he for sale?'

'Might be,' growled Quinn. 'If the price is right.'

The two men haggled over the sale until Frank appeared to reluctantly give in. 'All right. I think you've asked a bit over the odds,' he complained, 'but my boss could use him as a hunter. He's got a few quid, he can afford it.' He spat on the palm of his hand and held it out to Quinn. With a sly grin, Quinn repeated the gesture on his own hand and they shook on the deal.

'You'll have to come with me,' said Frank casually. 'My boss is over yonder, and he's the one with the cash.'

Quinn followed willingly and was taken completely by surprise as two men jumped on him, covering his head with a blanket, and rammed him into the back of a van.

Later that night, Quinn Gifford moaned with pain as he dragged himself along the quayside on his stomach. His face was swollen and he couldn't see out of one eye. He was sure a couple of his ribs were broken. He tried to stand, but the pain in his ankle made him cry out as he put his weight on it. Those bastards had broken it. He managed to get to his feet and leaned against a wall and held his side as he tried to breathe. It was agony.

He heard footsteps approaching, and fearful that George Coleman had returned, he pressed his back against the wall – and it was like this that the docks policeman found him.

He shone a torch in Quinn's face. 'Bloody hell!' he exclaimed when he saw his bruised and swollen features. 'What happened to you?' He blew his whistle to summon help.

'No, don't do that,' the gypsy protested.

'Now then, lad, best we get you to hospital. Can you walk?'

Quinn shook his head. 'Me ankle's busted.'

'Who did this to you?' asked the constable.

'I don't know,' he lied. 'Two men jumped me. After me money, I expect.'

The constable went through his pockets and frowned. He held out a wad of notes. 'How do you explain this then?'

'Perhaps they were disturbed. How the bloody hell should I know? Look at me! I can't remember everything that happened. I must have passed out.'

But he did remember, clearly. He knew who George Coleman was the minute he saw him, just before they threw a blanket over him at the horse-sale. He struggled in the back of the van, to no avail, thinking they were going to rob him, but when they eventually arrived at their destination, the real reason for his kidnap became apparent.

The three of them carried him kicking and fighting to the warehouse where they strapped him in a chair, then George stood in front of him.

'I believe you're being a nuisance to a friend of mine,' accused Coleman. 'I know you've been following Miss Lily Pickford and she's pissed off about it and rightly so. Now we can't have that, can we?' He hit Quinn across the mouth.

Quinn's anger was roused. 'Mind your own bloody business!' he yelled at the big man and got another thump for his cheek.

George looked at him with an ice-cold expression in his eyes. 'For my money I'd do for you and throw you in the docks, but Miss Lily won't hear of it. All she wants is to be left alone.' He kicked Quinn in the shin. 'Do I make myself clear?'

Quinn spat at him and struggled to break the bonds that held him, tipping the chair over. He was kicked in the ribs by Charlie as he lay on the ground; Frank then hauled him and the chair in an upright position.

'Now don't be a fool,' said George. 'I can beat you to within an inch of your life, leave you in such a way that you won't be any use to any woman . . . ever! Is that what you want?'

For once Quinn kept his head, knowing the man wasn't making an idle threat. He knew his reputation. 'No, I don't want that,' he growled.

With a cruel smile George said, 'I'm glad you're being sensible. But just to make sure, my boys will have to teach you a lesson. Then maybe you'll leave that poor girl alone.'

He nodded to Charlie and Frank and walked away. Then the beating began in earnest.

The ambulance arrived at the quayside and Quinn was placed carefully on a stretcher and taken to the South Hants Hospital. There his wounds were bathed and stitched, his ribs strapped up and his ankle put in plaster.

All the time he was being attended to, his anger festered.

The doctors decided to keep him in overnight, under observation. The dark hours seemed to stretch endlessly, the pain he was suffering, despite his medication, keeping him awake. But he spent his time, fuming and scheming.

George Coleman and his men had done their work well, but it didn't deter him. He wanted Lily more than ever now. She owed him. He'd taken a beating for her and he intended to be paid for it. He'd have to wait until his ankle was healed, but that was fine. It would give him time to plan. He tried to smile, but his face hurt too much. He'd thought of a way to ensure she'd come to him. But first he'd have to get fit.

The following day, he rang his brother Jake and asked him to collect him from the hospital. When Jake walked into the ward and saw Quinn, he was horrified.

'Christ Almighty! What the bleedin' hell happened to you? When you disappeared at the show, I thought you'd gone off to the pub.'

'Never mind that,' snapped Quinn. 'Help me out of this place – I want to go home. Then in time, I'll pay Lily Pickford back for this, 'cos she was behind it.'

'I don't understand you, Quinn,' Jake sighed. 'Lily Pickford ain't that special. There are plenty of other women you can have . . . forget her, mate.'

Quinn didn't answer, but took a cheroot from his pocket and lit it. Forget Lily? Never!

★ ★ ★

Detective Inspector Chadwick sat behind his desk at the Hampshire Constabulary and studied the report before him. He lit his pipe and puffed away on it with a satisfied smile. At last he could make his move. It had taken months of detective work, secretly following Gates and his own Sergeant, liaising with the London police. Informants had been paid, evidence gathered, and tonight, after midnight, his group of detectives, aided by the uniformed division, would strike.

He sat back in his chair. He couldn't wait to tell Lily Pickford, but he knew that until everything was covered and the raid successful, nothing was certain. Even the best-laid plans could backfire, he'd seen that for himself many a time. But not this time, he hoped. This time there should be no slip-ups.

That bloody Gates was a crafty bastard. He'd been very clever in covering his tracks and it was only that Sergeant Green had let something slip in a drunken conversation with one of his snouts that they had been able to piece things together.

Not only was Gates mixed up in a fraud with his dodgy roulette tables and marked cards, but he'd been smuggling in pornographic photographs from abroad. Dirty bugger! Chadwick had seen some of them. He and his detectives had had a laugh as they studied them.

'Bloody hell!' exclaimed one of his officers. 'If I tried that with my wife, I'd break my bleedin' neck.' And although it had given them all some amusement, there had been many showing sexual deviations that had turned all their stomachs. And the ones showing the abuse of small children sickened him. Chadwick was furious that this filth was being distributed around the streets on his patch. The ones sent to London were someone else's headache. But here, it was his.

He looked at his watch. Only another four hours to go. There were to be similar raids on local gambling houses and the same in London, all of whom were knowingly using the fixed tables. When all the dodgy dealers were brought to justice, no doubt all would name Gates in an effort to save their own skins. Pleading ignorance, as Lily had done. The only difference was that she was an innocent pawn, whereas the others were villains. It was to be quite a coup.

Two days later, DI Chadwick made his way to the Mariner's Hotel, a jaunty bounce in his stride. He couldn't wait to tell Lily the good news. As soon as he entered the hotel he was surprised at the change in the place. He knew it well. The police had been called to many an affray here over the years and he'd watched the hotel deteriorate. Now the reception area was freshly painted, a new carpet had been laid, and he grinned as he noted the flowers on the desk. That had to be Lily's touch.

The newly employed receptionist smiled pleasantly at him. 'Good morning, sir. Can I help you?'

My, he thought, things *are* looking up. 'I would like to speak with Miss Pickford, please.'

'Certainly, sir. What name shall I give?'

'Detective Inspector Chadwick.' He saw the look of alarm in her eyes. 'I'm an old friend of hers,' he added, and hid a smile at the relief on her pretty face.

The girl hurried away and soon returned with Lily.

He grinned broadly at her. 'I've got a bit of good news for you,' he said.

She looked puzzled for a moment. 'Come into the dining room,' she said, 'we'll have a bit of privacy there. Would you like a cup of coffee?'

'Yes, thanks. That would be very welcome.'

Heather the receptionist went to make it whilst Chadwick followed Lily. Inside the dining room, again he was impressed. The tables were laid, the tablecloths clean and the room looked inviting.

'Bloody hell, Lily. This place has taken on a new lease of life.'

She smiled happily at the compliment. 'What news have you got, then? You've made me very curious.'

'Percy Gates has been caught at last. As we speak he's locked in a cell awaiting trial.'

'No!'

Seeing the look of complete surprise on her face, he chuckled. 'I promised you I'd bring that bugger to justice, didn't I?'

There was a sudden expression of sadness in her eyes as she said, 'Yes, you did. What a pity it couldn't have happened sooner.'

They stopped talking as Heather brought in the coffee. When once again they were alone, he said, 'I'm really sorry you had to go inside. But Bill, the croupier who put you in the frame, has finally come good. He's willing to give evidence against Gates, which will leave you in the clear. Your good name will be restored.'

Lily didn't look as ecstatic as he'd anticipated. 'But at what cost, Mr Chadwick? My name might be cleared, but people will always remember that I spent six months in prison. They won't be interested that it was all a mistake – you know what folk are like. I'll always have that stain on my character.'

With a heavy heart, he knew that she spoke the truth.

Seeing his happiness fade, Lily felt a touch of guilt. After all, this lovely man had tried hard to bring Gates to justice as he had promised. Another detective might not have been so resolute. She put a hand on his arm. 'Thanks a million. You've done a great job.' There was a sudden fire of anger in her eyes. 'I hope that bugger has a hard time inside. He bloody well deserves it.'

'Don't you worry about that, Lily love. Rumour has it that he screwed one of the London villains for a lot of money. Being inside isn't going to save him from retribution, take my word for it.'

Lily was pleased to hear this. She felt no sympathy for the man who had lost her her freedom and been the cause of the suffering of her child. She hoped he'd get his just deserts.

Chadwick looked around. 'This place looks fine now but it isn't the Valletta, is it, love?'

She shook her head then she brightened. 'No, but I've got myself another job. A friend of mine has bought the old Regent Hotel and wants me to be his manageress.'

'Oh yes,' said Chadwick. 'I've been hearing about the chap. Sounds a real go-getter, just what Southampton needs. Well, my dear, I wish you luck.' He paused. 'You may be required to appear in court though, when Gates's case comes up.'

Lily's expression hardened. 'I'll be there, called or not. I want to see the bastard walk down the steps to the cells. I know how he'll be feeling and I want to be there to see it for myself.'

Chadwick grinned at her. 'Revenge is sweet, eh, Lily?'

'It bloody well is!' she replied. 'And I'm going to enjoy every moment of it. And whilst we're on the subject, what's happening about The Protection of Children Society? I haven't heard a thing about it.'

'We're building up a dossier.' He looked angry. 'Your Gladys Parker has a history of mental cruelty, and I'm afraid there are one or two others among the foster parents who haven't looked after their charges as they should. One of their inspectors will want to speak to Victoria in the near future, then we can take all the documents to the Director. He'll be forced to hold an enquiry.'

'About time too. It makes my blood boil every time I think about that woman.'

'Never mind, Lily. Everything is getting sorted, and you have a new job. Perhaps things are turning in your favour again.'

She grinned at him. 'I hope you're right.'

As Roger Chadwick walked away he hoped so too, for her sake. She'd been through a great deal for such a lovely young woman. It didn't seem fair. But sadly, that was life.

Chapter Sixteen

Lily had put off telling Eddie about her impending move, but knew she'd have to face up to it. She knocked on his office door and entered.

'What can I do for you, Lily?' he asked.

She sat down in what was now a very tidy and clean office. 'I've got the offer of another job and I have to take it. It's too good to turn down.'

There was a look of disappointment on his face. 'Tell me about it.'

She told him about Luke, the new hotel, and what she would be doing there. He smiled kindly at her. 'Good for you, girl. Let's face it, you don't belong here, especially after the Club Valletta.'

She looked at him in surprise; she'd never told him where she was from.

With a chuckle Eddie explained. 'I picked up the cutting from the paper that Dolly was waving around the day she quit. Funny, you know, I never twigged you were *that* Lily Pickford. Bloody stupid when you think about it. I suppose I didn't expect anyone like you to come to my place.'

'You gave me a fresh start,' said Lily. 'I'll never forget you for that. But I won't be leaving just yet. Luke has a lot to do before he needs me full-time. I'll let you know when.'

'Well, Lily my dear, you've smartened this place up.' He looked around the office and with a wry smile added, 'And me too. I owe you. But if you're leaving, you've just helped me to make a decision that I was dithering over.'

'And what's that?'

'I'm going to put the Mariner's on the market. Sell it. It looks pretty decent now, the clients are better, not so rough and ready and business is good. I'll take my doctor's advice, which will give him a surprise, and I'll retire.'

She was pleased for him. 'I think that's a wise decision. But keep in touch. You'll come to the new hotel when it opens, won't you?'

He grinned broadly at her. 'I'll get my best suit out of mothballs for the occasion.'

Luke rang Lily at the hotel later that morning and asked if there was any way she could be free for the evening. 'I know it's difficult with Victoria,' he said, 'but there's a dinner dance at the Dolphin this evening and I'd love to take you. You did tell me you had tonight off.'

Hearing his voice over the telephone made Lily long to see him. He'd been busy this past week and she kept wondering how things were going. She would love to go. It had been so long since she'd been anywhere, and she did have one evening dress left, hanging in her wardrobe. 'I'll ask Rachel to look after Victoria,' she said. 'She does have her to sleep over on occasion.'

'Wonderful! You mean I'll have you all to myself?'

She laughed. 'Yes, and I won't have to worry about my daughter.'

'I'll pick you up at seven-thirty.'

Rachel was only too delighted to oblige and after she had delivered Victoria to her friend, Lily rushed home to get ready. As she strip-washed in the scullery, she longed for the use of a decent bath and bathroom, remembering in times past when she'd soaked in hers with scented crystals in the water instead of the tin bath in front of the fire on a Friday.

She put on her black sequinned evening dress and a cheap paste arm bracelet she'd bought from the Penny Bazaar in a moment of madness, when she'd purchased a child's umbrella for Victoria. Luke would never know it was fake and it set off the dress beautifully. She no longer had any earrings, having sold all of her jewellery, but it didn't matter. She used the Chanel No. 5 he'd bought her and thought at last she would be wearing it in appropriate surroundings.

Luke arrived promptly and Lily left the house, locking the door behind her, and climbed into his car. He put his arm around her and kissed her cheek.

'You look enchanting,' he said softly.

The evening lived up to her expectations. The dinner was excellent, she especially enjoyed the Duck à l'orange and Peach Melba. The wine was good and the conversation fascinating. Luke was an excellent companion. He amused her, flattered her, intrigued her. And when he took her in his arms at the edge of the dance-floor, she felt she was in heaven. He was a wonderful dancer, moving around the floor so fluidly, his arm firm about her waist, leading her into the steps, steering her expertly around the other couples.

He didn't speak, but she could feel the warmth of his hand in the small of her back, his warm skin as his face brushed hers. The smell of his shaving lotion invaded her nostrils and she was aware of his strong body aligned with hers.

It was both wonderful and disconcerting. Yes, he'd kissed her before, but tonight she felt the full blast of his masculinity. How handsome he looked in his dinner jacket. How well he held himself. How much strength there was in his face.

She'd been attracted to him from the moment he'd walked into the Club Valletta, but whenever they'd met since, other things had got in the way. Prison, Victoria, her job. This was the first time they'd been together, by themselves. This was a real man and she wondered just how it would be to be really close to him, and felt herself go hot at the thought.

As the band played the 'Last Waltz', he held her close, his face against hers, his fingers caressing her back as they danced around the room. Her spine tingled at his touch and when they left the ballroom and he suggested a nightcap in his room, she went willingly.

He unlocked his door. The room was large, with a sitting area as well as a double bed. On a table in front of a small settee was an ice bucket with a bottle of champagne in it, waiting to be opened.

Luke drew her slowly to him and enfolded her into his warm embrace. 'Come here,' he murmured.

She revelled in his kisses, putting her arms around him, running her fingers through the short dark hair at the nape of his neck.

'Lily, oh Lily,' he whispered against her ear as he nuzzled it. 'I've wanted to do this all evening and once or twice I nearly did.' His mouth covered hers.

At last he released her and led her to the settee. He took the bottle of champagne, held it in a linen napkin and twisted it open; with a pop, the cork flew out. He filled the two glasses and handed her one, sitting beside her, his arm about her shoulders.

'To us,' he said, and clinked his glass against hers.

'To us . . . and the hotel,' she replied, and sipped from hers.

Luke put his glass down, removed his jacket, undid his bow tie and the top two buttons of his shirt. 'That's better.' He softly stroked her cheek. 'You look wonderful tonight. I'm so happy we could be together. Ever since we first met, you seem to be surrounded by other people. Now I have you all to myself.' He took her drink from her hand and put it on the table, then took her into his arms and kissed her again.

The feel of his mouth on hers stirred within Lily feelings she'd long forgotten. It had been almost four years since a man had held her, kissed her like this, and she knew what it could lead to. For a moment she tensed. She felt the gentle probing of his tongue as he teased her into a response. And at last she relaxed, slipped her fingers inside his open shirt and stroked his chest.

Luke smoothed her face softly, ran his fingers through her hair and said, 'We are going to have so much fun together in the future, you have no idea.'

'That would be nice,' she murmured, snuggled against him.

He lifted her chin until she looked into his eyes. 'Lily,' he whispered, 'I don't want this night to end like this. I want to take you to bed, hold you close, feel your smooth body against mine, touch you, tease you, make love to you. Will you let me?'

'Oh yes,' she whispered.

He rose from the settee and taking her by the hand, led her over to the bed. He slowly undressed her, caressing her as he undid the back of the dress and slipped it over her head. Picking her up in his strong arms, he placed her carefully on the bed and lay beside her. Gathering her to him, smoothing her bare shoulders, her hips, the soft mound of her stomach as he rained kisses on her, leaving her breathless and wanting more.

He took off her undergarments then his shirt, his trousers and when he too was naked, he pulled her to him, his bare skin against hers. He murmured words of love and desire as he nuzzled her neck, kissed her eyes, her mouth, her throat, her breasts.

Lily lay in his arms, the heat of desire rising from her depths as she returned his caresses, feeling beneath her sensitive fingers the strength of the man, his broad shoulders, muscular arms, his slender waist and slim hips.

As he gently cupped her left breast in his hand and suckled on her pert nipple, she gave a moan of delight, and when he slid his hand to her inner thighs and spread her legs, she was lost.

He softly brushed the triangle of curled hair and murmured hoarsely, 'Lily, I want you so much.' He rolled over and was astride her, after quickly fitting a condom to protect her. She arched her back to accommodate him as he slipped inside her.

She was floating in a world of passion, letting her needs carry her along this tide of love, matching his thrusting with her own until with a cry, she came.

Above her, head thrown back, Luke reached his own pinnacle, and exhausted, lowered his body onto hers. She could feel the heat of their bodies intermingle, as she opened her eyes and gazed into his.

He lay beside her, holding her close, stroking her hair. 'You are a wonderful woman. I think I began to fall in love with you the night I walked into the Club Valletta. When this elegant and beautiful woman walked over to our table, I was hooked. You have something about you, Lily darling, that gets under a man's skin. And tonight, you proved you are the woman for me.'

Lily's emotions were in turmoil. She was still under the spell of his lovemaking, yet when Luke declared his love for her, she was filled with dread. She could no longer hide her past from him. She had to be sure that he loved her for herself, not for the woman he believed her to be. How strong a man was he? Was his love deep enough to cope with it? She had to know.

'Luke,' she said as she ran her finger over his lips, 'there are things I have to say, before we go any further.'

He rose from the bed and grabbing a bath towel, put it around his waist. He sat on the bed, caressing her breast. 'What on earth do you mean?'

She caught hold of his hand to still the sensuous touch. Sitting up, she pulled the bedsheet up to cover her nakedness. 'There's a lot about me that you don't know.'

'The past is behind us, darling. The future is what is important now.'

'Luke! Will you *please* listen?'

He looked surprised at her insistence. 'I'm listening,' he said.

Taking a deep breath Lily began. 'My father, who'd abused me for years, kicked me out of the house on the eve of my sixteenth birthday. For a while I had to live on the streets, sleep rough. Rachel gave me a job but I was forced to leave, because her son Manny found out about my dad and threatened to tell him my whereabouts.' She saw Luke's smile fade. 'I was starving,' she went on quietly. 'I had no means of earning money. To buy food I had to sell my body.'

There was horror reflected in his eyes now.

'Please believe me, I hated every moment! When a stranger touched me, I felt dirty, degraded. But I didn't want to starve to death . . . I wanted to live!'

He didn't answer.

She held her head high. There was nothing left to hide now; she might as well continue. 'I lived with an ex-con, a pickpocket called Fred, for a while, who rescued me from the streets, but he died. Then I became the mistress of Vittorio Teglia, Victoria's father.'

'But I assumed you were married to him!'

'We were to be married, but he died too,' she explained.

Luke's jaw tightened. 'What business was he in?' he asked, remembering the tough character he'd seen calling on Lily.

Her gaze didn't falter. 'He ran a club that was a front for gambling and prostitution.'

Luke closed his eyes. 'Oh my God!' he said.

Lily felt sick inside when she saw the expression on his face. There was no flicker of love there now. No affection. Just a cold set look. A furrowed brow. Silence.

She got out of bed and slowly dressed, saying nothing.

He stood up. 'I'll drive you home,' he said.

'No. Just get me a taxi. I think that's for the best.'

He rang the reception and ordered a car. He quickly dressed and took her to the hotel entrance and paid the driver. As she was about to get into the back seat, he caught hold of her arm.

'I need some time to think, Lily,' he said.

She just nodded, unable to speak. She didn't turn and look at him but stared straight ahead through misty eyes at the back of the driver's head as he drove away.

Luke returned to his room, poured himself a glass of champagne, lit a cigarette and sat down. He was completely shattered by Lily's revelations. He'd wondered from time to time about her past, but he'd never imagined it had been quite so colourful. Having just made love to her, he couldn't bear to think that others had paid her money to do the same. The very idea sickened him. He closed his eyes to try to shut out the images that filled his mind. He got up and started to pace the room.

He should feel pity for her, forced as she was to fend for herself. He couldn't imagine her sleeping rough, not his elegant Lily. And she'd lived with two other men! He shook his head as if to clear it. What was he to do? He grabbed his jacket and car keys, and left the hotel.

Getting into his car, he switched on the engine, put on the headlights, the car into gear – and drove. Much later he found himself in Winchester. The streets were empty. By now, one-thirty in the morning, all good citizens were in their beds. He parked the car and headed for the grounds of the Cathedral. Sitting alone beneath the high walls of this sacred place seemed strangely to soothe his troubled soul.

As he rested in quiet contemplation, he visualised the look of hurt in Lily's eyes as she climbed into the taxi and was driven away. She'd been through so much, and he'd only added to her distress. He hated himself for it, but still found it impossible to come to terms with her past.

When Lily arrived home, she went straight to her room, thankful that Madge had already retired. She couldn't have faced an inquisition, however friendly. She sat on the edge of her bed asking herself why on earth she had chosen that moment to tell him the truth about herself. Tonight had been so wonderful and she'd ruined it. Her timing had been so bad. Perhaps she should have waited, maybe even kept her past to herself, but that would have been foolish. There were too many people in Southampton who knew all about her. It would have been worse if Luke had learned all this from a stranger. Her head was spinning, her heart was heavy. In her mind was etched the expression of distaste on his face when she had confessed that she had turned to prostitution to survive. Well, it was all out in the open now. She had to be loved for the person she was, not some figment of his imagination. She wasn't ashamed of her past. She wasn't proud of it either, but she had survived and that was what was important.

She undressed and hung her dress in the shabby wardrobe. No doubt that was the end of her job prospects, too. Tonight she'd lost a great deal. The man she was beginning to love, her future and Victoria's future too. She'd planned to save her money, get a better place to live, take her child away from the grit and grime of the docklands. Bring her up as a lady. Now she was to remain scrimping and scraping, and if Eddie sold the hotel there was no guarantee the new owners would keep her on.

As she lay in her bed, alone, she relived the happier moments of the evening. The meal, the dancing, the lovemaking. God! That had been so good. Vittorio had been a great lover but Luke had taken her even further. She closed her eyes. She could still feel his mouth on hers, the path his magical fingers had taken. The feel of him inside her. She let out a deep sigh. Luke would never be able to forget what she'd told him. She'd shattered his illusion completely and he would never forgive her.

Pulling the covers up to her neck she wondered, was there never to be a tomorrow for her? Something to really look forward to? Then she scolded herself. Whatever else she'd lost, she still had Victoria – and for her she'd fight tooth and nail. No matter what. But it wasn't until this moment she realised just how much she wanted Luke Longford. And now she'd lost him.

Chapter Seventeen

Ten days had elapsed without a word from Luke. As Lily cleared the breakfast tables at the Mariner's Hotel and relaid them for the evening meal, she wondered what he was doing.

At first she'd felt deeply hurt by his rejection, and then, disappointed, but now she was angry. What would he have done at the age of sixteen in her position? It was easy for men, they could run away to sea at an early age, but not a young girl. How simple it would have been for her if that had been possible!

But if her past was too much for Luke Longford, then so was she! Besides, she had other things to worry about. Today, an inspector from The Protection of Children Society was coming to question Victoria and she was worried about the effect that would have on her child.

So concerned was she about the outcome of this interview, that she walked out of the main door of the Mariner's after her morning shift with her eyes downcast and didn't see Luke standing by his car outside, waiting. It wasn't until she heard someone call her name, that she looked up.

He walked towards her. She could read nothing from his expression and wondered what he was going to say.

'Hello, Lily. How are you?'

He sounded like an acquaintance, someone she vaguely knew.

'Fine . . . and you?'

'Busy. I just wanted to say the position at the hotel is still open to you if you want it.'

'You still want me to work for you then?' She could feel the anger inside her bubbling.

'Yes, I admire your expertise, you know that.'

'But that's all you admire, is it?'

'Please, Lily. Don't make this any harder for me than it is.'

Hardship! she thought. He doesn't know the meaning of the word. But she did, and she wasn't going to let her emotions prevent her from getting the best for Victoria.

'Very well, Luke. I'll work for you, but I expect to be paid well my *expertise*. After all, I'm worth every penny. What do you want me to do, and when?' She could see he was having difficulty with this conversation but she wasn't going to make it easy for him.

'I've exchanged contracts and I would like you to come with me to choose the carpets and material for the drapes to be made. I have a note of the colour schemes we chose, and the measurements of all the windows.'

'Very well, but that won't take long. What happens after that?'

'I'd like you to start recruiting staff. I myself will see to the management as I have my own people lined up. In two weeks from now, I'll need you to work full-time, if that's all right? The builders and decorators will start work and I'll need you to help me, keeping tabs on everything. But of course I'll pay you from whichever day you start to assist me.'

Even though she was mad at him she searched his face for a glimmer of affection, but all she saw was grim determination. 'Very well. I'll be free from Monday of next week,' she said shortly. 'Just let me know when and where. I can't stop – I've got to pick up Victoria.'

'How is she?'

'Fine. We're both absolutely fine. Get in touch before next week or leave a message at the desk of the Mariner's.' She turned abruptly and walked away.

This unexpected meeting had shaken her to the core, and despite her fury and wounded pride, she still felt the attraction between them. Even though they conversed as strangers, there was still something, a frisson of chemistry. But Luke had made his decision. She would work for him, save her money and make her own plans. If she saved enough, perhaps later she could start a business of her own. Be independent again. Stand on her own two feet. Luke needed her to help him organise the new hotel – well, that was fine. She needed him to finance her future, and she'd work hard for her money. It was to be a means to an end. If being around him was difficult, she would just have to put up with it for as long as was necessary . . . and then she'd move on.

Whilst Lily was sorting out her future, Luke was sitting in his car, parked outside the bank. He had an appointment with the manager, but for the moment he was trying to cope with seeing Lily again. The anger in her cornflower-blue eyes as she stood before him had surprised him. Yet as he thought about it, he realised she had every reason to feel that way. He knew he'd handled the situation of their last meeting badly, but her revelations had shocked him, destroyed his image of her, and he was still trying to come to terms with all that. He admired her for her honesty, and knew it had taken a great deal of courage on her part to reveal such details, when she could have remained silent. If he were truthful, he wished she had done so, but of course it would have been far worse to discover all about her later, when perhaps he'd committed himself.

And today when she'd stood before him, angry and defiant, he knew he still wanted her. He banged the steering wheel in anger. Why couldn't he accept her for what she was? A wonderful, sparky woman. A woman who'd had to face so many traumas in her life and still survived. But try as he would, he couldn't forget she had sold her body to other men. It stuck in his craw and he couldn't erase the sordid pictures that invaded his thoughts every hour of the day. He got out of the car and went into the bank.

Lily waited nervously at home with Victoria. Knowing about the impending visit, Madge had tactfully taken herself off somewhere. Lily gave her daughter a boiled egg and a piece of bread and butter for lunch and then the two of them sat at the table drawing pictures.

In answer to a knock at the door, Lily opened it to reveal a kindly looking gentleman in his forties.

'Miss Pickford? I've come to see Victoria.'

She stepped back and allowed him into the kitchen.

He took off his trilby and slowly walked over to the child, admiring her pictures. She offered him a piece of paper and a crayon. The stranger sat beside her and started to draw.

Lily sat down and waited with bated breath.

The man drew a house, not unlike the one that belonged to Gladys Parker. 'Do you know who lives in here?' he asked.

Victoria glanced at it and returned to her drawing. 'No,' she said.

'Mrs Parker lives in it, the lady you stayed with.'

'I didn't like her!' declared the child, but continued to draw.

'And why was that?' he asked casually.

'She shouted at me and shut me in a cupboard.'

'That wasn't very nice, was it?'

'No,' said Victoria and drew a deep line across her picture. 'It was dark and I was frightened. I cried for my Mama, but she didn't come.'

Lily covered her mouth to smother the cry of anguish that rose in her throat.

'But you told the lady who came to see you that you were happy with Mrs Parker.'

'She told me to say that.'

'Did the nasty lady ever smack you?'

She shook her head.

'Why did she shut you in the cupboard, Victoria?'

Her bottom lip began to tremble. 'She said I was a naughty, dirty girl. But I was a good girl. I only cried because I wanted my Mama to take me home.' She left the table and ran over to Lily and clambered onto her knee.

The man smiled at her. 'You're happy now though.'

Victoria stared at him with her dark-brown eyes. 'I love my Mama, and she's *never* going to leave me again,' she added defiantly.

Lily held her close and said, 'No, I'm never going to leave you again. Ever.'

The man rose from his chair. 'Thank you, that'll be all.' He ruffled the top of Victoria's hair. 'Goodbye,' he said.

She didn't answer, but snuggled closer to Lily.

'Don't get up, I'll let myself out. I'm so sorry that this was necessary, but rest assured, Miss Pickford, this will not happen to another child if I have my way.' He left the house, closing the door behind him.

'Let's go for a walk,' suggested Lily to her daughter in an effort to distract her. 'I know, we'll go to the pier and watch the boats.'

Victoria jumped off her knee immediately. 'Oh yes, I'd like that. Come on, Mama, hurry.'

They left the house and walked together past the Maypole Dairy where Lily usually bought her ha'porth of tea and a pennyworth of broken biscuits. Past the posters advertising Rudolph Valentino in *Blood and Sand*. He'd died the month before and the cinemas were now showing all his films. Then along to the Esplanade, to the Royal Pier where they paid their penny entrance fee. Victoria peered through the slats of wood that she walked on, looking at the water swirling around the posts below.

There was an autumnal feel in the September air, but the sun shone brightly as the passengers for the ferry to the Isle of Wight queued up to board. Victoria watched with delight a little later as the big paddle of the steamer turned, churning the water, stirring the flotsam that had gathered, before the ferry moved away. People sat in deck chairs watching the passing scene, eating ice cream, socialising. There was a child's roundabout with animal figures, turning slowly, and Victoria sat on one of them waving at her mother each time she passed, until it stopped.

On the way home, Lily bought a penny box of Lyon's jam tarts as a special treat and thought, When I'm earning real money again, I'll be able to do this more often. And looking at Victoria's clean but nevertheless second-hand clothes, she smiled with satisfaction, knowing that once again she'd be able to walk into a shop and buy new things for her daughter, and that thought gave her great pleasure. She would have to come to an arrangement with Betty Logan as her hours would be different, once she started to work for Luke. She found herself wondering about Nanny Gordon. She'd had an occasional postcard from Scotland, saying that she was well, but oh how she wished that the nanny was back in Southampton, looking after Victoria as she used to.

She took her child on a tram to St Mary Street to visit Rachel. She'd confided in her about Luke's behaviour. The Jewess had been scathing.

'Men! All the same they are. It's all right for them to have women. If it wasn't for men, there would be no need for prostitutes!' She'd put an arm around Lily. 'Darling, if he really does love you, he'll come back.'

Well, at least now she could tell her her job was safe.

But Rachel wasn't impressed when she imparted her news on her arrival. 'Typical! Bloody typical. So now he needs you?' She shrugged her shoulders. 'But still he sits in judgement on you. St Peter at the Pearly Gates he thinks he is. Him with his smart suits, his pockets full of money. Ach!'

Lily began to chuckle. The little Jewish woman was a sight to behold when she was angry.

'So, what's so funny?'

'You are. If Luke Longford walked through the door now, you'd string him up.'

'By his balls I would!' Then she too began to laugh. 'My life! Such pain, and not a pretty sight. A naked man ain't so attractive. All those bits and pieces dangling.'

'Rachel! Don't be disgusting,' giggled Lily.

'But he can't do without you, darling, or perhaps he don't want to.'

'It doesn't matter,' said Lily. 'I'll make my money and save to open a business myself. Then I won't need him or any man.'

Rachel didn't quite believe her protestations. She knew that Lily didn't give herself lightly to any man. To have allowed Luke Longford to bed her showed the depth of feeling she had for him. But time would tell. She liked Luke. He was just the man for her lovely girl, but first he'd have to swallow his manly pride. And for him, that wouldn't be easy.

A week later, Lily deposited Victoria at Betty Logan's to stay and play with Daisy, then she made her way to Shepherd & Hedge's where she was due to meet Luke. She'd dressed with care in her best navy two-piece. Her hair was shining after she'd shampooed it the night before with Amami. The soft bob and fringe framed her lovely face. She'd applied her lipstick carefully and now was ready to face him.

His car was parked outside the shop, and as she passed she looked in the window and saw him talking to a salesman. Taking a deep breath, she pushed open the door and entered. Walking over to the two men she said, 'Good morning. Were you waiting for me?'

Luke looked at her with a veiled expression and a half-smile. 'Good morning, Lily.' He turned to the other man and said, 'This is Miss Pickford, my manageress.'

The strained atmosphere between them soon faded as they became embroiled in the business in hand. Lily was impressed that Luke had all the measurements of everything and all the colour schemes, even down to the patterns of the wallpaper. He was indeed efficient, and being the fine businesswoman that she was, she appreciated this.

They made a note of the carpets they liked, but Luke didn't place an order, saying he'd get back to the man when they had come to a final decision. Once outside he explained that he'd been given the address of a wholesaler who had a wider choice of stock. He opened the passenger door of his car for her to get in. They sat side by side. The atmosphere between them was suddenly tense once more.

As they silently drove to the outskirts of town, Lily couldn't bring herself to speak, but was very aware of Luke sitting beside her. She longed to glance across at him, to see his expression, but forced herself to keep her vision fixed firmly on the road ahead.

The wholesaler did indeed have a good selection and a wider range of colours. They chose carefully and Luke made a firm order, but asked them to hold the stock until he was ready to have the carpets fitted.

From there they returned to Southampton to a store that sold good quality furnishings and curtain material. Here Lily came into her own. She had very definite ideas, and Luke didn't disagree with any of her choices, even though she gave him the opportunity.

As they got into the car she said, 'It's good to know what quality stock these place have. It'll be useful when eventually one day I once again open my own business.'

He gave her a startled look. 'Your own business?'

'Of course,' she said. 'I don't intend to work for anyone else for the rest of my life. You must surely understand that.'

'Yes, yes, of course I do.'

She smothered a smile. He'd sounded so surprised that she knew she'd given him something to think about. Well, Mr Luke Longford, she thought triumphantly, you needn't think I'm going to be at your beck and call for ever . . . however much you're paying me. Then she realised she'd never actually discussed money with him. Well, she might as well get that sorted too.

'Before we go any further,' she said, 'I think it's about time you told me exactly what you are going to pay me . . . for my *expertise*.'

The corners of Luke's mouth twitched at her sarcasm. You had to hand it to Lily; she knew how to stand up for herself. 'How will five guineas a week suit you?'

Lily caught her breath. This was real money. 'Are there any bonus schemes?'

He looked at her. 'Bonus? What bonus?'

She sat back in the seat of the car. Vittorio always said she drove a hard bargain. 'Well, Luke, if the hotel does good business I would expect some consideration for all my hard work.'

He shook his head. 'We'll have to wait and see,' was his only concession to this outrageous demand.

He dropped her outside Betty Logan's house and offered to give her and Victoria a lift home, but she refused. 'No thank you, I can manage. I don't think you'd appreciate sticky fingers all over your car seats.'

'Very well. I'll expect you at the hotel in two weeks' time then.'

When she entered the house, Madge was sitting reading a copy of the *Daily Mirror*. 'How did you get on?' she asked.

'We saw some lovely stuff,' said Lily. She looked across at her friend. 'How do you fancy working at a new posh hotel when it opens?'

Madge's eyes widened. 'What are you talking about?'

'Soon I'll be recruiting staff. You're a first-class waitress now. What do you think? Are you interested?'

'Bloody hell! A posh place . . . I don't know. After all, I'm an ex-con.'

Lily burst out laughing. 'So am I, you silly sod. And I'm the manageress!'

She honestly didn't think Luke would be well pleased, but Madge was a good waitress and she was willing. She was very good with the customers and they liked her. Lily would happily employ her if the place was hers. What was good enough for her should be good enough for Luke. He'd just have to trust her judgement.

Chapter Eighteen

Lily sat on a chair in a corner of what was to be the foyer of Luke's hotel. Her head was bursting from the smell of paint and the destruction of a wall nearby, to enlarge the smoking room.

It had been almost a week since she'd said goodbye to Eddie and the Mariner's Hotel. And now she was surrounded by worksheets, lists of things to be done, another with jobs completed, all of which were covered in a film of dust. And she was finding it hard to concentrate.

Luke emerged from the residents' lounge without a jacket, sleeves rolled up, his tie discarded, and his hair awry. For one whose appearance was usually so immaculate, it was an unusual sight. He was in deep discussion with the foreman, which gave Lily a chance to watch him unobserved.

He ran his fingers through his hair with impatience and annoyance, that was evident from his expression. But his mouth was set in a determined line as he spoke to the man, who eventually nodded in agreement and walked away. Luke muttered beneath his breath, looked at the list in his hand, made a quick note, then glanced up and saw Lily watching him.

'Trouble?' she asked.

He walked over to her. 'You just wouldn't believe the

stupidity of some people! I give the man precise instructions about a job and he gets it wrong. Inefficiency drives me crazy! How are things going with you?'

She frowned. 'I have a million things to do. You want a list of linen requirements for the bedrooms and dining room, there are lists everywhere for everything and I need some assistance if I'm to see to it all!'

He looked at the chaos around her. 'And this doesn't help. When there is a room that the decorators have finished with, set yourself up there. Use it as an office until yours is ready. I'll have a telephone installed. Yes, by all means get someone to give you a hand. Ring up one of the agencies.'

'No need,' said Lily. 'I know just the right person.'

When Madge arrived home that night, Lily was waiting for her. 'Give your notice in to Eddie tomorrow morning,' she said. 'I've got a job for you.'

'But the hotel isn't open yet!' exclaimed her friend.

'I know, but I need an assistant and you'll fit the bill beautifully.'

There was an expression of concern on Madge's face. 'What will I have to do, if it isn't waitressing? That's the only thing I know, except nicking things,' she added with a grin.

'That's not funny, Madge,' Lily retorted.

'Go on then.'

'I have so much to do, I need someone I know and can trust who I can ask, say, to go to the printers and pick up the hotel stationery, for instance. Or to make me a cup of tea, check in the bedrooms and see if whatever has been done, make phone calls for me. Piddling things, but that would leave me free to concentrate on major items.'

'Well, if you think I can,' said Madge with a note of uncertainty.

'Of course I do. You're bright, why shouldn't you do it perfectly well?'

Madge preened. 'Why not indeed.' Then she chuckled. 'Blimey, Lily, I am going up in the world. If my mother could see me now, the old cow.'

'Just count your blessings that she can't. Any news of a buyer for the Mariner's?'

'A couple of people came round today. One seemed all right, but I didn't care for the other. He looked a right bastard. I wouldn't like to work for him.'

'Well, now you won't have to.' Lily gave her a hug. 'Didn't I tell you you could make a life for yourself?'

With a smile of affection, Madge said, 'Indeed you did, love. And thank God for you.'

Lily brushed her remarks aside, but she wondered just what Luke's reaction would be when he saw her new assistant.

He encountered Madge a few days later as he entered the hotel after a morning appointment with his solicitor. A figure hurried past him with a cheery, 'Good morning.' He answered her back without thinking, then did a double-take at her retreating figure, rushing across the park. He found Lily and demanded, 'What is your friend Madge doing here?'

Blithely she said, 'She's my assistant.'

'She what?'

Calmly she repeated, 'She's my assistant. Madge is ideal. She's bright, she's willing and she works hard . . . and I know and trust her. The hotel business will not be discussed outside this building.'

'But she's got a prison record!'

Lily glared at him. 'So have I, Luke. So have I.'

'But you were innocent, she wasn't.'

'And she's paid for it. Look, I need someone willing to do anything I ask without question. Madge is that person. I don't have the time to spend getting to know a stranger. You either trust my judgement or you don't have a manageress!'

He was speechless and stormed away.

With a slow satisfied smile Lily watched him go.

But as the days progressed and Madge proved her ability and her usefulness, Luke's attitude began slowly to change. He was a little abrupt still when he spoke to her, but he could see how invaluable she was to Lily and his hostility lessened.

'I have to go to London for the day tomorrow,' he announced one morning. 'I'll be away all day as I'm going to the auction warehouse I told you about to choose some furniture. Here is their card with the telephone number, if you need to contact me.'

'Is there anything in particular you want me to do?' she asked.

'Just make sure the workmen don't slack when I'm not about.'

Having learned, over the short time she'd worked for him, how much of a perfectionist and how demanding he was, she said caustically, 'As if they dare.'

He looked at her with a wide grin. 'Exactly!'

As one of the men demanded his attention, Lily realised that was the first time he'd shown any sign of humour since the night at his hotel when their relationship collapsed. His smile was heartstopping and she knew that she felt just the same about him now, as she had when he made love to her. But that was all in the past, and anyway she was far too busy for recriminations.

Thank God that at least Quinn Gifford had disappeared from the scene. Fleetingly, she wondered what had happened to him. Perhaps he was away with his brothers, visiting horse-fairs. Whatever the cause, she was grateful for his absence.

The one thing she did regret was that she wasn't spending as much time with Victoria as she wanted, but the child seemed happy and content at Betty's, playing with Daisy. She paid Betty extra money each week to compensate her for the longer hours, and until she could think of something else, the arrangement would have to stand.

Quinn Gifford waited impatiently at the South Hants Hospital to have his plaster removed. These past weeks had been frustrating for him, especially when Jake his brother had told him that Lily had a new job. Jake had made discreet enquiries about her and relayed the information to his brother.

Quinn had been furious. Lily was moving up in the world again and that didn't sit right with him. Whilst she was forced into poverty, his position was strong, or so he thought. He was able to offer her better things but now, she'd be less inclined to think about it. Well, there were many other ways to skin a cat.

With the plaster finally removed, he flexed his ankle. It felt weak as he tried to put his weight on it. Oh well. He'd waited this long, another week would make little difference.

He made Jake drive him to Cumberland Place and park the truck, so he could observe what was going on without being seen. There was massive activity. Builders' vans were parked outside, decorators in paint-splashed overalls came in and out, but of Lily there was no sign. His dark eyes narrowed. He'd have to find out her working hours, discover where her daughter was. He needed to know her every movement to put his plan into action.

DI Chadwick made a call on Lily the following day whilst

Luke was in London. He looked around at the chaos. 'Blimey, Lily! Will this place ever be ready?'

She chuckled. 'You won't know it when it is. What can I do for you?'

'I've two bits of news for you, my dear. I was able to furnish The Protection of Children Society with a very comprehensive dossier of complaints, and the Director held an enquiry. Gladys Parker has been black-listed, the Supervisor, Ethel Giles, has been fired, and there have been several staff changes. But most important of all, there are two new inspectors who will keep a tighter control on all the foster parents.'

'That's wonderful,' said Lily sincerely. 'At least no other child will suffer like my little Victoria. Thank you, you did a grand job. What's the other piece of news?'

'Percy Gates is up in court next week. You'll be called as a witness for the prosecution.'

'I can't wait until that bastard gets what he deserves. I'll be there, don't you worry.'

Luke returned from London, delighted with his purchases. 'You wouldn't believe the stuff they have there,' he told Lily enthusiastically the next morning. 'You'll love the leather chairs I ordered for the smoking room, and the chandeliers: I ordered five. There are also some lovely old pieces of furniture that will want refurbishing. When they arrive I'll need your advice on those. But they were of such quality I couldn't resist them.'

His green eyes shone as he told her about everything else he'd bought and Lily thought what a shame it would be when the time came for her to move on. Luke had thrown away so much. They would have been an ideal team. A successful one. She would have loved the responsibility of running this place, building it up, watching it grow as she was sure it would. Well, she would see a major part before she'd saved enough to start again on her own.

She told Luke that one day next week she was needed to appear in court. When she told him why, anger shone in his eyes. 'Not before time. That man cost you six months of your life!'

She was touched by his sentiment, but although he could accept that she was innocent of fraud, he still couldn't excuse the rest of her past, and that still hurt deep down.

'Would you like me to come with you?' he asked, to her surprise.

'No, thank you. I'm used to fighting my own battles.' She couldn't prevent a touch of bitterness from entering her voice and Luke didn't miss the implication.

'Very well,' he said.

The following week, Lily sat in court and saw Gates sent down for a long sentence. Bill the croupier gave his evidence which finally convicted Gates, and then he told the court that Lily had been set up and that she was innocent of any crime. At the end of the day she thanked him.

'I owed it to you, Miss Pickford. I'm really sorry you were sent down.'

'Well, now my solicitor says he can apply to clear my name.' At the despondency in his face she put a hand on his arm. 'No hard feelings, Bill.'

He looked relieved. 'Thanks. That's more than I deserve.'

One evening, Luke stood across the road from his hotel and surveyed the frontage. It was an elegant façade and he was filled with pride when he thought that now it belonged to him. His life savings were being invested here. Here was his future.

He mentally pictured all the items that had been purchased, placing the furniture in the rooms, the chandeliers hanging from the ceilings. He could envisage the dining room set up with the first-class linen – plain white damask to match the fine china.

The chef in charge of the kitchen was all-important, and he'd been in touch with one in London who was really interested in becoming part of the project. It would cost him dearly to pay the man's salary, but it would secure the culinary reputation of the hotel. *His* hotel.

Turning his head, Luke looked over at Watts Park, a glorious view that would be enjoyed by his residents. With its smooth green grass, tall trees, beautiful shrubs and neatly laid beds, it provided an oasis of calm and colour within a few walking steps of the hotel entrance. It was a perfect spot.

He was impatient for the opening, but knew that a great deal of work needed to be done first. Lily had proved to be invaluable and was taking a lot of the burden from him. She had such personality, and a fine head for business. How could they fail? But at the back of his mind he recalled her saying that she wanted her own business one day – that had taken him by surprise. It had been his plan that they would always be together, and the thought that she would one day leave was hard to accept. Despite everything, in his mind, she was part of all this, but of course, things between them had changed and this was his fault. He lit a cigarette in an effort to relax. Whenever he thought of her being on the streets, it churned him up inside. He thought of how he had held her in his arms, kissed her, touched her, and wondered how many other men had had the same privilege. He threw down the cigarette and ground it to smithereens beneath his foot. The same pictures in his mind, the same question. Was he never going to be able to erase it?

He saw Lily walk out of the hotel, knowing she was going to pick up Victoria. He could have offered to run her there, but he couldn't face sitting in his car in such close proximity to her. It drove him crazy. In the hotel it was different. There was so much going on. A car was too intimate. He watched her walk to the tram stop, and wandered back to the entrance of the hotel.

Lily waited at the stop, unaware that she was being observed, by Luke . . . and Quinn Gifford.

Chapter Nineteen

Quinn's carefully laid plans were put into disarray when Betty Logan caught influenza and Victoria had to go to the hotel every day with her mother. It was now almost the end of October and it had rained constantly every day. Lily and her daughter were sent home each night by taxi, and during the day remained safely inside the confines of the hotel, surrounded by workmen.

He himself had caught a cold, hanging around the park, keeping watch, and was miserable and bad-tempered. But at last the heavens cleared and although cold, the weather was dry and crisp and the forecast predicted that it would be so for the next few days.

Quinn had observed a woman taking Victoria for a walk in the park in the morning and afternoon, no doubt to get her from under the feet of those inside, and he knew he'd have to strike now or not at all.

'No, I won't do it! The whole thing is madness.' Jake glared at his older brother. 'You're obsessed with this woman. Why don't you see sense, for God's sake!'

Quinn grabbed Jake by the front of his jacket and pushed him up against a wall. They were outside a pub in the docklands. Jake had rushed out of the bar to get away from his brother and his crazy idea.

265

'You will do exactly as I say, without argument or you will never set foot on the farm again,' Quinn told him through gritted teeth. 'Bart will get your share of everything, I'll make sure of that!'

'That's blackmail!'

'No,' said Quinn grimly, 'that's a fact of life. Now get into the bloody truck and drive to Cumberland Place.'

Inside the hotel, great strides had been made. The myriad of painters were just putting the finishing touches to the bedrooms, and the main rooms on the lower floor were nearing completion. The electricians had hung the magnificent chandeliers: one in the main entrance hall, another in the enlarged smoking room, two in the dining room and the biggest one in the ballroom. They looked magnificent.

The rich maroon carpet and flocked wallpaper gave the smoking room a feel of warmth, and the brass fender and fire dogs gleamed. In one corner stood a handsome bookcase filled with volumes to match most tastes. Small tables sat next to the large leather chairs that Luke had ordered, and with the wall lights and table-lamps switched on, the ambience was very masculine, yet cosy. Lily had searched for pictures of hunting scenes and these now adorned the walls. She and Luke stood looking at the finished room.

'It's splendid,' he declared. 'I can see this being a favourite with the men.'

Lily smoothed the leather of one of the chairs, then sat in it. 'This is very comfortable. If ever I'm missing from my duties, this is probably where you'll find me.'

'Yes, with all of the men!' Luke had meant this as a jovial remark, but she shot him a searching look and he became embarrassed.

'Next Wednesday the fitters will come to lay the carpets in

266

the foyer, the dining room and the residents' lounge. The day after, all the drapes should arrive.'

'Yes, it's getting there,' she said. 'Once the kitchen has finally been finished, the rest is minor, in comparison.' She gazed at him. 'Is it the way you pictured it in your mind as that small bellboy?'

He rubbed his chin thoughtfully. 'To be honest, it's much better. That's largely thanks to you, Lily. Your eye for colour and furnishings is quite exceptional.'

She was surprised by his compliment. During the hectic days of the past weeks, neither of them had come anywhere near making personal remarks.

'That's what you pay me for,' she said shortly. She couldn't cope with flattery. She could handle being with Luke and working, because their relationship was purely on a business basis. But anything else would be too much.

'I have to go to a meeting this morning. I'll leave you to hold the fort until I return,' he said as they walked back to the foyer.

Here sat Victoria with her dolls and her toy teaset, laid out on a table used for wallpapering. Madge was beside her.

'Hello, Luke,' said the child.

He stooped down. 'Well, what have we here? Is this a tea party?'

'Yes,' she said, picking up the teapot, filled with water. 'Would you like some?'

He stood up and with a smile said, 'I'm sorry, darling, but I've got to go out on business. I'll have one when I come back. Is that all right?'

The small face looked annoyed. 'Then I'll have to make a fresh pot. This one will have gone cold!'

Luke chuckled softly. 'I'm very sorry to put you to so much trouble. What about if I bring back some fancy cakes with me, will you make it then?'

She clapped her hands gleefully. 'Oh yes, I will.'

Smiling to himself he left the building. Children! Such imaginations they had. He hadn't had a lot to do with them, being away at sea all his life, but Victoria was quite a character. She took after her mother, of course. At first when Lily had arrived at the hotel with Victoria in tow, he'd been irritated. Even when Lily explained the predicament of Betty's illness.

'Well, keep her out of everyone's way. There's saws, hammers and paint everywhere. This is no place for a child!'

Lily had leapt to Victoria's defence. And cross words had been exchanged, which hadn't helped the atmosphere between them. But to his relief, the child had been no trouble.

Quinn watched Luke Longford leave the building. By now he knew who the man was. The whole town knew about him. Him with his money, his flash car, his posh hotel. He was filled with jealousy, thinking that such an attractive man might just appeal to his Lily. Well, he'd very soon put a stop to that.

Jake was still wittering on, trying to make him change his mind. If he didn't shut up, he'd bloody soon thump him one! He sat up suddenly as he saw the woman and Lily's child leave the hotel. He nudged his brother. 'Come on.'

The two men got out of the truck and followed Madge at a discreet distance. To their dismay she didn't go to the park, but carried on to the shops. They hung around the entrance of the stores she visited, waiting, worried that they'd miss her. But eventually she made her various purchases and walked back towards Watts Park with Victoria, chatting away to her.

The park was fairly quiet. It was too cold for people to linger as they did in the summer. Those who took a short-cut through it, walked with their heads down, collars turned up, hurrying to their destinations. Not interested in anyone else.

Quinn and his brother closed the distance between them and their quarry.

Madge was unaware that she was being followed. Victoria wanted to play hide and seek and ran ahead to hide behind a shrub. Madge pretended to lose her, calling: 'Victoria! Where are you?' before pouncing on her, catching hold of the child by her coat to squeals of delight from the little one.

'Once more,' pleaded Victoria. 'Please!'

'All right then, but hurry up. Your mother will wonder where we are.'

The child ran behind a large evergreen, out of sight, to be caught by Jake who picked her up, putting his hand over her mouth to smother her screams.

When the little girl didn't come to her when she called, Madge approached the place where she had disappeared. 'Now that's enough, Victoria. Come on out. We're late and your mother will be cross.'

Just then she heard a muffled cry and ran to investigate, thinking the child had fallen. She was grabbed roughly by Quinn Gifford who threatened her with his closed fist. Over his shoulder she could see Victoria, being held by another stranger. The child was struggling, but the man was carrying her away across the park.

An envelope was thrust into Madge's hand and she was told, in low menacing tones: 'You give this letter to Lily Pickford. Don't say nothing to nobody or she'll never see the little one again. Understand?'

Trembling with fright, Madge nodded.

Quinn let her go. 'Now remember what I said. You only go to Lily.'

'Yes, I understand,' said Madge, her voice shaking.

As soon as Quinn started to walk quickly away, Madge took flight, running as fast as she could towards the hotel. She burst in the main door, but Lily wasn't there. She frantically searched all the lower rooms, to no avail. Then she flew up the stairs, taking them two at a time, calling wildly, 'Lily! Lily!' looking in all the bedrooms. She arrived at the top floor, out of breath, her legs almost giving way beneath her. She stopped and leaned panting against the wall of the corridor and yelled as loud as she could. '*Lily!*'

She came running out of a room, saw Madge and the state of her, and rushed over to her friend. 'Whatever is the matter?'

'It's Victoria,' she wheezed. 'They've taken her.' She held out the letter.

'Who's taken her?' Lily grabbed Madge's arm. 'Who? What are you talking about?'

Madge shoved the letter at her. 'He said you must read this.'

Lily tore at the envelope, and stiffened as she recognised Quinn's handwriting.

Lily. I have Victoria. She is with me at my farm. I you ever want to see her alive again, do not tell anyone. You tell the police and I will kill her. Come to the farm alone. Quinn.

She froze. Looking at her friend she whispered, 'Tell me exactly what happened.'

Madge told her everything. 'What are you going to do?' she asked.

'I'm going to call a taxi and go to Quinn Gifford's farm in Bitterne. Don't you dare say a word about this to a soul.'

'What'll I tell Luke when he comes back?'

Lily gripped her tighter. 'Make up some story – anything – but you must promise me not to breathe a word of this. My baby's life depends on it.'

'I swear.'

The two of them ran down the stairs. Lily grabbed her coat and telephoned for a taxi. Pacing the floor, wringing her hands, she waited impatiently. When the car arrived, she hugged her friend.

'For God's sake be careful,' called Madge as Lily ran out of the hotel and into the car.

Madge watched her drive away. Biting her bottom lip, she was terrified for Victoria, terrified for Lily and scared to death at the thought of Luke's return. What on earth was she going to say to him?

Jake held tightly to the struggling child, cursing his brother. 'You're bloody mad!' he cried. 'You'll get the lot of us locked up for this.'

'No I won't,' said Quinn with an evil grin. 'Lily will come rushing to the farm to get her brat back. She won't tell anyone, she'll be too frightened. When she gets there, she'll stay, you'll see.' He glared at Victoria who was beginning to whimper. 'Shut up!' he yelled.

Victoria's eyes widened in fright and she was quiet.

'That's better,' growled Quinn. 'I can't abide squawking kids.'

Jake knew his brother didn't like children at all and this worried him even more. Ever since Quinn had been beaten up, he'd been like a deranged man. Plotting, planning, going round the farmhouse muttering to himself, and Jake was more than a little concerned. They'd pulled many an unlawful stunt between them, he and the brothers, but kidnapping a child – well, that was going too far. He didn't like it at all. Where was it all going to end?

Quinn turned the truck into the farmyard, scattering the chickens and hens, frightening the ducks and making the dogs bark. He stopped with a loud squeal of brakes.

'Bring her inside,' he said as he strode towards the kitchen door.

Rosie his mother was standing by the sink, peeling vegetables, her clay pipe in her mouth, as he entered, followed by Jake and the terrified child. Rosie dropped the knife with a clatter as she looked at Victoria, then at Quinn. She took the pipe out of her mouth and pointed at Quinn with it. 'You bloody fool! Now look what you've gone and done!'

He glowered at her. 'Mind your own business, Ma.'

Her piercing eyes stared out of her wizened and lined face. 'This *is* my business. You'm going to bring us all down, my son.'

Jake turned to him, a note of panic in his voice. 'There – didn't I tell you? I don't want nothing to do with this!'

Quinn's wicked laugh seemed to fill the untidy kitchen, and Victoria cowered in fright. 'You're up to your neck in it, Jake. Who took the brat? You did!' There was a triumphant gleam in his dark eyes as he grinned at his brother.

'You forced me.'

Rosie said sharply, 'Shut up, the two of you.' She went over to Victoria and took her from Jake's grasp and led her over to a chair by the open log fire. 'You sit with me, my beauty. Don't you worry. Everything's going to be fine.' She sat the little figure on her lap.

Quinn leered and said, 'Yes, your mother's coming real soon.'

Victoria looked up at the old crone. 'Is my Mama coming here?' she whispered.

'Yes, darlin',' answered Rosie softly. 'She'll be here very soon, you'll see. Now you sit quietly, I'll take care of you. Pour the little one a cup of milk,' she said to Jake, who lumbered away to do his mother's bidding.

Quinn lit one of his cheroots and stood by the window, waiting.

The journey to Bitterne seemed endless to Lily. If Quinn Gifford had touched a hair of her child's head, she'd kill him! Then the fear that he might have already done so, made her feel sick. She prayed silently, eyes tightly closed, making all sorts of promises to God, if only He would deliver Victoria safely to her.

She'd thought she was safe from the gypsy, she hadn't seen hide nor hair of him for so long. What was he thinking of? This was his wicked way of getting her to his home – but what would she find when she got there? It didn't bear thinking about. What did he want from her? She knew the answer to that. She conjured up the vision of Quinn in her mind and shuddered, but acknowledged in her heart that she would do anything – *anything* – to keep Victoria safe.

After what seemed an age, the taxi arrived at the Giffords' farm. She paid off the driver and walked through the farm gate, which was hanging on its hinges. The place was a mess. Straw and mud littered the yard. Two large, fierce dogs strained at their chains as they growled and barked at her. Two cats started spitting at each other, fighting over a half-dead rat, and hens and chickens strutted around the place, pecking at the ground. There was a pungent smell wafting from the pigsty. Her heart sank as she walked towards the door which was ajar. She pushed it open slowly and saw Victoria sitting on the knee of an old woman. Her heart lifted.

'Victoria,' she cried and stepped inside.

The door slammed behind her.

She turned and looked into the face of Quinn Gifford.

There was a triumphant glare in his eyes as he said, 'You

took long enough!' He grabbed her arm in an iron grip which made her wince. 'I hope you weren't stupid enough to tell anyone where you was going.'

She shook free of his grasp and glared fiercely at him. 'No, of course I didn't.' She couldn't let him see she was scared. 'What the hell do you think you're doing, taking my child? How dare you do such a thing?'

He loved the fire in her. She was the girl for him, all right. He liked a woman with a bit of spirit. Most people were terrified of him, but look at her . . . facing up to him. She was like a tiger.

He puffed on his cheroot and grinned. 'I told you I would take care of you and yours. You didn't believe me, did you?' The grin was wiped off his face as he glared at her. 'Or maybe you did. Maybe that's why you set that bastard Coleman onto me.'

Seeing the tight line of his mouth, the angry glitter in his eyes, Lily was terrified. What had George done? But in her heart, she knew. 'I don't know what you're talking about,' she told him.

Quinn grasped hold of her wrist.

'Mama!' cried Victoria anxiously.

Lily turned to her. 'Shush, darling, everything's going to be fine.'

Quinn ignored the interruption. 'He and his thugs beat me up, put me in hospital. Broke me ribs and me ankle – I was in plaster for weeks. Don't tell me you didn't know – he told me it was because of *you*!'

'I didn't know!' she protested. 'Honestly.'

He let her go. 'Well, I think you're lying.' He smiled slowly. 'But no matter, you're here and this is where you'll stay, you and your brat. You'll pay me for the beating when I takes you to me bed.'

Lily went cold. She knew he meant every word.

He glared at her and licked his lips. 'You and me are gonna be wed, girl. You'll be Mrs Quinn Gifford and like it.'

She turned to the woman seated with Victoria, correctly guessing she was his mother. 'Can't you talk sense into him? This is crazy.'

The old woman just stared at her.

Lily turned to Quinn. 'You can't get away with this!'

His voice was quiet but it was so cold, it chilled her. 'You do as I ask or your babby will accidentally drown in the pond.'

Lily felt the blood drain from her body and she thought she was going to faint. She looked into the evil eyes of the gypsy and saw the madness and knew he wouldn't hesitate to fulfil his threats. She had to play for time. Make him think she'd go along with his plans and try to find a way out of this situation. She had to get Victoria to a place of safety somehow. Taking a deep breath, she said, 'Very well. I'll do as you ask, but on one condition. You don't touch my child.'

Quinn looked at her suspiciously. She had given in to his demands very quickly. What was she up to? 'You'd better not be lying to me, girl, or you'll be sorry.'

'And you'd better not be lying to me, Quinn Gifford. You touch one hair of Victoria's head and I'll kill you with my own bare hands!'

He laughed. That was more like it. They'd fill the farm with children, who would work for him, because he was really going to enjoy her. She'd be at his beck and call and he had a huge sexual appetite.

Chapter Twenty

Back at the hotel, Madge was beside herself with worry. She'd promised Lily she would remain silent – but what if she didn't return? What was she to do then?

A while later, Luke breezed in through the main entrance, clutching a box of cakes in his hand. He looked at the empty chair. Victoria's teaset was still laid out on the table.

'Go and find the little one, will you, please?' he asked Madge. 'Tell her the cakes are here.'

She stumbled over her words. 'I – I'm sorry. Lily had to take her home.'

There was a note of concern in his voice. 'Oh. Why was that?'

'Victoria wasn't well. She had a tummy-ache. Lily said she'd be back later if she could . . . or tomorrow,' she added, not sure how long her friend would be gone, and praying she'd return soon.

A frown creased Luke's brow. 'Was the child very poorly?'

'I don't know.'

'What do you mean? You were here, weren't you?'

'No, I was upstairs. She left a message with one of the workmen.'

Luke looked at her suspiciously. Lily wouldn't leave such a message with a workman. She would have found Madge, given her instructions of work to be done. He was sure the girl was lying, but why? What was Lily up to?

'Did she ask you to do anything in particular whilst she was away?'

Madge looked flummoxed. 'Er . . . no, not really.'

Luke was getting annoyed. 'Well, I have plenty you can do. For goodness' sake, if we're to open at all I can't have people disappearing without a word! Come with me.'

Back at the farm, the atmosphere wasn't any better than at the hotel. Lily was watching Quinn closely, unsure of his mental attitude, fearing for both herself and her child.

Rosie had given them a hunk of bread and cheese and told them to eat. Quinn had sat with his, drinking a glass of beer. When Victoria had wanted to go to the lavatory, he insisted his mother take her to the outside privy, keeping Lily in the kitchen beneath his watchful gaze.

Jake had taken his food to the barn with a feeling of impending doom, unable to cope with the heavy atmosphere that hung over those inside.

'I've painted our bedroom,' Quinn suddenly declared. 'And I've bought a new bed, sheets and blankets too, so you'll see I mean business.'

'That's nice of you,' she said. 'But we're not married yet, Quinn.'

'That didn't stop you before.' He looked at Victoria. 'You aren't trying to tell me you're an innocent virgin, are you?'

'No, of course not. But if I'm to be your bride,' she saw the look of happiness on his face at her words, 'if I'm to be your bride, don't you think it would be nice for us to get to know one another better?'

He leered at her. 'Now you're talking. We could go up now.'

'No, that's not what I meant.' She looked coyly at him. 'A girl likes to be courted, you know. You're a handsome man, Quinn. You've had your share of women.'

'I have that,' he boasted.

'Then, knowing so much about the ladies, you know about these things. Before you take a woman to your bed, you have to make her want to be with you, because she thinks you're something special. You treat her right, flatter her a little. Take things nice and slowly. Let her get to know you.' She saw him thinking about her words. 'After all, I only know you as a gambler. Nothing else. I'm sure there's a great deal more to know about Quinn Gifford, the man.'

He drained his glass and rose to his feet. 'Come with me,' he said, crossing the room and grabbing hold of her hand. Victoria clung tightly to the other one.

'You stay with Mrs Gifford,' Lily hastily told her. 'I promise I'll be back.' She looked at Rosie, pleading with her eyes.

'I'll look after her,' the old woman said as Quinn dragged her out of the house and into the farmyard.

He led her across the yard to the meadows beyond. There in the distance were six horses. Even to Lily's untrained eye, they looked fine specimens. He pointed to them. 'That's how I make me money, Lily. I have a nose for horse-flesh. A knowledge learned at me father's knee and one I'll pass on to our sons.' He pointed to a mare who was in foal. 'She's due at any moment. We put her in the stable at nights now, just in case.' He looked at them with pride. 'I broke them all in meself.'

'Isn't that dangerous?' she asked, trying to flatter him.

'Yes, of course, but there isn't a horse – or a woman – I can't tame.'

She looked up at him. 'Yes, I can see you're a powerful

man, a strong one, but a woman appreciates gentleness. She doesn't want to be handled like a horse.' She smiled softly at him. 'Gentleness brings its own rewards.'

He regarded her carefully. 'So you want to be treated gently, do you?' He caught hold of her arm and pulled her to him.

She was filled with revulsion but fought hard to hide her true feelings as he lowered his mouth to hers and kissed her. Softly. She made herself respond, but felt sick to her stomach as she felt the invasion of his tongue in her mouth. She pulled away, very carefully.

'There! You see – you can do it,' she said teasingly. 'You're a fine-looking man, Quinn Gifford, but you frighten some people. You don't let them see the other side of you. That's a shame.'

His piercing eyes studied her. He wasn't a fool. She was playing some sort of game, but she'd kissed him. Well, he would go along with it whilst it suited him . . . then he'd take her, any way he wanted.

Luke gazed at his watch. It was five o'clock and Lily certainly wouldn't be coming back this evening. He looked at Madge. 'Come on, I'll drive you home and then I can see how Victoria is.'

She was in a panic, knowing that the house was empty. 'No, it's all right,' she protested. 'I'm meeting some friends, I'm not going home. And I think you should leave Lily be; you may disturb Victoria. She'll probably be better after a good night's sleep. You know children – up one minute, down the next.'

Luke was an excellent judge of character and he knew that Madge was covering for Lily. But why? Why did she need to lie? If Lily was not at home, where the devil was she? His mouth narrowed in an angry line. He'd have something to say to her in the morning, that was for sure.

'Very well,' he snapped, 'but don't be late tomorrow. There's too much to do.'

She scuttled to the entrance. 'No, right. I'd best be off then.' She almost ran, she was so anxious to get away.

Luke drove to the Dolphin Hotel. Once his rooms were ready in his own place, he'd move in, but this suited him for the time being. He parked the car and made for the bar.

Sitting alone, he puzzled to himself over Lily. She'd worked like a Trojan these past weeks, but still there was this strong barrier between them. There were times when he longed to tear it down and take her into his arms. When she looked at him with those cornflower-blue eyes, he remembered the delight of holding her, making love to her, but always, always, her past got in the way.

He quickly downed his drink, walked outside and headed for the Esplanade, to gaze out over the water. How soothing it was to watch the rise and fall of the River Test as the ripples broke on the pebbles. How many times in different parts of the world had he done this on board some liner, standing by the ship's rails, looking out over the ocean, trying to sort out some problem or other. But for him, this time, there was no easy option. His own masculine pride stood in his way and no matter how hard he battled with it, he couldn't forget the sordid details of Lily's past life. He kicked angrily at the stones on the beach, then walked back to the hotel.

At the Giffords' farm, Lily was very tense. It was now dark and the night loomed ahead of her. Rosie had fed them with lamb stew. Victoria was fretting and had lost her appetite, but Lily had managed to get her to take a little sustenance. The child kept looking fearfully at Quinn who watched her with his brooding eyes and a look of impatience.

When Lily was sitting in one of the chairs beside the fire, Victoria had whispered to her, 'I don't like that nasty man, Mama.'

Lily held her close and murmured, 'It's all right, darling. Don't you worry. Mama will look after you.'

'When can we go home?'

'I don't know yet, Victoria. But very soon.'

Quinn had gone to bed the horses down for the night, leaving Jake on guard. Lily appealed to him.

'Jake, for God's sake, can't you put a stop to all this?'

He looked at her with a certain sympathy. 'I wish I could, Lily. But Quinn has planned to have you here for a long time. Then when he got beat up, he got angry. He'd kill me if I interfered.'

'Honestly, I didn't know anything about that. I wouldn't have that done to anyone. I know what George Coleman is capable of.'

Jake looked at her. 'Well, Quinn thinks you did.'

'Wouldn't Bart help you to talk to him?'

'Our Bart's away, visiting family.' He hesitated and said softly, 'You know, Quinn don't forgive easily. You watch yourself, girl.' He walked into the scullery as he heard his brother return.

Quinn walked in and looked from one to the other, then sat at the table. He gazed across at Lily. 'Soon be bedtime,' he said.

The expression on his face filled her with horror. Taking a deep breath she asked, 'Have you a bed for Victoria and me? The child is tired.'

'She can sleep in a cot in Ma's room. You'll sleep in my bed . . . *our* bed.'

'No, Quinn. Not tonight. I'm really tired. This has been

quite a day one way and another, and,' she looked at him beneath silky lashes, 'when I come to your bed, I want to be at my best. Then I can really please you.'

He hesitated and for one moment Lily thought he would refuse. He stared at her and she feigned a yawn. 'All right,' he conceded surprisingly. 'Just for tonight. You can use Bart's room. Come on, I'll show you.'

She followed him up the rickety wooden stairs, hardly daring to breathe. He pushed open the door and she entered. The bed was unmade, but what caught her eye was a high-backed chair, one that was stout enough to put under the handle of the door, and that to her was far more important.

She sat Victoria on the bed. 'Thank you, Quinn. Good-night.'

He pulled her to him roughly and kissed her hard, his mouth bruising hers. 'Don't try these games for too long, girl. I'm not a patient man.' He closed the door behind him.

Letting out a sigh of relief, Lily quickly put the chair under the door-handle. If he really wanted to barge in, nothing would stop him, but at least it would give her warning.

She tidied the bed, undressed Victoria to her knickers and Liberty bodice, but kept her own clothes on, removing only her stockings and shoes, just in case. Wearily, she climbed into bed and held Victoria close.

As her daughter fell into a deep sleep, Lily thought about Luke. What would he do if he knew of her predicament? He was a good man, a strong man, and now she knew she cared deeply for him. If only he could put her past behind him, they could have a wonderful life together. But reality stared her in the face. She had to escape from Quinn Gifford first, before she had *any* life. How the hell could she do it? If she could get away with Victoria, they were a long way from other houses. There was no near neighbour here. The dogs would bark if she slipped out now. Had she been alone, she might have taken the chance, but she couldn't ignore the threats to Victoria's safety.

Outside in the yard, Rosie was sitting on a pile of sacks, smoking. Quinn sat beside her. He gazed down at the cobbled stones of the yard, shining wet after the rain earlier in the day. He looked into the small puddles and studied the kaleidoscope of colours reflected in them from the oil-lamp beside him.

'I can't help meself, Ma,' he said quietly. 'It's as if something inside of me is driving me on. I just have to do . . . what I have to do.'

She turned then and looked at him, her eyes full of sorrow. 'And I have no choice either, son. Destiny is a cruel master.' She got up and walked slowly over to him, placed a comforting hand on the top of his head for a moment, then walked back towards the kitchen. Head down, shoulders bent.

The following morning, Lily dressed Victoria and then with great trepidation, walked downstairs to the kitchen. Quinn was sitting at the table consuming a large plate of bacon and eggs. He looked up at Lily.

'Take the kettle from the fire into the scullery. You can wash there. On the side is a towel.'

Holding Victoria's hand tightly she took the kettle and walked into the other room. She tried hard to behave normally for her daughter's sake, but she cast a furtive glance in Quinn's direction trying to gauge his mood. However, he was bent over his plate, shovelling food into his mouth.

The outside door opened and Rosie entered, carrying logs for the fire. She pointed to the stove and said, 'There's some eggs there if you want to boil some for you and the child.

And there's bread in the bread bin.' She went into the other room to stoke up the fire.

Lily perched Victoria on the draining board, washed her, gave herself a quick swill and set about preparing their breakfast.

Quinn put down his knife and fork and wiped the plate with a piece of bread. As he ate it he watched Lily as she busied herself at the stove. He saw that the pleats in her skirt were creased and so was her warm jumper. He gave a half-smile, realising that she'd slept in her clothes. No doubt she'd thought he would come to her room.

He lit a cheroot and sipped tea from his chipped mug. How often he'd pictured such a scene and now it was reality. Lily Pickford was in his scullery, in his house, and soon she'd be in his bed. His gaze went to the soft rounded shape of her breasts, taut against the wool of her jumper as she stretched for a saucepan. How soft and pliable her soft flesh would be. He couldn't wait to touch her, taste her, fuck her. He rose from his seat and walked into the scullery.

Victoria looked up anxiously as he entered. He ignored the child and walked over to the stove where Lily was standing and put an arm around her waist.

'That's just how I've pictured you, my girl. Standing in my house, cooking. You've no idea how happy this makes me. You behave yourself and we'll have a good life together.'

'But I'm ill prepared to stay. I've only the clothes I stand up in . . . and Victoria needs clean clothes as well, and her toys,' she said.

He looked at her skirt and jumper. But his eyes narrowed as he said, 'I suppose you want me to let you go and pack your things?'

'Well, it would make sense, wouldn't it?'

There was a harshness in his voice. 'You must think I'm a complete idiot! I let you walk out of here, you'll never come back. I'll find you something to wear. Something you can work in. Fine feathers have no place on a farm.' He cupped her chin in a firm grip. 'You're here to stay, Lily Pickford, until we're wed. I've warned you of the consequences.' He gazed towards Victoria, perched on the draining board. 'And I don't think you'll cross me. Now I've work to be done, but before I go, show me just how happy you are to be here.'

His mouth crushed hers and his strong arms pulled her close until her body was moulded with his. She was so startled, she didn't respond to him. His mouth released hers and he looked into her eyes, his own glittering with anger. 'Try a little harder, my girl. I need to be convinced, or else . . .'

She wound her arms around his neck and put her lips to his, fighting the feeling of nausea rising inside her. She closed her eyes tightly and tried to freeze her mind to the feel of him, the taste of him. When he at last released her, she gasped for breath, wanting to wipe the imprint of his mouth from hers, but not daring to.

With a slow lazy smile he said, 'That's much better. You'll soon get used to me, learn how to please me.' The smile disappeared. 'If you don't, you'll live to regret it, my dear. And so will the babby.'

He walked towards the door and paused. 'Ma! Give Lily a pinny and make her work. There's no place here for visitors and idle hands!' He slammed the door behind him.

Lily rushed to the sink and washed her mouth out. Then she splashed cold water over her face and the back of her neck. She felt faint, sick and terrified. She picked up Victoria and held her close.

'What did that nasty man do to you?' asked Victoria in a tearful voice.

Taking a deep breath, Lily tried to console her. 'Don't you worry about him, darling. He didn't hurt me. He likes me and what's why I kissed him. He's just a friend.'

'I want to go home,' wailed the child.

'Hush now. As soon as we can, I promise you we'll leave this place.' She carried Victoria into the kitchen and sat her at the table. 'We're going to have some breakfast before we do anything.'

Having settled her daughter, Lily forced herself to eat. She must keep up her strength. That much she had learned from her days in prison. She gazed around the untidy kitchen. Rosie handed her an old pinafore and a brush.

'Best sweep up in here,' she said. 'When Quinn comes back he'll be pleased if you do a good job. It's best not to upset him when he's in this kind of mood.' She gave Victoria a sheet of paper and a pencil. 'There, my beauty. You draw a picture for your mother.'

Lily set about cleaning the kitchen. She swept it thoroughly, putting the dust and pieces of straw onto the fire. She went into the small hallway to clean there and saw the telephone. If only she had a moment alone, she could call Madge at the hotel and get help. Without it she would be forced to share Quinn's bed this night. The thought of him touching her in an intimate way was horrifying, but to save Victoria, she'd do it if she had no other choice.

She wondered just how long Madge would wait before she told anyone of her whereabouts, but of course, knowing that Victoria's life was at stake, she'd be too scared to say a word to anyone.

Luke was striding about the foyer of the hotel, raging at

Madge, demanding to know what was going on. 'You lied to me yesterday,' he accused. 'Now tell me the truth. Where is Lily? Why isn't she here?'

With tears brimming in her eyes, Madge said, 'I don't know, honest I don't.'

He caught hold of her wrist. 'You don't know the true meaning of the word honesty. If you did, you wouldn't have gone to gaol!'

Normally she'd have been stung by his insult but she was beside herself with worry, wanting to tell Luke, longing for him to go to the farm and see what was happening, but terrified she'd endanger Victoria. She burst into tears and fled.

'Bloody women!' he fumed, and went off towards the kitchen to take out his anger on the workmen.

Madge locked herself in the linen cupboard and sobbed. How long must she wait? If things had been all right, Lily would have telephoned to tell her so, surely? Perhaps she could telephone the farm? But what if that dreadful man answered! She had been terrified of him and she guessed he was dangerous. It might put Lily in further jeopardy. But . . . she could look up the number, ring, and if anyone but Lily answered, she could hang up.

She made her way downstairs and looked up the number in the telephone directory, making a note of the address too. She could hear Luke's voice coming from the direction of the kitchen, and picking up the receiver, she dialled.

Lily was emptying the contents of the dustpan into the fire when the phone rang. As Rosie went to answer it, she cursed her bad luck. If she'd still been there, cleaning, she could have lifted the receiver and begged whoever was on the other end of the line to send help. She listened to Rosie, wondering who was calling.

288

'Hello. Hello . . . Well, say something, for Christ's sake!'

Lily heard her mutter to herself and replace the receiver. The old crone returned to the room muttering still, then picking up her mending she settled in the chair by the fire.

Chapter Twenty-One

Luke waited impatiently the next morning for Lily to arrive. He kept looking at his watch, gazing out of the window, walking up and down. When Madge entered the hotel, alone, he marched straight over to her. 'Well?'

She looked pale and there were dark rings under her eyes. 'Victoria was sick in the night and Lily's waiting for the doctor to call.'

'Is it serious?' he asked.

She shrugged. 'No, I don't think so, but Lily wants to be certain,' she lied.

His brow furrowed with concern. 'Right. I want you to ring this number and order the linen I've written down. I'll be back very soon.' He walked out of the hotel, climbed into his car and drove away.

He headed for the house which Lily shared with Madge and eventually drew up in front of it, parked the car, climbed out of the driving seat and knocked on the door. He waited and waited. No one came. He knocked again, peered through the net curtains at the window, bent and looked through the letter box and saw nothing. The house was quiet.

Frustrated, he drove to Rachel's house and knocked impatiently on the door. When the Jewess answered he demanded, 'Is Lily with you?'

She shook her head. 'Why would she be? She's usually at work at this time.' She saw the worried expression he wore and said, 'You'd better come in and tell me what's going on.'

He stepped inside the room and sat down, then told her of his concerns. 'I can't understand why I haven't heard from her. It's not like Lily at all. Madge knows something, I'm certain.'

'Then go back and question her again, and for the Lord's sake let me know what's happened,' she said anxiously. Climbing back into the car, he took out a cigarette and lit it. This was so unlike Lily that he began to worry. Something was going on, but what? Madge knew, he was sure, and by the state of her this morning, it was causing her some concern. Well, this time he'd *make* her tell him! Throwing away the cigarette, he switched on the ignition, put the car into gear and drove back to the hotel. But when he arrived, Madge too, had disappeared.

Clutching the address of the Giffords' farm, Madge sat in the back of a taxi heading for Bitterne. She couldn't wait around any longer, wondering and worrying. Lily would have contacted her by now if all had been well. She had to find out for herself, and if Lily was in danger, she needed to know. What she would do when she got to the farm she had no idea.

She made the driver stop the taxi just before her destination, so that her arrival would not be seen by anyone around the farmhouse. She paid him and waited for him to drive away before slowly and quietly approaching the gate, hiding behind the wall. She froze as she saw the two fierce dogs chained up. They would certainly make her appearance known. Turning, she cautiously made her way round the back of the building.

Hidden behind thick overgrown bushes, she waited and

watched. There was a window beside the back door. Along the pathway was an outside privy. Thank goodness for that, she thought. Everyone in the house would have to use it at some time, and perhaps she'd be able to call to Lily if she came out. She made herself comfortable and waited, peering through the branches, watching for any sign of movement.

Inside the farmhouse, Lily was helping Rosie prepare vegetables for the midday meal. Victoria was playing in front of the fire with one of the many farm cats.

'You'll learn that the men need to be well fed,' Rosie told her. 'Farming isn't an easy life.'

Lily stared hard at the woman. 'You know I can't stay here,' she declared. 'Yet you carry on as if everything is normal. How can you?'

Rosie looked back at her, her dark beady eyes bright and penetrating. 'You don't know about destiny, my girl. Your life, mine, everybody's, is all charted out from the time we are born. If you're meant to stay with my Quinn you will; if not, then there will be a way, you'll see. Just be patient, but don't rile my son, 'cos that'll put you in great danger.'

'Won't you help me to get away, to get my Victoria to a place of safety?'

'No harm will come to the babby,' Rosie said knowingly. 'So don't you fret yourself.'

'I could run away with Victoria now, if you would turn a blind eye,' pleaded Lily.

'That would be very foolish,' said the old woman. 'Quinn may not be here, but I can tell you he'll be working where he can watch everything that goes on. You push him and the consequences would be dire. Now I've some washing that needs putting through the mangle outside the back door. You do that. I'll keep the little one here with me in case you decide to be stupid and make a run for it.'

Madge sat up as she heard the back door open. Her heart lifted when she saw Lily, wearing an apron, carrying a large wooden basket filled with wet clothes. She remained hidden, watching, not wanting to reveal herself until she was sure it was safe.

An old woman came out and piled more clothes into the basket, then she helped Lily to mangle several sheets, holding the end so they wouldn't become soiled from the ground.

Madge watched impatiently, at the same time wondering where Victoria was. At that moment the child came to the door calling for her mother, only to be hustled back inside by the old woman. Madge heaved a sigh of relief. At least they were both alive. She inched forward, careful to remain hidden. She parted the branches of the hedge.

'Lily!' she called softly, hardly daring to breathe. 'Lily!'

Lily looked up, her gaze searching for a sign of the person calling her name.

Again Madge called; at the same time she stood up so her head was visible just above the hedge.

Lily's eyes widened as she saw her friend. She put a finger to her mouth and continued to mangle, but when she went to shake out the creases of the next garment she moved nearer to the hedge.

'Madge! Thank God you're here.'

Talking through the foliage, Madge told her how worried she was and how Luke had been having a fit at her disappearance.

'Go back and send help,' Lily told her. 'You must get us out of here before tonight. Go now and be careful.'

Madge ducked down as Rosie came outside again. The old woman looked across towards the hedge and Madge caught her breath expecting the woman to walk over and discover her whereabouts, but after a second the old crone turned and walked back into the building.

'I'll be back,' she whispered as she crawled away.

Lily continued with her chores with a lighter heart. Thank God. Now at least she knew that help would be on the way as soon as her friend could summon it. All she had to do was keep Quinn Gifford sweet and at arm's length. Pretend to go along with his wishes and keep him away from Victoria.

Madge kept low and out of sight until she was clear of the property. Then she stood up, clutching her back which had stiffened. Now where could she go? There were no houses nearby and the farm was out in the country. She'd head back towards Southampton. She knew she had a long walk ahead of her, but at least Lily and Victoria were all right. She must let Luke know. Now at last she could share the secret of Lily's whereabouts.

She trudged on relentlessly, slipping on the wet grass verges, the mud on the roads, side-stepping the cow pats, sweating beneath her coat despite the cold. Thankfully, the threatening rain had held off.

Eventually, in the far distance she espied smoke coming from a chimney and with a cry of joy headed on down the road until she came to a gate. The house at the end of the long winding drive was large and imposing. Inside the entrance was a cattle grid. The gate was locked and she climbed over it, but as she did so she slipped, twisting her ankle. She staggered and fell into a ditch, banging her head on the upturned root of a tree as she did so. Her senses swam, then the blackness took over.

Luke had had enough. In the hotel foyer he picked up the telephone and asked the operator to connect him to the main police station. 'This is Luke Longford,' he said. 'I'd like to talk to Detective Inspector Chadwick, please.' After a few moments' pause, he heard the voice of the policeman.

'Can you come to my hotel in Cumberland Place?' he asked. 'I think I've got a problem. Lily Pickford is missing.'

DI Chadwick was at the hotel within fifteen minutes. 'What's this all about?' he asked Luke.

He listened whilst Luke told him about the last two days. 'I can see your concern, Mr Longford, but at the moment there is little I can do. This Madge will probably return before long. After all, she was here this morning. She may have slipped out to do something for Lily or the child.'

'But they're not at the house!' Luke exclaimed. 'The doctor was supposed to be calling. I went to Rachel Cohen's, but Lily wasn't there either.'

'Do you know the doctor's name?'

Luke shook his head. 'No, of course not.'

'She may have taken Victoria to a hospital.'

'No,' said Luke. 'I rang them.' He glared at Chadwick. 'Look, I know something's wrong. This isn't like Lily.' He paused then asked, 'You've known her longer than I have. Can you shed any light on the matter?'

Chadwick shook his head. 'No, not really.' He rose to his feet. 'But I'll ask around. Make a few discreet enquiries, see if I can sniff out anything. I'll get back to you. Will you be here all day?'

'I'll be here until late tonight,' said Luke. 'There's so much to do.'

The policeman put a comforting hand on his shoulder. 'Try not to worry,' he said. 'If there's one thing I do know about Lily, it's that she can take care of herself. I'll be in touch.'

With a sense of frustration Luke watched him walk away. He didn't like mysteries. There had to be a good reason for Lily's absence. She had such a sense of duty, he felt she would have let him know why she wouldn't be around. He was beginning to feel really worried. God! If anything had happened to her, he'd never forgive himself. He'd treated her badly when she needed him most, and he was full of self-recrimination. But there was perhaps a beacon of hope. Madge, he was sure, knew what was going on, and as she wasn't here, perhaps the mystery would soon be solved and maybe soon, she and Lily would walk back into the hotel . . . Then he'd throttle her for giving him so much worry!

At lunchtime, Quinn and Jake came back to the farmhouse for their meal. As soon as he'd removed his Wellington boots, Quinn grabbed Lily and kissed her. 'I can't wait for tonight, my beauty,' he said hoarsely. 'There will be no more excuses. Tonight you sleep in my bed.'

She smiled at him. 'Of course I will, but I hope you'll have a bath first,' she said playfully.

'What do you mean?' he growled.

'Well, Quinn, you'll have been working all day. You'll smell of pigs and horses. I don't want to share the bed with a load of animals, only the man.'

He grinned with delight. 'Right then. You have a bath run for me when I come home. You can cook my supper whilst I have it, like a wife. Then after, we'll go to bed.' His expression darkened. 'You'd better tell your babby to behave. I don't want her grizzling when we go off to our room without her.'

'Don't you worry about Victoria,' she said.

His eyes gleamed with anticipation. 'I've wanted you for so long, Lily. You best not be tired. We have a long night ahead.'

Yes, longer than you think, Quinn Gifford, she thought. By then help will have arrived and I'll be long gone, but she smiled at him. 'I won't be tired,' she said. 'I promise.'

He and Jake devoured their food and returned to work. For Lily the long wait began.

As hour after hour passed, she became more agitated. Help should have been here by now. It was five o'clock and almost dark. Soon Quinn would be back expecting his bath, a meal and then . . . She hid her head in her hands. Oh my God! She was going to have to sleep with this monster. Luke *certainly* wouldn't want her then, but at least Victoria would be safe. But what on earth had happened to Madge? It would take her some time to get help. She would have had a long walk until she could have found public transport or a taxi but she should have done so, long since. Where was she? Where was Luke? Why didn't anyone come?

Madge gradually came to. Her head ached. She put her hand to the matted hair at the back of her head where there was a large bump. Her hand was wet. She smelt it and knew that it was covered in blood. It was now dark and she couldn't think where she was. She sat up and her head swam, her vision blurred. She tried to get to her feet but one ankle hurt so much she couldn't put any weight on it. Then she remembered. Lily! She'd left her late in the morning and she had no idea of the time now. Hours must have passed. Lily would be waiting. She must get help.

Gazing around she saw lights shining from the big house and remembered the long drive. She had to get up there somehow. She began to hop on one foot, then she tripped over, cursing, calling out with pain. But all she could think of was her friend, relying on her. She began to crawl, muttering to herself, 'Don't you worry, Lily. I'll make it.'

Quinn Gifford walked towards the door of the scullery, a big smile on his face. He'd have his bath, followed by a good meal, and then he'd take Lily to his bed. The very thought of her soft body lying next to his filled him with lust and longing. Village girls were all very well, and the odd prostitute had fulfilled his needs in the past, but this was different. The lovely Lily Pickford would be his. As he thought of how he'd thrust himself inside her, again and again, he felt himself harden and cursed the fact that he'd agreed to have a bath first. He wanted her now. But he could see how the smell of the animals might put her off and he wanted her to please him. Excite him. Satisfy him . . . so he would clean himself for her. He pushed open the scullery door.

Lily felt sick when she saw him. He grinned across the room at her and she saw the lustful expression in his eyes. There was to be no escape for her this night. As the hours had passed, she'd given up all hope of salvation. She'd prepared Victoria for sleeping in Rosie's room with the promise of the cat she liked so much sleeping with her. Now she prayed that the child would behave, knowing that Quinn would be furious if Victoria cried for her. She looked at Quinn and smiled.

'I've run your bath and your supper's in the oven.'

He walked over to her and grabbing her by the hair at the back of her head he kissed her roughly. 'I'll be down in twenty minutes.'

She rubbed his growth of beard. 'Have a shave too,' she said. Trying to think of every way to take up his time. At his angry look she added, 'I have a delicate skin, Quinn.' She tickled his chin softly. 'This will make my face sore, and you wouldn't like that, would you?'

He rubbed the three-day stubble. 'No. All right, I'll shave too.'

With a heavy heart she waited for him to come downstairs for his supper.

When he did join her, he'd changed into clean clothes. He'd cut himself shaving, she noticed, but made no comment as she laid the meat pie before him. 'There,' she said. 'Take your time. There's no hurry. I'll just put Victoria to bed. I'll tell her a story to settle her.'

'Make it a short one!' he snapped.

Lily tucked up her daughter in the cot beside Rosie's bed and put the cat on the bottom. She started to make up a tale of fairies and princesses, hardly knowing what she was saying, but within a short time, Victoria's eyes had closed. Lily kissed her forehead and went downstairs.

Quinn was sitting by the fire, smoking a cheroot and drinking a glass of beer. At the sight of Lily he threw the cheroot into the fire, downed his drink in one gulp and rising from his chair, he took her hand and walked to the stairs.

She followed him, her heart in her mouth. Quinn, she was sure, would be a rough lover. He was a hard man with no finesse about him and she wondered just what was ahead of her.

At that moment Jake came bursting into the kitchen.

'Quinn, come quickly! The mare is about to foal and she's having trouble. I think it's a breech birth. We could lose them both if we don't help her.'

Quinn swore loudly. 'Shit!' he glared at Jake, but he had no choice. The mare and foal were worth a lot of money. 'Go on up,' he told Lily. 'I'll come when I can.' He followed his brother out of the room.

She collapsed on the stairs and burst into tears of relief.

Chapter Twenty-Two

Her knees bleeding, her head aching, Madge clawed her way up the steps of the big house, somehow dragged herself unsteadily to her feet, and beat on the door with both fists. As it opened she fell forward in a swoon.

James Redfern looked at the bundle at his feet, and quickly bending down, felt for a pulse. He saw the swollen ankle and carefully examined it, calling for his wife as he did so. Then, picking Madge up in his strong arms, he carried her to the drawing room and laid her on the large sofa.

His wife rushed into the room. 'Goodness me. Who is it?' she asked.

James shook his head. 'I've never seen her before, but she's either sprained or broken her ankle and her knees are badly grazed. Bring a bowl of warm water, some cotton wool and my bag from the surgery, will you dear?'

It was some time later when Madge regained consciousness and looked up into the kindly eyes of a stranger. She made to get up, but he gently restrained her.

'Lie still, my dear,' he coaxed. 'You've been in the wars.'

She grabbed his hand and said, 'Please, you've got to help me. My friend's in danger. Have you a telephone?'

He nodded.

'Please, will you contact Luke Longford at the old Regent

Hotel in Cumberland Place? I've got to speak to him now.'

She was so agitated that the doctor was concerned. 'Now then, young lady, don't upset yourself so. Tell me slowly what is wrong then I'll be able to understand.'

Luke, weary from a long day with the builders and decorators and tormented by a mounting concern for Lily, was just leaving the hotel when the telephone rang. He picked up the receiver, hoping it was Chadwick with some news, but a stranger's voice answered.

'Mr Longford?'

'Yes, speaking.'

'I have a young lady here who wishes to speak to you. Hold on, I'll just pass the receiver to her.'

'Lily, is that you?' he asked anxiously.

'No, Luke, it's me – Madge. Quinn Gifford has got Lily and Victoria at his farm in Bitterne. He kidnapped Victoria when I took her out the other day and Lily had to go to him. I couldn't tell you because he threatened to hurt Victoria. Get the police, don't go alone, he's dangerous. Please hurry.' The words came pouring out.

Luke was shaken to the core, but he was a man of action not easily panicked in a situation. 'Where are you?'

But Madge didn't know; she handed the phone over to her host.

James Redfern explained who and where he was, and the condition of his patient. He also told Luke the location of the farm, warning him about the Giffords. 'Take the young lady's advice and inform the police. The Gifford brothers are renowned for their violence, Quinn in particular. You need to take care. I'll look after Madge until the morning. Good luck.'

302

Lily was huddled by the dying embers of the fire, cuddling Victoria who had woken from a nightmare. She'd made the child a warm drink of milk and one for herself. She had no idea of the time, but knew it was late. Across the yard she could see a soft light in the barn and prayed that Quinn would be there all night. She had no intention of waiting for him in his bed. Maybe when he did eventually return, he'd want just to sleep, but in her heart she knew that this would not be an option.

At that moment Rosie came down the stairs, an old tweed dressing gown bundled up around her, swamping her small frame. She looked at the fire and went outside and brought in a couple of logs.

'Want to freeze to death, do you?' she asked shortly.

'No,' said Lily, 'I just didn't want to go outside.'

'Frightened he might hear you?'

Lily nodded. This would have been a good opportunity for her to make her escape but it was a bitterly cold night and she was afraid that if they'd had to spend all night in the open, Victoria would have suffered. Whereas if she could get into Quinn's good books, even if it meant sharing his bed for one night, then he might not watch her so closely tomorrow. Then she'd try to get away, whilst he was filled with a false sense of security. Yet as she waited, she began to wish she'd taken the chance, but now with Rosie sitting opposite her, she'd burned her bridges. Resigned, she settled back in the chair with Victoria and closed her eyes.

In her mind she pictured the interior of St Michael's Church in Southampton. She'd gone there many years ago when the future had looked bleak. Now she visualised the altar beneath the steep arches and prayed fervently for a safe delivery from this terrible predicament.

★　★　★

Meanwhile, Luke was in touch with DI Chadwick, passing on the information that Madge had given him.

'That bastard!' said Chadwick. 'You were right to call me. I'll have two cars ready. I'll pick you up on the way.'

'I'll drive there myself,' said Luke.

'No, Mr Longford, you'll come with me,' declared the officer firmly. 'We don't want any heroics, thank you. I would like you near me, where I can keep an eye on you.'

Luke agreed, albeit unwillingly. Within minutes a car pulled up in front of the hotel and Luke climbed in the back beside the detective.

Whilst they were being driven towards Bitterne, the policeman outlined his plan. 'We've no intention of rushing in the place like a bull at a gate,' he warned. 'We keep out of sight and watch and observe. Any other way we put them all in danger. Understand, Mr Longford?'

'Yes, I do understand,' said Luke. 'I won't do anything, you have my word . . . until Lily and Victoria are safe, anyway.'

'You'll not do anything afterwards either, my son! I don't want to have to send you down for grievous bodily harm. You just let the professionals do their job.'

The journey seemed endless to Luke and he was filled with guilt for doubting Lily, and Madge. He remembered, to his shame, having told Madge she didn't know what honesty was. She must have bravely made her way alone to the Giffords' farm to find out for herself what had happened. Now she was injured. Not only was she honest but she was loyal – something that had been lacking in him. Had he been truly loyal to Lily, it wouldn't have mattered what had happened in her past. His own pride had stood in the way. What a false pride it had been! There was Madge and now Lily putting herself in the greatest of danger to save her child and he felt unworthy. He knew now that he truly loved her and wanted her to share his life, no matter what had befallen her before they met. He only hoped he hadn't waited too long to come to his senses. If anything happened to her and Victoria, he would never forgive his stupidity.

Mr Chadwick leaned forward and told the driver to pull in, shut off the headlights and cut the engine. Turning to Luke he said, 'We've arrived. Get out of the car and don't close the door. We don't want to alert anyone.'

He sent three men around the back of the building with orders to do absolutely nothing unless they heard him blow his whistle.

Four of them stealthily approached the front of the house, keeping low and out of sight behind the wall. Chadwick peered around the corner and saw the two sleeping dogs on the end of their chains. Well, at least should they need to rush in, they wouldn't be a problem. Apart from their barking.

He saw a faint light coming from the barn and heard a sound of movement inside. But who was there? They'd have to wait and see.

Lily was woken suddenly when the scullery door burst open. Quinn and his brother came in. They washed their hands before entering the kitchen. Lily held Victoria closer to her as she saw the thunderous expression on Quinn's face. His clean clothes were covered in blood and mucus. He walked over to the cupboard and took out a bottle of scotch and two glasses, then poured two heavy measures into them, handing one to Jake who had now joined him.

Quinn took a large swig of the liquor and cursed. 'Just my fucking bad luck! Those two were worth a small fortune.' He banged the table with his fist, making Lily and Victoria jump.

'So you lost them then?'

He looked over at Rosie. 'Yeah. My God, it was a battle. The foal was big. Jake and I had a real tussle to get it out, but it was too much for both of them.' He drank the remainder of his drink and poured another. Glaring at Lily he said, 'Why aren't you waiting for me in my bed, like I told you? And why is that brat down here?'

She tried to keep the tremor from her voice. 'I wasn't tired and Victoria woke up. And I was worried about the mare.'

He gave a sardonic grin. 'Becoming a right little farmer's wife, ain't you?'

She didn't answer, but watched with fear and trepidation as he finished his drink and poured another. His eyes became bleary, and his speech thick as he talked to Jake about the disposal of the carcasses in the barn.

Eventually, Jake got to his feet and wearily said, 'I'm off to bed.'

Quinn downed the last of his drink and belched. 'Yeah, me too.' He got awkwardly to his feet and staggered over to Lily. 'Come on, woman. Get up those stairs!'

She quickly took Victoria from her knee and handed her to Rosie. 'Sit there, darling,' she said. 'Be a good girl.' She looked at Quinn. 'What you need more at this moment is a good night's sleep. You look worn out.'

He grabbed her wrist. 'More of your bloody games, is it? Well, they don't work any more, my fine Lily. Don't think I'm good enough for you, is that it?'

'No, of course not. But you're upset. You've had a hard night. What you need is rest.'

He pulled Lily to her feet and laughed at her. 'What I need is a hard night with *you*. A good fuck will soon make me feel better.'

Lily tried to break away from his grasp, but he held her tighter, his eyes narrowing.

'Listen to me, bitch. I took a beating for you!'

She froze, the anger in his voice robbing her of movement.

'You set that bastard George Coleman on to me. He broke my ribs and my ankle. You owe me, my fine lady and now in my bed, by Christ you'll pay me back!'

'I didn't put Coleman on to you, I swear,' she pleaded. 'He saw us talking outside the Mariner's. He said he'd sort you out but I told him not to.'

He grabbed her by the shoulders and thrust his face close to hers. 'I don't believe you!' He kissed her savagely, then pushed her away from him. She staggered back and fell into the chair.

'Mama!' cried Victoria, her little face puckered up with fear as she looked at her mother.

'Stay where you are!' Quinn pointed to the child. 'Don't you dare move!'

Victoria looked at Lily with a fearful expression.

'Sit still, darling,' said Lily softly. 'Everything's all right.'

'He won't harm the child. I won't let him.' Rosie spoke for the first time.

Lily glared at her. 'Can't you put a stop to all this? You're his mother, after all.'

Rosie shook her head.

'I've seen you swanning around with that flashy Longford bloke,' said Quinn, his mouth in a cruel and evil smile. 'Driving around in his fancy car. I've seen the way he fusses over you. Well, he won't have the chance again. Now you're here to stay. You'll fuss over me instead.'

Outside, away from the main gate, Detective Inspector Chadwick gathered his men. They could hear angry voices coming from the kitchen, but they couldn't distinguish them. Luke was getting restless, but the detective calmed him. 'We'll know when, we always do. Just be patient a little longer.' He scratched his bald pate. 'Lily can be a cool customer in a crisis. It's not her I'm worried about, it's that mad bastard Gifford.' He stared at Luke. 'I might as well be honest with you, he's a dangerous man. He can turn in a second. That's why we must wait.' The policeman put his hand on Luke's arm. 'Listen, Mr Longford. If we make the wrong move, Lily and the child could be in real danger. I'm sure you don't want that?'

'No, of course not.'

Inside the building, Victoria stirred and in a plaintive voice said, 'Mama. I want to do a wee-wee.'

Lily made to move, but Quinn glared at her. He looked across at his mother. 'You take her,' he said.

Rosie got to her feet and picking up Victoria, held her close. Looking over at Lily, she said, 'Don't you fret none. I'll take care of the little one. She'll be safe with me.'

There was something in the expression of the old woman that eased Lily's fears. She nodded. Looking at her daughter she said gently, 'It's all right, darling. You go with the lady. She'll look after you.'

Rosie went out of the back door of the farm to the outside lavatory. As she walked towards it, she felt the presence of others, but she didn't hesitate, taking the child inside and seeing to her needs, comforting her. As she waited, her heart was heavy knowing that this awful situation would be brought to its inevitable conclusion all too soon. When Victoria had finished, she took her by the hand and they returned to the kitchen.

Victoria ran over to her mother. 'Can we go home now?'

Lily held her tight and whispered in her ear, 'Not yet, sweetheart. Just be patient a little longer.' She sat her on her knee and waited. What was Madge doing? she wondered. How long before someone came to their rescue?

Quinn became more aggressive. He glared across at Lily, his mouth twisted with anger. 'You always thought you were too good for me. I saw the way you used to look at me in the Club when I bought you drinks.'

Thinking to appease him, she said quietly, 'That's not true. You're imagining it.'

'You could have come to me when I wrote to you in prison, but oh no! Not Lily Pickford. Whore of The Maltese and for all I know, that ponce at the posh hotel too.' He grinned at her. 'I've been watching you carefully for a long time . . . except when that bastard Coleman put me in hospital!' He glowered at her. 'Just because you were the whore of The Maltese, you thought you could use his methods. Well, look where it got you!'

The scene was becoming ugly and Lily held her daughter tighter. She also felt the tension in Quinn's mother. It seemed to stretch across the divide. She looked past the hearth at the woman.

Rosie was observing Quinn closely.

The sudden change in the atmosphere affected Victoria and she started to whimper. 'Let's go home, Mama, please. I don't like that man. He frightens me.'

Hearing her words, Quinn angrily kicked a chair across the kitchen. He glared at Lily. 'Are you frightened of me too?'

She met his gaze bravely. 'No, Quinn,' she lied. 'I'm sorry for you.'

'Sorry!' he swiped the glass and bottle off the table, the breaking glass reaching the ears of the police outside, who were hidden, silent, listening for any sound from within.

Luke stiffened and looked at Chadwick. 'We can't wait any longer! God knows what's going on in there.'

Chadwick gripped his arm.

Quinn lurched across the floor, grabbing hold of the table to steady himself. 'I don't want your pity, woman.' He walked unsteadily towards her.

She pushed Victoria from her knee and towards Rosie. 'Go to the lady, please,' she said.

Quinn caught hold of Lily by her arm, hauling her to her feet. 'I've waited long enough for you,' he said. 'I want to enjoy what The Maltese and that flashy Longford had. You're coming upstairs with me now.'

'No!' Lily cried, trying to fight him off, but he was far too strong. He dragged her towards the rickety stairs. She could hear Victoria's cries of fright and knew that once Quinn got her to his room, all would be lost. She struggled harder, but found herself dragged to the foot of the staircase.

He grabbed her by the hair, his eyes bright with madness and anticipation. 'You're going to be mine. I want to see just what is under all those clothes you're wearing.'

'Mama! Mama!' cried Victoria. 'Let her go, you nasty man! You leave my Mama alone!'

Quinn, his face red with drink and anger, let out a demented cry of fury and roughly released Lily. He turned and snarled, 'You blasted little brat. I'll teach you a lesson you won't forget.'

It was then that Lily screamed.

The sound of her scream rent the air. Luke made to run towards the door, but a constable held him back. Detective Inspector Chadwick picked up his loudhailer.

'Quinn Gifford! This is Inspector Chadwick of the Hampshire Constabulary. Come out of the farmhouse now. I advise you to listen to me. I have the place surrounded.'

Hearing the sudden voice, Quinn stopped in his tracks. H

glared at Lily. 'You cunning bitch! You tricked me!'

'No! I didn't know they were there, honestly. How could I? You've had me shut up here.'

'Don't you lie to me.'

'Come out, Quinn Gifford,' the voice called again. 'Don't be a fool. No harm has been done. Don't make matters worse. Just come out of the house.'

Hearing the familiar voice of the policeman filled Lily with a sense of relief. Thank God! Madge had made it, after all. She looked across at Victoria, still beside Rosie, and prayed the child would remain silent.

Quinn Gifford went berserk. 'Come out?' he bellowed. 'The man must think I'm mad.' He shot a crazed look at Lily. 'I suppose you think you're safe now. So he wants me outside, does he? Wants to put me in prison, more like.' He moved quickly across the room and grabbed Victoria from his mother's clutches. 'Well, I'll give him what he wants all right.'

He dragged the screaming child to the door and threw it open. Stepping outside he walked forward, holding Victoria in front of him. The torchlight from the police officers shone on him, catching the gleam of madness in his eyes.

Lily ran to the door but stopped abruptly as she saw that Quinn had drawn a knife from his belt and was holding it to her daughter's throat.

His eyes glistening with anger, he yelled at Chadwick: 'You come near me and I'll cut her.'

There was absolute silence from the watchers.

Luke looked at the madman then at Lily. No one dared move.

Chadwick put down his hailer and in a quiet voice said, 'Now then, Gifford, this won't solve anything. Let the child go.'

A demoniacal laugh escaped the lips of the wild gypsy. 'Her safety is in your hands, you bastard. Go away and leave us alone. Lily and the babby are staying here with me.' He looked at Lily. 'Tell them,' he ordered.

She took a couple of steps forward. She saw Luke standing there, a look of anguish on his face. In a clear voice she said, 'That's right. I'm staying here – I promised. Go away, all of you.'

'You know we can't do that, Lily,' said the detective.

Lily was becoming demented, terrified for the life of her daughter. She looked at Quinn and realised that madness had taken him over completely. 'Please, Mr Chadwick, leave us alone. We'll be all right.' Out of the corner of her eye she saw a movement. Rosie was standing in the doorway of the farm.

'Quinn!' she called sharply.

The familiar voice of his mother broke through the gypsy's lunacy. He turned towards her, still holding Victoria in front of him. 'Ma?'

'Let her go, son,' said Rosie firmly. 'It's time to bring this to an end.'

Everyone held their breath.

'I can't do that, Ma,' he said coldly. He gripped the handle of the knife tighter. 'If I can't have Lily, then she can't have her babby.'

Lily put a hand to her mouth to smother the scream of terror that was rising in her throat.

'For the last time, Quinn. I'm telling you, let her go!'

'That's what they all want, but I can't let that happen, Ma.'

From behind her back, Rosie took a shotgun and before anyone realised her intentions, she called: 'Quinn! Look at me!'

He turned around as she held the gun to her shoulder and fired.

There was a look of surprise on the face of Quinn Gifford as his body sagged and blood began to flow from the hole in the middle of his forehead. The knife dropped from his grasp, and his hold on Victoria loosened as he slowly sank to the ground.

Lily rushed forward and grabbed her daughter.

There was a clatter on the cobblestones as Rosie Gifford dropped the shotgun. She walked slowly over to the body of her son and kneeling beside him, held his still form in her arms. 'Oh Quinn, my boy. Why wouldn't you listen to me?' She held him to her chest, her old and tattered dressing gown, turning red with his blood. She rocked back and forth, wailing quietly.

Luke ran over to Lily, whose tears were flowing down her cheeks. She hid Victoria's face so she couldn't see the terrible sight. As she looked down, she saw the child's clothes were spattered in blood.

'Come away, darling,' urged Luke. 'Please come away.'

Lily gazed into his eyes and saw the love shining there. 'Oh Luke!' Her voice filled with anguish as she asked, 'Where were you?'

His heart was full of shame and guilt as he took her into his arms and encompassed both her and Victoria. 'Oh Lily. Can you ever forgive me?'

She softly stroked his careworn face and gave a tearful smile. 'Take us home. Please take us home.'

He lifted Victoria from her arms and helped Lily to a police car parked outside the farm gates. He ushered her inside the vehicle and with Victoria still in his arms, he climbed in beside her and held them both. Patting Lily's back, like a baby, he made soothing noises as she sobbed into his chest.

Detective Inspector Chadwick put his head through the

open window. 'I'll get a driver to take you back to the Dolphin Hotel,' he told them, 'but I'll have to question Lily.'

'Tomorrow!' urged Luke.

'Yes, Mr Longford. Tomorrow will be soon enough.' He called an officer over and ordered him to drive them away from the scene.

All the way home, Luke held Lily tightly in his arms and in a soft voice he chatted to Victoria, trying to allay her childish fears, not quite knowing how much she had understood of the incident. But however much either of them had suffered, now they were in his care and if love alone would cure them, he had enough for both.

Chapter Twenty-Three

The police car drew up outside the locked iron gates of the Dolphin Hotel. Luke got out of the vehicle and rang the night porter's bell.

As he came to unlock the gates, the porter looked with surprise at Luke, who was carrying Victoria, and then at the still-distraught Lily, standing beside him.

As they entered the hotel, Luke asked the man to bring two large brandies and a glass of milk to his room, and a couple of blankets and pillows. 'The lady has been involved in an accident,' he explained, and handed the man a pound note.

Unlocking his door and entering the room, Luke gently deposited Victoria on the large comfortable settee. 'Sit there, darling,' he said, 'until the porter brings your milk.'

She looked up at him and plaintively asked, 'Can we stay here with you? We don't have to go back to that nasty man, do we?'

He bent down and hugged her. 'No. You'll never see him again. You and Mama will stay with me tonight, in this room. I'll be here all the time with you. Won't that be nice?'

The anxious look faded from her bright eyes. 'Yes, I'll like that.'

Luke turned to Lily and took her into his arms; he pulled her close to him. 'I need to hold you, feel you,' he said passionately. 'To know you're safe. God! What a nightmare. I don't know what I'd have done if anything had happened to either of you.' He was too full of emotion to say any more. He kissed the top of her head, stroked her hair and held her tightly until a knock on the door disturbed them.

'Come in.'

The night porter entered the room, put down the tray of glasses and the blankets and pillows.

'Thank you,' said Luke. 'Now we don't want to be disturbed.'

'Yes sir,' said the man, and left them alone.

Leading Lily gently to the settee beside her daughter, he handed her a brandy. 'Drink this,' he said, then gave Victoria her milk. He sat down and sipped his own drink, watching Lily talking softly to the child until eventually she undressed her.

Victoria turned up her nose when she looked at her blood-spattered dress. 'It's dirty,' she said.

'I'll buy you a nice new one in the morning,' Luke promised.

He helped Lily to make up a bed on the settee and settle the little one, kissing her goodnight. Victoria lay down, clasping Lily's hand. 'I didn't like it at that place, Mama,' she yawned.

'No, darling, neither did I. But now we're here with Luke.' She gazed across at him, but there was an expression of uncertainty in her eyes, which tore at his heart.

Victoria continued to tell her mother of her fears and the loud bang that had frightened her, but as the child poured out her worries, Lily was thankful to realise that her daughter hadn't seen the ugly vision of Quinn, after he'd been shot.

At last she fell asleep.

'Come here,' said Luke, holding out his hand.

Lily rose from the settee and walked over to him. He took her onto his knee and held her. 'She'll be all right,' he assured her. 'You were in time to hide her face. She doesn't realise what happened, but you, my darling, I'm worried about.'

She snuggled down in the comfort of his arms. 'I thought he was going to kill us both,' she confessed. Silent tears trickled down her face.

He gently wiped them away, soothing her. 'I thought I'd go crazy waiting outside the farmhouse, not knowing what was happening to you both. I wanted to rush in, but Mr Chadwick wouldn't let me.' He lifted her chin gently until she was looking at him. 'If that bastard had harmed either of you, I would have killed him!'

'What happened to Madge?' Lily covered her mouth with her hand. 'I'd forgotten all about dear Madge. How could I *do* such a thing? She came to the farm looking for me and went to get help. What happened to her?'

Luke told her the whole story. Then: 'She is someone else I misjudged, but I'll make it up to her somehow.' He gazed into Lily's eyes, his brow furrowed. 'I can't tell you how much I love you, my darling. I've been such a fool. Can you ever forgive me?'

With a sob in her voice, she reached up and kissed him. 'If only you knew how much I longed to see you walk into that kitchen. I prayed for you to come.'

'Oh, my darling, if I'd only known where you were, I'd have been there much sooner. You must have been terrified.' He closed his eyes with relief and to hide his own tears. He nuzzled the top of her head. 'I love you so much.'

'And I've wanted to hear you say that for so long,' she confessed, the barrier she'd built between them now destroyed. She looked up at him. 'There's nothing to forgive, but . . . can you ever forget what I have been in the past?'

He kissed her gently. 'The past is dead; we have only our future to consider.' He gazed tenderly at her. 'I can't face it without you. The hotel isn't important to me any more unless you're there by my side. Lily, will you marry me, share my life? Let me care for you and Victoria?'

'If you're really certain. I don't want you to regret this. I have to know you mean it.'

He kissed her eyes, her hair, her soft mouth. With a deep sigh he said, 'I don't deserve your love after the way I behaved. Please say you'll marry me. My life would be empty without you and Victoria.'

She looked into his eyes and saw the anguish there. 'Yes, of course I will.' And she kissed him with all her heart.

Seeing how pale and weary she looked, Luke felt guilty. 'Come to bed, darling,' he told her. 'What you need is a good night's sleep.'

They lay entwined in each other's arms throughout the night. Content to be together.

The following morning, Luke ordered breakfast to be served in the room. He fussed over his womenfolk, concerned about their mental state after such an ordeal, and when he felt it was right to do so, he left to buy Victoria a new dress. He came back a while later, laden with packages.

When she saw the amount of shopping, Lily asked, 'What's all this?'

'Open them and see,' he said with a broad smile.

She and Victoria opened the boxes with great excitement. There was underwear for Victoria, new socks and a pale blue woollen dress and matching heavier coat. The child was thrilled. Lily gasped with delight as she unpacked delicate camiknickers for herself, stockings and a beautiful fine woollen costume in emerald green. There was one large package left. She looked at Luke, then at the box.

He chuckled. 'Go on – open it. I know you're dying to.'

She tore the ribbon off and opened the lid. Inside, wrapped in tissue paper, was a short mink jacket. She took it out and held it up. 'Oh Luke . . . it's beautiful. Thank you.' She flung her arms around him and kissed him soundly.

He looked at Victoria. 'Do I get one from you, too?'

The child ran to him and gave him a smacking kiss.

Lily's eyes were shining with happiness. 'There is just one more thing,' he told her. He put his hand in the pocket of his jacket and pulled out a small box. 'Here.'

Lily took it from him and opened it. Inside was a half hoop of large diamonds. She was speechless.

Taking the box from her he removed the ring and carefully placed it on her finger. 'Let's get married very soon,' he whispered as he took her in his arms and held her close.

She looked up at him. 'I've always wanted to get married in St Michael's Church,' she said wistfully, 'but being an unmarried mother, that's probably expecting too much.'

'I'll go and see the vicar today,' he promised. 'Have a chat with him.' He reluctantly released her. 'Much as I want to stay, I have to go to the hotel. The men are coming to lay the carpets. Will you be all right? You can stay here if you like.' He looked anxiously at her, wondering if it was safe to leave them alone. 'I could get Rachel to come here,' he suggested.

'I'll be fine, honestly. After all, I don't have anything to be frightened of any more. Quinn Gifford is dead. Just give me time to dress Victoria and myself, then if you'll take us home, that would be best. I'd rather be there – there's things I have to see to. Then I'll let you go. But only for a few hours,' she teased. 'We've wasted so much time.'

'Thank God we've got the rest of our lives to catch up,' he said soberly.

She ran her finger across his full mouth. 'I don't think I can wait that long,' she whispered in his ear.

Luke drove them home and then left to get on with the business of the day. Lily walked around the small house, gazing lovingly at every shabby piece of furniture, touching it, knowing that at one time, she doubted she'd ever see it again.

There was the sound of a key in the door and voices. The door opened and Madge limped in, followed by a tall, distinguished-looking gentleman.

'Lily!' Madge opened her arms. The two friends embraced.

'Oh Madge, how can I ever thank you! But for you, God knows what would have happened.' She looked with concern at the bandage on Madge's foot, then at the stranger.

'How do you do,' he said, extending his hand. 'I'm Dr Redfern. It was to my house that your friend Madge came. Her ankle is badly sprained, unfortunately, but that's all. She just needs to rest it.'

Shaking his hand, Lily thanked him heartily. 'Can I get you a cup of tea?' she asked. But he refused, saying he had a surgery full of patients. 'I'm so glad that everything turned out so well, my dear,' he said as he made for the door.

Victoria ran over to Madge and clutched her around the knees. 'Well, what's all this then?' asked Madge. 'Can it be you're pleased to see me?'

'Oh yes, I am,' said Victoria. Then she twirled around. 'Do you like my new dress and coat?'

'Very stylish.'

'Luke bought it,' she declared proudly.

'Why don't you go upstairs and get your toys,' suggested Lily, anxious to find out her friend's news.

When they were alone, Madge regaled her with the events

that had occurred after she had left Lily at the farm, beginning with her fall.

'I thought I'd broken my bloody foot,' she said ruefully. 'Imagine me ending up at a doctor's house! Wasn't that a bit of luck? Now tell me what happened. I know Luke was going after you.'

As she listened to Lily's tale, her eyes grew wider. 'My God! You must have been terrified!'

Lily nodded.

'And now? Have you and Luke made up?'

She held out her hand and showed her the ring.

'Bloody hell! What did he do, rob the Crown Jewels?' She held Lily's hand and studied the diamonds. 'That cost a bleedin' fortune!' She looked at her friend. 'And you deserve every penny.' She hugged her. 'I nearly went out of my mind. Oh Lily, don't ever do anything like that to me again.'

'I'm worried about Quinn's mother,' said Lily, her voice filled with sadness.

'What a brave old girl. But the fact that she saved Victoria's life will stand her in good stead, surely?'

'I'll find out from Mr Chadwick,' said Lily. 'He wants to question me about what happened. You too, probably.'

Madge pulled a face. 'I don't like coppers . . . So when's the wedding?'

'Soon. That's all I know.' Lily's face lit up with happiness. 'The sooner the better – before he changes his mind!' she laughed.

'Change his mind? Never! You should have seen the state of the man when you went missing. He won't let you out of his sight in future, that I do know.'

A loud banging on the door made them both look round. It was thrown open and Rachel breezed in. 'My life! Such a worry you are,' she said as she embraced Lily. 'Luke told me what happened. Sheesh! Can't you live a quiet life for once?'

Both Madge and Lily burst out laughing.

It was a busy day. Detective Inspector Chadwick called and spoke to the two girls. He said that Rosie Gifford had hired a first-class lawyer, so her chances of a light sentence were good. And who knows,' he added, 'if they plead mitigating circumstances, which of course they will do, in the light of this tragedy, she may be put on probation.'

'I do hope so,' said Lily sincerely.

'You both need to come to the station and give a statement,' he said. 'Any time within the next two days.'

Then the local vicar, John Page, arrived. He sat and talked to Lily about her impending marriage.

'I understand you want to be married in my church, my dear?'

'I really would, but I think you ought to know all about me first.'

He held up his hand. 'I know who you are, and about your past. I get to hear a great deal about what goes on in my parish.'

Lily's honesty came to the fore. 'Do you know I was once on the game?'

His expression didn't change. 'No, I didn't.' He paused. 'You know that Christ forgave Mary Magdalene?'

She nodded.

'Then who am I to judge? I'll be happy to perform the ceremony.'

At that moment little Victoria ran into the room. 'This is my daughter,' said Lily. 'I was not married to the father.'

'Yes, I know about Vittorio Teglia. He lost his life trying to save another.' He looked at her with a soft smile. 'Not exactly the actions of a sinner, would you say? She'd make a charming bridesmaid, don't you think?'

Lily hugged the man who, though surprised at this show of affection, wasn't displeased by it.

'As soon as you and Luke can arrange a date for the wedding, I'll have the banns called.' He shook her hand. 'You'll make a radiant bride, I'm sure.'

It was early evening before Luke was free to call on his new fiancée. He arrived clutching two bouquets and four packets of fish and chips, wrapped in newspaper.

He gave one bouquet to Lily and then the other to Madge. 'I owe you an apology,' he told Madge quietly.

She flushed with embarrassment. 'No, you don't, really.'

'Believe me, I do. Without your intervention . . . well, it doesn't bear thinking about.'

They all sat around the table, eating the delicious impromptu meal. Luke's mouth twitched with amusement. 'Imagine, if anyone could see me now, about to open a hotel whose reputation for high cuisine is of the utmost importance, I'd lose my credibility!'

'I'm not sure what that means,' said Madge with a grin. 'But I won't tell if you won't!'

After the meal, Lily put Victoria to bed and Madge retired to her room, leaving the two lovers together.

Luke sat on the old battered settee, his arm around Lily, and told her about the hotel, what had happened during her absence. 'The carpets look really good,' he said, 'although the men haven't quite finished. It makes such a difference.'

He softly kissed her cheek. 'We're going to have a good life together. I'm going to rent a house for us until the time comes to buy our own.'

'But what about Madge?' asked Lily, a frown creasing her forehead. 'She won't be able to afford this place alone.'

'Yes, she will,' he assured her. 'I want to give her a

permanent job as your personal assistant, with a salary to match – if you're in agreement, of course.'

'Oh Luke! That's a marvellous idea!'

'In the first place, she's proved she's capable, and secondly, it's my way of thanking her.'

Lily told him about the vicar calling and how he'd agreed to marry them. 'I know,' he said. 'We had quite a chat. The problem is how to find the time, there is so much to do. But I do have a suggestion.'

'What's that?' she asked.

'I know it sounds crazy, but we need to be at the hotel every minute of the days leading up to the opening. However . . . on opening day, it will be just the final touches. I thought we could get married in the morning, then have our friends back to the hotel for the opening and lunch, and afterwards in a private side room we could cut the cake and hold a small reception. What do you think?'

She stroked his cheek. 'I think it's an inspired idea.'

He tickled her neck. 'In just over three weeks' time, you'll be Lily Longford. It has a nice ring about it, don't you think?'

She chuckled and with a mischievous twinkle in her eye said, 'It sounds too much like the Jersey Lily, Edward the Seventh's mistress!' At the look of dismay on Luke's face she added, 'But I love it. "Mrs Lily Longford." Mmm. Very nice. Very respectable.'

'Who will you ask to give you away?'

'There's only one person – my old friend Sandy. We've been through so many bad times together, it would be nice to share this happy day with him.' She gave an impish grin. 'He'll relish the role, he's such an old queen and loves to perform. I'll write to him in the morning.'

Luke gazed deep into her eyes. 'There is just one more thing I want to do.'

'And what's that?'

'I want to legally adopt Victoria. I'd be so proud to be her father, watch her grow, help her along life's path.'

Her voice was choked with emotion as she replied: 'That would be wonderful.' She clung to him, her eyes moist with tears of happiness. 'Oh Luke, I do love you. You'll make a wonderful father.'

They sat together in each other's arms, silent and content. Each lost in their own thoughts.

He looked at his watch. 'Darling, much as I hate to leave you I must go, I've a busy day tomorrow and need an early night.'

'Well, tomorrow, I'm coming back to work,' she said firmly.

He looked startled. 'Isn't that a bit soon? You've been through a very traumatic experience.'

She was adamant. 'No. I need to be occupied – and anyway, I have to keep an eye on things. Make sure you don't mess around with my colour schemes.'

'As if I'd dare!' He drew her to him. 'I just want to take you to bed,' he whispered as he nuzzled her ear. 'But I can't here, and it's driving me crazy.' He kissed her passionately, caressing her face, her neck, her soft breasts. 'I'd better go,' he said reluctantly. 'I'll see you tomorrow.'

She hugged him, before opening the door, telling herself it wouldn't be long before they would all be together for always.

As Lily entered the hotel the following morning, she was impressed at the change in its appearance. The rich green carpet that covered the foyer gave such a feel of opulence. There was a beautifully carved reception desk beside the entrance. Plush chairs were placed with a coffee table in between, for waiting guests. She thought a nice vase of flowers would make it complete and made a note to supply one.

'Come and see the kitchen,' urged Luke. 'It's finished now – and any chef would be happy to work there.' And she agreed with him. Every surface was in stainless steel, easy to clean and hygienic. It had been designed with an experienced eye, making it ideal for both cooking and serving.

'Luke, it's excellent.' She hugged him, feeling the excitement of it all.

He put his arm around her. 'All this is our future. Now come outside.'

They stood on the pavement and looked up at the frontage of the building. In large lettering a sign proclaimed: THE LONGFORD HOTEL.

'There you are, darling,' Luke declared. 'Your name in lights!'

Chapter Twenty-Four

The following three weeks were spent in frenzied activity, preparing for the wedding. Luke had rented a large house for them nearby, and much to Victoria's delight and Lily's great relief, Nanny Gordon was invited back and installed in the household.

Luke and Lily came home from the hotel each night in a state of exhaustion, but nevertheless, their lovemaking was tender and ardent. Little Victoria kept telling anyone who would listen that Luke was going to be her new daddy and how much she loved him. And he, whenever he had a moment, was completely enamoured with the child and would play with her, tell her stories of his travels and the things that he'd seen around the world.

Rachel was in her element, going around the shops, helping Lily choose her dress for the wedding and an outfit for herself.

'The mother of the bride, I feel,' she preened, and smiled proudly as Lily tried on yet another creation, having adamantly refused to be married in white as Rachel had suggested.

'How can you think of such a thing?' Lily chided. 'I have a four-year-old child, out of wedlock. Virginal I'm not!'

At last she chose a coffee-coloured silk dress with a

handkerchief hemline and a satin band around the dropped waist. To go with it she'd found a confection of a hat in straw, covered with delicate brown flecked feathers and a half-veil. A pair of shoes in soft beige leather and matching handbag completed the ensemble.

The two women took the outfit to the best florist in town to discuss what flowers to put in her bouquet. They decided on tea-coloured and pale cream roses, which the florist promised would look just right.

Then on to another store to buy the trousseau.

'I don't know when I had so much fun,' declared the elderly Jewess. 'My heart is so full that at last you're happy with a good man,' she told Lily, her eyes shining.

Luke too was tearing around, being measured for a three-piece suit in a dark grey, ordering buttonholes for the wedding guests, seeing that everything was perfect for this very special occasion.

He and Lily went together to the jeweller's to choose wedding rings.

'I'm so sorry that we have to wait for our honeymoon,' Luke told her, 'but once the hotel is up and running I'm taking you away to the South of France.'

Her eyes widened with surprise and joy. She'd never dreamed life could be so happy.

At last the day drew nearer and all was prepared. Victoria had a new green velvet dress and insisted on trying it on every day. Prancing around the room, practising to be the bridesmaid.

At the hotel, all the staff had now been recruited, references checked, and there was a definite buzz of excitement about the place as the last of the furniture began to arrive. Madge was proving her worth, running around like a scalded cat, carrying out Lily's instructions to the letter and using her own initiative when it was required.

Alex McGill, an old colleague of Luke's, was now installed as the restaurant manager. He was tall, fair-haired and distinguished-looking, and was blessed with a manner that would charm the most tiresome of clients. He was also extremely efficient.

The chef had duly been poached from one of London's top hotels and came with the highest references and reputation. As Luke told Lily, 'He's costing a small fortune, but he's essential to the success of the place.'

On the day all the beds arrived, Lily was busy with the housekeeper, arranging the furniture, handing out linen to the chambermaids, listing towel supplies.

As she walked down the broad staircase, choosing not to use the lift, she ran her hand lightly over the deeply flocked wallpaper and gazed in admiration at the wall mirrors with their ornate gold frames. Despite the chaos, the hotel was taking shape.

She walked into the dining room where Alex was tearing his hair with frustration. The carpet fitters were putting the finishing touches and he was anxious to arrange the tables and get organised.

'Will we make it in time, do you think?' asked Lily.

He chuckled. 'You have never seen an ocean liner the day before sailing, Lily. Cables and wires everywhere, but come sailing day, it is all pristine – as this will be, I promise.'

Luke appeared, cursing beneath his breath, his shirt-sleeves rolled up. He looked fraught; his hair was in disarray where he kept running his fingers through it.

'Whatever's the matter?' asked Lily.

'That bloody fool of a plumber! One of the gents' toilets in the bar has flooded because he didn't screw up some pipe properly. I've just told him if he doesn't fix it quickly I'll be screwing his neck!' And he rushed off.

'Oh dear,' she said.

'Don't you worry, it'll be fine,' Alex assured her.

'Yes, maybe, but what sort of state will my bridegroom be in?' she asked anxiously.

He put a comforting arm around her. 'Don't you worry about Luke. Your wedding is the most important thing to him, not the hotel. He won't let anything spoil that. He'd rather delay the opening!'

All too soon, the combined opening and wedding day was upon them.

It was six o'clock in the morning and pitch black, but lights blazed in the Longford Hotel as Lily arrived by taxi carrying her wedding finery. She was to change at the hotel, ready to go to the church.

The staff had been called in early on this auspicious day, and were scurrying about, vacuuming carpets, dusting imaginary specks off every surface. Straightening lamps, lighting fires, folding napkins, arranging flowers and hoping to meet the high standards of their meticulous employer, and mindful of the forthcoming nuptials which put all the female members of the staff in a state of flux.

Mid-morning, Lily made her way to the dining room where Alex was issuing orders briskly and efficiently. There was no feel of panic; everything was being attended to by competent professional staff who knew their job. The ambience of the room was just right. The dark green carpet complemented the paler green velvet drapes, which were edged with gold fringe and held back by heavy gold cords. The wall-lights, echoing the crystal chandeliers, glittered like huge teardrops, illuminating the lush pattern of the wallpaper.

The tables, now arranged for easy access to both the client and the waiting staff, were being laid with pristine white damask cloths. The fine china was also white, with a narrow gold rim; any delicate dish that was arranged on it would look superb. Napkins had been folded into intricate shapes, the heavy silver cutlery polished until it shone, and small arrangements of bronze and yellow chrysanthemums placed in the centre of the tables, enhancing the colour scheme of the room. Here was a place to relax and eat the finest dishes the chef could prepare, and where today, they would serve her wedding breakfast. Lily thought she couldn't have wished for better surroundings.

'You happy with everything, Alex?' Luke asked when he came in later.

'Yes, no problems. We're ready for the champagne reception at noon, and as you can see, the tables are laid for lunch. The large one is for your own personal wedding guests – I've made up one or two extra, just in case – and the private room is ready for your reception. The cake the chef has made is a work of art, but we're keeping it hidden from Lily.'

'Excellent,' said Luke. 'I'll just have a word with the chef, then I want everyone gathered together. Will you see to that? Here, in about ten minutes.' He walked purposefully towards the kitchen.

Inside, the kitchen staff were working as hard as everybody else. 'Any problems, Chef?' enquired Luke.

'Not in my kitchen, Mr Longford! I don't allow them,' he answered with a grin. 'Good luck for the wedding. I can assure you the food will be excellent.'

'I've no doubt it will. Now, can you and your staff spare me five minutes in the dining room? I'd like a word with everyone before we open.'

'Certainly, sir.' He gathered his team about him and followed Luke.

In the dining room the staff were standing round, waiting with expectation. Luke stood before them and made a short but encouraging speech, thanking them all for their hard work.

Lily touched his arm. 'I'd like to say something, too,' she said.

She stood before them, her eyes bright, her voice clear. 'I know from talking to you all individually that you have the success of the hotel at heart. We have something to be proud of in the Longford Hotel, but I just wanted to say how proud I am of all of *you* and the effort you have put in to making this a very special day. You are all very special people.'

There was a spontaneous burst of applause at the end of her speech and the staff went away, pleased that they were thought of so highly.

Lily walked over to Luke and gently touched his face. 'Why don't you go into your office and let me bring you some breakfast?' she asked. 'You look tired and it's going to be a long day.' As she saw him about to refuse, she urged, 'You can't manage without something. We don't want you fainting at the altar or getting drunk through drinking champagne on an empty stomach. What sort of an impression would that make?' she teased.

He capitulated, accepting the wisdom of her words. 'But nothing cooked, Lily. Toast and coffee will do. And you had better have some too.'

'I will, later,' she said, and kissed him briefly before making her way to the kitchen to see to it. On her way she passed Madge.

'Oh Lily! This is so exciting, isn't it?' Her friend didn't wait for an answer but rushed off in the opposite direction.

Lily smiled to herself and shook her head. Who'd have thought it. From a prison cell to a prestigious hotel! How strange a thing was fate!

At ten o'clock, Luke and Lily went to his suite to change their clothes ready for the wedding. He opened the bottle of champagne that was waiting in a bucket of ice and poured them a glass each. 'To us,' he whispered as he kissed her. 'All morning I've been thinking of waiting at the altar for you to arrive. I've never known the time drag so much. Don't be late, will you – I don't think I could stand it!'

She hugged him. 'You are an idiot.' But shortly after, when he was changed, Lily hustled him towards the door, saying, 'It's unlucky to see the bride on her wedding day as it is. You're not seeing my dress as well!'

He gallantly kissed the back of her hand. 'Nothing is going to spoil our wedding, I promise, Miss Pickford.'

'For goodness' sake, touch wood when you say that!' she exclaimed.

'The depth of love I have for you, my darling, can overcome everything.'

Nevertheless, she pushed him out of the room.

Soon afterwards, there was a knock on the door. 'Come in!' she called. And when her old friend Sandy stepped inside: 'Hello, you old tart!' She ran forwards and flung her arms around him. 'Oh Sandy! It's so good to see you.'

He walked over to the wardrobe and looked at the dress hanging there, ready for her to put on. 'Darling, how *very* stylish. And how expensive.'

She poured him a glass of champagne. 'Now talk to me while I get dressed. How's your sister? Are you well? And how's *your* lovelife?'

'Well, if you'd only pause to take a breath I'll tell you!' he scolded.

At last it was time to leave. The hotel staff were all gathered at the entrance to see Lily off in her horse-drawn carriage. They cheered and waved as she moved off and she was near to tears as she waved back, a proud Sandy at her side and Victoria, dressed in her new velvet frock with matching sash and silk ribbons, clutching a small posy of rosebuds to match the ones in her mother's bouquet.

Eventually they arrived at the church. As Sandy helped her down he joked, 'Come on, dearie. I've been trying to give you away for years – at least today I can do it legally.'

Lily clutched hold of his arm with one hand and her bouquet with the other. He saw the nervous expression on her face and said, 'The only trouble is, you look better than me – and you know I like to be the star turn!' He smoothed his bottle-green velvet jacket and tweaked the carnation in his buttonhole. 'Come on, ducky, we've done a double act before.'

Lily burst out laughing, thus dispelling her nerves. 'If you trip when you're mincing down the aisle, I'll kill you!' she said with a wide grin.

He looked behind at Victoria, holding her small posy. 'Ready, darling? Big smile. We're on stage now.'

Victoria's eyes lit up with excitement. 'Will I have to sing like Mama used to? I know "The Spaniard That Blighted My Life"!'

Lily started to giggle at the look of horror on her friend's face.

'Good God, no!' he exclaimed. 'You only do that when you're at home. Now promise me you'll be a quiet little girl.'

'Yes, all right,' she said with a note of disappointment.

He looked at Lily. 'The vicar would love that! Right, ready?'

She nodded.

Sandy did her proud. He walked beside her with great dignity. Lily saw many familiar faces in the pews – Madge, Rachel, with a broad smile and handkerchief at the ready, Eddie Chapman who winked at her as she passed, but she got the surprise of her life when she saw DI Roger Chadwick standing beside Luke as his best man.

Luke, tall, handsome and immaculate in his attire, stepped forward and took her hand in his, giving it a quick squeeze.

She looked at him and smiled.

The ceremony to Lily was like a dream, almost unreal. She vaguely heard herself say her wedding vows, but she clearly heard the vicar declare: 'I now pronounce you man and wife.'

Luke tilted her chin and kissed her. 'Hello, Mrs Longford,' he whispered.

They returned to the hotel, ready to receive their guests. As they waited, Luke took her into his arms and kissed her passionately. 'If only we had the time,' he said.

She pushed him gently away. 'We'll make up for it tonight. I've ordered a bottle of our best champagne. You and I are going to have a night of unbridled passion.'

He playfully nuzzled her neck. 'It sounds as if I've married a wanton woman. How very satisfying!'

At noon, the first residents began to arrive at the hotel, its elegant façade bedecked with bunting. They were welcomed by Lily and Luke, who looked very stylish in their finery – Luke in his new suit and Lily in her wedding dress, minus the hat. Around her neck a long string of pearls.

They invited the newly arrived residents to the champagne reception and luncheon, to their delight. After they'd signed the register, the porter picked up their cases and led them towards the lift.

Luke looked at Lily with a broad grin and gave her a quick hug. 'It's started! We're on our way.'

At that moment, Rachel swept through the entrance, with Sandy on her arm. Lily threw her arms about him.

'Oh Sandy, you were marvellous. I don't think I'd have made that walk down the aisle without you.'

'Of course you would have, darling,' he said. 'You were always a performer.' He hugged her and kissed her cheek. 'I know you'll be very happy. What's it like to be married to such a beautiful man? He looks so capable, dearie . . . in *every* direction!' He winked at her.

She smacked him playfully. 'Behave! You are in exalted company.'

He raised himself to his full height and said most regally, 'And I'm perfectly at home.'

Lily ushered them into the residents' lounge and sent a waiter over to look after them.

The next guest to arrive was Eddie Chapman. 'Congratulations, you are a beautiful bride,' he said warmly. 'I've missed you, my dear, but looking around this place I can well understand why you took the job. And now you've married the boss! It was time you had some good luck, Lily.'

'Thanks for coming. It's so good to see you again. How's the Mariner's Hotel?' she asked.

He beamed at her. 'I sold it a few weeks ago. I'm now retired and thinking of taking up golf or cricket – or something. I've not made up my mind.'

'Come and have some champagne and meet some friends of mine. You'll be sitting at our special table with them at lunch. We have to entertain our business guests now, but afterwards we'll all be going into a smaller room to cut the cake.' She led Eddie over to Rachel and Sandy and introduced them to each other, knowing they would look after her old employer. Little Victoria, accompanied by Nanny Gordon, was to be allowed to sit with Sandy and was wildly excited.

Soon, more people had arrived and the place was filling up with specially invited guests, including the town's most prominent businessmen, bankers, the Mayor and his wife, adorned with Mayoral chains. Waiters moved silently among them with trays of champagne and canapés. The guests were all favourably impressed with the furnishings, the décor, the service, the ambience.

Roger Chadwick walked in with his wife, a middle-aged lady wearing a smart costume, an expression of excitement in her eyes. Lily immediately crossed over to them and the Inspector introduced his wife. Then he leaned forward and kissed Lily's cheek. 'I'm allowed as best man to kiss the bride,' he said.

She smiled at him then turning to his wife said, 'I hope you enjoy your lunch, Mrs Chadwick,' as she stopped a passing waiter and gave them each a glass of bubbly. 'Try some of these,' she said as the canapés were offered.

The woman tucked into them and looked around, her eyes getting wider by the minute. 'I would really like to stay here for a night, Mrs Longford,' she said gleefully. 'We usually stay in small hotels when we take a holiday, but this is so elegant.'

Lily looked at the policeman and with a cheeky grin said, 'Well, I think you'd better start saving your pennies, Inspector!'

'Pounds more like, Lily. Now don't you start putting ideas into her head.'

When Alex announced that luncheon would now be

served, the guests made their way to the dining room. The doors had been closed until now and as the people entered, the comments about the opulence were all very satisfying.

Lily grinned at Luke. 'I think they like it.'

The luncheon was going well. Luke and Lily were sitting at a large round table with the Mayor and Mayoress on either side of them. The food was superb, every course cooked to perfection. The Beef Consommé had a delicate flavour, the Sole Véronique was excellent and the saddle of lamb, pink and tender.

The Charlotte Russe had been eaten, with Scotch Woodcock to finish. Eventually the dishes were cleared, the coffee and petits fours served, and the liqueurs chosen by the diners. The meal was nearly over. Lily breathed a sigh of relief.

There was a halt to the buzz of conversation as the Mayor got to his feet. 'Ladies and gentlemen,' he began. 'I'm sure you are all as impressed as I am with the excellent meal we have just enjoyed?' There were murmurs of assent all round. 'I would like to thank Mr and Mrs Longford for their hospitality today and to wish them every success with this fabulous hotel. It's just the sort of place we need in Southampton. And I would like to take this opportunity to congratulate them on their very recent marriage. Please raise your glasses and let us toast . . . the Longford Hotel.'

Glasses were raised and the toast made, to loud applause.

Luke rose from his chair. 'My Lord Mayor, Lady Mayoress, ladies and gentlemen, thank you for your good wishes. This hotel has been my dream ever since I was a young lad, a bellboy with the Cunard Company. Today has seen the fruition of it. But today could not have been so successful without my staff, who have all worked so very hard to make it happen. In particular, my good friend Alex McGill, the restaurant manager, Charles our talented chef and the lovely lady who, this morning, became my wife.'

There was enthusiastic applause. Alex grinned across at Lily, who blushed.

As the applause died down, Luke said, 'Thank you all. Please avail yourselves of the public rooms – the bar of course, is open.'

The two of them mingled with their guests. Luke in deep conversation with various businessmen, agreeing to them using his hotel for their business functions, Lily discussing with another group the matter of a wedding reception, and both of them together, holding hands, talking with their special friends.

Rachel looked about her and said to Luke, 'Mazeltov! How beautiful this place is. It must have cost you a fortune!'

Lily looked aghast at her friend. 'Rachel!' she chided.

The elderly Jewess wasn't at all fazed. 'So what's so wrong? The bottom line in all business is money.' Turning to Luke she said, 'Am I right?'

His face was wreathed in smiles. 'Absolutely. I expect to make a pile.'

'There!' she said, looking at Lily. 'He ain't embarrassed by money talk, so why should you be?'

Lily hugged her. 'You are such a cheeky devil. I can't take you anywhere.'

'Darling, in my lifetime, I've been most places!'

When the time came for the cake-cutting, their friends were ushered into a private room for their own celebration. Luke led Lily to the table where the two-tiered wedding cake stood and she gasped with surprise. The chef had decorated it with lilies, in her honour, and on the top tier was a small cut-glass vase containing small fresh lilies. She looked around and saw Charles watching anxiously.

'Thank you,' she said. 'It's absolutely magnificent.'

He flushed with pleasure.

Roger Chadwick made a short but delightful speech, saying how honoured he was to be the best man. How he knew that the young couple were going to be happy and successful in their future, and wondering if, as best man, would he get special rates as his wife was badgering him to stay in the hotel!

Luke and Lily burst out laughing, Luke assuring him that something could certainly be arranged.

'How did Roger become your best man?' she asked.

'I would liked to have asked Alex,' he explained, 'but he had to be left to look after the place while we were at the church. Roger Chadwick is a man of integrity, someone I admire, and when I asked him, he was delighted.'

The cake was cut, more champagne drunk and after an hour, Luke made his excuses and taking Lily by the hand, led her into his office, closing the door behind him. 'Come here,' he said. She went willingly to his arms. He held her close and nestled his cheek against her hair.

'Oh my darling,' he sighed. 'This has been such a special day, in every way, but I couldn't have done it without you.'

'Of course you could. Well, not the wedding, of course. I did have a particular role to play there.' She kissed him softly, and with twinkling eyes added, 'But as for the hotel, you could have managed, but maybe the décor would have lacked a certain touch!'

He chuckled. 'I'm sure you're right. Oh Lily, we are going to be so happy. We have a wonderful future ahead of us. It's going to be hard work for a while, and I'm sorry we have to wait for a honeymoon, but I promise it will eventually be one you won't forget.'

At that moment Victoria burst into the room. 'Mama,' she cried. 'Can I sing "The Spaniard That Blighted My Life" now?'

Both Luke and Lily burst out laughing. He picked the child up in his arms and kissed her. 'Not just yet, darling,' he said. Then turning to his bride he added, 'Perhaps in a few years' time, she could be the cabaret?'

Lily felt Luke's strong arms encompass them both. She looked at her new gold wedding band, at her new husband and knew that there would definitely be many tomorrows for them all.

Miss You Forever

Josephine Cox

One winter's night, Rosie finds a woman who has been severely beaten by thugs. At a glance, Kathleen looks like an unkempt, aged vagabond, carrying all her worldly possessions in a grubby tapestry bag. Her only friend is the mangy old dog who accompanies her; the sum of her life is in the diaries she so jealously guards. Yet close up, Rosie can see that Kathleen has a gracious beauty – the 'look' of a respectable lady of means.

Moved by Rosie's care and compassion, Kathleen entrusts the precious diaries to her. In the soft glow of a night-lamp, Rosie opens the first page. Captivated through the small hours, she uncovers a heartrending tale of stolen dreams, undying love, heartache and loss. Once, a lifetime ago, Kathleen had a promising future, a family and a reason to hope. But is this really the end of her dreams?

'Vivid characters' *Express*

'Guaranteed to tug at the heartstrings' *Sunday Post*

'A heartwarming tale' *Sunderland Echo*

'Another sure-fire winner' *Woman's Weekly*

0 7472 4958 X

HEADLINE

Liverpool Songbird

Lyn Andrews

Alice O'Connor's family is the poorest of the poor in Benledi Street, the heart of Liverpool's toughest slum. Her bullying father drinks away what little he earns, whilst Nelly, her careworn mother, works when she can and begs when she can't. Since she was five young Alice has also begged in the streets around the docks but she has managed to hold on to the hope of something better, a stubborn optimism that keeps her head held high even in her lowest moments.

For Alice knows she has a gift that allows her to rise above the fate that made her life so bitterly hard. Alice O'Connor can sing like an angel . . .

It is a gift that will take her far, though it is to Liverpool she will always return. But is it enough to bring her the success she needs – and the love and happiness she so desperately craves?

'Spellbinding . . . the Catherine Cookson of Liverpool' *Northern Echo*; 'Enormously popular' *Liverpool Echo*; 'A compelling read' *Woman's Realm*

0 7472 5174 6

HEADLINE